THE MIRROR OF INFINITY

THE MIRROR
OF INFINITY

A Critics' Anthology of Science Fiction

edited by

Robert Silverberg

HARPER & ROW, PUBLISHERS
New York, Evanston, and London

Contents

vi   CONTENTS

Introduction

Science fiction is as old as dreaming. The man who first, upon seeing the moon's scarred face one night, allowed himself a sudden fantasy of journeying to that other world, was the first to indulge in the substance of science fiction. To reach beyond the set bounds of space and time, to attempt to walk for a moment in infinity's shadow, is science fiction's essential goal.

As a literary form it can be traced back at least to Lucian of Samosata, the genre's often-invoked progenitor, who in the second century A.D. sent his hero on a lunar voyage via oceanic waterspout. But undoubtedly there were earlier writers who toyed with speculative ideas of this sort. A case could be made for *The Odyssey,* that wondrous travelogue, as a kind of proto-science-fiction. And Plato's dialogues on Atlantis, *Timaeus* and *Critias,* are science-fictional in theme even if they are not cast in the mode of fiction.

In the sixteenth and seventeenth centuries many writers turned to science fiction as a useful vehicle for criticism of society. Thomas More's *Utopia* (1515–16) created a sub-genre within science fiction by providing an imaginary scene for the depiction of an ideal society. Bishop Francis Godwin's *The Man in the Moone* (1638) and Cyrano de Bergerac's *A Voyage to the Moon* (1657) chose a lunar standpoint from which to examine the flaws of Europe. Jonathan Swift's *Gulliver's Travels* (1726) inverted More's tactic, offering fantastic communities in which man's flaws and not his virtues were magnified for satiric purposes.

As prose fiction came to take its place as a medium for popular entertainment, science fiction found a special niche as the literature of soaring imagination and uninhibited speculative thinking. Jules Verne, one of its first professional practitioners, reduced science fiction to the level of formularized boys' adventure stories in the nineteenth century, but his insistence on plausibility of invention and his respect for scientific detail are virtues that compensate for the poverty of his fiction. Verne's example has guided many modern science-fiction writers, those who feel that one cannot begin to extrapolate meaningfully from existing scientific ideas without a firm grasp on those ideas.

Later in the nineteenth century, H. G. Wells began to produce his "scientific romances," which went far beyond Verne both in literary attainment and in scope of imagination. It was Wells, within a span of less than twenty years, who systematically conceived and explored each of the major themes of modern science fiction: the conflict between worlds, the social consequences of great inventions, the voyage in time, the possibility of the world's destruction, the future of warfare, and much else. Lucian of Samosata notwithstanding, Wells is the true father of today's science fiction, for it was he who set the canons of subject and technique that most contemporary writers follow. When Swift sent Gulliver off to Brobdingnag and Laputa, it was for the sake of mocking the pretensions and follies of Swift's own society; but while social commentary is implicit in Wells and in most modern science fiction, it is *the voyage for its own sake*, not the editorial criticism of society, that now concerns the writer. When Wells' Time Traveler vaults into a far future occupied by idle Eloi and depraved Morlocks, Wells undoubtedly intends to make a point about the class struggle in nineteenth-century Great Britain, but mere economic platitudes would not have kept *The Time Machine* in print for four generations. Wells also is offering a vision of time to come, a dream of futurity, and it is that vision that gives his work continuing life. Any of us could hold forth for hours on the proper relationship between labor and management, but only Wells was capable of showing us the hideous crabs crawling on that somber beach at the end of time.

Unfortunately, the shift from science fiction as satire to science fiction as vision can be carried too far; the retreat from editorial content may lead to a retreat from content of any sort, so that the grand voyage of science fiction becomes mere motion for motion's sake, hollow and pointless adventure fiction. This is one of the things that happened to science fiction when it became a part of commercial magazine publishing in the twentieth century. The first magazine completely devoted to science fiction—Hugo Gernsback's *Amazing Stories,* founded in 1926—attempted to preserve the older traditions. Leaning heavily on reprinted Verne and Wells, Gernsback also sought technologically oriented writers who would produce new stories depicting the worlds to come. The stiff gray pages of Gernsback's magazine glittered with fanciful gadgetry and bold predictions; but the prose, alas, was stiff and gray as well, since the men who could dream the dreams Gernsback wanted to print were not men who understood much about the narrative art. The awkward tales of this pioneering science-fiction magazine could captivate only a reader so thirsty for wonders that he could overlook a total lack of literary skill.

Gernsback's writers produced, for this special audience, lame gadget fiction after the manner of Verne, lame utopian satire after the manner of More, and lame visionary fiction after the manner of Wells. Inevitably, other magazine publishers sought to fill the niche Gernsback left vacant, by introducing an element of mass appeal. They replaced the dreary professors of *Amazing*'s typical stories with two-fisted reporters, adventurers, or space pilots; they junked the lengthy speculations on the future of technology and called upon the formulas of conventional pulp-magazine action fiction. Writers who in an earlier era would have been churning out dime novels now tooled up for the production of heroic epics of the spaceways. An empty, juvenile, superficially exciting science fiction, a debased Wellsian stuff that was all action and no content, began to appear.

The first magazine offering such fiction was founded in 1930: *Astounding Stories of Super Science.* Its contents were as gaudy as its title and its monster-bedecked covers; ray guns flashed, villains hissed, terrified maidens trembled as ghastly Things assailed their virtue. The puerility of the magazine's stories and the flamboyance of its illustrations helped to give science fiction a stigma of foolishness which it is only now losing. Naturally, *Astounding* immediately found a wide audience.

The Depression killed it, and when it was reborn under new management *Astounding* took a somewhat more mature approach.

By 1940, ironically, it stood alone as a source of adult science fiction in a sea of trash. By then, somewhat more demurely re-named *Astounding Science Fiction*, it was edited by John W. Campbell, one of the best writers of the Gernsback era. Campbell demanded from his contributors a consistency of thought and a breadth of vision not previously required. He wanted a fiction of ideas and imagination that could engage the reader's interest as ordinary fiction might do; that is, he wanted a fiction of characters, events, and style. One had to know how to think—the basic Gernsback criterion—but one also had to know how to write.

By this roundabout route, by this lengthy detour into trashiness, science fiction found its way back toward literary respectability. The pulp-magazine episode of the 1930s and 1940s now seems like a momentary aberration in a literary tradition of high antiquity. Today's science-fiction writers are makers of new myths, creators of unique dreams, explorers of time to come; but they are *not,* except for a reactionary few, purveyors of supersonic hackwork.

It has slowly become apparent to students of literature that science fiction deserves serious attention, not as a manifestation of pop culture but as an expressive and distinctive branch of the narrative art. Universities have begun to offer courses in the fiction of speculative thought. At first these courses kept piously to the sanctified classics—Cyrano, Bishop Godwin, Thomas More, Wells, Aldous Huxley, George Orwell—but gradually the academic investigation has extended even unto those who have worked within the established boundaries of science fiction as a publishing genre. The novels of such science-fictionists as Arthur C. Clarke, Walter M. Miller, Jr., Robert A. Heinlein, Alfred Bester, and others have lately found their way onto college reading lists.

The modern science-fiction short story has not yet had much consideration from the literary critics, however, and one of the purposes of the present book is to offer a selection of such stories by way of demonstrating the liveliness of the genre. Of the thirteen stories included, eleven appeared in specialized science-fiction magazines; the only exceptions are those of H. G. Wells—to show the point of departure for modern science fiction—and Jorge Luis Borges—to show how the form can be extended in the hands of a writer working entirely outside the magazine-fiction traditions. The others, published originally between 1934 and 1967, display the evolution of science fiction from the days of *Astounding Stories* to the current period of experiment and transition.

The special feature of this collection is the critical commentary attached to each story. No science-fiction anthology of the past, I believe, has ever attempted this kind of interpretive function. All thirteen essays here are the work of men who have previously published critiques of science fiction, ranging from articles in scholarly journals to entire books of analysis. Four of the contributors (Clareson, McNelly, Rogers, and Franklin) deal with science fiction in the classroom, in their capacities as professors of literature. Seven others (Blish, Knight, Panshin, Budrys, Conquest, Harrison, and Aldiss) are not only critics but also practicing science-fiction writers of high achievement. One (Williamson) bridges both groups, for he is a professor of literature who also has long been accounted an outstanding science-fiction writer.

In their brief forewords these contributors attempt to discern the criteria for excellence in science-fiction writing, and to show why the stories they have chosen meet those criteria. Both implicitly—in the stories—and explicitly—in the commentary—I think it is made clear that the attention science fiction has lately received has not been misplaced. The makers of myths must never be spurned; and in science fiction, which accepts no limitations of time or space and uniquely liberates the imagination, I believe we will find the governing myths of the dawning age of galactic man.

ROBERT SILVERBERG

THE STAR

by H. G. WELLS

FOREWORD
by Jack Williamson

THE AUTHOR

H. G. WELLS (1866–1946) was the author of a great many works of popularized history, philosophy, and science, and also wrote a series of "scientific romances" that are considered the foundation of modern science fiction. His best-known science-fiction novels include *The War of the Worlds, The Time Machine, The Island of Dr. Moreau,* and *When the Sleeper Wakes.* "The Star" was first published in 1897.

THE CRITIC

JACK WILLIAMSON's first science-fiction story, "The Metal Man," was published in Hugo Gernsback's *Amazing Stories* in 1928. In the mid-1930s his novel *The Legion of Space* was accorded classic status almost immediately upon publication; his story "With Folded Hands" (1947) and its sequel, *The Humanoids,* won him new fame a decade later; and he remains active as a writer, most recently collaborating with Frederik Pohl on a trilogy of novels.

Having left college without a degree in 1931, Williamson returned to get his B.A. twenty-six years later, and in 1960 joined the faculty of Eastern New Mexico University, where he is now a professor in English literature. In 1964 he received his doctorate at the University of Colorado. The topic of his thesis was *H. G. Wells: Critic of Progress.*

Foreword

"The Star" is a terror story of the most genuine stamp. Its terror springs from no vague Victorian ghosts, but from something that has touched us all.

"Now and then, though I rarely admit it," Wells commented, "the universe projects itself toward me in a grimace." One such grimace became *The Island of Dr. Moreau,* his black fable of man's jungle nature.

"The Star" must have sprung from another leer of the cosmos, for it leers at all of us. As literary artist—though he says he is no artist—Wells answers the demon. He wrestles it in the dark, and transforms its terror into a kind of delight.

Most nineteenth-century science fiction has gone with the gazebo. The science is rusty and the plots creak and the style is too ripe for our palates. Wells' early work is the exception.

Remarkable even today, Wells was dazzling in 1897, when "The Star" appeared in the Christmas *Graphic.* Pouring out such stories as this and such novels as *The Time Machine* and *The War of the Worlds,* he was more than anybody else the creator of modern science fiction.

Others before him, of course, had written tales of science and the future. There was the great Frenchman Jules Verne. There was the American Edgar Allan Poe, who inspired Verne. There was Swift and his Gulliver. There was even Plato, who planned a Greek utopia.

But Plato's *Republic* is philosophy, not science fiction. With troubles enough in his own time, Swift was satirizing the world he knew. Poe perhaps invented science fiction, but he didn't live to perfect it. Though Verne wrote thrilling adventure tales of new machines, he was too conservative to see the future as Wells did.

Unlike Verne, Wells could think as a scientist. He tells in his autobiography of his stirring year of study under Thomas Henry Huxley, who opened his eyes to the method and the power of

3

science. Huxley was Darwin's champion, and the facts of biological evolution must have given Wells his modern sense of the meaning of change.

Notions of change were not exactly new, but most of them had been mystical glimpses of supernatural motion toward the millennium or toward Armageddon. The processes of natural change, described by discoverable laws of nature, had first been firmly established by such men as Darwin and Huxley.

Now science fiction is about change. More exactly, it's about the human consequences of scientific progress. That's why the genre is so new. Though the rates of change have now become a mad stampede, they were invisible in Plato's day and oxcart-slow in Swift's. In worlds where tomorrow could only replay yesterday, science fiction had no place.

Aware of change, Wells was one of the first intelligent men to take a serious look at the future from the new viewpoint of science. In his significant lecture "The Discovery of the Future," he observed that we can investigate things to come, from a study of the relevant available evidence, in very much the same way that historians investigate the past.

He applied his forecasting techniques in a nonfiction book, *Anticipations,* and then in the great novel *When the Sleeper Wakes,* whose grim social predictions already seem to be hitting uncomfortably close to the truth.

We can be either optimists or pessimists about the outcome of change. Falsely, for a whole generation, Wells has been called an easy optimist. His name has been misused, in such phrases as "crass Wellsianism," to describe a blind devotion to material progress.

In a doctoral study of Wells, I tried to show up this error. A biologist, Wells knew that no species survives forever. He saw that the human species is in danger of extinction. He explores the danger, in his early science fiction, and marks out the limits of human progress.

Some limits are in ourselves. *The Island of Dr. Moreau* is a terrible parable of the animal nature of man. Moreau is a symbolic god, created somewhat in Huxley's image. Through vivisection, he transforms animals into things like men. When he is killed, his creatures revert into a dreadful parody of humanity.

Our greatest danger springs out of our own nature, as Wells is clearly aware. (He began writing about uranium fission bombs in 1914.) Yet, as he points out, even if we survive our own bent for self-destruction, we still have external dangers to face.

"The Star" offers a terrifying symbol of man and his cosmos. The unknown planetary object, "rushing without warning out of the black mystery of the sky," stands for all the dark indifference of a universe not made for human comfort, where nothing at all survives forever.

With even deeper pessimism, Wells points out in many stories that all progress is relative and self-limiting. His Martians have advanced so far that they are killed by the simplest germs. His future human beings, in *The Time Machine,* have built their whole social order on murder and cannibalism. Nature cares only for survivors, and our humane ideals are even more vulnerable than the species itself.

Ironically, the image of Wells as the stupidly cheerful utopian arose from his darkest premonitions. Spurred to desperate effort, he fought to save mankind. He wrote his later utopian novels as blueprints for possible survival. He toiled over thick books on history and biology and economics, textbooks to train citizens of the world state he fought for. He died almost in despair, feeling that his long fight had been lost.

In his middle years, deep in that struggle, Wells gave up his art for propaganda and indulged in a famous quarrel with Henry James over the use of literature. *Boom* was a deadly stab at James. Most of his propaganda novels have been forgotten, but he was still an artist when he wrote "The Star." It remains decidedly alive.

Goodness in fiction is hard to define, because artistic values, like snowflakes, tend to disappear under examination. But, among other things, literature is a record of response to experience. As I. A. Richards observed, some responses are better than others. Here Wells has set down a good response.

The experience is one of those jeering faces that we all sometimes glimpse in the cosmic dark, the piercing awareness that our world was not made for us and that all our futures lie beyond prediction and control. Most of us drop our eyes and try to say the demon isn't really there.

Writing as artist, Wells faces the monster, drags it out of the shadows, cages it for all of us to inspect. So exhibited under the objective controls of form and style, it loses half its leering terror.

As science fiction, "The Star" has its own special effects. One of these is wonder. Creating wonder takes more than something strange or extraordinary. It takes identification and emotional involvement. Vicariously sharing adventure, the reader feels the shock of unexpected discovery, the fear of unknown danger, the hope of new fulfillment.

"The Star" has wonder enough. When planets are twisted from their orbits to visit earth with fire and flood, the reader fears the extinction of the race and hopes for its survival.

This sense of wonder flows out of what Coleridge called "that willing suspension of disbelief for the moment, which constitutes poetic faith." To sustain his vital illusion, the writer must do far more than avoid clumsy violation of accepted scientific fact. For fact alone doesn't really matter.

Wells' *Invisible Man* is a case in point. The hero becomes invisible by making his body tissues transparent. Wells understood that transparent eyes would be blind, but for the sake of the novel he chose to ignore that inconvenience.

In "The Star" he ignores other difficulties of the same sort. In strict scientific fact, if a colliding body stopped the planet Neptune in its orbit in the way he describes, the incandescent mass would take years instead of days to fall into the sun.

For the sake of pace and tension, he squeezes literal fact into more dramatic truth. His craftsmanship justifies itself.

Early, Wells perfected what is still the basic pattern of science fiction. In his own words, it's "the method of bringing some fantastically possible or impossible thing into a commonplace group of people, and working out their reactions with the greatest gravity and reasonableness."

The invention, he says, is nothing in itself. "The thing that makes such imaginations interesting is their translation into commonplace terms and a rigid exclusion of other marvels from the story. Then it becomes human."

Here his formula proves itself. The invention, the invader out of the dark, can scarcely be questioned, now when we are discovering such objects as quasars and pulsars. Accepting the premise, we're trapped at once in the spell of poetic faith.

His language has rhythm and emotion and rich detail. "And upon all the mountains of the earth the snow and ice began to melt that night, and all the rivers coming out of high country flowed thick and turbid, and soon—in their upper reaches—with swirling trees and the bodies of beasts and men."

The terror here is real, because it springs from a shared sense that we are nothing against the ultimate unknown—that, in spite of all our cunning, we are as surely mortal as any other species.

But Wells uses style to make this terror tolerable. The ironic detachment of his point of view suggests the final insignificance of man, to underline his theme. He sets us at a safe distance, both aesthetic and astronomical, to watch the plight of earth in company with the scientists of Mars.

With superb craftsmanship, he uses everything about the story to support his dominant theme that the cosmos cares nothing for man. There is no characterization. No character is even named—because, from Wells' cosmic point of view, no human being is worth a second glance. The vastness of the astronomical setting contrasts with the infinite smallness of man. The plot problem is solved by the coincidental chance movement of planets rolling in their orbits like balls in roulette wheels, and not by any human effort—which is Wells' way of saying that human effort means nothing at all. Even the brevity of the story underlines the theme. Mankind is worth no more attention.

"The Star" is fine science fiction.

THE STAR

It was on the first day of the new year that the announcement was made, almost simultaneously from three observatories, that the motion of the planet Neptune, the outermost of all the planets that wheel about the sun, had become very erratic. Ogilvy had already called attention to a suspected retardation in its velocity in December. Such a piece of news was scarcely calculated to interest a world the greater portion of whose inhabitants were unaware of the existence of the planet Neptune, nor outside the astronomical profession did the subsequent discovery of a faint remote speck of light in the region of the perturbed planet cause any very great excitement. Scientific people, however, found the intelligence remarkable enough, even before it became known that the new body was rapidly growing larger and brighter, that its motion was quite different from the orderly progress of the planets, and that the deflection of Neptune and its satellite was becoming now of an unprecedented kind.

Few people without a training in science can realize the huge isolation of the solar system. The sun with its specks of planets, its dust of planetoids, and its impalpable comets, swims in a vacant immensity that almost defeats the imagination. Beyond the orbit of Neptune there is space, vacant so far as human observation has penetrated, without warmth or light or sound, blank emptiness, for twenty million times a million miles. That is the smallest estimate of the distance to be traversed before the very nearest of the stars is attained. And, saving a few comets more unsubstantial than the thinnest flame, no matter had ever to human knowledge crossed this gulf of space, until early in the twentieth century this strange wanderer appeared. A vast mass of matter it was, bulky, heavy, rushing without warning out of the black mystery of the sky into the radiance of the sun. By the second day it was clearly visible to any decent instrument, as a speck with a barely sensible diameter, in the constellation Leo near Regulus. In a little while an opera glass could attain it.

On the third day of the new year the newspaper readers of two hemispheres were made aware for the first time of the real importance of this unusual apparition in the heavens. "A Planetary Collision," one London paper headed the news, and proclaimed Duchaine's opinion that this strange new planet would probably collide with Neptune. The leader writers enlarged upon the topic. So that in most of the capitals of the world, on January 3rd, there was an expectation, however vague, of some imminent phenomenon in the sky; and as the night followed the sunset round the globe, thousands of men turned their eyes skyward to see—the old familiar stars just as they had always been.

Until it was dawn in London and Pollux setting and the stars overhead grown pale. The Winter's dawn it was, a sickly filtering accumulation of daylight, and the light of gas and candles shone yellow in the windows to show where people were astir. But the yawning policemen saw the thing, the busy crowds in the markets stopped agape, workmen going to their work early, milkmen, the drivers of news-carts, dissipation going home jaded and pale, homeless wanderers, sentinels on their beats, and in the country, laborers trudging afield, poachers slinking home, all over the dusky quickening country it could be seen—and out at sea by seamen watching for the day—a great white star, come suddenly into the westward sky!

Brighter it was than any star in our skies; brighter than the evening star at its brightest. It still glowed out white and large, no mere twinkling spot of light, but a small round clear shining disc, an hour after the day had come. And where science has not reached, men stared and feared, telling one another of the wars and pestilences that are foreshadowed by these fiery signs in the heavens. Sturdy Boers, dusky Hottentots, Gold Coast Negroes, Frenchmen, Spaniards, Portuguese, stood in the warmth of the sunrise watching the setting of this strange new star.

And in a hundred observatories there had been suppressed excitement, rising almost to shouting pitch, as the two remote bodies had rushed together, and a hurrying to and fro, to gather photographic apparatus and spectroscope, and this appliance and that, to record this novel astonishing sight, the destruction of a world. For it was a world, a sister planet of our earth, far greater than our earth indeed, that had so suddenly flashed into flaming death. Neptune it was, had been struck, fairly and squarely, by the strange planet from outer space and the heat of the concussion had incontinently turned two solid globes into one vast mass of incandescence. Round the world that day, two hours before the dawn, went the pallid great white star, fading only as it sank westward and the sun mounted above it. Everywhere men marvelled at it, but of all those who saw it none could have marvelled more than those sailors, habitual watchers of the stars, who far away at sea had heard nothing of its advent and saw it now rise like a pigmy moon and climb zenithward and hang overhead and sink westward with the passing of the night.

And when it next rose over Europe everywhere were crowds of watchers on hilly slopes, on house-roofs, in open spaces, staring eastward for the rising of the great new star. It rose with a white glow in front of it, like the glare of a white fire, and those who had seen it come into existence the night before cried out at the sight of it. "It is larger," they cried. "It is brighter!" And, indeed, the moon a quarter full and sinking in the west was in its apparent size beyond comparison, but scarcely in all its breadth had it as much brightness now as the little circle of the strange new star.

"It is brighter!" cried the people clustering in the streets. But in the dim observatories the watchers held their breath and peered at one another. *"It is nearer,"* they said. *"Nearer!"*

And voice after voice repeated, "It is nearer," and the clicking telegraph took that up, and it trembled along telephone wires, and in a thousand cities grimy compositors fingered the type. "It is nearer." Men writing in offices, struck with a strange realization, flung down their pens, men talking in a thousand places suddenly came upon a grotesque possibility in those words, "It is nearer." It hurried along awakening streets, it was shouted down the frost-stilled ways of quiet villages, men who had read these things from the throbbing tape stood in yellow-lit doorways shouting the news to the passers-by. "It is nearer." Pretty women, flushed and glittering, heard the news told jestingly between the dances, and feigned an intelligent interest they did not feel. "Nearer! Indeed. How curious! How very, very clever people must be to find out things like that!"

Lonely tramps faring through the wintry night murmured those words to comfort themselves—looking skyward. "It has need to be nearer, for the night's as cold as charity. Don't seem much warmth from it if it *is* nearer, all the same."

"What is a new star to me?" cried the weeping woman kneeling beside her dead.

The schoolboy, rising early for his examination work, puzzled it out for himself—with the great white star, shining broad and bright through the frost-flowers of his window. "Centrifugal, centripetal," he said, with his chin on his fist. "Stop a planet in its flight, rob it of its centrifugal force, what then? Centripetal has it, and down it falls into the sun! And this—!

"Do *we* come in the way? I wonder—"

The light of that day went the way of its brethren, and with the later watches of the frosty darkness rose the strange star again. And it was now so bright that the waxing moon seemed but a pale yellow ghost of itself, hanging huge in the sunset. In a South African city a great man had married, and the streets were alight to welcome his return with his bride. "Even the skies have illuminated," said the flatterer. Under Capricorn, two Negro lovers, daring the wild beasts and the evil spirits, for love of one another, crouched together in a canebrake where the fire-flies hovered. "That is our star," they whispered, and felt strangely comforted by the sweet brilliance of its light.

The master mathematician sat in his private room and pushed the papers from him. His calculations were already finished. In a small white phial there still remained a little of the drug that had kept him awake and active for four long nights. Each day, serene, explicit, patient as ever, he had given his lecture to his students, and then had come back at once to this momentous calculation. His face was grave, a little drawn and hectic from his drugged activity. For some time he seemed lost in thought. Then he went to the window, and the blind went up with a click. Halfway up the sky, over the clustering roofs, chimneys and steeples of the city, hung the star.

He looked at it as one might look into the eyes of a brave enemy. "You may kill me," he said after a silence. "But I can hold you—and all the universe for that matter—in the grip of this little brain. I would not change. Even now."

He looked at the little phial. "There will be no need of sleep again," he said. The next day at noon, punctual to the minute, he entered his lecture theater, put his hat on the end of the table, as his habit was, and carefully selected a large piece of chalk. It was a joke among his students that he could not lecture without that piece of chalk to fumble in his fingers, and once he had been stricken to impotence by their hiding his supply. He came and looked under his gray eyebrows at the rising tiers of young fresh faces, and spoke with his accustomed studied commonness of phrasing. "Circumstances have arisen—circumstances beyond my control," he said and paused, "which will debar me from completing the course I had designed. It would seem, gentlemen, if I may put the thing clearly and briefly, that—Man has lived in vain."

The students glanced at one another. Had they heard aright? Mad? Raised eyebrows and grinning lips there were, but one or two faces remained intent upon his calm gray-fringed face. "It will be interesting," he was saying, "to devote this morning to an exposition, so far as I can make it clear to you, of the calculations that have led me to this conclusion. Let us assume—"

He turned toward the blackboard, meditating a diagram in the way that was usual to him. "What was that about 'lived in vain'?" whispered one student to another. "Listen," said the other, nodding toward the lecturer.

And presently they began to understand.

That night the star rose later, for its proper eastward motion had carried it some way across Leo toward Virgo, and its brightness was so great that the sky became a luminous blue as it rose, and every star was hidden in its turn, save only Jupiter near the zenith, Capella, Aldebaran, Sirius and the pointers of the Bear. It was very white and beautiful. In many parts of the world that night a pallid halo encircled it about. It was perceptibly larger; in the clear refractive sky of the tropics it seemed as if it were nearly a quarter the size of the moon. The frost was still on the ground in England, but the world was as brightly lit as if it were midsummer moonlight. One could see to read quite ordinary print by that cold clear light, and in the cities the lamps burnt yellow and wan.

And everywhere the world was awake that night, and throughout Christendom a somber murmur hung in the keen air over the countryside like the belling of bees in the heather, and this murmurous tumult grew to a clangor in the cities. It was the tolling of the bells in a million belfry towers and steeples, summoning the people to sleep no more, to sin no more, but to gather in their churches and pray. And overhead, growing larger and brighter, as the earth rolled on its way and the night passed, rose the dazzling star.

And the streets and houses were alight in all the cities, the shipyards glared, and whatever roads led to high country were lit and crowded all night long. And in all the seas about the civilized lands, ships with throbbing engines, and ships with bellying sails, crowded with men and living creatures, were standing out to ocean and the north. For already the warning of the master mathematician had been telegraphed all over the world, and translated into a hundred tongues. The new planet and Neptune, locked in a fiery embrace, were whirling headlong, ever faster and faster toward the sun. Already every second this blazing mass flew a hundred miles, and every second its terrific velocity increased. As it flew now, indeed, it must pass a hundred million miles wide of the earth and scarcely affect it. But near its destined path, as yet only slightly perturbed, spun the mighty planet Jupiter and his moons sweeping splendid round the sun. Every moment now the attraction between the fiery star and the greatest of the planets grew stronger. And the result of that attraction? Inevitably Jupiter would be deflected from its orbit into an elliptical path, and the burning star, swung by his attraction wide of its sunward rush, would "describe a curved path" and perhaps collide with, and certainly pass very close to, our earth. "Earthquakes, volcanic outbreaks, cyclones, sea waves, floods, and a steady rise in temperature to I know not what limit"— so prophesied the master mathematician.

And overhead, to carry out his words, lonely and cold and livid, blazed the star of the coming doom.

To many who stared at it that night until their eyes ached, it seemed that it was visibly approaching. And that night, too, the weather changed, and the frost that had gripped all Central Europe and France and England softened toward a thaw.

But you must not imagine because I have spoken of people praying through the night and people going aboard ships and people fleeing toward mountainous country that the whole world was already in a terror because of the star. As a matter of fact, use and wont still ruled the world, and save for the talk of idle moments and the splendor of the night, nine human beings out of ten were still busy at their common occupations. In all the cities the shops, save one here and there, opened and closed at their proper hours, the doctor and the undertaker plied their trades, the workers gathered in the factories, soldiers drilled, scholars studied, lovers sought one another, thieves lurked and fled, politicians planned their schemes. The presses of the newspapers roared through the nights, and many a priest of this church and that would not open his holy building to further what he considered a foolish panic. The newspapers insisted on the lesson of the year 1000—for then, too, people had anticipated the end. The star was no star—mere gas—a comet; and were it a star it could not possibly strike the earth. There was no precedent for such a thing. Common sense was sturdy everywhere, scornful, jesting, a little inclined to persecute the obdurate fearful. That night, at seven-fifteen by Greenwich time, the star would be at its nearest to Jupiter. Then the world would see the turn things would take. The master mathematician's grim warnings were treated by many as so much mere elaborate self-advertisement. Common sense at last, a little heated by argument, signified its unalterable convictions by going to bed. So, too, barbarism and savagery, already tired of the novelty, went about their nightly business, and save for a howling dog here and there, the beast world left the star unheeded.

And yet, when at last the watchers in the European States saw the star rise, an hour later it is true, but no larger than it had been the night before, there were still plenty awake to laugh at the master mathematician—to take the danger as if it had passed.

But hereafter the laughter ceased. The star grew—it grew with a terrible steadiness hour after hour, a little larger each hour, a little nearer the midnight zenith, and brighter and brighter, until it had turned night into a second day. Had it come straight to the earth instead of a curved path, had it lost no velocity to Jupiter, it must have leapt the intervening gulf in a day, but as it was it took five days altogether to come by our planet. The next night it had become a third the size of the moon before it set to English eyes, and the thaw was assured. It rose over America near the size of the moon, but blinding white to look at, and *hot;* and a breath of hot wind blew now with its rising and gathering strength, and in Virginia, and Brazil, and down the St. Lawrence valley, it shone intermittently through a driving reek of thunder-clouds, flickering violet lightning, and hail unprecedented. In Manitoba was a thaw, and devastating floods. And upon all the mountains of the earth the snow and ice began to melt that night, and all the rivers coming out of high country flowed thick and turbid, and soon—in their upper reaches—with swirling trees and the bodies of beasts and men. They rose steadily, steadily in the ghostly brilliance, and came trickling over their banks at last, behind the flying population of their valleys. And along the coast of Argentina and up the South Atlantic the tides were higher than had ever been in the memory of man, and the storms drove the waters in many cases scores of miles inland, drowning whole cities. And so great grew the heat during the night that the rising of the sun was like the coming of a shadow. The earthquakes began and grew until all down America, from the Arctic Circle to Cape Horn, hillsides were sliding, fissures were opening, and houses and walls crumbling to destruction. The whole side of Cotopaxi slipped out in one vast convulsion, and a tumult of lava poured out so high and broad and swift and liquid that in one day it reached the sea.

So the star, with the wan moon in its wake, marched across the Pacific, trailed the thunderstorms like the hem of a robe, and the growing tidal wave that toiled behind it, frothing and eager, poured over island and island and swept them clear of men. Until that wave came at last—in a blinding light and with the breath of a furnace, swift and terrible it came—a wall of water, fifty feet high, roaring hungrily, upon the long coasts of Asia, and swept inland across the plains of China. For a space the star, hotter now and larger and brighter than the sun in its strength, showed with pitiless brilliance the wide and populous country; towns and villages with their pagodas and trees, roads, wide cultivated fields, millions of sleepless people staring in helpless terror at the incandescent sky; and then, low and growing, came the murmur of the flood. And thus it was with millions of men that night—a flight nowhither, with limbs heavy with heat and breath fierce and scant, and the flood like a wall swift and white behind. And then death.

China was lit glowing white, but over Japan and Java and all the islands of Eastern Asia the great star was a ball of dull red fire because of the steam and smoke and ashes the volcanoes were spouting forth to salute its coming. Above was the lava, hot gases and ash, and below the seething floods, and the whole earth swayed and rumbled with the earthquake shocks. Soon the immemorial snows of Tibet and the Himalayas were melting and pouring down by ten million deepening converging channels upon the plains of Burma and Hindustan. The tangled summits of the Indian jungles were aflame in a thousand places, and below the hurrying waters around the stems were dark objects that still struggled feebly and reflected the blood-red tongues of fire. And in a rudderless confusion a multitude of men and women fled down the broad river-ways to that one last hope of men—the open sea.

Larger grew the star, and larger, hotter, and brighter with a terrible swiftness now. The tropical ocean had lost its phosphorescence, and the whirling steam rose in ghostly wreaths from the black waves that plunged incessantly, speckled with storm-tossed ships.

And then came a wonder. It seemed to those who in Europe watched for the rising of the star that the world must have ceased its rotation. In a thousand open spaces of down and upland the people who had fled thither from the floods and the falling houses and sliding slopes of hill watched for that rising in vain. Hour followed hour through a terrible suspense, and the star rose not. Once again men set their eyes upon the old constellations they had counted lost to them forever. In England it was hot and clear overhead, though the ground quivered perpetually, but in the tropics, Sirius and Capella and Aldebaran showed through a veil of steam. And when at last the great star rose near ten hours late, the sun rose close upon it, and in the center of its white heart was a disc of black.

Over Asia it was as if the star had begun to fall behind the movement of the sky, and then suddenly, as it hung over India, its light had been veiled. All the plain of India from the mouth of the Indus to the mouth of the Ganges was a shallow waste of shining water that night, out of which rose temples and palaces, mounds and hills, black with people. Every minaret was a clustering mass of people, who fell one by one into the turbid waters, as heat and terror overcame them. The whole land seemed a-wailing, and suddenly there swept a shadow across that furnace of despair, and a breath of cold wind, and a gathering of clouds, out of the cooling air. Men looking up, near blinded, at the star, saw that a black disc was creeping across the light. It was the moon, coming between the star and the earth. And even as men cried to God at this respite, out of the East with a strange inexplicable swiftness sprang the sun. And then star, sun and moon rushed together across the heavens.

So it was that presently, to the European watchers, star and sun rose close upon each other, drove headlong for a space and then slower, and at last came to rest, star and sun merged into one glare of flame at the zenith of the sky. The moon no longer eclipsed the star but was lost to sight in the brilliance of the sky. And though those who were still alive regarded it for the most part with that dull stupidity that hunger, fatigue, heat and despair engender, there were still men who could perceive the meaning of these signs. Star and earth had been at their nearest, had swung about one another, and the star had passed. Already it was receding, swifter and swifter, in the last stage of its headlong journey downward into the sun.

And then the clouds gathered, blotting out the vision of the sky, the thunder and lightning wove a garment round the world; all over the earth was such a downpour of rain as men had never before seen, and where the volcanoes flared red against the cloud canopy there descended torrents of mud. Everywhere the waters were pouring off the land, leaving mud-silted ruins, and the earth littered like a storm-worn beach with all that had floated, and the dead bodies of the men and brutes, its children.

For days the water streamed off the land, sweeping away soil and trees and houses in the way, and piling huge dikes and scooping out Titanic gullies over the countryside. Those were the days of darkness that followed the star and the heat. All through them, and for many weeks and months, the earthquakes continued.

But the star had passed, and men, hunger-driven and gathering courage only slowly, might creep back to their ruined cities, buried granaries, and sodden fields. Such few ships as had escaped the storms of that time came stunned and shattered and sounding their way cautiously through the new marks and shoals of once familiar ports. And as the storms subsided men perceived that everywhere the days were hotter than of yore, and the sun larger, and the moon, shrunk to a third of its former size, took now fourscore days between its new and new.

But of the new brotherhood that grew presently among men, of the saving of laws and books and machines, of the strange change that had come over Iceland and Greenland and the shores of Baffin's Bay, so that the sailors coming there presently found them green and gracious, and could scarce believe their eyes, this story does not tell. Nor of the movement of mankind now that the earth was hotter, northward and southward toward the poles of the earth. It concerns itself only with the coming and the passing of the Star.

The Martian astronomers—for there are astronomers on Mars, although they are very different beings from men—were naturally profoundly interested by these things. They saw them from their own standpoint of course. "Considering the mass and temperature of the missile that was flung through our solar system into the sun," one wrote, "it is astonishing what little damage the earth, which it missed so narrowly, has sustained. All the familiar continental markings and the masses of the seas remain intact, and indeed the only difference seems to be a shrinkage of the white discoloration (supposed to be frozen water) round either pole." Which only shows how small the vastest of human catastrophes may seem, at a distance of a few million miles.

TWILIGHT

by JOHN W. CAMPBELL

FOREWORD

by Algis Budrys

THE AUTHOR

JOHN W. CAMPBELL, born in 1910, began writing science fiction when he was still an undergraduate at the Massachusetts Institute of Technology; his first story, "When the Atoms Failed," was published in *Amazing Stories* for January, 1930. Though he has a degree in physics from Duke University, he has been professionally involved in science fiction for most of his adult life, first as a leading author and then (since 1937) as the editor of the magazine now called *Analog,* formerly *Astounding Science Fiction.* His fiction under his own name includes such novels as *The Mightiest Machine* and *The Black Star Passes,* but he won more attention for his stories under the pseudonym of "Don A. Stuart," particularly "Who Goes There?," "Twilight," and "Night." "Twilight" was first published in 1934.

THE CRITIC

ALGIS BUDRYS, born in Prussia in 1931 to Lithuanian parents, came to the United States five years later, and after a varied education became a professional science-fiction writer in 1952. Many of his early stories appeared in John W. Campbell's *Astounding.* Among Budrys' best-known work are the novels *Rogue Moon* and *The Falling Torch,* and the stories "The End of Summer," "The Executioner," and "Walk to the World." In recent years he has worked for public-relations firms in the Chicago area, and has served as book reviewer for *Galaxy Science Fiction.*

Foreword

There is no story in science fiction more influential than "Twilight."
I think you should have read it before delving any farther into
this essay. If you have not read it recently, I even more strongly
suggest that you read it now, for this story possesses two of the
hallmarks of literature, at least: (1) it gives the impression of
being totally memorable; and (2) it rewards each rereading with
a revelation of how much more it contains than your memory can.

Now, then. This story, by Don A. Stuart, is famous for having
been written in 1932 by John W. Campbell, Jr., who was running
E. E. Smith a very close second as a factory of super-science tales
of thrilling and gory (but bloodless) adventure 'mongst the
galaxies. Everyone, just about, knows the tale of how this gently
told vignette was rejected by every publication in the field, and of
how Campbell had to create the Stuart byline to ease the shock of
its radically different style. And, of course, when it finally appeared,
in the November, 1934, *Astounding Stories* (along with an announcement that the magazine would shortly be serializing *The
Mightiest Machine* by the fabulous planet wrecker John W. Campbell, Jr.), it began a revolution which soon saw Campbell as editor
of *Astounding,* and *Astounding* founding a truly golden age of
stories in the mode of "Twilight," and not at all like *The Mightiest Machine.*

But I wonder, now, if this might not be too facile a legend.

There is no doubt of the bare facts of when and how the story
was written. If you ask Campbell, he will tell you that he wrote
it in 1932, after having mulled over a novel by C. E. Scoggins
called *The Red Gods Call.* This book, he recalls, contains a description of modern Indians working as laborers in an archaeological
excavation of Inca monuments. What struck Campbell, apparently
after having struck Scoggins as a valid observation of an identifi-
able quality of man, was that the Indian laborers grubbing out
the dirt betrayed no sense of kinship with their jungled-over

ancestral glories. And of the thousands who read Scoggins' book, Campbell alone, the science-fiction writer, was moved then to write "Twilight," and moved as well to accept responsibility for all that was discovered to follow from it.

But this is a bit odd, because if you look at "Twilight" you find things in it that have nothing to do, even in parallel, with sweaty Indians and the static past; they have to do, in fact, with educability, which is a much different, and supposedly abstract, subject.

If you will put aside the legend, and regard only the story—a truly good, effective story, betraying not a line or blemish of its venerable age—I think you will find in it many evocations not of Scoggins but of the mood and tone of the latter half of H. G. Wells' *The Time Machine,* which also has to do with a man from the past who cannot persuade the people of the future to adopt his morality.

This is not, I believe, what either "Twilight" or *The Time Machine* is usually supposed to be about. But if you read very many critical essays about works of art—particularly about the same works of art, and most particularly about works of art that you have gone and observed for yourself—you will find that generally speaking there is little disagreement that a particular piece is effective. The disputes arise—in volume corresponding to the effectiveness of the piece—over questions related to resolving what the work is about.

This phenomenon offers the clues that (1) even art is not immune to the common human trait of finding the proper box in which to store the memory of each event, and (2) that these discussions are totally unrelated to the preceding artistic process, even when the artist himself gets involved in the discussions.

All this relates to "Twilight" as follows:

If you read the story, you may well be struck by the author's attention to significant detail as he depicts the verbal interplay among the twentieth-century small-town wise men coping with the reported phenomenon of the man from the future, and his story. You may be struck, as well, by the many times in the story in which we have an incident of failed communication—between scientist and his experiment, between traveler and machine, between the past and the future, between the future and the past, and even between the supposedly contemporary individuals of the little group of village elders mulling over the central question of whether what has happened is going to be good or bad for the Chamber of Commerce. And when one comes to the stuffed dog in his glass case, one cannot help also thinking that there are a great many places in this story in which the author touches on the fact that information is the embalming fluid of history.

There's a veritable feast of critical clues from which you are free to draw any conclusion you may arrange, and of which you may construct whatever edifice or artifice may appeal to you. I have constructed mine, and mine is that John W. Campbell, Jr., felt something when he read about Scoggins' Indians; that he was moved, that he had to explain to himself why and how he was moved, and that, being an artist (not a dirty word, by the way), he took what he felt and related it to everything he had ever felt before—and expressed himself.

He must have been profoundly moved to write something so apparently different from what was not only successful but accustomed, and to nurture it for years. But my point now is that this does not necessarily mean that what he was moved to do was what he thought he was moved to do. The events testify only to the intensity of his emotion.

If you will look at the other Don A. Stuart stories that followed —"Forgetfulness," "Who Goes There?," "Blindness," and the many others—you will often find them fundamentally different from "Twilight," and from each other. (They are usually also very good stories.) They do not in fact express any consistent rational view of the world; they reflect only a consistent rational mood, quite different from the precise little boxes in which John W. Campbell stacks his editorial expressions and his reasons why.

I think John W. Campbell, Jr., found that the Don A. Stuart mode was exciting; that "Twilight" was an event—a signal event— and that much of what has followed after it in the history of this field is the result of how John W. Campbell, Jr., reacted to the event of "Twilight."

But that is something very different from "Twilight" itself, which is a work of art, enduring and effective on its own merits, more permanent than criticism, more valid than an essay; a moment in time in which you and an artist's expression meet, and then each go your separate ways, with you richer in whatever good coin you were equipped to accept at the time.

TWILIGHT

"Speaking of hitch-hikers," said Jim Bendell in a rather bewildered way, "I picked up a man the other day that certainly was a queer cuss." He laughed, but it wasn't a real laugh. "He told me the queerest yarn I ever heard. Most of them tell you how they lost their good jobs and tried to find work out here in the wide spaces of the West. They don't seem to realize how many people we have out here. They think all this great beautiful country is uninhabited."

Jim Bendell's a real estate man, and I knew how he could go on. That's his favorite line, you know. He's real worried because there's a lot of homesteading plots still open out in our state. He talks about the beautiful country, but he never went farther into the desert than the edge of town. 'Fraid of it actually. So I sort of steered him back on the track.

"What did he claim, Jim? Prospector who couldn't find land to prospect?"

"That's not very funny, Bart. No; it wasn't only what he claimed. He didn't even claim it, just said it. You know, he didn't say it was true, he just said it. That's what gets me. I know it ain't true, but the way he said it—Oh I don't know."

By which I knew he didn't. Jim Bendell's usually pretty careful about his English—real proud of it. When he slips, that means he's disturbed. Like the time he thought the rattlesnake was a stick of wood and wanted to put it on the fire.

Jim went on: And he had funny clothes, too. They looked like silver, but they were soft as silk. And at night they glowed just a little.

I picked him up about dusk. Really picked him up. He was lying off about ten feet from the South Road. I thought, at first, somebody had hit him, and then hadn't stopped. Didn't see him very clearly, you know. I picked him up, put him in the car, and started on. I had about three hundred miles to go, but I thought I could drop him at Warren Spring with Doc Vance. But he came to in about five minutes, and opened his eyes. He looked straight off, and he looked first at the car, then at the Moon. "Thank God!" he says, and then looks at me. It gave me a shock. He was beautiful. No; he was handsome.

He wasn't either one. He was magnificent. He was about six feet two, I think, and his hair was brown, with a touch of red-gold. It seemed like fine copper wire that's turned brown. It was crisp and curly. His forehead was wide, twice as wide as mine. His features were delicate, but tremendously impressive; his eyes were gray, like etched iron, and bigger than mine—a lot.

That suit he wore—it was more like a bathing suit with pajama trousers. His arms were long and muscled smoothly as an Indian's. He was white, though, tanned lightly with a golden, rather than a brown, tan.

But he was magnificent. Most wonderful man I ever saw. I don't know, damn it!

"Hello!" I said. "Have an accident?"

"No; not this time, at least."

And his voice was magnificent, too. It wasn't an ordinary voice. It sounded like an organ talking, only it was human.

"But maybe my mind isn't quite steady yet. I tried an experiment. Tell me what the date is, year and all, and let me see," he went on.

"Why—December 9, 1932," I said.

And it didn't please him. He didn't like it a bit. But the wry grin that came over his face gave way to a chuckle.

"Over a thousand—" he says reminiscently. "Not as bad as seven million. I shouldn't complain."

"Seven million what?"

"Years," he said, steadily enough. Like he meant it. "I tried an experiment once. Or I will try it. Now I'll have to try again. The experiment was—in 3059. I'd just finished the release experiment. Testing space then. Time—it wasn't that, I still believe. It was space. I felt myself caught in that field, but I couldn't pull away. Field gamma-H 481, intensity 935 in the Pellman range. It sucked me in, and I went out.

"I think it took a short cut through space to the position the solar system will occupy. Through a higher dimension, effecting a speed exceeding light and throwing me into the future plane."

He wasn't telling me, you know. He was just thinking out loud. Then he began to realize I was there.

"I couldn't read their instruments, seven million years of evolution changed everything. So I overshot my mark a little coming back. I belong in 3059.

"But tell me, what's the latest scientific invention of this year?"

He startled me so, I answered almost before I thought. "Why, television, I guess. And radio and airplanes."

"Radio—good. They will have instruments."

"But see here—who are you?"

"Ah—I'm sorry. I forgot," he replied in that organ voice of his. "I am Ares Sen Kenlin. And you?"

"James Waters Bendell."

"Waters—what does that mean? I do not recognize it."

"Why—it's a name, of course. Why should you recognize it?"

"I see—you have not the classification, then. 'Sen' stands for science."

"Where did you come from, Mr. Kenlin?"

"Come from?" He smiled, and his voice was slow and soft. "I came out of space across seven million years or more. They had lost count—the men had. The machines had eliminated the unneeded service. They didn't know what year it was. But before that—my home is in Neva'th City in the year 3059."

That's when I began to think he was a nut.

"I was an experimenter," he went on. "Science, as I have said. My father was a scientist, too, but in human genetics. I myself am an experiment. He proved his point, and all the world followed suit. I was the first of the new race.

"The new race—oh, holy destiny—what has—what will—

"What is its end? I have seen it—almost. I saw them—the little men—bewildered—lost. And the machines. Must it be—can't anything sway it?

"Listen—I heard this song."

He sang the song. Then he didn't have to tell me about the people. I knew them. I could hear their voices, in the queer, crackling, un-English words. I could read their bewildered longings. It was in a minor key, I think. It called, it called and asked, and hunted hopelessly. And over it all the steady rumble and whine of the unknown, forgotten machines.

The machines that couldn't stop, because they had been started, and the little men had forgotten how to stop them, or even what they were for, looking at them and listening—and wondering. They couldn't read or write any more, and the language had changed, you see, so that the phonic records of their ancestors meant nothing to them.

But that song went on, and they wondered. And they looked out across space and they saw the warm, friendly stars—too far away. Nine planets they knew and inhabited. And locked by infinite distance, they couldn't see another race, a new life.

And through it all—two things. The machines. Bewildered forgetfulness. And maybe one more. Why?

That was the song, and it made me cold. It shouldn't be sung around people of today. It almost killed something. It seemed to kill hope. After that song—I—well, I believed him.

When he finished the song, he didn't talk for a while. Then he sort of shook himself.

You won't understand (he continued). Not yet—but I have seen them. They stand about, little misshapen men with huge heads. But their heads contain only brains. They had machines that could think—but somebody turned them off a long time ago, and no one knew how to start them again. That was the trouble with them. They had wonderful brains. Far better than yours or mine. But it must have been millions of years ago when they were turned off, too, and they just haven't thought since then. Kindly little people. That was all they knew.

When I slipped into that field it grabbed me like a gravitational field whirling a space transport down to a planet. It sucked me in—and through. Only the other side must have been seven million years in the future. That's where I was. It must have been in exactly the same spot on Earth's surface, but I never knew why.

It was night then, and I saw the city a little way off. The Moon was shining on it, and the whole scene looked wrong. You see, in seven million years, men had done a lot with the positions of the planetary bodies, what with moving space liners, clearing lanes through the asteroids, and such. And seven million years is long enough for natural things to change positions a little. The Moon must have been fifty thousand miles farther out. And it was rotating on its axis. I lay there a while and watched it. Even the stars were different.

There were ships going out of the city. Back and forth, like things sliding along a wire, but there was only a wire of force, of course. Part of the city, the lower part, was brightly lighted with what must have been mercury vapor glow, I decided. Blue-green. I felt sure men didn't live there—the light was wrong for eyes. But the top of the city was so sparsely lighted.

Then I saw something coming down out of the sky. It was brightly lighted. A huge globe, and it sank straight to the center of the great black-and-silver mass of the city.

I don't know what it was, but even then I knew the city was deserted. Strange that I could even imagine that, I who had never seen a deserted city before. But I walked the fifteen miles over to it and entered it. There were machines going about the streets, repair machines, you know. They couldn't understand that the city didn't need to go on functioning, so they were still working. I found a taxi machine that seemed fairly familiar. It had a manual control that I could work.

I don't know how long that city had been deserted. Some of the men from the other cities said it was a hundred and fifty thousand years. Some went as high as three hundred thousand years. Three hundred thousand years since human foot had been in that city. The taxi machine was in perfect condition, functioned at once. It was clean, and the city was clean and orderly. I saw a restaurant and I was hungry. Hungrier still for humans to speak to. There were none, of course, but I didn't know.

The restaurant had the food displayed directly, and I made a choice. The food was three hundred thousand years old, I suppose. I didn't know, and the machines that served it to me didn't care, for they made things synthetically, you see, and perfectly. When the builders made those cities, they forgot one thing. They didn't realize that things shouldn't go on forever.

It took me six months to make my apparatus. And near the end I was ready to go; and, from seeing those machines go blindly, perfectly, on in orbits of their duties with the tireless, ceaseless perfection their designers had incorporated in them, long after those designers and their sons, and their sons' sons had no use for them—

When Earth is cold, and the Sun has died out, those machines will go on. When Earth begins to crack and break, those perfect, ceaseless machines will try to repair her—

I left the restaurant and cruised about the city in the taxi. The machine had a little, electric-power motor, I believe, but it gained its power from the great central power radiator. I knew before long that I was far in the future. The city was divided into two sections, a section of many strata where machines functioned smoothly, save for a deep humming beat that echoed through the whole city like a vast unending song of power. The entire metal framework of the place echoed with it, transmitted it, hummed with it. But it was soft and restful, a reassuring beat.

There must have been thirty levels above ground, and twenty more below, a solid block of metal walls and metal floors and metal and glass and force machines. The only light was the blue-green glow of the mercury vapor arcs. The light of mercury vapor is rich in high-energy-quanta, which stimulate the alkali metal atoms to photo-electric activity. Or perhaps that is beyond the science of your day? I have forgotten.

But they had used that light because many of their worker machines needed sight. The machines were marvelous. For five hours I wandered through the vast power plant on the very lowest level, watching them, and because there was motion, and that pseudo-mechanical life, I felt less alone.

The generators I saw were a development of the release I had discovered—when? The release of the energy of matter, I mean, and I knew when I saw that for what countless ages they could continue.

The entire lower block of the city was given over to the machines. Thousands. But most of them seemed idle, or, at most, running under light load. I recognized a telephone apparatus, and not a single signal came through. There was no life in the city. Yet when I pressed a little stud beside the screen on one side of the room, the machine began working instantly. It was ready. Only no one needed it any more. The men knew how to die, and be dead, but the machines didn't.

Finally I went up to the top of the city, the upper level. It was a paradise.

There were shrubs and trees and parks, glowing in the soft light that they had learned to make in the very air. They had learned it five million years or more before. Two million years ago they forgot. But the machines didn't, and they were still making it. It hung in the air, soft, silvery light, slightly rosy, and the gardens were shadowy with it. There were no machines here now, but I knew that in daylight they must come out and work on these gardens, keeping them a paradise for masters who had died, and stopped moving, as they could not.

In the desert outside the city it had been cool, and very dry. Here the air was soft, warm and sweet with the scent of blooms that men had spent several hundreds of thousands of years perfecting.

Then somewhere music began. It began in the air, and spread softly through it. The Moon was just setting now, and as it set, the rosy-silver glow waned and the music grew stronger.

It came from everywhere and from nowhere. It was within me. I do not know how they did it. And I do not know how such music could be written.

Savages make music too simple to be beautiful, but it is stirring. Semisavages write music beautifully simple, and simply beautiful. Your Negro music was your best. They knew music when they heard it and sang it as they felt it. Semicivilized peoples write great music. They are proud of their music, and make sure it is known for great music. They make it so great it is top-heavy.

I had always thought our music good. But that which came through the air was the song of triumph, sung by a mature race, the race of man in its full triumph! It was man singing his triumph in majestic sound that swept me up; it showed me what lay before me; it carried me on.

And it died in the air as I looked at the deserted city. The machines should have forgotten that song. Their masters had, long before.

I came to what must have been one of their homes; it was a dimly-seen doorway in the dusky light, but as I stepped up to it, the lights which had not functioned in three hundred thousand years illuminated it for me with a green-white glow, like a firefly, and I stepped into the room beyond. Instantly something happened to the air in the doorway behind me; it was as opaque as milk. The room in which I stood was a room of metal and stone. The stone was some jet-black substance with the finish of velvet, and the metals were silver and gold. There was a rug on the floor, a rug of just such material as I am wearing now, but thicker and softer. There were divans about the room, low and covered with these soft metallic materials. They were black and gold and silver, too.

I had never seen anything like that. I never shall again, I suppose, and my language and yours were not made to describe it.

The builders of that city had right and reason to sing that song of sweeping triumph, triumph that swept them over the nine planets and the fifteen habitable moons.

But they weren't there any more, and I wanted to leave. I thought of a plan and went to a subtelephone office to examine a map I had seen. The old World looked much the same. Seven or even seventy million years don't mean much to old Mother Earth. She may even succeed in wearing down those marvelous machine cities. She can wait a hundred million or a thousand million years before she is beaten.

I tried calling different city centers shown on the map. I had quickly learned the system when I examined the central apparatus.

I tried once—twice—thrice—a round dozen times. Yawk City, Lunon City, Paree, Shkago, Singpor, others. I was beginning to feel that there were no more men on all Earth. And I felt crushed, as at each city the machines replied and did my bidding. The machines were there in each of those far vaster cities, for I was in the Neva City of their time. A small city. Yawk City was more than eight hundred kilometers in diameter.

In each city I had tried several numbers. Then I tried San Frisco. There was someone there, and a voice answered and the picture of a human appeared on the little glowing screen. I could see him start and stare in surprise at me. Then he started speaking to me. I couldn't understand, of course. I can understand your speech, and you mine, because your speech of this day is largely recorded on records of various types and has influenced our pronunciation.

Some things are changed; names of cities, particularly, because names of cities are apt to be polysyllabic, and used a great deal. People tend to elide them, shorten them. I am in—Nee-vah-dah—as you would say? We say only Neva. And Yawk State. But it is Ohio and Iowa still. Over a thousand years, effects were small on words, because they were recorded.

But seven million years had passed, and the men had forgotten the old records, used them less as time went on, and their speech varied till the time came when they could no longer understand the records. They were not written any more, of course.

Some men must have arisen occasionally among that last of the race and sought for knowledge, but it was denied them. An ancient writing can be translated if some basic rule is found. An ancient voice, though—and when the race has forgotten the laws of science and the labor of mind.

So his speech was strange to me as he answered over that circuit. His voice was high in pitch, his words liquid, his tones sweet. It was almost a song as he spoke. He was excited and called others. I could not understand them, but I knew where they were. I could go to them.

So I went down from the paradise of gardens, and as I prepared to leave, I saw dawn in the sky. The strange-bright stars winked and twinkled and faded. Only one bright rising star was familiar—Venus. She shone golden now. Finally, as I stood watching for the first time that strange heaven, I began to understand what had first impressed me with the wrongness of the view. The stars, you see, were all different.

In my time—and yours, the solar system is a lone wanderer that by chance is passing across an intersection point of Galactic traffic. The stars we see at night are the stars of moving clusters, you know. In fact our system is passing through the heart of the Ursa Major group. Half a dozen other groups center within five hundred light-years of us.

But during those seven millions of years, the Sun had moved out of the group. The heavens were almost empty to the eye. Only here and there shone a single faint star. And across the vast sweep of black sky swung the band of the Milky Way. The sky was empty.

That must have been another thing those men meant in their songs—felt in their hearts. Loneliness—not even the close, friendly stars. We have stars within half a dozen light-years. They told me that their instruments, which gave directly the distance to any star, showed that the nearest was one hundred and fifty light-years away. It was enormously bright. Brighter even than Sirius of our heavens. And that made it even less friendly, because it was a blue-white supergiant. Our sun would have served as a satellite for that star.

I stood there and watched the lingering rose-silver glow die as the powerful blood-red light of the Sun swept over the horizon. I knew by the stars now that it must have been several millions of years since my day; since I had last seen the Sun sweep up. And that blood-red light made me wonder if the Sun itself was dying.

An edge of it appeared, blood-red and huge. It swung up, and the color faded, till in half an hour it was the familiar yellow-gold disk.

It hadn't changed in all that time.

I had been foolish to think that it would. Seven million years—that is nothing to Earth, how much less to the Sun? Some two thousand thousand thousand times it had risen since I last saw it rise. Two thousand thousand thousand days. If it had been that many years—I might have noticed a change.

The universe moves slowly. Only life is not enduring; only life changes swiftly. Eight short millions of years. Eight days in the life of Earth—and the race was dying. It had left something: machines. But they would die, too, even though they could not understand. So I felt. I—may have changed that. I will tell you. Later.

For when the Sun was up, I looked again at the sky and the

ground, some fifty floors below. I had come to the edge of the city.

Machines were moving on that ground, leveling it, perhaps. A great wide line of gray stretched off across the level desert straight to the east. I had seen it glowing faintly before the Sun rose—a roadway for ground machines. There was no traffic on it.

I saw an airship slip in from the east. It came with a soft, muttering whine of air, like a child complaining in sleep; it grew to my eyes like an expanding balloon. It was huge when it settled in a great port-slip in the city below. I could hear now the clang and mutter of machines, working on the materials brought in, no doubt. The machines had ordered raw materials. The machines in other cities had supplied. The freight machines had carried them here.

San Frisco and Jacksville were the only two cities on North America still used. But the machines went on in all the others, because they couldn't stop. They hadn't been ordered to.

Then high above, something appeared, and from the city beneath me, from a center section, three small spheres rose. They, like the freight ship, had no visible driving mechanisms. The point in the sky above, like a black star in a blue space, had grown to a moon. The three spheres met it high above. Then together they descended and lowered into the center of the city, where I could not see them.

It was a freight transport from Venus. The one I had seen land the night before had come from Mars, I learned.

I moved after that and looked for some sort of a taxi-plane. They had none that I recognized in scouting about the city. I searched the higher levels, and here and there saw deserted ships, but far too large for me, and without controls.

It was nearly noon—and I ate again. The food was good.

I knew then that this was a city of the dead ashes of human hopes. The hopes not of *a* race, not the whites, nor the yellow, nor the blacks, but the human race. I was mad to leave the city. I was afraid to try the ground road to the west, for the taxi I drove was powered from some source in the city, and I knew it would fail before many miles.

It was afternoon when I found a small hangar near the outer wall of the vast city. It contained three ships. I had been searching through the lower strata of the human section—the upper part. There were restaurants and shops and theatres there. I entered one place where, at my entrance, soft music began, and colors and forms began to rise on a screen before me.

They were the triumph songs in form and sound and color of a mature race, a race that had marched steadily upward through five millions of years—and didn't see the path that faded out ahead, when they were dead and had stopped, and the city itself was dead—but hadn't stopped. I hastened out of there—and the song that had not been sung in three hundred thousand years died behind me.

But I found the hangar. It was a private one, likely. Three ships. One must have been fifty feet long and fifteen in diameter. It was a yacht, a space yacht, probably. One was some fifteen feet long and five feet in diameter. That must have been the family air machine. The third was a tiny thing, little more than ten feet long and two in diameter. I had to lie down within it, evidently.

There was a periscopic device that gave me a view ahead and almost directly above. A window that permitted me to see what lay below—and a device that moved a map under a frosted-glass screen and projected it onto the screen in such a way that the cross-hairs of the screen always marked my position.

I spent half an hour attempting to understand what the makers of that ship had made. But the men who made that were men who held behind them the science and knowledge of five millions of years and the perfect machines of those ages. I saw the release mechanism that powered it. I understood the principles of that and, vaguely, the mechanics. But there were no conductors, only pale beams that pulsed so swiftly you could hardly catch the pulsations from the corner of the eye. They had been glowing and pulsating, some half dozen of them, for three hundred thousand years at least; probably more.

I entered the machine, and instantly half a dozen more beams sprang into being; there was a slight suggestion of a quiver, and a queer strain ran through my body. I understood in an instant, for the machine was resting on gravity nullifiers. That had been my hope when I worked on the space fields I discovered after the release.

But they had had it for millions of years before they built that perfect deathless machine. My weight entering it had forced it to readjust itself and simultaneously to prepare for operation. Within, an artificial gravity equal to that of Earth had gripped me, and the neutral zone between the outside and the interior had caused the strain.

The machine was ready. It was fully fueled, too. You see they were equipped to tell automatically their wants and needs. They were almost living things, every one. A caretaker machine kept them supplied, adjusted, even repaired them when need be, and when possible. If it was not, I learned later, they were carried away in a service truck that came automatically; replaced by an exactly similar machine; and carried to the shops where they were made, and automatic machines made them over.

The machine waited patiently for me to start. The controls were simple, obvious. There was a lever at the left that you pushed forward to move forward, pulled back to go back. On the right a horizontal, pivoted bar. If you swung it left, the ship spun left; if right, the ship spun right. If tipped up, the ship followed it, and likewise for all motions other than backward and forward. Raising it bodily raised the ship, as depressing it depressed the ship.

I lifted it slightly, a needle moved a bit on a gauge comfortably before my eyes as I lay there, and the floor dropped beneath me. I pulled the other control back, and the ship gathered speed as it moved gently out into the open. Releasing both controls into neutral, the machine continued till it stopped at the same elevation, the motion absorbed by air friction. I turned it about, and another dial before my eyes moved, showing my position. I could not read it, though. The map did not move, as I had hoped it would. So I started toward what I felt was west.

I could feel no acceleration in that marvelous machine. The ground simply began leaping backward, and in a moment the city was gone. The map unrolled rapidly beneath me now, and I saw that I was moving south of west. I turned northward slightly, and watched the compass. Soon I understood that, too, and the ship sped on.

I had become too interested in the map and the compass, for suddenly there was a sharp buzz and, without my volition, the machine rose and swung to the north. There was a mountain ahead of me; I had not seen, but the ship had.

I noticed then what I should have seen before—two little knobs that could move the map. I started to move them and heard a sharp clicking, and the pace of the ship began decreasing. A moment and it had steadied at a considerably lower speed, the machine swinging to a new course. I tried to right it, but to my amazement the controls did not affect it.

It was the map, you see. It would either follow the course, or the course would follow it. I had moved it and the machine had taken over control of its own accord. There was a little button I could have pushed—but I didn't know. I couldn't control the ship until it finally came to rest and lowered itself to a stop six inches from the ground in the center of what must have been the ruins of a great city, Sacramento, probably.

I understood now, so I adjusted the map for San Frisco, and the ship went on at once. It steered itself around a mass of broken stone, turned back to its course, and headed on, a bullet-shaped, self-controlled dart.

It didn't descend when it reached San Frisco. It simply hung in the air and sounded a soft musical hum. Twice. Then it waited. I waited, too, and looked down.

There were people here. I saw the humans of that age for the first time. They were little men—bewildered—dwarfed, with heads disproportionately large. But not extremely so.

Their eyes impressed me most. They were huge, and when they looked at me there was a power in them that seemed sleeping, but too deeply to be roused.

I took the manual controls then and landed. And no sooner had I got out than the ship rose automatically and started off by itself. They had automatic parking devices. The ship had gone to a public hangar, the nearest, where it would be automatically serviced and cared for. There was a little call set I should have taken with me when I got out. Then I could have pressed a button and called it to me—wherever I was in that city.

The people about me began talking—singing almost—among themselves. Others were coming up leisurely. Men and women—

but there seemed no old and few young. What few young there were, were treated almost with respect, carefully taken care of lest a careless footstep on their toes or a careless step knock them down.

There was reason, you see. They lived a tremendous time. Some lived as long as three thousand years. Then—they simply died. They didn't grow old, and it never had been learned why people died as they did. The heart stopped, the brain ceased thought—and they died. But the young children, children not yet mature, were treated with the utmost care. But one child was born in the course of a month in that city of one hundred thousand people. The human race was growing sterile.

And I have told you that they were lonely? Their loneliness was beyond hope. For, you see, as man strode toward maturity, he destroyed all forms of life that menaced him. Disease. Insects. Then the last of the insects, and finally the last of the man-eating animals.

The balance of nature was destroyed then, so they had to go on. It was like the machines. They started them—and now they can't stop. They started destroying life—and now it wouldn't stop. So they had to destroy weeds of all sorts, then many formerly harmless plants. Then the herbivora, too, the deer and the antelope and the rabbit and the horse. They were a menace, they attacked man's machine-tended crops. Man was still eating natural foods.

You can understand. The thing was beyond their control. In the end they killed off the denizens of the sea, also, in self-defense. Without the many creatures that had kept them in check, they were swarming beyond bounds. And the time had come when synthetic foods replaced natural. The air was purified of all life about two and a half million years after our day, all microscopic life.

That meant that the water, too, must be purified. It was— and then came the end of life in the ocean. There were minute organisms that lived on bacterial forms, and tiny fish that lived on the minute organisms, and small fish that lived on the tiny fish, and big fish that lived on the small fish—and the beginning of the chain was gone. The sea was devoid of life in a generation. That meant about one thousand and five hundred years to them. Even the sea plants had gone.

And on all Earth there was only man and the organisms he had protected—the plants he wanted for decoration, and certain ultra-hygienic pets, as long-lived as their masters. Dogs. They must have been remarkable animals. Man was reaching his maturity then, and his animal friend, the friend that had followed him through a thousand millenniums to your day and mine, and another four thousand millenniums to the day of man's early maturity, had grown in intelligence. In an ancient museum—a wonderful place, for they had, perfectly preserved, the body of a great leader of mankind who had died five and a half million years before I saw him—in that museum, deserted then, I saw one of those canines. His skull was nearly as large as mine. They had simple ground machines that dogs could be trained to drive, and they held races in which the dogs drove those machines.

Then man reached his full maturity. It extended over a period of a full million years. So tremendously did he stride ahead, the dog ceased to be a companion. Less and less were they wanted. When the million years had passed, and man's decline began, the dog was gone. It had died out.

And now this last dwindling group of men still in the system had no other life form to make its successor. Always before when one civilization toppled, on its ashes rose a new one. Now there was but one civilization, and all other races, even other species, were gone save in the plants. And man was too far along in his old age to bring intelligence and mobility from the plants. Perhaps he could have in his prime.

Other worlds were flooded with man during that million years —the million years. Every planet and every moon of the system had its quota of men. Now only the planets had their populations, the moons had been deserted. Pluto had been left before I landed, and men were coming from Neptune, moving in toward the Sun, and the home planet, while I was there. Strangely quiet men, viewing, most of them, for the first time, the planet that had given their race life.

But as I stepped from that ship and watched it rise away from me, I saw why the race of man was dying. I looked back at the faces of those men, and on them I read the answer. There was one single quality gone from the still-great minds—minds far greater than yours or mine. I had to have the help of one of them in solving some of my problems. In space, you know, there are twenty coordinates, ten of which are zero, six of which have fixed values, and the four others represent our changing, familiar dimensions in space-time. That means that integrations must proceed in not double, or triple, or quadruple—but ten integrations.

It would have taken me too long. I would never have solved all the problems I must work out. I could not use their mathematics machines; and mine, of course, were seven million years in the past. But one of those men was interested and helped me. He did quadruple and quintuple integration, even quadruple integration between varying exponential limits—in his head.

When I asked him to. For the one thing that had made man great had left him. As I looked in their faces and eyes on landing I knew it. They looked at me, interested at this rather unusual-looking stranger—and went on. They had come to see the arrival of a ship. A rare event, you see. But they were merely welcoming me in a friendly fashion. They were not curious! Man had lost the instinct of curiosity.

Oh, not entirely! They wondered at the machines, they wondered at the stars. But they did nothing about it. It was not wholly lost to them yet, but nearly. It was dying. In the six short months I stayed with them, I learned more than they had learned in the two or even three thousand years they had lived among the machines.

Can you appreciate the crushing hopelessess it brought to me? I, who love science, who see in it, or have seen in it, the salvation, the raising of mankind—to see those wondrous machines, of man's triumphant maturity, forgotten and misunderstood. The wondrous, perfect machines that tended, protected, and cared for those gentle, kindly people who had—forgotten.

They were lost among it. The city was a magnificent ruin to them, a thing that rose stupendous about them. Something not understood, a thing that was of the nature of the world. It was. It had not been made; it simply was. Just as the mountains and the deserts and the waters of the seas.

Do you understand—can you see that the time since those machines were new was longer than the time from our day to the birth of the race? Do we know the legends of our first ancestors? Do we remember their lore of forest and cave? The secret of chipping a flint till it had a sharp-cutting edge? The secret of trailing and killing a saber-toothed tiger without being killed one-self?

They were now in similar straits, though the time had been longer, because the language had taken a long step towards perfection, and because the machines maintained everything for them through generation after generation.

Why, the entire planet of Pluto had been deserted—yet on Pluto the largest mines of one of their metals were located; the machines still functioned. A perfect unity existed throughout the system. A unified system of perfect machines.

And all those people knew was that to do a certain thing to a certain lever produced certain results. Just as men in the Middle Ages knew that to take a certain material, wood, and place it in contact with other pieces of wood heated red, would cause the wood to disappear, and become heat. They did not understand that wood was being oxidized with the release of the heat of formation of carbon dioxide and water. So those people did not understand the things that fed and clothed and carried them.

I stayed with them there for three days. And then I went to Jacksville. Yawk City, too. That was enormous. It stretched over—well, from well north of where Boston is today to well south of Washington—that was what they called Yawk City.

I never believed that, when he said it, said Jim, interrupting himself. I knew he didn't. If he had, I think he'd have bought land somewhere along there and held for a rise in value. I know Jim. He'd have the idea that seven million years was something like seven hundred, and maybe his great-grandchildren would be able to sell it.

Anyway, went on Jim, he said it was all because the cities had spread so. Boston spread south. Washington, north. And Yawk

City spread all over. And the cities between grew into them.

And it was all one vast machine. It was perfectly ordered and perfectly neat. They had a transportation system that took me from the North End to the South End in three minutes. I timed it. They had learned to neutralize acceleration.

Then I took one of the great space liners to Neptune. There were still some running. Some people, you see, were coming the other way.

The ship was huge. Mostly it was a freight liner. It floated up from Earth, a great metal cylinder three-quarters of a mile long, and a quarter of a mile in diameter. Outside the atmosphere it began to accelerate. I could see Earth dwindle. I have ridden one of our own liners to Mars, and it took me, in 3048, five days. In half an hour on this liner Earth was just a star, with a smaller, dimmer star near it. In an hour we passed Mars. Eight hours later we landed on Neptune. M'reen was the city. Large as the Yawk City of my day—and no one living there.

The planet was cold and dark—horribly cold. The Sun was a tiny, pale disk, heatless and almost lightless. But the city was perfectly comfortable. The air was fresh and cool, moist with the scent of growing blossoms, perfumed with them. And the whole giant metal framework trembled just slightly with the humming, powerful beat of the mighty machines that had made and cared for it.

I learned from records I deciphered, because of my knowledge of the ancient tongue that their tongue was based on, and the tongue of that day when man was dying, that the city was built three million seven hundred and thirty thousand one hundred and fifty years after my birth. Not a machine had been touched by the hand of man since that day.

Yet the air was perfect for man. And the warm, rose-silver glow hung in the air here and supplied the only illumination.

I visited some of their other cities where there were men. And there, on the retreating outskirts of man's domain, I first heard The Song of Longings, as I called it.

And another, The Song of Forgotten Memories. Listen:

He sang another of those songs. There's one thing I know, declared Jim. That bewildered note was stronger in his voice, and by that time I guess I pretty well understood his feelings. Because, you have to remember, I heard it only second hand from an ordinary man, and Jim had heard it from an eye-and-ear witness that was not ordinary, and heard it in that organ voice. Anyway, I guess Jim was right when he said: "He wasn't any ordinary man." No ordinary man could think of those songs. They weren't right. When he sang that song, it was full of more of those plaintive minors. I could feel him searching his mind for something he had forgotten, something he desperately wanted to remember—something he knew he should have known—and I felt it eternally elude him. I felt it get further away from him as he sang. I heard that lonely, frantic searcher attempting to recall that thing—that thing that would save him.

And I heard him give a little sob of defeat—and the song ended. Jim tried a few notes. He hasn't a good ear for music—but that was too powerful to forget. Just a few hummed notes. Jim hasn't much imagination, I guess, or when that man of the future sang to him he would have gone mad. It shouldn't be sung to modern men; it isn't meant for them. You've heard those heart-rending cries some animals give, like human cries, almost? A loon, now—he sounds like a lunatic being murdered horribly.

That's just unpleasant. That song made you feel just exactly what the singer meant—because it didn't just sound human—it was human. It was the essence of humanity's last defeat, I guess. You always feel sorry for the chap who loses after trying hard. Well, you could feel the whole of humanity trying hard—and losing. And you knew they couldn't afford to lose, because they couldn't try again.

He said he'd been interested before. And still not wholly upset by those machines that couldn't stop. But that was too much for him.

I knew after that, he said, that these weren't men I could live among. They were dying men, and I was alive with the youth of the race. They looked at me with the same longing, hopeless wonder with which they looked at the stars and the machines. They knew what I was, but couldn't understand.

I began to work on leaving.

It took six months. It was hard because my instruments were

gone, of course, and theirs didn't read in the same units. And there were few instruments, anyway. The machines didn't read instruments; they acted on them. They were sensory organs to them.

But Reo Lantal helped where he could. And I came back.

I did just one thing before I left that may help. I may even try to get back there sometime. To see, you know.

I said they had machines that could really think? But that someone had stopped them a long time ago, and no one knew how to start them?

I found some records and deciphered them. I started one of the latest and best of them and started it on a great problem. It is only fitting it should be done. The machine can work on it, not for a thousand years, but for a million, if it must.

I started five of them actually, and connected them together as the records directed.

They are trying to make a machine with something that man had lost. It sounds rather comical. But stop to think before you laugh. And remember that Earth as I saw it from the ground level of Neva City just before Reo Lantal threw the switch.

Twilight—the sun has set. The desert out beyond, in its mystic, changing colors. The great, metal city rising straight-walled to the human city above, broken by spires and towers and great trees with scented blossoms. The silvery-rose glow in the paradise of gardens above.

And all that great city-structure throbbing and humming to the steady gentle beat of perfect, deathless machines built more than three million years before—and never touched since that time by human hands. And they go on. The dead city. The men that have lived, and hoped, and built—and died to leave behind them those little men who can only wonder and look and long for a forgotten kind of companionship. They wander through the vast cities their ancestors built, knowing less of them than the machines themselves.

And the songs. Those tell the story best, I think. Little, hopeless, wondering men amid vast, unknowing, blind machines that started three million years before—and just never knew how to stop. They are dead—and can't die and be still.

So I brought another machine to life, and set it to a task which, in time to come, it will perform.

I ordered it to make a machine which would have what man had lost. A curious machine.

And then I wanted to leave quickly and go back. I had been born in the first full light of man's day. I did not belong in the lingering, dying glow of man's twilight.

So I came back. A little too far back. But it will not take me long to return—accurately this time.

"Well, that was his story," Jim said. "He didn't *tell* me it was true—didn't say anything about it. And he had me thinking so hard I didn't even see him get off in Reno when we stopped for gas.

"But—he wasn't an ordinary man," repeated Jim, in a rather belligerent tone.

Jim claims he doesn't believe the yarn, you know. But he does; that's why he always acts so determined about it when he says the stranger wasn't an ordinary man.

No, he wasn't, I guess. I think he lived and died, too, probably, sometime in the thirty-first century. And I think he saw the twilight of the race, too.

NIGHTFALL

by ISAAC ASIMOV

FOREWORD

by Harry Harrison

THE AUTHOR

ISAAC ASIMOV, born in Russia in 1920, came to the United States when he was three. He studied biochemistry at Columbia University, where he received his Ph.D. in 1948. Afterward he became an assistant professor of biochemistry at Boston University School of Medicine, teaching and doing cancer research, and in 1958 he left that position to devote his time to writing. Asimov's first science-fiction story was published in 1939; he is the author of scores of stories and novels, including *The Caves of Steel, The Currents of Space,* the *Foundation* trilogy, and *I, Robot.* More recently he has turned to books on scientific subjects, among them *Asimov's Biographical Encyclopedia of Science and Technology* and *The Intelligent Man's Guide to Science.* "Nightfall" was first published in 1941.

THE CRITIC

HARRY HARRISON has been an editor and an illustrator of science fiction as well as a writer and a critic. Raised in New York City, he has lived in many parts of the world and at last report was located, with wife and children, near San Diego, California. Among his recent science-fiction novels are *Captive Universe, Deathworld,* and *Make Room! Make Room!* He edits an annual anthology of the year's best s-f short stories, and, together with Brian W. Aldiss, publishes an occasional little magazine, *SF Horizons,* devoted to science-fiction criticism and review.

Foreword

A quote from Ralph Waldo Emerson opens "Nightfall," and is perhaps the genesis of this story. Nightfall does come in the manner described in the quotation, though after two thousand and forty-nine years, not a thousand, but the story itself goes far beyond Emerson's "believe and adore . . . the remembrance of the city of God!" This is just one factor in the story, although an important one. It is as though the author felt the Emerson surmise was incomplete and wished to show what really would happen given the stated conditions.

This he did, in a story that is a perfect example of an era that has been called the golden age of *Astounding Science Fiction*. During the early 1940s this magazine reached a zenith of quality and originality that has never been equaled. Great numbers of stories, in fact all of the stories from at least one entire issue, have been anthologized. The editor, John W. Campbell, was broadening the horizons of science fiction by bringing in new writers and inducing the best of the older writers to join his literary crusade. The excitement can still be felt when you go through issues of the magazine from this period. The stories are alive and pulsating with new concepts and directions. But they are always stories— entertainment—and always a pleasure to read.

"Nightfall" has all the strengths, and weaknesses, of its time. The weaknesses are relatively unimportant: some dated slang; a pulp-inherited tendency to move the story through violence; the device of having one character ask a question of another, so that the answer can feed needed background information to the reader as well as the wide-eyed listener. The strengths *are* important, in that they are typical of the very best science fiction being written at that time. Equally important: the story is just as exciting when read today, some three decades later.

The prose is not flashy or evocative; it is quiet and efficient, because that is the best way to present a story of ideas. The pace is fast, and is sustained without letup right to the very end. As one problem is partially resolved, another is presented, all of them building toward the awaited climax. And when the climax does arrive we are not cheated. The reader is totally involved, even though he suspects beforehand what the ending will be. But the author goes beyond these expectations and, with the reader safely in hand, permits himself something beyond stark prose for the first time:

—Lagash was in the center of a giant cluster. Thirty thousand mighty suns shone down in a soul-searing splendor that was more frighteningly cold in its awful indifference than the bitter wind that shivered across the cold, horribly bleak world. . . . The bright walls of the universe were shattered and their awful black fragments were falling down to crush and squeeze and obliterate him.

How different this is from "You double-crossing rat!" of the previous page. Too much can be made of artistic language and the avoidance of clichés and common expressions. The average reader, and the younger reader, will never notice these things. Most of us, in conversation, will say "big as a house" or "strong as an ox," although we might be put off by them on the printed page. We expect better things of our authors, wordsmiths by trade, and well we should. Yet I feel that science fiction is an exception to this general rule. In science fiction, a fiction basically of ideas and not character development in the usual fictional sense, the familiar in speech may even smooth the way to enjoyment of the story by taking our attention away from literary novelty and per-mitting us to focus it upon the developing concept—where it be-longs. This is particularly true of the era in science fiction represented by this story, where the most exciting concepts were presented in the most banal prose. The pulp tradition still put a heavy hand upon the quality of the narrative, so that it was *idea*, not skill of presentation, that made the impact. (This, incidentally, provides the material for what might be called second-generation science-fiction writers who are better equipped, technically or artistically, to explore in greater depth concepts only briefly con-sidered or proposed in the earlier days.)

Careful note should be taken of the furnishings of this story; they are there although no great point is made of them. Heming-way said that what you leave out of a story is more important

than what you put in, and Asimov practices this dictum. He has
worked out his alien culture in great detail—but he suggests this
culture rather than describing it to us. Yet all of the developments
within the story relate to this greater concept, and are all relevant.
Through them we can get a good idea of the level of this society.
They are culturally advanced, with institutes of higher education,
and highly developed in mathematics and observational astronomy.
They use electricity, although they have never developed the
electric light—undoubtedly because they never had reason to.
Theirs is an old language, with roots dating back some thousands
of year before the last "fall." They are psychologically different
from us; one out of ten is driven to insanity by a short period of
darkness, and they are unaware of limitations to their points of
view, considering them universal. (They believe that life could
not exist on a planet with only one sun.)

Science fiction of this era was firmly entrenched in the "what
if?" proposition, and it derived its great satisfaction from the
rigorous development of ideas. Style was unimportant—or, rather,
the starkest, simplest "lack of style" was the one best suited for
the presentation and development of ideas. After the first simple
"what if?" the author elaborates in great detail all the related ifs
that follow. The basic concept in this story is the once-an-era
nightfall. In order to tell about this, the astronomy of the multi-
solar system had to be worked out. To get complete blackness
an eclipse was needed, and this required a satellite and the mathematics to permit this eclipse to occur only at great intervals.
Scientists were needed to explain the astronomy to the reader, a
psychology to explain civilization's downfall, a level of culture to
support the science, linguistic concepts to motivate the religious
cult. And all of this had to be presented in the form of a moving
story that would grip the reader's attention. It is a monument to
the author's ability that he has succeeded on all counts.

Asimov has indeed gone beyond Emerson, who was being
entirely too simplistic. Perhaps Emerson meant his lines to be
symbolic. But even if he did they read like a statement of fact—
an incomplete one. Asimov agrees that yes, this monumental nightfall and the stars would indeed be remembered for a thousand
years—but in a distorted manner by a not too respected cult.
This is a far more realistic concept than all the hosannas and
adoration. And, more important, what else would be caused by the
millennial nightfall? As Asimov considered the possibilities, they

must have become more and more interesting, until the fleshed-out background for the story was in his head. That was the first half of his task. The second was the turning of all these vague ideas and extrapolations into a story. That he performed both of these functions satisfactorily makes him a science-fiction writer. That he did it so well makes him a major science-fiction writer, and makes this story a landmark in the development of the entire genre.

NIGHTFALL

If the stars should appear one night in a thousand
years, how would men believe and adore, and preserve for many generations the remembrance of the
city of God!—EMERSON

Aton 77, director of Saro University, thrust out a belligerent lower
lip and glared at the young newspaperman in a hot fury.

Theremon 762 took that fury in his stride. In his earlier days,
when his now widely syndicated column was only a mad idea in a
cub reporter's mind, he had specialized in "impossible" interviews.
It had cost him bruises, black eyes, and broken bones; but it had
given him an ample supply of coolness and self-confidence.

So he lowered the outthrust hand that had been so pointedly
ignored and calmly waited for the aged director to get over the
worst. Astronomers were queer ducks, anyway, and if Aton's
actions of the last two months meant anything, the same Aton was
the queer-duckiest of the lot.

Aton 77 found his voice, and though it trembled with restrained
emotion, the careful, somewhat pedantic, phraseology, for which
the famous astronomer was noted, did not abandon him.

"Sir," he said, "you display an infernal gall in coming to me
with that impudent proposition of yours."

The husky telephotographer of the Observatory, Beenay 25,
thrust a tongue's tip across dry lips and interposed nervously,
"Now, sir, after all——"

The director turned to him and lifted a white eyebrow. "Do
not interfere, Beenay. I will credit you with good intentions in

55

bringing this man here; but I will tolerate no insubordination now."

Theremon decided it was time to take a part. "Director Aton, if you'll let me finish what I started saying I think—"

"I don't believe, young man," retorted Aton, "that anything you could say now would count much as compared with your daily columns of these last two months. You have led a vast newspaper campaign against the efforts of myself and my colleagues to organize the world against the menace which it is now too late to avert. You have done your best with your highly personal attacks to make the staff of this Observatory objects of ridicule."

The director lifted the copy of the Saro City *Chronicle* on the table and shook it at Theremon furiously. "Even a person of your well-known impudence should have hesitated before coming to me with a request that he be allowed to cover today's events for his paper. Of all newsmen, you!"

Aton dashed the newspaper to the floor, strode to the window and clasped his arms behind his back.

"You may leave," he snapped over his shoulder. He stared moodily out at the skyline where Gamma, the brightest of the planet's six suns, was setting. It had already faded and yellowed into the horizon mists, and Aton knew he would never see it again as a sane man.

He whirled. "No, wait, come here!" He gestured peremptorily. "I'll give you your story."

The newsman had made no motion to leave, and now he approached the old man slowly. Aton gestured outward, "Of the six suns, only Beta is left in the sky. Do you see it?"

The question was rather unnecessary. Beta was almost at zenith, its ruddy light flooding the landscape to an unusual orange as the brilliant rays of setting Gamma died. Beta was at aphelion. It was small; smaller than Theremon had ever seen it before, and for the moment it was undisputed ruler of Lagash's sky.

Lagash's own sun, Alpha, the one about which it revolved, was at the antipodes; as were the two distant companion pairs. The red dwarf Beta—Alpha's immediate companion—was alone, grimly alone.

Aton's upturned face flushed redly in the sunlight. "In just under four hours," he said, "civilization, as we know it, comes to an end. It will do so because, as you see, Beta is the only sun in the sky." He smiled grimly. "Print that! There'll be no one to read it."

"But if it turns out that four hours pass—and another four—and nothing happens?" asked Theremon softly.

"Don't let that worry you. Enough will happen."

"Granted! And *still*—if nothing happens?"

For a second time, Beenay 25 spoke, "Sir, I think you ought to listen to him."

Theremon said, "Put it to a vote, Director Aton."

There was a stir among the remaining five members of the Observatory staff, who till now had maintained an attitude of wary neutrality.

"That," stated Aton flatly, "is not necessary." He drew out his pocket watch. "Since your good friend, Beenay, insists so urgently, I will give you five minutes. Talk away."

"Good! Now, just what difference would it make if you allowed me to take down an eyewitness account of what's to come? If your prediction comes true, my presence won't hurt; for in that case my column would never be written. On the other hand, if nothing comes of it, you will just have to expect ridicule or worse. It would be wise to leave that ridicule to friendly hands."

Aton snorted. "Do you mean yours when you speak of friendly hands?"

"Certainly!" Theremon sat down and crossed his legs. "My columns may have been a little rough at times, but I gave you people the benefit of the doubt every time. After all, this is not the century to preach 'the end of the world is at hand' to Lagash. You have to understand that people don't believe the 'Book of Revelations' any more, and it annoys them to have scientists turn about-face and tell us the Cultists are right after all—"

"No such thing, young man," interrupted Aton. "While a great deal of our data has been supplied us by the Cult, our results contain none of the Cult's mysticism. Facts are facts, and the Cult's so-called 'mythology' *has* certain facts behind it. We've exposed them and ripped away their mystery. I assure you that the Cult hates us now worse than you do."

"I don't hate you. I'm just trying to tell you that the public is in an ugly humor. They're angry."

Aton twisted his mouth in derision. "Let them be angry."

"Yes, but what about tomorrow?"

"There'll be no tomorrow!"

"But if there is. Say that there is—just to see what happens. That anger might take shape into something serious. After all, you know, business has taken a nose dive these last two months. Investors don't really believe the world is coming to an end, but just the same they're being cagy with their money until it's all over. Johnny Public doesn't believe you, either, but the new spring furniture might as well wait a few months—just to make sure.

"You see the point. Just as soon as this is all over, the business interests will be after your hide. They'll say that if crack-pots— begging your pardon—can upset the country's prosperity any time they want simply by making some cockeyed prediction—it's up to the planet to prevent them. The sparks will fly, sir."

The director regarded the columnist sternly. "And just what were you proposing to do to help the situation?"

"Well," grinned Theremon, "I was proposing to take charge of the publicity. I can handle things so that only the ridiculous side will show. It would be hard to stand, I admit, because I'd have to make you all out to be a bunch of gibbering idiots, but if I can get people laughing at you, they might forget to be angry. In return for that, all my publisher asks is an exclusive story."

Beenay nodded and burst out, "Sir, the rest of us think he's right. These last two months we've considered everything but the million-to-one chance that there is an error somewhere in our theory or in our calculations. We ought to take care of that, too."

There was a murmur of agreement from the men grouped about the table, and Aton's expression became that of one who found his mouth full of something bitter and couldn't get rid of it.

"You may stay if you wish, then. You will kindly refrain, however, from hampering us in our duties in any way. You will also remember that I am in charge of all activities here, and in spite of your opinions as expressed in your columns, I will expect full co-operation and full respect—"

His hands were behind his back, and his wrinkled face thrust forward determinedly as he spoke. He might have continued indefinitely but for the intrusion of a new voice.

"Hello, hello, hello!" It came in a high tenor, and the plump cheeks of the newcomer expanded in a pleased smile. "What's this morgue-like atmosphere about here? No one's losing his nerve, I hope."

Aton started in consternation and said peevishly, "Now what the devil are you doing here, Sheerin? I thought you were going to stay behind in the Hideout."

Sheerin laughed and dropped his tubby figure into a chair. "Hideout be blowed! The place bored me. I wanted to be here, where things are getting hot. Don't you suppose I have my share of curiosity? I want to see these Stars the Cultists are forever speaking about." He rubbed his hands and added in a soberer tone, "It's freezing outside. The wind's enough to hang icicles on your nose. Beta doesn't seem to give any heat at all, at the distance it is."

The white-haired director ground his teeth in sudden exasperation, "Why do you go out of your way to do crazy things, Sheerin? What kind of good are you around here?"

"What kind of good am I around there?" Sheerin spread his palms in comical resignation. "A psychologist isn't worth his salt in the Hideout. They need men of action and strong, healthy women that can breed children. Me? I'm a hundred pounds too heavy for a man of action, and I wouldn't be a success at breeding children. So why bother them with an extra mouth to feed? I feel better over here."

Theremon spoke briskly, "Just what is the Hideout, sir?"

Sheerin seemed to see the columnist for the first time. He frowned and blew his ample cheeks out, "And just who in Lagash are you, redhead?"

Aton compressed his lips and then muttered sullenly, "That's Theremon 762, the newspaper fellow. I suppose you've heard of him."

The columnist offered his hand. "And, of course, you're Sheerin 501 of Saro University. I've heard of *you*." Then he repeated, "What is this Hideout, sir?"

"Well," said Sheerin, "we have managed to convince a few

people of the validity of our prophecy of—er—doom, to be spectacular about it, and those few have taken proper measures. They
consist mainly of the immediate members of the families of the
Observatory staff, certain of the faculty and a few outsiders. Altogether, they number about three hundred, but three-quarters are
women and children."

"I see! They're supposed to hide where the Darkness and the—
er—Stars can't get at them, and then hold out when the rest of
the world goes poof."

"If they can. It won't be easy. With all of mankind insane; with
the great cities going up in flames—environment will not be
conducive to survival. But they have food, water, shelter, and
weapons—"

"They've got more," said Aton. "They've got all our records,
except for what we will collect today. Those records will mean
everything to the next cycle, and *that's* what must survive. The rest
can go hang."

Theremon whistled a long, low whistle and sat brooding for
several minutes. The men about the table had brought out a
multichess board and started a six-member game. Moves were
made rapidly and in silence. All eyes bent in furious concentration
on the board. Theremon watched them intently and then rose and
approached Aton, who sat apart in whispered conversation with
Sheerin.

"Listen," he begun, "let's go somewhere where we won't bother
the rest of the fellows. I want to ask some questions."

The aged astronomer frowned sourly at him, but Sheerin
chirped up, "Certainly. It will do me good to talk. It always does.
Aton was telling me about your ideas concerning world reaction
to a failure of the prediction—and I agree with you. I read your
column pretty regularly, by the way, and as a general thing I like
your views."

"Please, Sheerin," growled Aton.

"Eh? Oh, all right. We'll go into the next room. It has softer
chairs, anyway."

There *were* softer chairs in the next room. There were also thick
red curtains on the windows and a maroon carpet on the floor.

With the bricky light of Beta pouring in, the general effect was one of dried blood.

Theremon shuddered, "Say, I'd give ten credits for a decent dose of white light for just a second. I wish Gamma or Delta were in the sky."

"What are your questions?" asked Aton. "Please remember that our time is limited. In a little over an hour and a quarter we're going upstairs, and after that there will be no time for talk."

"Well, here it is." Theremon leaned back and folded his hands on his chest. "You people seem so all-fired serious about this that I'm beginning to believe you. Would you mind explaining what it's all about?"

Aton exploded, "Do you mean to sit there and tell me that you've been bombarding us with ridicule without even finding out what we've been trying to say?"

The columnist grinned sheepishly. "It's not that bad, sir. I've got the general idea. You say that there is going to be a world-wide Darkness in a few hours and that all mankind will go violently insane. What I want to know is the science behind it."

"No, you don't. No, you don't," broke in Sheerin. "If you ask Aton for that—supposing him to be in the mood to answer at all —he'll trot out pages of figures and volumes of graphs. You won't make head or tail of it. Now if you were to ask *me*, I could give you the layman's standpoint."

"All right; I ask you."

"Then first I'd like a drink." He rubbed his hands and looked at Aton.

"Water?" grunted Aton.

"Don't be silly!"

"Don't you be silly. No alcohol today. It would be too easy to get my men drunk. I can't afford to tempt them."

The psychologist grumbled wordlessly. He turned to Theremon, impaled him with his sharp eyes, and began.

"You realize, of course, that the history of civilization on Lagash displays a cyclic character—but I mean, *cyclic!*"

"I know," replied Theremon cautiously, "that that is the current archaeological theory. Has it been accepted as a fact?"

"Just about. In this last century it's been generally agreed upon.

This cyclic character is—or, rather, was—one of *the* great mysteries. We've located series of civilizations, nine of them definitely, and indications of others as well, all of which have reached heights comparable to our own, and all of which, without exception, were destroyed by fire at the very height of their culture.

"And no one could tell why. All centers of culture were thoroughly gutted by fire, with nothing left behind to give a hint as to the cause."

Theremon was following closely. "Wasn't there a Stone Age, too?"

"Probably, but as yet, practically nothing is known of it, except that men of that age were little more than rather intelligent apes. We can forget about that."

"I see. Go on!"

"There have been explanations of these recurrent catastrophes, all of a more or less fantastic nature. Some say that there are periodic rains of fire; some that Lagash passes through a sun every so often; some even wilder things. But there is one theory, quite different from all of these, that has been handed down over a period of centuries."

"I know. You mean this myth of the 'Stars' that the Cultists have in their 'Book of Revelations.'"

"Exactly," rejoined Sheerin with satisfaction. "The Cultists said that every two thousand and fifty years Lagash entered a huge cave, so that all the suns disappeared, and there came *total darkness all over the world!* And then, they say, things called Stars appeared, which robbed men of their souls and left them unreasoning brutes, so that they destroyed the civilization they themselves had built up. Of course, they mix all this up with a lot of religio-mystic notions, but that's the central idea."

There was a short pause in which Sheerin drew a long breath. "And now we come to the Theory of Universal Gravitation." He pronounced the phrase so that the capital letters sounded—and at that point Aton turned from the window, snorted loudly, and stalked out of the room.

The two stared after him, and Theremon said, "What's wrong?"

"Nothing in particular," replied Sheerin. "Two of the men were due several hours ago and haven't shown up yet. He's terrifically short-handed, of course, because all but the really essential men have gone to the Hideout."

"You don't think the two deserted, do you?"

"Who? Faro and Yimot? Of course not. Still, if they're not back within the hour, things would be a little sticky." He got to his feet suddenly, and his eyes twinkled. "Anyway, as long as Aton is gone—"

Tiptoeing to the nearest window, he squatted, and from the low window box beneath withdrew a bottle of red liquid that gurgled suggestively when he shook it.

"I *thought* Aton didn't know about this," he remarked as he trotted back to the table. "Here! We've only got one glass so, as the guest, you can have it. I'll keep the bottle." And he filled the tiny cup with judicious care.

Theremon rose to protest, but Sheerin eyed him sternly. "Respect your elders, young man."

The newsman seated himself with a look of pain and anguish on his face. "Go ahead, then, you old villain."

The psychologist's Adam's apple wobbled as the bottle upended, and then, with a satisfied grunt and a smack of the lips, he began again.

"But what do you know about gravitation?"

"Nothing, except that it is a very recent development, not too well established, and that the math is so hard that only twelve men in Lagash are supposed to understand it."

"*Tcha!* Nonsense! Baloney! I can give you all the essential math in a sentence. The Law of Universal Gravitation states that there exists a cohesive force among all bodies of the universe, such that the amount of this force between any two given bodies is proportional to the product of their masses divided by the square of the distance between them."

"Is that all?"

"That's enough! It took four hundred years to develop it."

"Why that long? It sounded simple enough, the way you said it."

"Because great laws are not divined by flashes of inspiration, whatever you may think. It usually takes the combined work of a world full of scientists over a period of centuries. After Genovi 41 discovered that Lagash rotated about the sun Alpha, rather than vice versa—and that was four hundred years ago—astronomers have been working. The complex motions of the six suns were recorded and analyzed and unwoven. Theory after theory was advanced and checked and counterchecked and modified and abandoned and revived and converted to something else. It was a devil of a job."

Theremon nodded thoughtfully and held out his glass for more liquor. Sheerin grudgingly allowed a few ruby drops to leave the bottle.

"It was twenty years ago," he continued after remoistening his own throat, "that it was finally demonstrated that the Law of Universal Gravitation accounted exactly for the orbital motions of the six suns. It was a great triumph."

Sheerin stood up and walked to the window, still clutching his bottle, "And now we're getting to the point. In that last decade, the motions of Lagash about Alpha were computed according to gravity, and *it did not account for the orbit observed;* not even when all perturbations due to the other suns were included. Either the law was invalid, or there was another, as yet unknown, factor involved."

Theremon joined Sheerin at the window and gazed out past the wooded slopes to where the spires of Saro City gleamed bloodily on the horizon. The newsman felt the tension of uncertainty grow within him as he cast a short glance at Beta. It glowered redly at zenith, dwarfed and evil.

"Go ahead, sir," he said softly.

Sheerin replied, "Astronomers stumbled about for years, each proposed theory more untenable than the one before—until Aton had the inspiration of calling in the Cult. The head of the Cult, Sor 5, had access to certain data that simplified the problem considerably. Aton set to work on a new track.

"What if there were another nonluminous planetary body such as Lagash? If there were, you know, it would shine only by reflected light, and if it were composed of bluish rock, as Lagash itself largely is, then, in the redness of the sky, the eternal blaze of the suns would make it invisible—drown it out completely."

Theremon whistled, "What a screwy idea!"

"You think *that's* screwy? Listen to this: Suppose this body rotated about Lagash at such a distance in such an orbit and had such a mass that its attraction would exactly account for the deviations of Lagash's orbit from theory—do you know what would happen?"

The columnist shook his head.

"Well, sometimes this body would get in the way of a sun." And Sheerin emptied what remained in the bottle at a draft.

"And it does, I suppose," said Theremon flatly.

"Yes! But only one sun lies in its plane of revolutions." He jerked a thumb at the shrunken sun above. "Beta! And it has been shown that the eclipse will occur only when the arrangement of the suns is such that Beta is alone in its hemisphere and at maximum distance, at which time the moon is invariably at minimum distance. The eclipse that results, with the moon seven times the apparent diameter of Beta, covers all of Lagash and lasts well over half a day, so that no spot on the planet escapes the effects. *That eclipse comes once every two thousand and forty-nine years."*

Theremon's face was drawn into an expressionless mask. "And that's my story?"

The psychologist nodded. "That's all of it. First the eclipse—which will start in three-quarters of an hour—then universal Darkness, and, maybe, these mysterious Stars—then madness, and end of the cycle."

He brooded. "We had two months' leeway—we at the Observatory—and that wasn't enough time to persuade Lagash of the danger. Two centuries might not have been enough. But our records are at the Hideout, and today we photograph the eclipse. The next cycle will *start off* with the truth, and when the next eclipse comes, mankind will at least be ready for it. Come to think of it, that's part of your story, too."

A thin wind ruffled the curtains at the window as Theremon opened it and leaned out. It played coldly with his hair as he stared at the crimson sunlight on his hand. Then he turned in sudden rebellion.

"What is there in darkness to drive *me* mad?"

Sheerin smiled to himself as he spun the empty liquor bottle with abstracted motions of his hand. "Have you ever experienced Darkness, young man?"

The newsman leaned against the wall and considered. "No. Can't say I have. But I know what it is. Just—uh—" He made vague motions with his fingers, and then brightened. "Just no light. Like in caves."

"Have you ever been in a cave?"

"In a *cave!* Of course not!"

"I thought not. *I* tried last week—just to see—but I got out in a hurry. I went in until the mouth of the cave was just visible as a blur of light, with black everywhere else. I never thought a person of my weight could run that fast."

Theremon's lip curled. "Well, if it comes to that, I guess I wouldn't have run, if I had been there."

The psychologist studied the young man with an annoyed frown.

"My, don't you talk big! I dare you to draw the curtain."

Theremon looked his surprise and said, "What for? If we had four or five suns out there we might want to cut the light down a bit for comfort, but now we haven't enough light as it is."

"That's the point. Just draw the curtain; then come here and sit down."

"All right." Theremon reached for the tasseled ring and jerked. The red curtain slid across the wide window, the brass rings hissing their way along the crossbar, and a dusk-red shadow clamped down on the room.

Theremon's footsteps sounded hollowly in the silence as he made his way to the table, and then they stopped halfway. "I can't see you, sir," he whispered.

"Feel your way," ordered Sheerin in a strained voice.

"But I can't see you, sir." The newsman was breathing harshly. "I can't see anything."

"What did you expect?" came the grim reply. "Come here and sit down!"

The footsteps sounded again, waveringly, approaching slowly. There was the sound of someone fumbling with a chair. Theremon's voice came thinly, "Here I am. I feel . . . *ulp* . . . all right."

"You like it, do you?"

"No-no. It's pretty awful. The walls seem to be—" He paused.

"They seem to be closing in on me. I keep wanting to push them away. But I'm not going *mad*! In fact, the feeling isn't as bad as it was."

"All right. Draw the curtain back again."

There were cautious footsteps through the dark, the rustle of Theremon's body against the curtain as he felt for the tassel, and then the triumphant *ro-o-o-osh* of the curtain slithering back. Red light flooded the room, and with a cry of joy Theremon looked up at the sun.

Sheerin wiped the moistness off his forehead with the back of a hand and said shakily. "And that was just a dark room."

"It can be stood," said Theremon lightly.

"Yes, a dark room can. But were you at the Jonglor Centennial Exposition two years ago?"

"No, it so happens I never got around to it. Six thousand miles was just a bit too much to travel, even for the exposition."

"Well, I was there. You remember hearing about the 'Tunnel of Mystery' that broke all records in the amusement area—for the first month or so, anyway?"

"Yes. Wasn't there some fuss about it?"

"Very little. It was hushed up. You see, that Tunnel of Mystery was just a mile-long tunnel—with no lights. You got into a little open car and jolted along through Darkness for fifteen minutes. It was very popular—while it lasted."

"Popular?"

"Certainly. There's a fascination in being frightened *when it's part of a game*. A baby is born with three instinctive fears: of loud noises, of falling, and of the absence of light. That's why it's considered so funny to jump at someone and shout 'Boo!' That's why it's such fun to ride a roller coaster. And that's why that Tunnel of Mystery started cleaning up. People came out of that Darkness shaking, breathless, half dead with fear, but they kept on paying to get in."

"Wait awhile, I remember now. Some people came out dead, didn't they? There were rumors of that after it shut down."

The psychologist snorted. "Bah! Two or three died. That was nothing! They paid off the families of the dead ones and argued the Jonglor City Council into forgetting it. After all, they said, if people with weak hearts want to go through the tunnel, it was at their own risk—and besides, it wouldn't happen again. So they put a doctor in the front office and had every customer go through a physical examination before getting into the car. That actually *boosted* ticket sales."

"Well, then?"

"But, you see, there was something else. People sometimes came out in perfect order, except that they refused to go into buildings—any buildings; including palaces, mansions, apartment houses, tenements, cottages, huts, shacks, lean-tos, and tents."

Theremon looked shocked. "You mean they refused to come in out of the open. Where'd they sleep?"

"In the open."

"They should have *forced* them inside."

"Oh, they did, they did. Whereupon these people went into violent hysterics and did their best to bat their brains out against the nearest wall. Once you got them inside, you couldn't keep them there without a strait jacket and a shot of morphine."

"They must have been crazy."

"Which is exactly what they were. One person out of every ten who went into that tunnel came out that way. They called in the psychologists, and we did the only thing possible. We closed down the exhibit." He spread his hands.

"What was the matter with these people?" asked Theremon finally.

"Essentially the same thing that was the matter with you when you thought the walls of the room were crushing you in the dark. There is a psychological term for mankind's instinctive fear of the absence of light. We call it 'claustrophobia,' because the lack of light is always tied up with inclosed places, so that fear of one is fear of the other. You see?"

"And those people of the tunnel?"

"Those people of the tunnel consisted of those unfortunates whose mentality did not quite possess the resiliency to overcome the claustrophobia that overtook them in the Darkness. Fifteen minutes without light is a long time; you only had two or three minutes and I believe you were fairly upset.

"The people of the tunnel had what is called 'claustrophobic fixation.' Their latent fear of Darkness and inclosed places had crystallized and become active, and, as far as we can tell, permanent. *That's* what fifteen minutes in the dark will do."

There was a long silence, and Theremon's forehead wrinkled slowly into a frown. "I don't believe it's that bad."

"You mean you don't want to believe," snapped Sheerin. "You're afraid to believe. Look out the window!"

Theremon did so, and the psychologist continued without pausing, "Imagine Darkness—everywhere. No light, as far as you can see. The houses, the trees, the fields, the earth, the sky—*black!* And Stars thrown in, for all I know—whatever *they* are. Can you conceive it?"

"Yes, I can," declared Theremon truculently.

And Sheerin slammed his fist down upon the table in sudden passion. "You lie! You can't conceive that. Your brain wasn't built for the conception any more than it was built for the conception of infinity or of eternity. You can only talk about it. A fraction of the reality upsets you, and when the real thing comes, your brain is going to be presented with a phenomenon outside its limits of comprehension. You will go mad, completely and permanently! There is no question of it!"

He added sadly, "And another couple of millenniums of painful struggle comes to nothing. Tomorrow there won't be a city standing unharmed in all Lagash."

Theremon recovered part of his mental equilibrium. "That doesn't follow. I still don't see that I can go loony just because there isn't a sun in the sky—but even if I did, and everyone else did, how does that harm the cities? Are we going to blow them down?"

But Sheerin was angry, too. "If you were in Darkness, what would you want more than anything else; what would it be that every instinct would call for? Light, damn you, *light!*"

"Well?"

"And how would you get light?"

"I don't know," said Theremon flatly.

"What's the *only* way to get light, short of the sun?"

"How should I know?"

They were standing face to face and nose to nose.

Sheerin said, "You burn something, mister. Ever see a forest fire? Ever go camping and cook a stew over a wood fire? Heat isn't the only thing burning wood gives off, you know. It gives off light, and people know that. And when it's dark they want light, and they're going to *get it*."

"So they burn wood?"

"So they burn whatever they can get. They've got to have light. They've got to burn something, and wood isn't handy—so they'll burn whatever is nearest. They'll have their light—and every center of habitation goes up in flames!"

Eyes held each other as though the whole matter were a personal affair of respective will powers, and then Theremon broke away wordlessly. His breathing was harsh and ragged, and he scarcely noted the sudden hubbub that came from the adjoining room behind the closed door.

Sheerin spoke, and it was with an effort that he made it sound matter-of-fact. "I think I heard Yimot's voice. He and Faro are probably back. Let's go in and see what kept them."

"Might as well!" muttered Theremon. He drew a long breath and seemed to shake himself. The tension was broken.

The room was in an uproar, with members of the staff clustering about the two young men who were removing outer garments as they parried the miscellany of questions being thrown at them.

Aton bustled through the crowd and faced the newcomers angrily. "Do you realize that it's less than half an hour before deadline. Where have you two been?"

Faro 24 seated himself and rubbed his hands. His cheeks were red with the outdoor chill. "Yimot and I have just finished carrying through a crazy little experiment of our own. We've been trying to see if we couldn't construct an arrangement by which we could simulate the appearance of Darkness and Stars so as to get an advance notion as to how it looked."

There was a confused murmur from the listeners, and a sudden look of interest entered Aton's eyes. "There wasn't anything said of this before. How did you go about it?"

"Well," said Faro, "the idea came to Yimot and myself long ago, and we've been working it out in our spare time. Yimot knew of a low one-story house down in the city with a domed roof—it had once been used as a museum, I think. Anyway, we bought it—"

"Where did you get the money?" interrupted Aton peremptorily.

"Our bank accounts," grunted Yimot 70. "It cost two thousand credits." Then, defensively, "Well, what of it? Tomorrow, two thousand credits will be two thousand pieces of paper. That's all."

"Sure," agreed Faro. "We bought the place and rigged it up with black velvet from top to bottom so as to get as perfect a Darkness as possible. Then we punched tiny holes in the ceiling and through the roof and covered them with little metal caps, all of which could be shoved aside simultaneously at the close of a switch. At least, we didn't do that part ourselves; we got a carpenter and an electrician and some others—money didn't count. The point was that we could get the light to shine through those holes in the roof, so we could get a starlike effect."

Not a breath was drawn during the pause that followed. Aton said stiffly:

"You had no right to make a private—"

Faro seemed abashed. "I know, sir—but, frankly, Yimot and I thought the experiment was a little dangerous. If the effect really worked, we half expected to go mad—from what Sheerin says about all this, we thought that would be rather likely. We wanted to take the risk ourselves. Of course, if we found we could retain sanity, it occurred to us that we might develop immunity to the real thing, and then expose the rest of you to the same thing. But things didn't work out at all—"

"Why, what happened?"

It was Yimot who answered. "We shut ourselves in and allowed our eyes to get accustomed to the dark. It's an extremely creepy feeling because the total Darkness makes you feel as if the walls and ceiling are crushing in on you. But we got over that and pulled the switch. The caps fell away and the roof glittered all over with little dots of light—"

"Well?"

"Well—nothing. That was the whacky part of it. Nothing happened. It was just a roof with holes in it, and that's just what it looked like. We tried it over and over again—that's what kept us so late—but there just isn't any effect at all."

There followed a shocked silence, and all eyes turned to Sheerin, who sat motionless, mouth open.

Theremon was the first to speak. "You know what this does to this whole theory you've built up, Sheerin, don't you?" He was grinning with relief.

But Sheerin raised his hand. "Now wait a while. Just let me think this through." And then he snapped his fingers, and when he lifted his head there was neither surprise nor uncertainty in his eyes. "Of course—"

He never finished. From somewhere up above there sounded a sharp clang, and Beenay, starting to his feet, dashed up the stairs with a "What the devil!"

The rest followed after.

Things happened quickly. Once up in the dome, Beenay cast one horrified glance at the shattered photographic plates and at the man bending over them; and then hurled himself fiercely at the intruder, getting a death grip on his throat. There was a wild threshing, and as others of the staff joined in, the stranger was swallowed up and smothered under the weight of half a dozen angry men.

Aton came up last, breathing heavily. "Let him up!"

There was a reluctant unscrambling and the stranger, panting harshly, with his clothes torn and his forehead bruised, was hauled to his feet. He had a short yellow beard curled elaborately in the style affected by the Cultists.

Beenay shifted his hold to a collar grip and shook the man savagely. "All right, rat, what's the idea? These plates—"

"I wasn't after them," retorted the Cultist coldly. "That was an accident."

Beenay followed his glowering stare and snarled, "I see. You were after the cameras themselves. The accident with the plates was a stroke of luck for you, then. If you had touched Snapping Bertha or any of the others, you would have died by slow torture. As it is—" He drew his fist back.

Aton grabbed his sleeve. "Stop that! Let him go!"

The young technician wavered, and his arm dropped reluctantly. Aton pushed him aside and confronted the Cultist. "You're Latimer, aren't you?"

The Cultist bowed stiffly and indicated the symbol upon his hip. "I am Latimer 25, adjutant of the third class to his serenity, Sor 5."

"And"—Aton's white eyebrows lifted—"you were with his serenity when he visited me last week, weren't you?"

Latimer bowed a second time.

"Now, then, what do you want?"

"Nothing that you would give me of your own free will."

"Sor 5 sent you, I suppose—or is this your own idea?"

"I won't answer that question."

"Will there be any further visitors?"

"I won't answer that, either."

Aton glanced at his timepiece and scowled. "Now, man, what is it your master wants of me? I have fulfilled my end of the bargain."

Latimer smiled faintly, but said nothing.

"I asked him," continued Aton angrily, "for data only the Cult could supply, and it was given to me. For that, thank you. In return, I promised to prove the essential truth of the creed of the Cult."

"There was no need to prove that," came the proud retort. "It stands proven by the 'Book of Revelations.' "

"For the handful that constitute the Cult, yes. Don't pretend to mistake my meaning. I offered to present scientific backing for your beliefs. And I did!"

The Cultist's eyes narrowed bitterly. "Yes, you did—with a fox's subtlety, for your pretended explanation backed our beliefs, and at the same time removed all necessity for them. You made of the Darkness and of the Stars a natural phenomenon, and re-moved all its real significance. That was blasphemy."

"If so, the fault isn't mine. The facts exist. What can I do but state them?"

"Your 'facts' are a fraud and a delusion."

Aton stamped angrily. "How do *you* know?"

And the answer came with the certainty of absolute faith. "I *know!*"

The director purpled and Beenay whispered urgently. Aton waved him silent. "And what does Sor 5 want us to do? He still thinks, I suppose, that in trying to warn the world to take measures against the menace of madness, we are placing innumerable souls in jeopardy. We aren't succeeding, if that means anything to him."

"The attempt itself has done harm enough, and your vicious effort to gain information by means of your devilish instruments must be stopped. We obey the will of the Stars, and I only regret that my clumsiness prevented me from wrecking your infernal devices."

"It wouldn't have done you too much good," returned Aton. "All our data, except for the direct evidence we intended collecting right now, is already safely cached and well beyond possibility of harm." He smiled grimly. "But that does not affect your present status as an attempted burglar and criminal."

He turned to the man behind him. "Someone call the police at Saro City."

There was a cry of distaste from Sheerin. "Damn it, Aton, what's wrong with you? There's no time for that. Here"—he bustled his way forward—"let me handle this."

Aton stared down his nose at the psychologist. "This is not the time for your monkeyshines, Sheerin. Will you please let me handle this my own way? Right now you are a complete outsider here, and don't forget it."

Sheerin's mouth twisted eloquently. "Now why should we go to the impossible trouble of calling the police—with Beta's eclipse a matter of minutes from now—when this young man here is perfectly willing to pledge his word of honor to remain and cause no trouble whatsoever."

The Cultist answered promptly, "I will do no such thing. You're free to do what you want, but it's only fair to warn you that just as soon as I get my chance I'm going to finish what I came out here to do. If it's my word of honor you're relying on, you'd better call the police."

Sheerin smiled in a friendly fashion. "You're a determined cuss, aren't you? Well, I'll explain something. Do you see that young man at the window? He's a strong, husky fellow, quite handy with his fists, and he's an outsider besides. Once the eclipse starts there will be nothing for him to do except keep an eye on you. Besides him, there will be myself—a little too stout for active fisticuffs, but still able to help."

"Well, what of it?" demanded Latimer frozenly.

"Listen and I'll tell you," was the reply. "Just as soon as the eclipse starts, we're going to take you, Theremon and I, and deposit you in a little closet with one door, to which is attached one giant lock and no windows. You will remain there for the duration."

"And afterward," breathed Latimer fiercely, "there'll be no one to let me out. I know as well as you do what the coming of the Stars means—I know it far better than you. With all your minds gone, you are not likely to free me. Suffocation or slow starvation, is it? About what I might have expected from a group of scientists. But I don't give my word. It's a matter of principle, and I won't discuss it further."

Aton seemed perturbed. His faded eyes were troubled. "Really, Sheerin, locking him—"

"Please!" Sheerin motioned him impatiently to silence. "I don't think for a moment things will go that far. Latimer has just tried a clever little bluff, but I'm not a psychologist just because I like the sound of the word." He grinned at the Cultist. "Come now, you don't really think I'm trying anything as crude as slow starvation. My dear Latimer, if I lock you in the closet, you are not going to see the Darkness, and you are not going to see the Stars. It does not take much of a knowledge of the fundamental creed of the Cult to realize that for you to be hidden from the Stars when they appear means the loss of your immortal soul. Now, I believe you to be an honorable man. I'll accept your word of honor to make no further effort to disrupt proceedings if you'll offer it."

A vein throbbed in Latimer's temple, and he seemed to shrink within himself as he said thickly, "You have it!" And then he added with swift fury, "But it is my consolation that you will all be damned for your deeds of today." He turned on his heel and stalked to the high three-legged stool by the door.

Sheerin nodded to the columnist. "Take a seat next to him, Theremon—just as a formality. Hey, Theremon!"

But the newspaperman didn't move. He had gone pale to the lips.

"Look at that!" The finger he pointed toward the sky shook, and his voice was dry and cracked.

There was one simultaneous gasp as every eye followed the pointing finger and, for one breathless moment, stared frozenly.

Beta was chipped on one side!

The tiny bit of encroaching blackness was perhaps the width of a fingernail, but to the staring watchers it magnified itself into the crack of doom.

Only for a moment they watched, and after that there was a shrieking confusion that was even shorter of duration and which gave way to an orderly scurry of activity—each man at his pre-scribed job. At the crucial moment there was no time for emotion. The men were merely scientists with work to do. Even Aton had melted away.

Sheerin said prosaically, "First contact must have been made fifteen minutes ago. A little early, but pretty good considering the uncertainties involved in the calculation." He looked about him and then tiptoed to Theremon, who still remained staring out the window, and dragged him away gently.

"Aton is furious," he whispered, "so stay away. He missed first contact on account of this fuss with Latimer, and if you get in his way he'll have you thrown out the window."

Theremon nodded shortly and sat down. Sheerin stared in surprise at him.

"The devil, man," he exclaimed, "you're shaking."

"Eh?" Theremon licked his dry lips and then tried to smile. "I don't feel very well, and that's a fact."

The psychologist's eyes hardened. "You're not losing your nerve?"

"No!" cried Theremon in a flash of indignation. "Give me a chance, will you? I haven't really believed this rigmarole—not way down beneath, anyway—till just this minute. Give me a chance to get used to the idea. *You've* been preparing yourself for two months or more."

"You're right, at that," replied Sheerin thoughtfully. "Listen! Have you got a family—parents, wife, children?"

Theremon shook his head. "You mean the Hideout, I suppose.

No, you don't have to worry about that. I have a sister, but she's two thousand miles away. I don't even know her exact address."

"Well, then, what about yourself? You've got time to get there, and they're one short anyway, since I left. After all, you're not needed here and you'd make a darned fine addition—"

Theremon looked at the other wearily. "You think I'm scared stiff, don't you? Well, get this, mister, I'm a newspaperman and I've been assigned to cover a story. I intend covering it."

There was a faint smile on the psychologist's face. "I see. Professional honor, is that it?"

"You might call it that. But, man, I'd give my right arm for another bottle of that sockeroo juice even half the size of the one *you* hogged. If ever a fellow needed a drink, I do."

He broke off. Sheerin was nudging him violently. "Do you hear that? Listen!"

Theremon followed the motion of the other's chin and stared at the Cultist, who, oblivious to all about him, faced the window, a look of wild elation on his face, droning to himself the while in singsong fashion.

"What's he saying?" whispered the columnist.

"He's quoting 'Book of Revelations,' fifth chapter," replied Sheerin. Then, urgently, "Keep quiet and listen, I tell you."

The Cultist's voice had risen in a sudden increase of fervor:

" 'And it came to pass that in those days the sun, Beta, held lone vigil in the sky for ever longer periods as the revolutions passed; until such time as for full half a revolution, it alone, shrunken and cold, shone down upon Lagash.

" 'And men did assemble in the public squares and in the highways, there to debate and to marvel at the sight, for a strange depression had seized them. Their minds were troubled and their speech confused, for the souls of men awaited the coming of the Stars.

" 'And in the city of Trigon, at high noon, Vendret 2 came forth and said unto the men of Trigon, "Lo, ye sinners! Though ye scorn the ways of righteousness, yet will the time of reckoning come. Even now the Cave approaches to swallow Lagash; yea, and all it contains."

" 'And even as he spoke the lip of the Cave of Darkness passed the edge of Beta so that to all Lagash it was hidden from sight. Loud were the cries of men as it vanished, and great the fear of soul that fell upon them.

" 'It came to pass that the Darkness of the Cave fell upon Lagash, and there was no light on all the surface of Lagash. Men were even, as blinded, nor could one man see his neighbor, though he felt his breath upon his face.

" 'And in this blackness there appeared the Stars, in countless numbers, and to the strains of ineffable music of a beauty so wondrous that the very leaves of the trees turned to tongues that cried out in wonder.

" 'And in that moment the souls of men departed from them, and their abandoned bodies became even as beasts; yea, even as brutes of the wild; so that through the blackened streets of the cities of Lagash they prowled with wild cries.

" 'From the Stars there then reached down the Heavenly Flame, and where it touched, the cities of Lagash flamed to utter destruction, so that of man and of the works of man nought remained.

" 'Even then—' "

There was a subtle change in Latimer's tone. His eyes had not shifted, but somehow he had become aware of the absorbed attention of the other two. Easily, without pausing for breath, the timbre of his voice shifted and the syllables became more liquid.

Theremon, caught by surprise, stared. The words seemed on the border of familiarity. There was an elusive shift in the accent, a tiny change in the vowel stress; nothing more—yet Latimer had become thoroughly unintelligible.

Sheerin smiled slyly. "He shifted to some old-cycle tongue, probably their traditional second cycle. That was the language in which the 'Book of Revelations' had originally been written, you know."

"It doesn't matter; I've heard enough." Theremon shoved his chair back and brushed his hair back with hands that no longer shook. "I feel much better now."

"You do?" Sheerin seemed mildly surprised.

"I'll say I do. I had a bad case of jitters just a while back. Listening to you and your gravitation and seeing that eclipse start almost finished me. But this"—he jerked a contemptuous thumb at the yellow-bearded Cultist—"*this* is the sort of thing my nurse used to tell me. I've been laughing at that sort of thing all my life. I'm not going to let it scare me *now*."

He drew a deep breath and said with a hectic gaiety, "But if I expect to keep on the good side of myself, I'm going to turn my chair away from the window."

Sheerin said, "Yes, but you'd better talk lower. Aton just lifted his head out of that box he's got it stuck into and gave you a look that should have killed you."

Theremon made a mouth. "I forgot about the old fellow." With elaborate care he turned the chair from the window, cast one distasteful look over his shoulder and said, "It has occurred to me that there must be considerable immunity against this Star madness."

The psychologist did not answer immediately. Beta was past its zenith now, and the square of bloody sunlight that outlined the window upon the floor had lifted into Sheerin's lap. He stared at its dusky color thoughtfully and then bent and squinted into the sun itself.

The chip in its side had grown to a black encroachment that covered a third of Beta. He shuddered, and when he straightened once more his florid cheeks did not contain quite as much color as they had had previously.

With a smile that was almost apologetic, he reversed his chair also. "There are probably two million people in Saro City that are all trying to join the Cult at once in one gigantic revival." Then, ironically, "The Cult is in for an hour of unexampled prosperity. I trust they'll make the most of it. Now, what was it you said?"

"Just this. How do the Cultists manage to keep the 'Book of Revelations' going from cycle to cycle, and how on Lagash did it get written in the first place? There must have been some sort of immunity, for if everyone had gone mad, who would be left to write the book?"

Sheerin stared at his questioner ruefully. "Well, now, young man, there isn't any eyewitness answer to that, but we've got a few damned good notions as to what happened. You see, there are three kinds of people who might remain relatively unaffected. First, the very few who don't see the Stars at all; the blind, those who drink themselves into a stupor at the beginning of the eclipse and remain so to the end. We leave them out—because they aren't really witnesses.

"Then there are children below six, to whom the world as a whole is too new and strange for them to be *too* frightened at Stars and Darkness. They would be just another item in an already surprising world. You see that, don't you?"

The other nodded doubtfully. "I suppose so."

"Lastly, there are those whose minds are too coarsely grained to be entirely toppled. The very insensitive would be scarcely affected—oh, such people as some of our older, workbroken peasants. Well, the children would have fugitive memories, and that, combined with the confused, incoherent babblings of the half-mad morons, formed the basis for the 'Book of Revelations.'

"Naturally, the book was based, in the first place, on the testimony of those least qualified to serve as historians; that is, children and morons; and was probably extensively edited and re-edited through the cycles."

"Do you suppose," broke in Theremon, "that they carried the book through the cycles the way we're planning on handing on the secret of gravitation?"

Sheerin shrugged. "Perhaps, but their exact method is unimportant. They do it, somehow. The point I was getting at was that the book can't help but be a mass of distortion, even if it is based on fact. For instance, do you remember the experiment with the holes in the roof that Faro and Yimot tried—the one that didn't work?"

"Yes."

"You know why it didn't w—" He stopped and rose in alarm, for Aton was approaching, his face a twisted mask of consternation. *"What's happened?"*

Aton drew him aside and Sheerin could feel the fingers on his elbow twitching.

"Not so loud!" Aton's voice was low and tortured. "I've just gotten word from the Hideout on the private line."

Sheerin broke in anxiously, "They are in trouble?"

"Not *they*." Aton stressed the pronoun significantly. "They sealed themselves off just a while ago, and they're going to stay buried till day after tomorrow. They're safe. But the *city,* Sheerin —it's a shambles. You have no idea—" He was having difficulty in speaking.

"Well?" snapped Sheerin impatiently. "What of it? It will get worse. What are you shaking about?" Then, suspiciously, "How do you feel?"

Aton's eyes sparked angrily at the insinuation, and then faded to anxiety once more. "You don't understand. The Cultists are active. They're rousing the people to storm the Observatory— promising them immediate entrance into grace, promising them salvation, promising them anything. What are we to do, Sheerin?"

Sheerin's head bent, and he stared in long abstraction at his toes. He tapped his chin with one knuckle, then looked up and said crisply, "Do? What is there to do? Nothing at all! Do the men know of this?"

"No, of course not!"

"Good! Keep it that way. How long till totality?"

"Not quite an hour."

"There's nothing to do but gamble. It will take time to organize any really formidable mob, and it will take more time to get them out here. We're a good five miles from the city—"

He glared out the window, down the slopes to where the farmed patches gave way to clumps of white houses in the suburbs; down to where the metropolis itself was a blur on the horizon—a mist in the waning blaze of Beta.

He repeated without turning. "It will take time. Keep on working and pray that totality comes first."

Beta was cut in half, the line of division pushing a slight concavity into the still-bright portion of the sun. It was like a gigantic eyelid shutting slantwise over the light of a world.

The faint clatter of the room in which he stood faded into oblivion, and he sensed only the thick silence of the fields outside. The very insects seemed frightened mute. And things were dim.

He jumped at the voice in his ear. Theremon said, "Is something wrong?"

"Eh? Er—no. Get back to the chair. We're in the way." They

slipped back to their corner, but the psychologist did not speak for a time. He lifted a finger and loosened his collar. He twisted his neck back and forth but found no relief. He looked up suddenly.

"Are you having any difficulty in breathing?"

The newspaperman opened his eyes wide and drew two or three long breaths. "No. Why?"

"I looked out the window too long, I suppose. The dimness got me. Difficulty in breathing is one of the first symptoms of a claustrophobic attack."

Theremon drew another long breath. "Well, it hasn't got me yet. Say, here's another of the fellows."

Beenay had interposed his bulk between the light and the pair in the corner, and Sheerin squinted up at him anxiously. "Hello, Beenay."

The astronomer shifted his weight to the other foot and smiled feebly. "You won't mind if I sit down awhile and join in on the talk. My cameras are set, and there's nothing to do till totality." He paused and eyed the Cultist, who fifteen minutes earlier had drawn a small, skin-bound book from his sleeve and had been poring intently over it ever since. "That rat hasn't been making trouble, has he?"

Sheerin shook his head. His shoulders were thrown back and he frowned his concentration as he forced himself to breathe regularly. He said, "Have you had any trouble breathing, Beenay?"

Beenay sniffed the air in his turn. "It doesn't seem stuffy to me."

"A touch of claustrophobia," explained Sheerin apologetically.

"Oh-h-h! It worked itself differently with me. I get the impression that my eyes are going back on me. Things seem to blur and—well, nothing is clear. And it's cold, too."

"Oh, it's cold, all right. That's no illusion." Theremon grimaced. "My toes feel as if I've been shipping them cross country in a refrigerating car."

"What we need," put in Sheerin, "is to keep our minds busy with extraneous affairs. I was telling you a while ago, Theremon, why Faro's experiments with the holes in the roof came to nothing."

"You were just beginning," replied Theremon. He encircled a knee with both arms and nuzzled his chin against it.

"Well, as I started to say, they were misled by taking the 'Book of Revelations' literally. There probably wasn't any sense in attaching any physical significance to the Stars. It might be, you know, that in presence of total Darkness, the mind finds it absolutely necessary to create light. This illusion of light might be all the Stars there really are."

"In other words," interposed Theremon, "you mean the Stars are the results of the madness and not one of the causes. Then, what good will Beenay's photographs be?"

"To prove that it is an illusion, maybe; or to prove the opposite, for all I know. Then again—"

But Beenay had drawn his chair closer, and there was an expression of sudden enthusiasm on his face. "Say, I'm glad you two got on to this subject." His eyes narrowed and he lifted one finger. "I've been thinking about these Stars and I've got a really cute notion. Of course, it's strictly ocean foam, and I'm not trying to advance it seriously, but I think it's interesting. Do you want to hear it?"

He seemed half reluctant, but Sheerin leaned back and said, "Go ahead! I'm listening."

"Well, then, supposing there were other suns in the universe." He broke off a little bashfully. "I mean suns that are so far away that they're too dim to see. It sounds as if I've been reading some of that fantastic fiction, I suppose."

"Not necessarily. Still, isn't that possibility eliminated by the fact that, according to the Law of Gravitation, they would make themselves evident, by their attractive forces?"

"Not if they were far enough off," rejoined Beenay, "really far off—maybe as much as four light-years, or even more. We'd never be able to detect perturbations then, because they'd be too small. Say that there were a lot of suns that far off; a dozen or two, maybe."

Theremon whistled melodiously. "What an idea for a good Sunday supplement article. Two dozen suns in a universe eight light-years across. Wow! That would shrink *our* universe into insignificance. The readers would eat it up."

"Only an idea," said Beenay with a grin, "but you see the point. During eclipse, these dozen suns would become visible, because there'd be no *real* sunlight to drown them out. Since they're so far off, they'd appear small, like so many little marbles. Of course, the Cultists talk of millions of Stars, but that's probably exaggeration. There just isn't any place in the universe you could put a million suns—unless they touch each other."

Sheerin had listened with gradually increasing interest. "You've hit something there, Beenay. And exaggeration is just exactly what would happen. Our minds, as you probably know, can't grasp directly any number higher than five; above that there is only the concept of 'many.' A dozen would become a million just like that. A damn good idea!"

"And I've got another cute little notion," Beenay said. "Have you ever thought what a simple problem gravitation would be if only you had a sufficiently simple system? Supposing you had a universe in which there was a planet with only one sun. The planet would travel in a perfect ellipse and the exact nature of the gravitational force would be so evident it could be accepted as an axiom. Astronomers on such a world would start off with gravity probably before they even invent the telescope. Naked-eye observation would be enough."

"But would such a system be dynamically stable?" questioned Sheerin doubtfully.

"Sure! They call it the 'one-and-one' case. It's been worked out mathematically, but it's the philosophical implications that interest me."

"It's nice to think about," admitted Sheerin, "as a pretty abstraction—like a perfect gas or absolute zero."

"Of course," continued Beenay, "there's the catch that life would be impossible on such a planet. It wouldn't get enough heat and light, and if it rotated there would be total Darkness half of each day. You couldn't expect life—which is fundamentally dependent upon light—to develop under those conditions. Besides—"

Sheerin's chair went backward as he sprang to his feet in a rude interruption. "Aton's brought out the lights."

Beenay said, "Huh," turned to stare, and then grinned halfway around his head in open relief.

There were half a dozen foot-long, inch-thick rods cradled in Aton's arms. He glared over them at the assembled staff members.

"Get back to work, all of you. Sheerin, come here and help me!"

Sheerin trotted to the older man's side and, one by one, in utter silence, the two adjusted the rods in makeshift metal holders suspended from the walls.

With the air of one carrying through the most sacred item of a religious ritual, Sheerin scraped a large, clumsy match into sputtering life and passed it to Aton, who carried the flame to the upper end of one of the rods.

It hesitated there a while, playing futilely about the tip, until a sudden, crackling flare cast Aton's lined face into yellow highlights. He withdrew the match and a spontaneous cheer rattled the window.

The rod was topped by six inches of wavering flame! Methodically the other rods were lighted, until six independent fires turned the rear of the room yellow.

The light was dim, dimmer than the tenuous sunlight. The flames reeled crazily, giving birth to drunken, swaying shadows. The torches smoked devilishly and smelled like a bad day in the kitchen. But they emitted yellow light.

There is something *to* yellow light—after four hours of somber, dimming Beta. Even Latimer had lifted his eyes from his book and stared in wonder.

Sheerin warmed his hands at the nearest, regardless of the soot that gathered upon them in a fine, gray powder and muttered ecstatically to himself, "Beautiful! Beautiful! I never realized before what a wonderful color yellow is."

But Theremon regarded the torches suspiciously. He wrinkled his nose at the rancid odor and said, "What are those things?"

"Wood," said Sheerin shortly.

"Oh, no, they're not. They aren't burning. The top inch is charred and the flame just keeps shooting up out of nothing."

"That's the beauty of it. This is a really efficient artificial-light mechanism. We made a few hundred of them, but most went to the

Hideout, of course. You see"—he turned and wiped his blackened hands upon his handkerchief—"you take the pithy core of coarse water reeds, dry them thoroughly and soak them in animal grease. Then you set fire to it and the grease burns, little by little. These torches will burn for almost half an hour without stopping. Ingenious, isn't it? It was developed by one of our own young men at Saro University."

After the momentary sensation, the dome had quieted. Latimer had carried his chair directly beneath a torch and continued reading, lips moving in the monotonous recital of invocations to the Stars. Beenay had drifted away to his cameras once more, and Theremon seized the opportunity to add to his notes on the article he was going to write for the Saro City *Chronicle* the next day— a procedure he had been following for the last two hours in a perfectly methodical, perfectly conscientious and, as he was well aware, perfectly meaningless fashion.

But, as the gleam of amusement in Sheerin's eyes indicated, careful note-taking occupied his mind with something other than the fact that the sky was gradually turning a horrible deep purple-red, as if it were one gigantic, freshly peeled beet; and so it fulfilled its purpose.

The air grew, somehow, denser. Dusk, like a palpable entity, entered the room, and the dancing circle of yellow light about the torches etched itself into ever-sharper distinction against the gathering grayness beyond. There was the odor of smoke and the presence of little chuckling sounds that the torches made as they burned; the soft pad of one of the men circling the table at which he worked, on hesitant tiptoes; the occasional indrawn breath of someone trying to retain composure in a world that was retreating into the shadow.

It was Theremon who first heard the extraneous noise. It was a vague, unorganized *impression* of sound that would have gone unnoticed but for the dead silence that prevailed within the dome.

The newsman sat upright and replaced his notebook. He held his breath and listened; then, with considerable reluctance, threaded his way between the solaroscope and one of Beenay's cameras and stood before the window.

The silence ripped to fragments at his startled shout:
"Sheerin!"

Work stopped! The psychologist was at his side in a moment. Aton joined him. Even Yimot 70, high in his little leanback seat at the eyepiece of the gigantic solaroscope, paused and looked downward.

Outside, Beta was a mere smoldering splinter, taking one last desperate look at Lagash. The eastern horizon, in the direction of the city, was lost in Darkness, and the road from Saro to the Observatory was a dull red line bordered on both sides by wooded tracts, the trees of which had somehow lost individuality and merged into a continuous shadowy mass.

But it was the highway itself that held attention, for along it there surged another, and infinitely menacing shadowy mass.

Aton cried in a cracked voice, "The madmen from the city! They've come!"

"How long to totality?" demanded Sheerin.

"Fifteen minutes, but . . . but they'll be here in five."

"Never mind, keep the men working. We'll hold them off. This place is built like a fortress. Aton, keep an eye on our young Cultist just for luck. Theremon, come with me."

Sheerin was out the door, and Theremon was at his heels. The stairs stretched below them in tight, circular sweeps about the central shaft, fading into a dank and dreary grayness.

The first momentum of their rush had carried them fifty feet down, so that the dim, flickering yellow from the open door of the dome had disappeared and both up above and down below the same dusky shadow crushed in upon them.

Sheerin paused, and his pudgy hand clutched at his chest. His eyes bulged and his voice was a dry cough. "I can't . . . breathe . . . go down . . . yourself. Close all doors—"

Theremon took a few downward steps, then turned. "Wait! Can you hold out a minute?" He was panting himself. The air passed in and out of his lungs like so much molasses, and there was a little germ of screeching panic in his mind at the thought of making his way into the mysterious Darkness below by himself.

Theremon, after all, was afraid of the dark!

"Stay here," he said. "I'll be back in a second." He dashed upward two steps at a time, heart pounding—not altogether from the exertion—tumbled into the dome and snatched a torch from its holder. It was foul-smelling, and the smoke smarted his eyes almost blind, but he clutched that torch as if he wanted to kiss it for joy, and its flame streamed backward as he hurtled down the stairs again.

Sheerin opened his eyes and moaned as Theremon bent over him. Theremon shook him roughly. "All right, get a hold on yourself. We've got light."

He held the torch at tiptoe height and, propping the tottering psychologist by an elbow, made his way downward in the middle of the protecting circle of illumination.

The offices on the ground floor still possessed what light there was, and Theremon felt the horror about him relax.

"Here," he said brusquely, and passed the torch to Sheerin. "You can hear *them* outside."

And they could. Little scraps of hoarse, wordless shouts.

But Sheerin was right; the Observatory *was* built like a fortress. Erected in the last century, when the neo-Gavottian style of architecture was at its ugly height, it had been designed for stability and durability, rather than for beauty.

The windows were protected by the grillwork of inch-thick iron bars sunk deep into the concrete sills. The walls were solid masonry that an earthquake couldn't have touched, and the main door was a huge oaken slab reinforced with iron at the strategic points. Theremon shot the bolts and they slid shut with a dull clang.

At the other end of the corridor, Sheerin cursed weakly. He pointed to the lock of the back door which had been neatly jimmied into uselessness.

"That must be how Latimer got in," he said.

"Well, don't stand there," cried Theremon impatiently. "Help drag up the furniture—and keep that torch out of my eyes. The smoke's killing me."

He slammed the heavy table up against the door as he spoke, and in two minutes had built a barricade which made up for what it lacked in beauty and symmetry by the sheer inertia of massiveness.

Somewhere, dimly, far off, they could hear the battering of naked fists upon the door; and the screams and yells from outside had a sort of half reality.

That mob had set off from Saro City with only two things in mind: the attainment of Cultist salvation by the destruction of the Observatory, and a maddening fear that all but paralyzed them. There was no time to think of ground cars, or of weapons, or of leadership, or even of organization. They made for the Observatory on foot and assaulted it with bare hands.

And now that they were there, the last flash of Beta, the last ruby-red drop of flame, flickered feebly over a humanity that had left only stark, universal fear!

Theremon groaned, "Let's get back to the dome!"

In the dome, only Yimot, at the solaroscope, had kept his place. The rest were clustered about the cameras, and Beenay was giving his instructions in a hoarse, strained voice.

"Get it straight, all of you. I'm snapping Beta just before totality and changing the plate. That will leave one of you to each camera. You all know about . . . about times of exposure—"

There was a breathless murmur of agreement.

Beenay passed a hand over his eyes. "Are the torches still burning? Never mind, I see them!" He was leaning hard against the back of a chair. "Now remember, don't . . . don't try to look for good shots. Don't waste time trying to get t-two stars at a time in the scope field. One is enough. And . . . and if you feel yourself going, *get away from the camera.*"

At the door, Sheerin whispered to Theremon, "Take me to Aton. I don't see him."

The newsman did not answer immediately. The vague forms of the astronomers wavered and blurred, and the torches overhead had become only yellow splotches.

"It's dark," he whimpered.

Sheerin held out his hand, "Aton." He stumbled forward. "Aton!"

Theremon stepped after and seized his arm. "Wait, I'll take you." Somehow he made his way across the room. He closed his eyes against the Darkness and his mind against the chaos within it.

No one heard them or paid attention to them. Sheerin stumbled against the wall. "Aton!"

The psychologist felt shaking hands touching him, then withdrawing, and a voice muttering, "Is that you, Sheerin?"

"Aton!" He strove to breathe normally. "Don't worry about the mob. The place will hold them off."

Latimer, the Cultist, rose to his feet, and his face twisted in desperation. His word was pledged, and to break it would mean placing his soul in mortal peril. Yet that word had been forced from him and had not been given freely. The Stars would come soon; he could not stand by and allow— And yet his word was pledged.

Beenay's face was dimly flushed as it looked upward at Beta's last ray, and Latimer, seeing him bend over his camera, made his decision. His nails cut the flesh of his palms as he tensed himself.

He staggered crazily as he started his rush. There was nothing before him but shadows; the very floor beneath his feet lacked substance. And then someone was upon him and he went down with clutching fingers at his throat.

He doubled his knee and drove it hard into his assailant. "Let me up or I'll kill you."

Theremon cried out sharply and muttered through a blinding haze of pain, "You double-crossing rat!"

The newsman seemed conscious of everything at once. He heard Beenay croak, "I've got it. At your cameras, men!" and then there was the strange awareness that the last thread of sunlight had thinned out and snapped.

Simultaneously he heard one last choking gasp from Beenay, and a queer little cry from Sheerin, a hysterical giggle that cut off in a rasp—and a sudden silence, a strange deadly silence from outside.

And Latimer had gone limp in his loosening grasp. Theremon peered into the Cultist's eyes and saw the blankness of them, staring upward, mirroring the feeble yellow of the torches. He saw the bubble of froth upon Latimer's lips and heard the low animal whimper in Latimer's throat.

With the slow fascination of fear, he lifted himself on one arm and turned his eyes toward the bloodcurdling blackness of the window.

Through it shone the Stars!

Not Earth's feeble thirty-six hundred Stars visible to the eye—Lagash was in the center of a giant cluster. Thirty thousand mighty suns shone down in a soul-searing splendor that was more frighteningly cold in its awful indifference than the bitter wind that shivered across the cold, horribly bleak world.

Theremon staggered to his feet, his throat constricting him to breathlessness, all the muscles of his body writhing in a tensity of terror and sheer fear beyond bearing. He was going mad, and knew it, and somewhere deep inside a bit of sanity was screaming, struggling to fight off the hopeless flood of black terror. It was very horrible to go mad and know that you were going mad—to know that in a little minute you would be here physically and yet all the real essence would be dead and drowned in the black madness. For this was the Dark—the Dark and the Cold and the Doom. The bright walls of the universe were shattered and their awful black fragments were falling down to crush and squeeze and obliterate him.

He jostled someone crawling on hands and knees, but stumbled somehow over him. Hands groping at his tortured throat, he limped toward the flame of the torches that filled all his mad vision.

"Light!" he screamed.

Aton, somewhere, was crying, whimpering horribly like a terribly frightened child. "Stars—all the Stars—we didn't know at all. We didn't know anything. We thought six Stars is a universe is something the Stars didn't notice is Darkness forever and ever and ever and the walls are breaking in and we didn't know we couldn't know and anything—"

Someone clawed at the torch, and it fell and snuffed out. In the instant, the awful splendor of the indifferent Stars leaped nearer to them.

On the horizon outside the window, in the direction of Saro City, a crimson glow began growing, strengthening in brightness, that was not the glow of a sun.

The long night had come again.

PRIVATE EYE

by LEWIS PADGETT

FOREWORD
by James Blish

THE AUTHOR

LEWIS PADGETT was a pseudonym employed by Henry Kuttner (1914–58), usually writing in collaboration, to some degree, with his wife, Catherine L. Moore. Kuttner, born in Los Angeles, spent most of his life as a free-lance writer, chiefly of science fiction and fantasy; his first story appeared in 1936. His early work was skillful but undistinguished action fiction, but his growth was rapid, and his writing took on a new richness after his marriage to Miss Moore in 1940. An outstanding fantasy writer in her own right, she also shared in the creation of Kuttner's work until it became impossible to determine the individual contributions of each. "Lewis Padgett," perhaps the most celebrated of their innumerable pseudonyms, won considerable fame before his nonexistence was revealed. "Private Eye" was first published in 1948.

THE CRITIC

JAMES BLISH is not only an important science-fiction writer (see page 167) but also one of the field's most formidable critical intelligences. Under the byline of "William Atheling, Jr.," he was responsible for a series of vigorous analyses of science-fiction stories, collected in 1964 by Advent: Publishers under the title of *The Issue at Hand*. His critical work has appeared in the Aldiss-Harrison *SF Horizons,* the *Hudson Review, Warhoon*, and many other magazines.

Foreword

The more supercilious critics of science fiction sometimes complain of it that it shows its pulp-magazine origins all too clearly. The most interesting aspect of this criticism is not that it is true—though it is—but that it is substantially in favor of the genre.

The old pulp magazines cared very little for style or characterization, but they absolutely required that their authors know how to plot. This is a craft that is viewed with indifference, if not with outright scorn, by most publishers of the art story, though there is no objection to it in the slick magazines. Even in science fiction, we have today a whole generation of writers which has grown up unexposed to the rigorous plotting demands of the (now extinct) pulps, considerably to their loss, and the readers'.

For this reason I think it worth while to sketch briefly here the basic plot structure of common practice. The reader will observe that this is not a formula but a skeleton; there are very few good stories of any kind that are not built on it. It requires, first of all, a sympathetic viewpoint character with whom the reader can identify. Second, it requires that he be confronted with a serious problem—one which threatens his life, his values, or someone he loves, not just his commissions or his collection of old billiard cues. The quicker the problem is stated, the better, for the main body of the story is the complication section, where each of the hero's attempts to solve the problem makes it worse. This leads at last to a crisis, in which the problem seems quite insoluble to the reader; and finally to a solution, which must come out of the hero's own efforts and abilities (no landings by the Marines, please), be a surprise to the reader, and at the same time emerge logically from what has gone before.

There are thousands of possible variants, of which the most obvious is the story of the villain who goes from success to success until he is defeated by his own efforts and weaknesses (sometimes called the "biter bit" story). Double plotting, which is tougher, confronts the hero with two apparently independent problems, so that any effort to solve one worsens the other; it is aesthetically most satisfying when both problems turn out to have a single solution. The modern art story, perhaps influenced by Joyce's emphasis on epiphanies, most often confronts the reader directly with the crisis, leaving all the preceding material to the reader's imagination. This is obviously the most difficult way to tackle plotting, but few contemporary mainstream writers seem to be aware of any other.

There was nothing in fiction that Henry Kuttner did not do well, but at plotting he was an outright virtuoso, as the following story shows. In addition, he worked out an interesting and viable solution to the problem of story line.

The story line is not the plot, but the *whole* story, including everything that has happened before the story begins to put the characters in the situation in which we find them, and to shape them so that their actions are characteristic of them, not arbitrary whims of the author. Getting this material over to the reader is one of the hardest jobs the writer faces. By far the most common way out of it is to have the characters lecture each other interminably about matters they clearly already know—sometimes with speeches that actually begin, "As you know . . ."

Obviously this is no solution at all, and these days it is considered equally unsatisfactory for the omniscient author to lay out the precedent material, *à la* Trollope. Kuttner, however, never took any of the technicalities of writing for granted, and after close examination of the machinery, he worked out a way of rehabilitating the omniscient author. His method was to start the story not with the usual narrative hook ("Autumn was descending on U.S. Highway 66 when John met the naked princess") but with a genuine sub-crisis, and within the space of about a thousand words develop it into a resounding paradox. While the reader is wondering what the answer to the paradox could possibly be, Kuttner drops the story for about a thousand words of straight lecture on the background of the situation, confident that the reader, captured by the paradox, will sit still for it.

Point of view is another technical trap for the unwary. Since Flaubert, almost all editors have required that the short story be told from a single point of view, usually that of the hero, though one or more additional viewpoints may be involved in the novel or in double plotting. The major difficulty here is that the story often requires the reader to know some things about the situation that the hero obviously cannot. One of Kuttner's many solutions to this difficulty consisted, characteristically, in turning it into a strength—usually an adjunct of characterization. Thus, a complex Kuttner story often is told partly from the point of view of the protagonist and partly from the point of view of another character (or several) who is attempting to figure him out. This sounds simple, but bringing it off is another matter, for it means that despite the wealth of information now available to the reader, he must still be surprised by the solution—as must *both* sets of characters.

I have stressed Kuttner's technical virtuosity here in part because it is rare and partly because plotting is a subject one seldom sees discussed in criticism these days. He had many other strengths, among the greatest of which was the enormous sympathy with which he viewed his characters, even those who were in an advanced state of moral decay. This sometimes appears laid out in almost classically Freudian terms, but Kuttner was never doctrinaire or obtrusive about his psychology, and I think he would have been equally at home in any system; the sympathy was a part of his nature, not the product of a school of thought or otherwise imposed from the outside. He was too witty to be a pedant about anything.

Some of the strengths you will find in this story, however, are not actually his. Almost all of his mature work was written in collaboration with his wife, Catherine L. Moore. There seldom seemed to be much foreplanning in this collaboration, especially in its last years; one of them would simply leave a story in the typewriter, so to speak, and return to find that it had been advanced several thousand words by the other. Viewing stories written individually by each of them, one can see what each of them gave the other: Henry by himself had no particular eye for sensory detail, while Catherine had a relatively weak plot sense and could not write clean, pointed dialogue.

The combination was ideal, and resulted in some of the best science fiction ever written by anybody (as well as an excellent suspense novel, *Man Drowning*). Their productivity was enormous, too; at one time the Kuttners operated so many pen names that almost any new writer was automatically suspected of being another of their masks. I myself in 1948 received a letter which, once out of the envelope, turned out to begin, "Dear Mr. Kuttner." I forwarded it to him, thus beginning a ten-year correspondence from which I learned more about writing than I have ever learned from any other person. The story which follows shows why.

PRIVATE EYE

The forensic sociologist looked closely at the image on the wall screen. Two figures were frozen there, one in the act of stabbing the other through the heart with an antique letter cutter, once used at Johns Hopkins for surgery. That was before the ultra-microtome, of course.

"As tricky a case as I've ever seen," the sociologist remarked. "If we can make a homicide charge stick on Sam Clay, I'll be a little surprised." *137850*

The tracer engineer twirled a dial and watched the figures on the screen repeat their actions. One—Sam Clay—snatched the letter cutter from a desk and plunged it into the other man's heart. The victim fell down dead. Clay started back in apparent horror. Then he dropped to his knees beside the twitching body and said wildly that he didn't mean it. The body drummed its heels upon the rug and was still.

"That last touch was nice," the engineer said.

"Well, I've got to make the preliminary survey," the sociologist sighed, settling in his dictachair and placing his fingers on the keyboard. "I doubt if I'll find any evidence. However, the analysis can come later. Where's Clay now?"

"His mouthpiece put in a *habeas mens*."

"I didn't think we'd be able to hold him. But it was worth trying. Imagine, just one shot of scop and he'd have told the truth. Ah, well. We'll do it the hard way, as usual. Start the tracer, will you? It won't make sense till we run it chronologically, but one must start somewhere. Good old Blackstone," the sociologist said, as, on the screen, Clay stood up, watching the corpse revive and arise, and then pulled the miraculously clean paper cutter out of its heart, all in reverse.

"Good old Blackstone," he repeated. "On the other hand, some-times I wish I'd lived in Jeffreys' time. In those days, homicide was homicide."

Telepathy never came to much. Perhaps the developing faculty went underground in response to a familiar natural law after the new science appeared—omniscience. It wasn't really that, of course. It was a device for looking into the past. And it was limited to a fifty-year span; no chance of seeing the arrows at Agincourt or the homunculi of Bacon. It was sensitive enough to pick up the "fingerprints" of light and sound waves imprinted on matter, descramble and screen them, and reproduce the image of what had happened. After all, a man's shadow can be photographed on con-crete, if he's unlucky enough to be caught in an atomic blast. Which is something. The shadow's about all there is left.

However, opening the past like a book didn't solve all problems. It took generations for the maze of complexities to iron itself out, though finally a tentative check-and-balance was reached. The right to kill has been sturdily defended by mankind since Cain rose up against Abel. A good many idealists quoted, "The voice of thy brother's blood crieth unto me from the ground." But that didn't stop the lobbyists and the pressure groups. Magna Carta was quoted in reply. The right to privacy was defended desperately.

And the curious upshot of this imbalance came when the act of homicide was declared nonpunishable, unless intent and fore-thought could be proved. Of course, it was considered at least naughty to fly in a rage and murder someone on impulse, and there was a nominal punishment—imprisonment, for example —but in practice this never worked, because so many defenses were possible. Temporary insanity. Undue provocation. Self-defense. Manslaughter, second-degree homicide, third degree, fourth degree —it went on like that. It was up to the State to prove that the killer had planned his killing in advance; only then would a jury convict. And the jury, of course, had to waive immunity and take a scop test, to prove the box hadn't been packed. But no defendant ever waived immunity.

A man's home wasn't his castle—not with the Eye able to enter it at will and scan his past. The device couldn't interpret, and it couldn't read his mind; it could only see and listen. Consequently the sole remaining fortress of privacy was the human mind. And that was defended to the last ditch. No truth serum, no hypo-analysis, no third degree, no leading questions.

If, by viewing the prisoner's past actions, the prosecution could prove forethought and intent, O.K.

Otherwise, Sam Clay would go scot-free. Superficially, it appeared as though Andrew Vanderman had, during a quarrel, struck Clay across the face with a stingaree whip. Anyone who has been stung by a Portuguese man-of-war can understand that, at this point, Clay could plead temporary insanity and self-defense, as well as undue provocation and possible justification. Only the curious cult of the Alaskan Flagellantes, who make the stingaree whips for their ceremonials, know how to endure the pain. The Flagellantes even like it; the pre-ritual drug they swallow trans-mutes pain into pleasure. Not having swallowed this drug, Sam Clay very naturally took steps to protect himself—irrational steps, perhaps, but quite logical and defensible ones.

Nobody but Clay knew that he had intended to kill Vanderman all along. That was the trouble. Clay couldn't understand why he felt so let down.

The screen flickered. It went dark. The engineer chuckled.

"My, my. Locked up in a dark closet at the age of four. What one of those old-time psychiatrists would have made of that. Or do I mean obimen? Shamans? I forget. They interpreted dreams, anyway."

"You're confused. It—"

"Astrologers! No, it wasn't either. The ones I mean went in for symbolism. They used to spin prayer wheels and say 'A rose is a rose is a rose,' didn't they? To free the unconscious mind?"

"You've got the typical layman's attitude toward antique psy-chiatric treatments."

"Well, maybe they had something, at that. Look at quinine and digitalis. The United Amazon natives used those long before science discovered them. But why use eye of newt and toe of frog? To impress the patient?"

"No, to convince themselves," the sociologist said. "In those days the study of mental aberrations drew potential psychotics, so naturally there was unnecessary mumbo-jumbo. Those medicos were trying to fix their own mental imbalance while they treated their patients. But it's a science today, not a religion. We've found out how to allow for individual psychotic deviation in the psychiatrist himself, so we've got a better chance of finding true north. However, let's get on with this. Try ultraviolet. Oh, never mind. Somebody's letting him out of that closet. The devil with it. I think we've cut back far enough. Even if he was frightened by a thunderstorm at the age of three months, that can be filed under Gestalt and ignored. Let's run through this chronologically. Give it the screening for . . . let's see. Incidents involving these persons: Vanderman, Mrs. Vanderman, Josephine Wells—and these places: the office, Vanderman's apartment, Clay's place—"

"Got it."

"Later we can recheck for complicating factors. Right now we'll run the superficial survey. Verdict first, evidence later," he added, with a grin. "All we need is a motive—"

"What about this?"

A girl was talking to Sam Clay. The background was an apartment, grade B-2.

"I'm sorry, Sam. It's just that . . . well, these things happen."

"Yeah. Vanderman's got something I haven't got, apparently."

"I'm in love with him."

"Funny. I thought all along you were in love with me."

"So did I . . . for a while."

"Well, forget it. No, I'm not angry, Bea. I'll even wish you luck. But you must have been pretty certain how I'd react to this."

"I'm sorry—"

"Come to think of it, I've always let you call the shots. Always."

Secretly—and this the screen could not show—he thought: Let her? I wanted it that way. It was so much easier to leave the decisions up to her. Sure, she's dominant, but I guess I'm just the opposite. And now it's happened again.

It always happens. I was loaded with weight-cloths from the start. And I always felt I had to toe the line, or else. Vanderman— that cocky, arrogant air of his. Reminds me of somebody. I was

locked up in a dark place, I couldn't breathe. I forget. What . . .
who . . . my father. No, I don't remember. But my life's been like
that. He always watched me, and I always thought someday I'd do
what *I* wanted—but I never did. Too late now. He's been dead
quite a while.

He was always so sure I'd knuckle under. If I'd only defied him
once—

Somebody's always pushing me in and closing the door. So I
can't use my abilities. I can't prove I'm competent. Prove it to
myself, to my father, to Bea, to the whole world. If only I could—
I'd like to push Vanderman into a dark place and lock the door.
A dark place, like a coffin. It would be satisfying to surprise him
that way. It would be fine if I killed Andrew Vanderman.

"Well, that's the beginning of a motive," the sociologist said.
"Still, lots of people get jilted and don't turn homicidal. Carry on."

"In my opinion, Bea attracted him because he wanted to be
bossed," the engineer remarked. "He'd given up."

"Protective passivity."

The wire-tapes spun through the screening apparatus, A new
scene showed on the oblong panel. It was the Paradise Bar.

Anywhere you sat in the Paradise Bar, a competent robot
analyzer instantly studied your complexion and facial angles, and
switched on lights, in varying tints and intensities, that showed you
off to best advantage. The joint was popular for business deals.
A swindler could look like an honest man there. It was also popular
with women and slightly passé teleo talent. Sam Clay looked rather
like an ascetic young saint. Andrew Vanderman looked noble,
in a grim way, like Richard Coeur-de-Leon offering Saladin his
freedom, though he knew it wasn't really a bright thing to do.
Noblesse oblige, his firm jaw seemed to say, as he picked up the
silver decanter and poured. In ordinary light, Vanderman looked
slightly more like a handsome bulldog. Also, away from the Paradise Bar, he was redder around the chops, a choleric man.

"As to that deal we were discussing," Clay said, "you can go
to—"

The censoring juke box blared out a covering bar or two.

Vanderman's reply was unheard as the music got briefly louder, and the lights shifted rapidly to keep pace with his sudden flush.

"It's perfectly easy to outwit these censors," Clay said. "They're keyed to familiar terms of profane abuse, not to circumlocutions. If I said that the arrangement of your chromosomes would have surprised your father . . . you see?" He was right. The music stayed soft.

Vanderman swallowed nothing. "Take it easy," he said. "I can see why you're upset. Let me say first of all—"

"*Hijo*—"

But the censor was proficient in Spanish dialects. Vanderman was spared hearing another insult.

"—that I offered you a job because I think you're a very capable man. You have potentialities. It's not a bribe. Our personal affairs should be kept out of this."

"All the same, Bea was engaged to me."

"Clay, are you drunk?"

"Yes," Clay said, and threw his drink into Vanderman's face. The music began to play Wagner very, very loudly. A few minutes later, when the waiters interfered, Clay was supine and bloody, with a mashed nose and a bruised cheek. Vanderman had skinned his knuckles.

"That's a motive," the engineer said.

"Yes, it is, isn't it? But why did Clay wait a year and a half? And remember what happened later. I wonder if the murder itself was just a symbol? If Vanderman represented, say, what Clay considered the tyrannical and oppressive force of society in general— synthesized in the representative image . . . oh, nonsense. Obviously Clay was trying to prove something to himself, though. Suppose you cut forward now. I want to see this in normal chronology, not backward. What's the next selection?"

"Very suspicious. Clay got his nose fixed up and then went to a murder trial."

He thought: I can't breathe. Too crowded in here. Shut up in a box, a closet, a coffin, ignored by the spectators and the vested authority on the bench. What would I do if I were in the dock, like that chap? Suppose they convicted? That would spoil it all. Another dark place—If I'd inherited the right genes, I'd have been strong enough to beat up Vanderman. But I've been pushed around too long.

I keep remembering that song.

> *Stray in the herd and the boss said kill it,*
> *So I shot him in the rump with the handle of a skillet.*

A deadly weapon that's in normal usage wouldn't appear dangerous. But if it could be used homicidally—no, the Eye could check on that. All you can conceal these days is motive. But couldn't the trick be reversed? Suppose I got Vanderman to attack me with what he thought was the handle of a skillet, but which I knew was a deadly weapon—

The trial Sam Clay was watching was fairly routine. One man had killed another. Counsel for the defense contended that the homicide had been a matter of impulse, and that, as a matter of fact, only assault and battery plus culpable negligence, at worst, could be proved, and the latter was canceled by an Act of God. The fact that the defendant inherited the decedent's fortune, in Martial oil, made no difference. Temporary insanity was the plea.

The prosecuting attorney showed films of what had happened before the fact. True, the victim hadn't been killed by the blow, merely stunned. But the affair had occurred on an isolated beach, and when the tide came in—

Act of God, the defense repeated hastily.

The screen showed the defendant some days before his crime, looking up the tide-table in a news tape. He also, it appeared, visited the site and asked a passing stranger if the beach was often crowded. "Nope," the stranger said, "it ain't crowded after sundown. Gits too cold. Won't do you no good, though. Too cold to swim then."

One side matched *Actus non facit reum, nisi mens sit rea*—"The act does not make a man guilty, unless the mind be also guilty"—against *Acta exteriora indicant interiora secreta*—"By the outward acts we are to judge of the inward thoughts." Latin legal basics were still valid, up to a point. A man's past remained sacrosanct, provided—and here was the joker—that he possessed the right of citizenship. And anyone accused of a capital crime was automatically suspended from citizenship until his innocence had been established.

Also, no past-tracing evidence could be introduced into a trial unless it could be proved that it had direct connection with the crime. The average citizen did have a right of privacy against tracing. Only if accused of a serious crime was that forfeit, and even then evidence uncovered could be used only in correlation with the immediate charge. There were various loopholes, of course, but theoretically a man was safe from espionage as long as he stayed within the law.

Now a defendant stood in the dock, his past opened. The prosecution showed recordings of a ginger blonde blackmailing him, and that clinched the motive and the verdict—guilty. The condemned man was led off in tears. Clay got up and walked out of the court. From his appearance, he seemed to be thinking.

He was. He had decided that there was only one possible way in which he could kill Vanderman and get away with it. He couldn't conceal the deed itself, nor the actions leading up to it, nor any written or spoken word. All he could hide were his own thoughts. And, without otherwise betraying himself, he'd have to kill Vanderman so that his act would appear justified. Which meant covering his tracks for yesterday as well as for tomorrow and tomorrow.

Now, thought Clay, this much can be assumed: If I stand to lose by Vanderman's death instead of gaining, that will help considerably. I must juggle that somehow. But I mustn't forget that at present I have an obvious motive. First, he stole Bea. Second, he beat me up.

So I must make it seem as though he's done me a favor—somehow.

I must have an opportunity to study Vanderman carefully, and it must be a normal, logical, waterproof opportunity. Private secretary. Something like that. The Eye's in the future now, after the fact, but it's watching me—

I must remember that. *It's watching me now!*

All right. Normally, I'd have thought of murder, at this point. That can't and shouldn't be disguised. I must work out of the mood gradually, but meanwhile—

He smiled.

Going off to buy a gun, he felt uncomfortable, as though that prescient Eye, years in the future, could with a wink summon the police. But it was separated from him by a barrier of time that only the natural processes could shorten. And, in fact, it had been watching him since his birth. You could look at it that way—

He could defy it. The Eye couldn't read thoughts.

He bought the gun and lay in wait for Vanderman in a dark alley. But first he got thoroughly drunk. Drunk enough to satisfy the Eye.

After that—

"Feel better now?" Vanderman asked, pouring another coffee.

Clay buried his face in his hands.

"I was crazy," he said, his voice muffled. "I must have been. You'd better t-turn me over to the police."

"We can forget about that end of it, Clay. You were drunk, that's all. And I . . . well, I—"

"I pull a gun on you . . . try to kill you . . . and you bring me up to your place and—"

"You didn't use that gun, Clay. Remember that. You're no killer. All this has been my fault. I needn't have been so blasted tough with you," Vanderman said, looking like Coeur-de-Leon in spite of uncalculated amber fluorescence.

"I'm no good. I'm a failure. Every time I try to do something, a man like you comes along and does it better. I'm a second-rater."

"Clay, stop talking like that. You're just upset, that's all. Listen to me. You're going to straighten up. I'm going to see that you do. Starting tomorrow, we'll work something out. Now drink your coffee."

"You know," Clay said, "you're quite a guy."

So the magnanimous idiot's fallen for it, Clay thought, as he was drifting happily off to sleep. Fine. That begins to take care of the Eye. Moreover, it starts the ball rolling with Vanderman. Let a man do you a favor and he's your pal. Well, Vanderman's going to do me a lot more favors. In fact, before I'm through, I'll have every motive for wanting to keep him alive.

Every motive visible to the naked Eye.

Probably Clay had not heretofore applied his talents in the right direction, for there was nothing second-rate about the way he executed his homicide plan. In that, he proved very capable. He needed a suitable channel for his ability, and perhaps he needed a patron. Vanderman fulfilled that function; probably it salved his conscience for stealing Bea. Being the man he was, Vanderman needed to avoid even the appearance of ignobility. Naturally strong and ruthless, he told himself he was sentimental. His sentimentality never reached the point of actually inconveniencing him, and Clay knew enough to stay within the limits.

Nevertheless it is nerve-racking to know you're living under the scrutiny of an extratemporal Eye. As he walked into the lobby of the V Building a month later, Clay realized that light-vibrations reflected from his own body were driving irretrievably into the polished onyx walls and floor, photographing themselves there, waiting for a machine to unlock them, some day, some time, for some man perhaps in this very city, who as yet didn't know even the name of Sam Clay. Then, sitting in his relaxer in the spiral lift moving swiftly up inside the walls, he knew that those walls were capturing his image, stealing it, like some superstition he remembered . . . ah?

Vanderman's private secretary greeted him. Clay let his gaze wander freely across that young person's neatly-dressed figure and mildly attractive face. She said that Mr. Vanderman was out, and the appointment was for three, not two, wasn't it? Clay referred to a notebook. He snapped his fingers.

"Three—you're right, Miss Wells. I was so sure it was two I didn't even bother to check up. Do you think he might be back sooner? I mean, is he out, or in conference?"

"He's out, all right, Mr. Clay," Miss Wells said. "I don't think he'll be back much sooner than three. I'm sorry."

"Well, may I wait in here?"

She smiled at him efficiently. "Of course. There's stereo and the magazine spools are in that case."

She went back to her work, and Clay skimmed through an article about the care and handling of lunar filchards. It gave him an opportunity to start a conversation by asking Miss Wells if she liked filchards. It turned out that she had no opinion whatsoever of filchards but the ice had been broken.

This is the cocktail acquaintance, Clay thought. I may have a broken heart, but, naturally, I'm lonesome.

The trick wasn't to get engaged to Miss Wells so much as to fall in love with her convincingly., The Eye never slept. Clay was beginning to wake at night with a nervous start and lie there looking up at the ceiling. But darkness was no shield.

"The question is," said the sociologist at this point, "whether or not Clay was acting for an audience."

"You mean us?"

"Exactly. It just occurred to me. Do you thing he's been behaving perfectly naturally?"

The engineer pondered.

"I'd say yes. A man doesn't marry a girl only to carry out some other plan, does he? After all, he'd get himself involved in a whole new batch of responsibilities."

"Clay hasn't married Josephine Wells yet, however," the sociologist countered. "Besides, that responsibility angle might have applied a few hundred years ago, but not now." He went off at random. "Imagine a society where, after divorce, a man was forced to support a perfectly healthy, competent woman! It was vestigial, I know—a throwback to the days when only males could earn a living—but imagine the sort of women who were willing to accept such support. That was reversion to infancy if I ever—"

The engineer coughed.

"Oh," the sociologist said. "Oh . . . yes. The question is, would Clay have got himself engaged to a woman unless he really—"

"Engagements can be broken."

"This one hasn't been broken yet, as far as we know. And *we know*."

"A normal man wouldn't plan on marrying a girl he didn't care anything about, unless he had some stronger motive—I'll go along that far."

"But how normal is Clay?" the sociologist wondered. "Did he know in advance we'd check back on his past? Did you notice that he cheated at solitaire?"

"Proving?"

"There are all kinds of trivial things you don't do if you think people are looking. Picking up a penny in the street, drinking soup out of the bowl, posing before a mirror—the sort of foolish or petty things everyone does when alone. Either Clay's innocent, or he's a very clever man—"

He was a very clever man. He never intended the engagement to get as far as marriage, though he knew that in one respect marriage would be a precaution. If a man talks in his sleep, his wife will certainly mention the fact. Clay considered gagging himself at night if the necessity should arise. Then he realized that if he talked in his sleep at all, there was no insurance against talking too much the very first time he had an auditor. He couldn't risk such a break. But there was no necessity, after all. Clay's problem, when he thought it over, was simply: How can I be sure I don't talk in my sleep?

He solved that easily enough by renting a narcohypnotic supplementary course in common trade dialects. This involved studying while awake and getting the information repeated in his ear during slumber. As a necessary preparation for the course, he was instructed to set up a recorder and chart the depth of his sleep, so the narcohypnosis could be keyed to his individual rhythms. He did this several times, rechecked once a month thereafter, and was satisfied. There was no need to gag himself at night.

He was glad to sleep provided he didn't dream. He had to take sedatives after a while. At night, there was relief from the knowledge that an Eye watched him always, an Eye that could bring him to justice, an Eye whose omnipotence he could not challenge in the open. But he dreamed about the Eye.

Vanderman had given him a job in the organization, which was enormous. Clay was merely a cog, which suited him well enough, for the moment. He didn't want any more favors yet. Not till he had found out the extent of Miss Wells' duties—Josephine, her Christian name was. That took several months, but by that time friendship was ripening into affection. So Clay asked Vanderman for another job. He specified. It wasn't obvious, but he was asking for work that would, presently, fit him for Miss Wells' duties.

Vanderman probably still felt guilty about Bea; he'd married her and she was in Antarctica now, at the Casino. Vanderman was due to join her, so he scribbled a memorandum, wished Clay good luck, and went to Antarctica, bothered by no stray pangs of conscience. Clay improved the hour by courting Josephine ardently.

From what he had heard about the new Mrs. Vanderman, he felt secretly relieved. Not long ago, when he had been content to remain passive, the increasing dominance of Bea would have satisfied him, but no more. He was learning self-reliance, and liked it. These days, Bea was behaving rather badly. Given all the money and freedom she could use, she had too much time on her hands. Once in a while Clay heard rumors that made him smile secretly. Vanderman wasn't having an easy time of it. A dominant character, Bea—but Vanderman was no weakling himself.

After a while Clay told his employer he wanted to marry Josephine Wells. "I guess that makes us square," he said. "You took Bea away from me and I'm taking Josie away from you."

"Now wait a minute," Vanderman said. "I hope you don't—"

"My fiancée, your secretary. That's all. The thing is, Josie and I are in love." He poured it on, but carefully. It was easier to deceive Vanderman than the Eye, with its trained technicians and forensic sociologists looking through it. He thought, sometimes, of those medieval pictures of an immense eye, and that reminded him of something vague and distressing, though he couldn't isolate the memory.

After all, what could Vanderman do? He arranged to have Clay given a raise. Josephine, always conscientious, offered to keep on working for a while, till office routine was straightened out, but it never did get straightened out, somehow. Clay deftly saw to that by keeping Josephine busy. She didn't have to bring work home to her apartment, but she brought it, and Clay gradually began to help her when he dropped by. His job, plus the narcohypnotic courses, had already trained him for this sort of tricky organizational work. Vanderman's business was highly specialized—planet-wide exports and imports, and what with keeping track of specific groups, seasonal trends, sectarian holidays, and so forth, Josephine, as a sort of animated memorandum book for Vanderman, had a more than full-time job.

She and Clay postponed marriage for a time. Clay—naturally enough—began to appear mildly jealous of Josephine's work, and she said she'd quit soon. But one night she stayed on at the office, and he went out in a pet and got drunk. It just happened to be raining that night. Clay got tight enough to walk unprotected through the drizzle, and to fall asleep at home in his wet clothes. He came down with influenza. As he was recovering, Josephine got it.

Under the circumstances, Clay stepped in—purely a temporary job—and took over his fiancée's duties. Office routine was extremely complicated that week, and only Clay knew the ins and outs of it. The arrangement saved Vanderman a certain amount of inconvenience, and, when the situation resolved itself, Josephine had a subsidiary job and Clay was Vanderman's private secretary.

"I'd better know more about him," Clay said to Josephine. "After all, there must be a lot of habits and foibles he's got that need to be catered to. If he wants lunch ordered up, I don't want to get smoked tongue and find out he's allergic to it. What about his hobbies?"

But he was careful not to pump Josephine too hard, because of the Eye. He still needed sedatives to sleep.

The sociologist rubbed his forehead.

"Let's take a break," he suggested. "Why does a guy want to commit murder anyway?"

"For profit, one sort or another."

"Only partly, I'd say. The other part is an unconscious desire to be punished—usually for something else. That's why you get accident prones. Ever think about what happens to murderers who feel guilty and yet who aren't punished by the law? They must live a rotten sort of life—always accidentally stepping in front of speedsters; cutting themselves with an ax—accidentally; accidentally touching wires full of juice—"

"Conscience, eh?"

"A long time ago, people thought God sat in the sky with a telescope and watched everything they did. They really lived pretty carefully, in the Middle Ages—the first Middle Ages, I mean. Then there was the era of disbelief, where people had nothing to believe in very strongly—and finally we get this." He nodded toward the screen. "A universal memory. By extension, it's a universal social conscience, an externalized one. It's exactly the same as the medieval concept of God—omniscience."

"But not omnipotence."

"Mm."

All in all, Clay kept the Eye in mind for a year and a half. Before he said or did anything whatsoever, he reminded himself of the Eye, and made certain that he wasn't revealing his motive to the judging future. Of course, there was—would be—an Ear, too, but that was a little too absurd. One couldn't visualize a large, disembodied Ear decorating the wall like a plate in a plate holder. All the same, whatever he said would be as important evidence—sometime—as what he did. So Sam Clay was very careful indeed, and behaved like Caesar's wife. He wasn't exactly defying authority, but he was certainly circumventing it.

Superficially Vanderman was more like Caesar, and his wife was not above reproach, these days. She had too much money to play with. And she was finding her husband too strong-willed a person to be completely satisfactory. There was enough of the matriarch in Bea to make her feel rebellion against Andrew Vanderman, and there was a certain lack of romance. Vanderman had little time for her. He was busy these days, involved with a whole string of deals which demanded much of his time. Clay, of course, had something to do with that. His interest in his new work was most laudable. He stayed up nights plotting and planning as though expecting Vanderman to make him a full partner. In fact, he even suggested this possibility to Josephine. He wanted it on the record. The marriage date had been set, and Clay wanted to move before then; he had no intention of being drawn into a marriage of convenience after the necessity had been removed.

One thing he did, which had to be handled carefully, was to

get the whip. Now, Vanderman was a fingerer. He liked to have something in his hands while he talked. Usually it was a crystalline paper weight, with a miniature thunderstorm in it, complete with lightening, when it was shaken. Clay put this where Vanderman would be sure to knock it off and break it. Meanwhile, he had plugged one deal with Callisto Ranches for the sole purpose of getting a whip for Vanderman's desk. The natives were proud of their leatherwork and their silversmithing, and a nominal make-weight always went with every deal they closed. Thus, presently, a handsome miniature whip, with Vanderman's initials on it, lay on the desk, coiled into a loop, acting as a paper weight except when he picked it up and played with it while he talked.

The other weapon Clay wanted was already there—an antique paper knife, once called a surgical scalpel. He never let his gaze rest on it too long, because of the Eye.

The other whip came. He absent-mindedly put it in his desk and pretended to forget it. It was a sample of the whips made by the Alaskan Flagellantes for use in their ceremonies, and was wanted because of some research being made into the pain-neutralizing drugs the Flagellantes used. Clay, of course, had engineered this deal, too. There was nothing suspicious about that; the firm stood to make a sound profit. In fact, Vanderman had promised him a percentage bonus at the end of the year on every deal he triggered. It would be quite a lot. It was December; a year and a half had passed since Clay first recognized that the Eye would seek him out.

He felt fine. He was careful about the sedatives, and his nerves, though jangled, were nowhere near the snapping point. It had been a strain, but he had trained himself so that he would make no slips. He visualized the Eye in the walls, in the ceiling, in the sky, every-where he went. It was the only way to play completely safe. And very soon now it would pay off. But he would have to do it soon; such a nervous strain could not be continued indefinitely.

A few details remained. He carefully arranged matters—under the Eye's very nose, so to speak—so that he was offered a well-paying position with another firm. He turned it down.

And, one night, an emergency happened to arise so that Clay, very logically, had to go to Vanderman's apartment.

Vanderman wasn't there. Bea was. She had quarreled violently with her husband. Moreover, she had been drinking. (This, too, he had expected.) If the situation had not worked out exactly as he wanted, he would have tried again—and again—but there was no need.

Clay was a little politer than necessary. Perhaps too polite; certainly Bea, that incipient matriarch, was led down the garden path, a direction she was not unwilling to take. After all, she had married Vanderman for his money, found him as dominant as herself, and now saw Clay as an exaggerated symbol of both romance and masculine submissiveness.

The camera eye hidden in the wall, in a decorative bas-relief, was grinding away busily, spooling up its wire-tape in a way that indicated Vanderman was a suspicious as well as a jealous husband. But Clay knew about this gadget, too. At the suitable moment he stumbled against the wall in such a fashion that the device broke. Then, with only that other Eye spying on him, he suddenly became so virtuous that it was a pity Vanderman couldn't witness his *volte-face*.

"Listen, Bea," he said, "I'm sorry, but I didn't understand. It's no good. I'm not in love with you any more. I was once, sure, but that was quite a while ago. There's somebody else, and you ought to know it by now."

"You still love me," Bea said with intoxicated firmness. "We belong together."

"Bea. Please. I hate to have to say this, but I'm grateful to Andrew Vanderman for marrying you. I . . . well, you got what you wanted, and I'm getting what I want. Let's leave it at that."

"I'm used to getting what *I* want, Sam. Opposition is something I don't like. Especially when I know you really—"

She said a good deal more, and so did Clay—he was perhaps unnecessarily harsh. But he had to make the point, for the Eye, that he was no longer jealous of Vanderman.

He made the point.

The next morning he got to the office before Vanderman, cleaned up his desk, and discovered the stingaree whip still in its box. "Oops," he said, snapping his fingers—the Eye watched, and this was the crucial period. Perhaps it would all be over within the hour. Every move from now on would have to be specially calculated in advance, and there could be no slightest deviation. The Eye was everywhere—literally everywhere.

He opened the box, took out the whip, and went into the inner sanctum. He tossed the whip on Vanderman's desk, so carelessly that a stylus rack toppled. Clay rearranged everything, leaving the stingaree whip near the edge of the desk, and placing the Callistan silver-leather whip at the back, half concealed behind the inter-office visor-box. He didn't allow himself more than a casual sweeping glance to make sure the paper knife was still there.

Then he went out for coffee.

Half an hour later he got back, picked up a few letters for signature from the rack, and walked into Vanderman's office. Vanderman looked up from behind his desk. He had changed a little in a year and a half; he was looking older, less noble, more like an aging bulldog. Once, Clay thought coldly, this man stole my fiancée and beat me up.

Careful. Remember the Eye.

There was no need to do anything but follow the plan and let events take their course. Vanderman had seen the spy films, all right, up to the point where they had gone blank, when Clay fell against the wall. Obviously he hadn't really expected Clay to show up this morning. But to see the louse grinning hello, walking across the room, putting some letters down on his desk—!

Clay was counting on Vanderman's short temper, which had not improved over the months. Obviously the man had been simply sitting there, thinking unpleasant thoughts, and just as Clay had known would happen, he'd picked up the whip and begun to finger it. But it was the stingaree whip this time.

"Morning," Clay said cheerfully to his stunned employer. His smile became one-sided. "I've been waiting for you to check this letter to the Kirghiz kovar-breeders. Can we find a market for two thousand of those ornamental horns?"

It was at this point that Vanderman, bellowing, jumped to his feet, swung the whip, and sloshed Clay across the face. There is probably nothing more painful than the bite of a stingaree whip.

Clay staggered back. He had not known it would hurt so much. For an instant the shock of the blow knocked every other consideration out of his head, and blind anger was all that remained.

Remember the Eye!

He remembered it. There were dozens of trained men watching everything he did just now. Literally he stood on an open stage surrounded by intent observers who made notes on every expression of his face, every muscular flection, every breath he drew.

In a moment Vanderman would be dead—but Sam Clay would not be alone. An invisible audience from the future was fixing him with cold, calculating eyes. He had one more thing to do and the job would be over. Do it—carefully, carefully!—while they watched.

Time stopped for him. *The job would be over.*

It was very curious. He had rehearsed this series of actions so often in the privacy of his mind that his body was going through with it now without further instructions. His body staggered back from the blow, recovered balance, glared at Vanderman in shocked fury, poised for a dive at that paper knife in plain sight on the desk.

That was what the outward and visible Sam Clay was doing. But the inward and spiritual Sam Clay went through quite a different series of actions.

The job would be over.

And what was he going to do after that?

The inward and spiritual murderer stood fixed with dismay and surprise, staring at a perfectly empty future. He had never looked beyond this moment. He had made no plans for his life beyond the death of Vanderman. But now—he had no enemy but Vanderman. When Vanderman was dead, what would he fix upon to orient his life? What would he work at then? His job would be gone, too. And he liked his job.

Suddenly he knew how much he liked it. He was good at it. For the first time in his life, he had found a job he could do really well.

You can't live a year and a half in a new environment without acquiring new goals. The change had come imperceptively. He was a good operator; he'd discovered that he could be successful. He didn't have to kill Vanderman to prove that to himself. He'd proved it already without committing murder.

In that time-stasis which had brought everything to a full stop he looked at Vanderman's red face and he thought of Bea, and of Vanderman as he had come to know him—and he didn't want to be a murderer.

He didn't want Vanderman dead. He didn't want Bea. The thought of her made him feel a little sick. Perhaps that was because he himself had changed from passive to active. He no longer wanted or needed a dominant woman. He could make his own decisions. If he were choosing now, it would be someone more like Josephine—

Josephine. That image before his mind's stilled eye was suddenly very pleasant. Josephine with her mild, calm prettiness, her admiration for Sam Clay, the successful businessman, the rising young importer in Vanderman, Inc. Josephine whom he was going to marry— Of course he was going to marry her. He loved Josephine. He loved his job. All he wanted was the status quo, exactly as he had achieved it. Everything was perfect right now—as of maybe thirty seconds ago.

But that was a long time ago—thirty seconds. A lot can happen in half a minute. A lot had happened. Vanderman was coming at him again, the whip raised. Clay's nerves crawled at the anticipation of its burning impact across his face a second time. If he could get hold of Vanderman's wrist before he struck again—if he could talk fast enough—

The crooked smile was still on his face. It was part of the pattern, in some dim way he did not quite understand. He was acting in response to conditioned reflexes set up over a period of many months of rigid self-training. His body was already in action. All that had taken place in his mind had happened so fast there was no physical hiatus at all. His body knew its job and it was doing the job. It was lunging forward toward the desk and the knife, and he could not stop it.

All this had happened before. It had happened in his mind, the only place where Sam Clay had known real freedom in the past year and a half. In all that time he had forced himself to realize that the Eye was watching every outward move he made. He had planned each action in advance and schooled himself to carry it through. Scarcely once had he let himself act purely on impulse.

Only in following the plan exactly was there safety. He had in-doctrinated himself too successfully.

Something was wrong. This wasn't what he'd wanted. He was still afraid, weak, failing—

He lurched against the desk, clawed at the paper knife, and, knowing failure, drove it into Vanderman's heart.

"It's a tricky case," the forensic sociologist said to the engineer. "Very tricky."

"Want me to run it again?"

"No, not right now. I'd like to think it over. Clay . . . that firm that offered him another job. The offer's withdrawn now, isn't it? Yes, I remember—they're fussy about the morals of their employ-ees. It's insurance or something, I don't know. Motive. Motive, now."

The sociologist looked at the engineer.

The engineer said: "A year and a half ago he had a motive. But a week ago he had everything to lose and nothing to gain. He's lost his job and that bonus, he doesn't want Mrs. Vanderman any more, and as for that beating Vanderman once gave him . . . ah?"

"Well, he did try to shoot Vanderman once, and he couldn't, remember? Even though he was full of Dutch courage. But—some-thing's wrong. Clay's been avoiding even the appearance of evil a little too carefully. Only I can't put my finger on anything, blast it."

"What about tracing back his life further? We only got to his fourth year."

"There couldn't be anything useful that long ago. It's obvious he was afraid of his father and hated him, too. Typical stuff, basic psych. The father symbolizes judgment to him. I'm very much afraid Sam Clay is going to get off scot-free."

"But if you think there's something haywire—"

"The burden of proof is up to us," the sociologist said.

The visor sang. A voice spoke softly.

"No, I haven't got the answer yet. Now? All right. I'll drop over."

He stood up.

"The D.A. wants a consultation. I'm not hopeful, though. I'm afraid the State's going to lose this case. That's the trouble with the externalized conscience—"

He didn't amplify. He went out, shaking his head, leaving the engineer staring speculatively at the screen. But within five minutes he was assigned to another job—the bureau was understaffed—and he didn't have a chance to investigate on his own until a week later. Then it didn't matter any more.

For, a week later, Sam Clay was walking out of the court an acquitted man. Bea Vanderman was waiting for him at the foot of the ramp. She wore black, but obviously her heart wasn't in it.

"Sam," she said.

He looked at her.

He felt a little dazed. It was all over. Everything had worked out exactly according to plan. And nobody was watching him now. The Eye had closed. The invisible audience had put on its hats and coats and left the theater of Sam Clay's private life. From now on he could do and say precisely what he liked, with no censoring watcher's omnipresence to check him. He could act on impulse again.

He had outwitted society. He had outwitted the Eye and all its minions in all their technological glory. He, Sam Clay, private citizen. It was a wonderful thing, and he could not understand why it left him feeling so flat.

That had been a nonsensical moment, just before the murder. The moment of relenting. They say you get the same instant's frantic rejection on the verge of a good many important decisions —just before you marry, for instance. Or—what was it? Some other common instance he'd often heard of. For a second it eluded him. Then he had it. The hour before marriage—and the instant after suicide. After you've pulled the trigger, or jumped off the bridge. The instant of wild revulsion when you'd give anything to undo the irrevocable. Only, you can't. It's too late. The thing is done.

Well, he'd been a fool. Luckily, it *had* been too late. His body took over and forced him to success he'd trained it for. About the job—it didn't matter. He'd get another. He'd proved himself capable. If he could outwit the Eye itself, what job existed he couldn't lick if he tried? Except—nobody knew exactly how good he was.

How could he prove his capabilities? It was infuriating to achieve such phenomenal success after a lifetime of failures, and never to get the credit for it. How many men must have tried and failed where he had tried and succeeded? Rich men, successful men, brilliant men who had yet failed in the final test of all—the contest with the Eye, their own lives at stake. Only Sam Clay had passed that most important test in the world—and he could never claim credit for it.

". . . knew they wouldn't convict," Bea's complacent voice was saying.

Clay blinked at her. "What?"

"I said I'm so glad you're free, darling. I knew they wouldn't convict you. I knew that from the very beginning." She smiled at him, and for the first time it occurred to him that Bea looked a little like a bulldog. It was something about her lower jaw. He thought that when her teeth were closed together the lower set probably rested just outside the upper. He had an instant's impulse to ask her about it. Then he decided he had better not.

"You knew, did you?" he said.

She squeezed his arm. What an ugly lower jaw that was. How odd he'd never noticed it before. And behind the heavy lashes, how small her eyes were. How mean.

"Let's go where we can be alone," Bea said, clinging to him. "There's such a lot to talk about."

"We *are* alone," Clay said, diverted for an instant to his original thoughts. "Nobody's watching." He glanced up at the sky and down at the mosaic pavement. He drew a long breath and let it out slowly. "Nobody," he said.

"My speeder's parked right over here. We can—"

"Sorry, Bea."

"What do you mean?"

"I've got business to attend to."

"Forget business. Don't you understand that we're free now, both of us?"

He had a horrible feeling he knew what she meant.

"Wait a minute," he said, because this seemed the quickest way to end it. "I killed your husband, Bea. Don't forget that."

"You were acquitted. It was self-defense. The court said so."

"It—" He paused, glanced up quickly at the high wall of the Justice Building, and began a one-sided, mirthless smile. It was all right; there was no Eye now. There never would be again. He was unwatched.

"You mustn't feel guilty, even within yourself," Bea said firmly. "It wasn't your fault. It simply wasn't. You've got to remember that. You *couldn't* have killed Andrew except by accident, Sam, so—"

"What? What do you mean by that?"

"Well, after all. I know the prosecution kept trying to prove you'd planned to kill Andrew all along, but you mustn't let what they said put any ideas in your head. I know you, Sam. I knew Andrew. You couldn't have planned a thing like that, and even if you had, it wouldn't have worked."

The half-smile died.

"It wouldn't?"

She looked at him steadily.

"Why, you couldn't have managed it," she said. "Andrew was the better man, and we both know it. He'd have been too clever to fall for anything—"

"Anything a second-rater like me could dream up?" Clay swallowed. His lips tightened. "Even you—What's the idea? What's your angle now—that we second-raters ought to get together?"

"Come on," she said, and slipped her arm through his. Clay hung back for a second. Then he scowled, looked back at the Justice Building, and followed Bea toward her speeder.

The engineer had a free period. He was finally able to investigate Sam Clay's early childhood. It was purely academic now, but he liked to indulge his curiosity. He traced Clay back to the dark closet, when the boy was four, and used ultraviolet. Sam was huddled in a corner, crying silently, staring up with frightened eyes at a top shelf.

What was on that shelf the engineer could not see.

He kept the beam focused on the closet and cast back rapidly through time. The closet often opened and closed, and sometimes Sam Clay was locked in it as punishment, but the upper shelf held its mystery until—

It was in reverse. A woman reached to that shelf, took down an object, walked backward out of the closet to Sam Clay's bedroom, and went to the wall by the door. This was unusual, for generally it was Sam's father who was warden of the closet.

She hung up a framed picture of a single huge staring eye floating in space. There was a legend under it. The letters spelled out: THOU GOD SEEST ME.

The engineer kept on tracing. After a while it was night. The child was in bed, sitting up wide-eyed, afraid. A man's footsteps sounded on the stair. The scanner told all secrets but those of the inner mind. The man was Sam's father, coming up to punish him for some childish crime committed earlier. Moonlight fell upon the wall beyond which the footsteps approached, showing how the wall quivered a little to the vibrations of the feet, and the Eye in its frame quivered, too. The boy seemed to brace himself. A defiant half-smile showed on his mouth, crooked, unsteady.

This time he'd keep that smile, no matter what happened. When it was over he'd still have it, so his father could see it, and the Eye could see it and they'd know he hadn't given in. He hadn't . . . he—

The door opened.

He couldn't help it. The smile faded and was gone.

"Well, what was eating him?" the engineer demanded.

The sociologist shrugged. "You could say he never did really grow up. It's axiomatic that boys go through a phase of rivalry with their fathers. Usually that's sublimated; the child grows up and wins, in one way or another. But Sam Clay didn't. I suspect he developed an externalized conscience very early. Symbolizing partly his father, partly God, an Eye and society—which fulfills the role of protective, punishing parent, you know."

"It still isn't evidence."

"We aren't going to get any evidence on Sam Clay. But that doesn't mean he's got away with anything, you know. He's always been afraid to assume the responsibilities of maturity. He never took on an optimum challenge. He was afraid to succeed at anything because that symbolic Eye of his might smack him down. When he was a kid, he might have solved his entire problem by kicking his old man in the shins. Sure, he'd have got a harder whaling, but he'd have made some move to assert his individuality. As it is, he waited too long. And then he defied the wrong thing, and it wasn't really defiance, basically. Too late now. His formative years are past. The thing that might really solve Clay's problem would be his conviction for murder—but he's been acquitted. If he'd been convicted, then he could prove to the world that he'd hit back. He'd kicked his father in the shins, kept that defiant smile on his face, killed Andrew Vanderman. I think that's what he actually has wanted all along—recognition. Proof of his own ability to assert himself. He had to work hard to cover his tracks —if he made any—but that was part of the game. By winning it he's lost. The normal ways of escape are closed to him. He always had an Eye looking down at him."

"Then the acquittal stands?"

"There's still no evidence. The State's lost its case. But I . . . I don't think Sam Clay has won his. Something will happen." He sighed. "It's inevitable, I'm afraid. Sentence first, you see. Verdict afterward. The sentence was passed on Clay a long time ago."

Sitting across from him in the Paradise Bar, behind a silver decanter of brandy in the center of the table, Bea looked lovely and hateful. It was the lights that made her lovely. They even managed to cast their shadows over that bulldog chin, and under her thick lashes the small, mean eyes acquired an illusion of beauty. But she still looked hateful. The lights could do nothing about that. They couldn't cast shadows into Sam Clay's private mind or distort the images there.

He thought of Josephine. He hadn't made up his mind fully yet about that. But if he didn't quite know what he wanted, there was no shadow of doubt about what he *didn't* want—no possible doubt whatever.

"You need me, Sam," Bea told him over her brimming glass.

"I can stand on my own feet. I don't need anybody."

It was the indulgent way she looked at him. It was the smile that showed her teeth. He could see as clearly as if he had X-ray vision how the upper teeth would close down inside the lower when she shut her mouth. There would be a lot of strength in a jaw like that. He looked at her neck and saw the thickness of it, and thought how firmly she was getting her grip upon him, how she maneuvered for position and waited to lock her bulldog clamp deep into the fabric of his life again.

"I'm going to marry Josephine, you know," he said.

"No, you're not. You aren't the man for Josephine. I know that girl, Sam. For a while you may have had her convinced you were a go-getter. But she's bound to find out the truth. You'd be miserable together. You need me, Sam darling. You don't know what you want. Look at the mess you got into when you tried to act on your own. Oh, Sam, why don't you stop pretending? You know you never were a planner. You . . . what's the matter, Sam?"

His sudden burst of laughter had startled both of them. He tried to answer her, but the laughter wouldn't let him. He lay back in his chair and shook with it until he almost strangled. He had come so close, so desperately close to bursting out with a boast that would have been confession. Just to convince the woman. Just to shut her up. He must care more about her good opinion than he had realized until now. But that last absurdity was too much. It was only ridiculous now. Sam Clay not a planner!

How good it was to let himself laugh, now. To let himself go, without having to think ahead. Acting on impulse again, after those long months of rigid repression. No audience from the future was clustering around this table, analyzing the quality of his laughter, observing that it verged on hysteria, measuring it against all possible occasions in the past that could not explain its exact depth and duration.

All right, so it was hysteria. Who cared? He deserved a little blowoff like this, after all he'd been through. He'd risked so much, and achieved so much—and in the end gained nothing, not even glory except in his own mind. He'd gained nothing, really, except the freedom to be hysterical if he felt like it. He laughed and laughed and laughed, hearing the shrill note of lost control in his own voice and not caring.

People were turning to stare. The bartender looked over at him uneasily, getting ready to move if this went on. Bea stood up, leaned across the table, shook him by the shoulder.

"Sam, what's the matter! Sam, do get hold of yourself! You're making a spectacle of me, Sam! What *are* you laughing at?"

With a tremendous effort he forced the laughter back in his throat. His breath still came heavily and little bursts of merriment kept bubbling up so that he could hardly speak, but he got the words out somehow. They were probably the first words he had spoken without rigid censorship since he first put his plan into operation. And the words were these.

"I'm laughing at the way I fooled you. I fooled everybody! You think I didn't know what I was doing every minute of the time? You think I wasn't planning, every step of the way? It took me eighteen months to do it, but I killed Andrew Vanderman with malice aforethought, and nobody can ever prove I did it." He giggled foolishly. "I just wanted you to know," he added in a mild voice.

And it wasn't until he got his breath back and began to experience that feeling of incredible, delightful, incomparable relief that he knew what he had done.

She was looking at him without a flicker of expression on her face. Total blank was all that showed. There was a dead silence for a quarter of a minute. Clay had the feeling that his words must have rung from the roof, that in a moment the police would come in to hale him away. But the words had been quietly spoken. No one had heard but Bea.

And now, at last, Bea moved. She answered him, but not in words. The bulldog face convulsed suddenly and overflowed with laughter.

As he listened, Clay felt all that flood of glorious relief ebbing away. For he saw that she did not believe him. And there was no way he could prove the truth.

"Oh, you silly little man," Bea gasped when words came back to her. "You had me almost convinced for a minute. I almost believed you. I—" Laughter silenced her again; consciously silvery laughter made heads turn. That conscious note in it warned him that she was up to something. Bea had had an idea. His own thoughts outran hers and he knew in an instant before she spoke exactly what the idea was and how she would apply it. He said:

"I *am* going to marry Josephine," in the very instant that Bea spoke.

"You're going to marry me," she said flatly. "You've got to. You don't know your own mind, Sam. I know what's best for you and I'll see you do it. Do you understand me, Sam?

"The police won't realize that was only a silly boast," she told him. "They'll believe you. You wouldn't want me to tell them what you just said, would you, Sam?"

He looked at her in silence, seeing no way out. This dilemma had sharper horns than anything he could have imagined. For Bea did not and would not believe him, no matter how he yearned to convince her, while the police undoubtedly would believe him, to the undoing of his whole investment in time, effort, and murder. He had said it. It was engraved upon the walls and in the echoing air, waiting for that invisible audience in the future to observe. No one was listening now, but a word from Bea could make them reopen the case.

A word from Bea.

He looked at her, still in silence, but with a certain cool calculation beginning to dawn in the back of his mind.

For a moment Sam Clay felt very tired indeed. In that moment he encompassed a good deal of tentative future time. In his mind he said yes to Bea, married her, lived an indefinite period as her husband. And he saw what that life would be like. He saw the mean small eyes watching him, the relentlessly gripping jaw set, the tyranny that would emerge slowly or not slowly, depending on the degree of his subservience, until he was utterly at the mercy of the woman who had been Andrew Vanderman's widow.

Sooner or later, he thought clearly to himself, *I'd kill her.*

He'd have to kill. That sort of life, with that sort of woman, wasn't a life Sam Clay could live, indefinitely. And he'd proved his ability to kill and go free.

But what about Andrew Vanderman's death?

Because they'd have another case against him then. This time it had been qualitative: the next time, the balance would shift toward quantitative. If Sam Clay's wife died, Sam Clay would be investigated no matter how she died. Once a suspect, always a suspect in the eyes of the law. The Eye of the law. They'd check back. They'd return to this moment, while he sat there revolving thoughts of death in his mind. And they'd return to five minutes ago, and listen to him boast that he had killed Vanderman.

A good lawyer might get him off. He could claim it wasn't the truth. He could say he had been goaded to an idle boast by the things Bea said. He might get away with that, and he might not. Scop would be the only proof, and he couldn't be compelled to take scop.

But—no. That wasn't the answer. That wasn't the way out. He could tell by the sick, sinking feeling inside him. There had been just one glorious moment of release, after he'd made his confession to Bea, and from then on everything seemed to run downhill again.

But that moment had been the goal he'd worked toward all this time. He didn't know what it was, or why he wanted it. But he recognized the feeling when it came. He wanted it back.

This helpless feeling, this impotence—was this the total sum of what he had achieved? Then he'd failed, after all. Somehow, in some strange way he could only partly understand, he had failed; killing Vanderman hadn't been the answer at all. He wasn't a success. He was a second-rater, a passive, helpless worm whom Bea would manage and control and drive, eventually, to—

"What's the matter, Sam?" Bea asked solicitously.

"You think I'm a second-rater, don't you?" he said. "You'll never believe I'm not. You think I couldn't have killed Vanderman except by accident. You'll never believe I could possibly have defied—"

"What?" she asked, when he did not go on.

There was a new note of surprise in his voice.

"But it wasn't defiance," he said slowly. "I just hid and dodged. Circumvented. I hung dark glasses on an Eye, because I was afraid of it. But—that wasn't defiance. So—what I really was trying to prove—"

She gave him a startled, incredulous stare as he stood up.

"Sam! What are you doing?" Her voice cracked a little.

"Proving something," Clay said, smiling crookedly, and glancing up from Bea to the ceiling. "Take a good look," he said to the Eye as he smashed her skull with the decanter.

THE SENTINEL

by ARTHUR C. CLARKE

FOREWORD

by Thomas D. Clareson

THE AUTHOR

ARTHUR C. CLARKE is equally well known as a science-fiction writer and as a popular prophet of the age of space. In such nonfiction works as *The Exploration of Space* and *The Promise of Space,* he has guided a vast public into the intricacies of interplanetary travel, while his science-fiction novels, such as *Childhood's End, The City and the Stars,* and *Prelude to Space,* have attracted an equally broad and not entirely identical audience. Born in England in 1918, Clarke now makes his home in Ceylon, though he spends much of his time in London, New York, and Cape Kennedy. His story "The Sentinel," first published in 1951, served as the inspiration for the motion picture *2001: A Space Odyssey,* on which Clarke collaborated in the screenplay with Stanley Kubrick.

THE CRITIC

THOMAS D. CLARESON is a professor of English literature at the College of Wooster in Wooster, Ohio. Since 1959 he has edited the twice-yearly periodical *Extrapolation,* the Newsletter of the Conference on Science Fiction of the Modern Language Association, to which he has contributed material on Aldous Huxley, early science fiction, and other topics. He has taken an active role in the seminars and forums on science fiction now held as part of the annual meetings of the Modern Language Association.

Foreword

Arthur C. Clarke, the author during the past twenty years of books ranging from the nonfiction *The Exploration of Space* to the novel *Childhood's End,* really needs no further introduction. Nor does the inclusion of a story by him in this anthology need explanatory justification. That the story, "The Sentinel" (1951), provided the idea for the symbolic monolith which structures the film *2001: A Space Odyssey* adds to but does not determine its importance. That final importance lies in the merit of "The Sentinel" itself.

Both in narrative technique and in theme it shows, I think, Clarke at his finest: what I call the essential Clarke.

All fiction (all art) depends, of course, upon selection. Moreover, all fiction—because it is imaginary, not real—must eventually be read as the author's metaphor of the condition of man, as, for example, in Dickens' *Bleak House* or Hemingway's *The Old Man and the Sea.* The task of the writer, then, is to find the best way to tell his story, to state his metaphor. This Clarke has achieved in "The Sentinel."

After you have read the story, imagine it told dramatically, with extensive dialogue and psychological realism, in the "here and now" of distinct scenes: the day-by-day account of crises faced by the men crossing Mare Crisium, the personal antagonisms between members of the crew, the debate whether or not to expend fuel and supplies while checking out the metallic gleam, urgent messages to the base, interspersed instructions. As such, the story could easily become another chronicle of a step in man's conquest of space. As such, it also destroys the sentinel.

Clarke gives us the reflective narrative of a man—Wilson, named only once, indirectly, and we learn that he is an experienced, older man—recalling a discovery that he made some

131

twenty years earlier. Yet as we read, even though the narrator
carefully recalls specific aspects of that journey "in the late summer of 1996" into the Mare Crisium, we realize that it is not the
act of discovery that is important, but rather the significance of
what is discovered. By using summary narrative, though rich in
particular detail, the narrator/Clarke increasingly concentrates
our attention upon first the crystalline pyramid itself and then
its implications. Only a sensitive narrator telling his story in the
first person can convincingly measure those implications for us.
The story cannot be told in the third person.

Nor has Clarke been less successful in helping the reader to
accept as real—as probable—as inevitable—his line of action. In
writing of one of Wilkie Collins' novels, Henry James commended
him for bringing the unusual to our doorstep amid a hundred
familiar details, thereby making the unusual more effective. Clarke
has a more difficult task than Collins; he does not have an English
estate or a London town house to frame his action. So Clarke
begins by suggesting ,"The next time you see the full Moon high in
the south," look for a particular point which "anyone with normal
eyesight can find. . . ." Gently we are placed on the "great walled
plain" of the Mare Crisium within "a ring of magnificent mountains." As soon as we are acquainted with our setting and our
geologist-narrator, we are lulled by "the buzzing of electric razors"
and "short-wave radio from Earth"; our narrator stands by "the
frying pan, waiting, like any terrestrial housewife, for the sausages
to brown." All is made very human, very familiar, although details remind us almost subconsciously perhaps that we are on another world. Improbable? Unacceptable? In afterthought one
doubts that even lunar-based astronaut-explorers will ever have
sausages for breakfast. But the important thing is acceptance
while reading; Clarke does not want us to give up our willing suspension of disbelief until he has had his full say.

A mastery of narrative technique provides only one measure
of "The Sentinel's" excellence. It also enunciates one of Clarke's
two basic themes. The first is best expressed, I believe, in the very
brief "If I Forget Thee, O Earth . . ." A moon colonist takes
his young son from the subterranean base to see the rising of the
earth. "It was beautiful, and it called to his heart across the abyss
of space." Then the boy "saw that the portion of the disk that
should have been in darkness was gleaming faintly with evil
phosphorescence. He was looking upon the funeral pyre of a

world—upon the radioactive aftermath of Armageddon." Not for centuries would "the great ships that were still waiting here on the silent, dusty plains . . . lift once more into space, along the road that led to home." The boy realizes that one day he will pass this dream to his son in such an earth-rise, and goes to "rejoin his people in their long exile," people alone "as no men had ever been alone before." Once again, not the action but the significance of a discovery becomes important.

The anguish and loneliness of "If I Forget Thee, O Earth . . ." is complemented by the melancholy pervading Clarke's second theme, so well expressed in "The Sentinel." Perhaps he states it most succinctly at the end of the Prologue of the novel *Childhood's End* (1935): "The human race was no longer alone." As Clarke's protagonists look out across the sea of stars, across the "hundred thousand million stars . . . turning in the circle of the Milky Way," they know a cosmic loneliness. If there were but someone else, however alien, to share man's thoughts and look with him "out across infinity," what might not be? But this theme is no panacea of angelic hosts rescuing man, for it is man who must meet the final "double challenge." It is, then, from this anguish and this loneliness that Clarke shapes his metaphor of twentieth-century man, as he has done so well in "The Sentinel."

THE SENTINEL

The next time you see the full Moon high in the south, look carefully at its right-hand edge and let your eye travel upwards along the curve of the disk. Round about two o'clock you will notice a small, dark oval: anyone with normal eyesight can find it quite easily. It is the great walled plain, one of the finest on the Moon, known as the Mare Crisium—the Sea of Crises. Three hundred miles in diameter, and almost completely surrounded by a ring of magnificent mountains, it had never been explored until we entered it in the late summer of 1996.

Our expedition was a large one. We had two heavy freighters which had flown our supplies and equipment from the main lunar base in the Mare Serenitatis, five hundred miles away. There were also three small rockets which were intended for short-range transport over regions which our surface vehicles couldn't cross. Luckily, most of the Mare Crisium is very flat. There are none of the great crevasses so common and so dangerous elsewhere, and very few craters or mountains of any size. As far as we could tell, our powerful caterpillar tractors would have no difficulty in taking us wherever we wished to go.

I was geologist—or selenologist, if you want to be pedantic—in charge of the group exploring the southern region of the Mare. We had crossed a hundred miles of it in a week, skirting the foothills of the mountains along the shore of what was once the ancient sea, some thousand million years before. When life was beginning on Earth, it was already dying here. The waters were retreating down the flanks of those stupendous cliffs, retreating into the empty heart of the Moon. Over the land which we were crossing, the tideless ocean had once been half a mile deep, and

135

now the only trace of moisture was the hoarfrost one could some-times find in caves which the searing sunlight never penetrated.

We had begun our journey early in the slow lunar dawn, and still had almost a week of Earth-time before nightfall. Half a dozen times a day we would leave our vehicle and go outside in the space-suits to hunt for interesting minerals, or to place markers for the guidance of future travellers. It was an uneventful routine. There is nothing hazardous or even particularly exciting about lunar exploration. We could live comfortably for a month in our pressurised tractors, and if we ran into trouble we could always radio for help and sit tight until one of the spaceships came to our rescue.

I said just now that there was nothing exciting about lunar exploration, but of course that isn't true. One could never grow tired of those incredible mountains, so much more rugged than the gentle hills of Earth. We never knew, as we rounded the capes and promontories of that vanished sea, what new splendors would be revealed to us. The whole southern curve of the Mare Crisium is a vast delta where a score of rivers once found their way into the ocean, fed perhaps by the torrential rains that must have lashed the mountains in the brief volcanic age when the Moon was young. Each of these ancient valleys was an invitation, challenging us to climb into the unknown uplands beyond. But we had a hundred miles still to cover, and could only look longingly at the heights which others must scale.

We kept Earth-time aboard the tractor, and precisely at 22.00 hours the final radio message would be sent out to Base and we would close down for the day. Outside, the rocks would still be burning beneath the almost vertical Sun, but to us it was night until we awoke again eight hours later. Then one of us would pre-pare breakfast, there would be a great buzzing of electric razors, and someone would switch on the short-wave radio from Earth. Indeed, when the smell of frying sausages began to fill the cabin, it was sometimes hard to believe that we were not back on our own world—everything was so normal and homely, apart from the feeling of decreased weight and the unnatural slowness with which objects fell.

It was my turn to prepare breakfast in the corner of the main cabin that served as a galley. I can remember that moment quite vividly after all these years, for the radio had just played one of my favourite melodies, the old Welsh air, "David of the White Rock." Our driver was already outside in his space-suit, inspecting our caterpillar treads. My assistant, Louis Garnett, was up forward in the control position, making some belated entries in yesterday's log.

As I stood by the frying pan waiting, like any terrestrial house-wife, for the sausages to brown, I let my gaze wander idly over the mountain walls which covered the whole of the southern horizon, marching out of sight to east and west below the curve of the Moon. They seemed only a mile or two from the tractor, but I knew that the nearest was twenty miles away. On the Moon, of course, there is no loss of detail with distance—none of that almost imperceptible haziness which softens and sometimes trans-figures all far-off things on Earth.

Those mountains were ten thousand feet high, and they climbed steeply out of the plain as if ages ago some subterranean eruption had smashed them skywards through the molten crust. The base of even the nearest was hidden from sight by the steeply curving sur-face of the plain, for the Moon is a very little world, and from where I was standing the horizon was only two miles away.

I lifted my eyes towards the peaks which no man had ever climbed, the peaks which, before the coming of terrestrial life, had watched the retreating oceans sink sullenly into their graves, taking with them the hope and the morning promise of a world. The sun-light was beating against those ramparts with a glare that hurt the eyes, yet only a little way above them the stars were shining steadily in a sky blacker than a winter midnight on Earth.

I was turning away when my eye caught a metallic glitter high on the ridge of a great promontory thrusting out into the sea thirty miles to the west. It was a dimensionless point of light, as if a star had been clawed from the sky by one of those cruel peaks, and I imagined that some smooth rock surface was catching the sunlight and heliographing it straight into my eyes. Such things were not uncommon. When the Moon is in her second quarter, observers on Earth can sometimes see the great ranges in the Oceanus Procel-larum burning with a blue-white iridescence as the sunlight flashes from their slopes and leaps again from world to world. But I was curious to know what kind of rock could be shining so brightly up there, and I climbed into the observation turret and swung our four-inch telescope round to the west.

I could see just enough to tantalise me. Clear and sharp in the field of vision, the mountain peaks seemed only half a mile away, but whatever was catching the sunlight was still too small to be resolved. Yet it seemed to have an elusive symmetry, and the summit upon which it rested was curiously flat. I stared for a long time at that glittering enigma, straining my eyes into space, until presently a smell of burning from the galley told me that our breakfast sausages had made their quarter-million-mile journey in vain.

All that morning we argued our way across the Mare Crisium while the western mountains reared higher in the sky. Even when we were out prospecting in the space-suits, the discussion would continue over the radio. It was absolutely certain, my companions argued, that there had never been any form of intelligent life on the Moon. The only living things that had ever existed there were a few primitive plants and their slightly less degenerate ancestors. I know that as well as anyone, but there are times when a scientist must not be afraid to make a fool of himself.

"Listen," I said at last, "I'm going up there, if only for my own peace of mind. That mountain's less than twelve thousand feet high—that's only two thousand under Earth gravity—and I can make the trip in twenty hours at the outside. I've always wanted to go up into those hills, anyway, and this gives me an excellent excuse."

"If you don't break your neck," said Garnett, "you'll be the laughing-stock of the expedition when we get back to Base. That mountain will probably be called Wilson's Folly from now on."

"I won't break my neck," I said firmly. "Who was the first man to climb Pico and Helicon?"

"But weren't you rather younger in those days?" asked Louis gently.

"That," I said with great dignity, "is as good a reason as any for going."

We went to bed early that night, after driving the tractor to within half a mile of the promontory. Garnett was coming with me in the morning; he was a good climber, and had often been with me on such exploits before. Our driver was only too glad to be left in charge of the machine.

At first sight, those cliffs seemed completely unscalable, but to anyone with a good head for heights, climbing is easy on a world where all weights are only a sixth of their normal value. The real danger in lunar mountaineering lies in over-confidence; a six-hundred-foot drop on the Moon can kill you just as thoroughly as a hundred-foot fall on Earth.

We made our first halt on a wide ledge about four thousand feet above the plain. Climbing had not been very difficult, but my limbs were stiff with the unaccustomed effort, and I was glad of the rest. We could still see the tractor as a tiny metal insect far down at the foot of the cliff, and we reported our progress to the driver before starting on the next ascent.

Inside our suits it was comfortably cool, for the refrigeration units were fighting the fierce sun and carrying away the body-heat of our exertions. We seldom spoke to each other, except to pass climbing instructions and to discuss our best plan of ascent. I do not know what Garnett was thinking, probably that this was the craziest goose-chase he had ever embarked upon. I more than half agreed with him, but the joy of climbing, the knowledge that no man had ever gone this way before and the exhilaration of the steadily widening landscape gave me all the reward I needed.

I don't think I was particularly excited when I saw in front of us the wall of rock I had first inspected through the telescope from thirty miles away. It would level off about fifty feet above our heads, and there on the plateau would be the thing that had lured me over these barren wastes. It was, almost certainly, nothing more than a boulder splintered ages ago by a falling meteor, and with its cleavage planes still fresh and bright in this incorruptible, un-changing silence.

There were no hand-holds on the rock face, and we had to use a grapnel. My tired arms seemed to gain new strength as I swung the three-pronged metal anchor round my head and sent it sailing up towards the stars. The first time it broke loose and came falling slowly back when we pulled the rope. On the third attempt, the prongs gripped firmly and our combined weights could not shift it.

Garnett looked at me anxiously. I could tell that he wanted to go first, but I smiled back at him through the glass of my helmet and shook my head. Slowly, taking my time, I began the final ascent.

Even with my space-suit, I weighed only forty pounds here, so I pulled myself up hand over hand without bothering to use my feet. At the rim I paused and waved to my companion, then I scrambled over the edge and stood upright, staring ahead of me.

You must understand that until this very moment I had been almost completely convinced that there could be nothing strange or unusual for me to find here. Almost, but not quite; it was that haunting doubt that had driven me forward. Well, it was a doubt no longer, but the haunting had scarcely begun.

I was standing on a plateau perhaps a hundred feet across. It had once been smooth—too smooth to be natural—but falling meteors had pitted and scored its surface through immeasurable eons. It had been levelled to support a glittering, roughly pyramidal structure, twice as high as a man, that was set in the rock like a gigantic, many-faceted jewel.

Probably no emotion at all filled my mind in those first few seconds. Then I felt a great lifting of my heart, and a strange, inexpressible joy. For I loved the Moon, and now I knew that the creeping moss of Aristarchus and Eratosthenes was not the only life she had brought forth in her youth. The old, discredited dream of the first explorers was true. There had, after all, been a lunar civilisation—and I was the first to find it. That I had come perhaps a hundred million years too late did not distress me; it was enough to have come at all.

My mind was beginning to function normally, to analyse and to ask questions. Was this a building, a shrine—or something for which my language had no name? If a building, then why was it erected in so uniquely inaccessible a spot? I wondered if it might be a temple, and I could picture the adepts of some strange priest-hood calling on their gods to preserve them as the life of the Moon ebbed with the dying oceans, and calling on their gods in vain.

I took a dozen steps forward to examine the thing more closely, but some sense of caution kept me from going too near. I knew a little of archaeology, and tried to guess the cultural level of the civilisation that must have smoothed this mountain and raised the glittering mirror surfaces that still dazzled my eyes.

The Egyptians could have done it, I thought, if their workmen had possessed whatever strange materials these far more ancient architects had used. Because of the thing's smallness, it did not occur to me that I might be looking at the handiwork of a race more advanced than my own. The idea that the Moon had possessed intelligence at all was still almost too tremendous to grasp, and my pride would not let me take the final, humiliating plunge.

And then I noticed something that set the scalp crawling at the back of my neck—something so trivial and so innocent that many would never have noticed it at all. I have said that the plateau was scarred by meteors; it was also coated inches-deep with the cosmic dust that is always filtering down upon the surface of any world where there are no winds to disturb it. Yet the dust and the meteor scratches ended quite abruptly in a wide circle enclosing the little pyramid, as though an invisible wall was protecting it from the ravages of time and the slow but ceaseless bombardment from space.

There was someone shouting in my earphones, and I realised that Garnett had been calling me for some time. I walked unsteadily to the edge of the cliff and signalled him to join me, not trusting myself to speak. Then I went back towards that circle in the dust. I picked up a fragment of splintered rock and tossed it gently towards the shining enigma. If the pebble had vanished at that invisible barrier I should not have been surprised, but it seemed to hit a smooth, hemispherical surface and slide gently to the ground.

I knew then that I was looking at nothing that could be matched in the antiquity of my own race. This was not a building, but a machine, protecting itself with forces that had challenged Eternity. Those forces, whatever they might be, were still operating, and perhaps I had already come too close. I thought of all the radiations man had trapped and tamed in the past century. For all I knew, I might be as irrevocably doomed as if I had stepped into the deadly, silent aura of an unshielded atomic pile.

I remember turning then towards Garnett, who had joined me and was now standing motionless at my side. He seemed quite oblivious to me, so I did not disturb him but walked to the edge of the cliff in an effort to marshal my thoughts. There below me lay the Mare Crisium—Sea of Crises, indeed—strange and weird to most men, but reassuringly familiar to me. I lifted my eyes towards the crescent Earth, lying in her cradle of stars, and I wondered what her clouds had covered when these unknown builders had finished their work. Was it the steaming jungle of the Carboniferous, the bleak shore-line over which the first amphibians must crawl to conquer the land—or, earlier still, the long loneliness before the coming of life?

Do not ask me why I did not guess the truth sooner—the truth that seems so obvious now. In the first excitement of my discovery, I had assumed without question that this crystalline apparition had been built by some race belonging to the Moon's remote past, but suddenly, and with overwhelming force, the belief came to me that it was as alien to the Moon as I myself.

In twenty years we had found no trace of life but a few degenerate plants. No lunar civilisation, whatever its doom, could have left but a single token of its existence.

I looked at the shining pyramid again, and the more remote it seemed from anything that had to do with the Moon. And suddenly I felt myself shaking with a foolish, hysterical laughter, brought on by excitement and over-exertion: for I had imagined that the little pyramid was speaking to me and was saying: "Sorry, I'm a stranger here myself."

It has taken us twenty years to crack that invisible shield and to reach the machine inside those crystal walls. What we could not understand, we broke at last with the savage might of atomic power and now I have seen the fragments of the lovely, glittering thing I found up there on the mountain.

They are meaningless. The mechanisms—if indeed they are mechanisms—of the pyramid belong to a technology that lies far beyond our horizon, perhaps to the technology of paraphysical forces.

The mystery haunts us all the more now that the other planets have been reached and we know that only Earth has ever been the home of intelligent life in our Universe. Nor could any lost civilisation of our own world have built that machine, for the thickness of the meteoric dust on the plateau has enabled us to measure its age. It was set there upon its mountain before life had emerged from the seas of Earth.

When our world was half its present age, *something* from the stars swept through the Solar System, left this token of its passage, and went again upon its way. Until we destroyed it, that machine was still fulfilling the purpose of its builders; and as to that purpose, here is my guess.

Nearly a hundred thousand million stars are turning in the circle of the Milky Way, and long ago other races on the worlds of other suns must have scaled and passed the heights that we have reached. Think of such civilisations, far back in time against the fading afterglow of Creation, masters of a universe so young that life as yet had come only to a handful of worlds. Theirs would have been a loneliness we cannot imagine, the loneliness of gods looking out across infinity and finding none to share their thoughts.

They must have searched the star-clusters as we have searched the planets. Everywhere there would be worlds, but they would be empty or peopled with crawling, mindless things. Such was our Earth, the smoke of the great volcanoes still staining the skies, when that first ship of the peoples of the dawn came sliding in from the abyss beyond Pluto. It passed the frozen outer worlds, knowing that life could play no part in their destinies. It came to rest among the inner planets, warming themselves around the fire of the Sun and waiting for their stories to begin.

Those wanderers must have looked on Earth, circling safely in the narrow zone between fire and ice, and must have guessed that it was the favourite of the Sun's children. Here, in the distant future, would be intelligence; but there were countless stars before them still, and they might never come this way again.

So they left a sentinel, one of millions they have scattered throughout the Universe, watching over all worlds with the promise of life. It was a beacon that down the ages has been patiently signalling the fact that no one had discovered it.

Perhaps you understand now why that crystal pyramid was set upon the Moon instead of on the Earth. Its builders were not concerned with races still struggling up from savagery. They would be interested in our civilisation only if we proved our fitness to survive—by crossing space and so escaping from the Earth, our cradle. That is the challenge that all intelligent races must meet, sooner or later. It is a double challenge, for it depends in turn upon the conquest of atomic energy and the last choice between life and death.

Once we had passed that crisis, it was only a matter of time before we found the pyramid and forced it open. Now its signals have ceased, and those whose duty it is will be turning their minds upon Earth. Perhaps they wish to help our infant civilisation. But they must be very, very old, and the old are often insanely jealous of the young.

I can never look now at the Milky Way without wondering from which of those banked clouds of stars the emissaries are coming. If you will pardon so commonplace a simile, we have set off the fire-alarm and have nothing to do but to wait.

I do not think we will have to wait for long.

SPECIALIST

by ROBERT SHECKLEY

FOREWORD
by Robert Conquest

THE AUTHOR

ROBERT SHECKLEY, born in New York in 1928, dabbled in a variety of transient employments (bartender, milkman, pretzel salesman, soldier) before entering New York University at the age of twenty-one. Soon after his graduation in 1952 he sold his first science-fiction story, and since then he has been a free-lance writer, noted for the lively inventiveness of his approach. Though he has concentrated on the short story, he has written a number of science-fiction and mystery novels, notably *Journey Beyond Tomorrow* and *Immortality, Inc.* His story "Seventh Victim" was the basis of the Italian motion picture *The Tenth Victim.* Currently he divides his time between New York City and Spain. "Specialist" was first published in 1953.

THE CRITIC

ROBERT CONQUEST, a resident of London, is the author of a number of books on Soviet subjects, including *The Great Terror, The Pasternak Affair,* and *Power and Policy in the U.S.S.R.* He has published three books of verse, a number of science-fiction short stories, and one science-fiction novel, *A World of Difference* (1964). With Kingsley Amis he has edited the *Spectrum* series of s-f anthologies. His critical writings include "Science Fiction and Literature" in *Critical Quarterly,* and other pieces.

Foreword

In the past few decades, the short story has on the whole been a sphere either for rather *fainéant* exercises in technical shading or for attempts to achieve significance by frenzy—the disruption of sense, or the extreme representation of extreme situations, or both. There have been few stories which have retained (or developed in a newer mode) the disciplines of the art. And a very high proportion of these are to be found in science fiction, a genre of which Robert Sheckley is one of the most striking representatives. The reason seems to be that in science fiction, and in the minds of those concerned to write or read it, intellectual concern, objective curiosity, and a sense of the phenomena persist far more strongly than in ordinary fiction. An exaggeration of the values of adolescence, of the virtues of introspection, has produced an enormous disproportion in mainstream literature—and more particularly in literary criticism, where the introspective canons are stronger. This is not to urge the abolition of introspection in literature or elsewhere. All the same, much of the greatest art has been created by sensitive extroverts—even (as Mr. G. S. Fraser has written) by sensitive Philistines.

Robert Sheckley is a stylist. That is to say he writes in good, clear English with an unmistakably personal tone (and not, as the term sometimes seems to suggest, bad, clotted, flashy English which might have been produced—and may be yet—on an evilly programed computer). He is ingenious. He has a wide-ranging intelligence. He has achieved that combination of excellence and readability which too many critics seem to feel impossible, or unwelcome.

In choosing "Specialist" to represent Sheckley, while not maintaining that it is by most tests his best story, I may be thought to be acting perversely. I must explain my reasons.

"Specialist" was, I think, the first of Sheckley's stories that I read. The most immediately striking thing about it was that it presented a new idea, with its spaceship consisting of a collaboration of living organisms. Truly new notions are very rare in science fiction; this is one of the reasons that the layman, with what he conceives to be a bright invention, will quite often write "science fiction" charged with smugness about its novelty which is wholly unjustified.

But, of course, Sheckley does not show a trace of self-congratulation about this, justified or not. His whole method is that of making the extravagant credible by sheer matter-of-factness. Science fiction in general attains its effect by one of two different methods. It can work through the most careful "realism," the utmost clarity and focus. Or it can achieve its result by sheer high-paced obsessiveness. Sheckley operates, usually, within the first convention. But various tones are possible, even within those limits. This can be seen by comparing Sheckley with, for example, another extremely fine science-fiction writer of a very different style, James Schmitz. Schmitz, too, takes the extremely strange just as it comes. But he conveys much more of terror and of wonder than is usual for Sheckley. (One does not want to compartmentalize these two fine writers, both of whom have a wider range than these few sentences might suggest, but only to describe their most typical tones.)

With this unpretentious attitude (far subtler than it looks at first sight), Sheckley achieves first of all the main aim of all fiction —the creation of a consistent, believable world with its own internal consistency, and its own achievement of the suspension of disbelief. This is not of course a criterion of science fiction merely. Even the most plodding piece of alleged semi-reportage is nonetheless the establishment of an internally consistent and externally credible field of imaginative construction, or it is nothing.

The means by which a work of art is created, and produces its effect on us, are of a depth and a complexity which have not yet yielded their secrets, and probably cannot until that far-off day when psychology becomes a true science. Attempts to produce rigorous aesthetic theories have simply led to a superficial pro-graming at the accessible levels. Meanwhile, it is perhaps worth saying just once more that a work of art does not necessarily depend on the emotional intensity of its content, or on the pressure and insistence of its method. A still life by Chardin conveys more to us than "Love Locked Out" by Holman Hunt. A Claude landscape is more moving—more sublime—than any of Martin's not by any means despicable Apocalypses.

I would also argue that "experimentalist" prose (which even in other fields may be thought to give its effects only to palates so coarse that they need, in Wordsworth's phrase, "outrageous stimulation" before they can taste anything) is scarcely tolerable in science fiction. The only exceptions I can think of are when dislocated language is used, as in some passages in Alfred Bester's *The Demolished Man,* to indicate mental or sensuous disintegration. And in the nature of things this can hardly take up a high proportion of a science-fiction story.

"Qu'il insiste peu" was Gide's praise of Stendhal. "Naturalists" had complained that a night love scene in *Le Rouge et le Noir* omitted all the properties of night, its odors and its voluptuousnesses. Stendhal did not need them: he conveyed their presence in a few dry words. In his day it was a relief not to have to go through the whole naturalist rigmarole. Nowadays it is a relief not to be told at length about neurotic motivations. (As Cyril Connolly points out in *The Unquiet Grave,* it is a mistake to think that neurosis is interesting—an admission all the more admirable coming from one who is himself admittedly much concerned with it.)

How little Sheckley, too, "insists"—at his best, at any rate. He writes for the audience that enjoys a science-fiction story. His work does not derive its effect by indulging the reader in the feeling that he is doing something superior, that he and the author are one up on all those peasants. Intellectual and aesthetic self-congratulation doubtless provides one form of enjoyment, but it is one which in principle is wholly destructive of the art of fiction—and other arts, too.

Moreover, Sheckley for his part clearly *likes* the sphere of science fiction. He enjoys what he is doing. And he is completely at home in it. There is never a trace of the stupefying attitude that science fiction is, or can be made, an instrument of some conscious, external program of aesthetic or social self-righteousness. As Yeats remarked, in a similar context, of the true attitude of the creative:

> *Players and painted stage took all my love*
> *And not those things that they were emblems of.*

When one speaks of social satire in present-day fiction, what a vision of tedium it usually conjures up—everything from the high school frivolity of *MacBird!* to the reform school frivolity of *Last Exit to Brooklyn*, in either case uncivilized, po'-faced, self-righteous—beset, too, as often as not, with the trashy gimmickry of chic kitsch. There is science fiction like this, or at least writing which describes itself as science fiction. But, on the whole, genuine science fiction has remained in its satirical aspect in or around the tradition of Swift. Clarity, careful realization, and the *reductio ad absurdum* have been its weapons.

Sheckley has written a splendid *Erewhon*-style social satire in "Ticket to Tranai," and a deadly projection of some of the horrors of our time in "The Prize of Peril." He has given us stories which raise the whole question of the nature and the "purpose" of life —as in "Ask a Foolish Question." He has given us extraordinary psychological comedies, in which (for example) the heroes are severely bitten and almost killed by monsters they know perfectly well to be their own personal delusions. At the other pole, we find the restrainedly tragic, the sinister interweaving of fantasy and reality in "Store of the Worlds."

In "Specialist," Sheckley seems to divest himself (almost it might be on purpose) of all these resources of the writer. There is no tragedy. There is no sex. It can hardly be said that there is no characterization, but it is perfunctory, as the seriocomic stance demands. Nor can it be claimed that "Specialist" is particularly profound at a philosophical level—or as social comment.

In fact, the story is effective without any of the properties conventionally thought necessary. It is science fiction stripped to the bone, using none but the elements it shares with no other genre. As parts of the rural Midlands have been called "unmitigated England," and as C. S. Lewis spoke of "mere Christianity," this story might be accurately praised as "mere science fiction," "unmitigated science fiction." In the context of this book, that seems particularly important. At the same time, I feel that "Specialist" is valuable as a locus of the high spirits, ease, good writing, and dry tone which are among Sheckley's great contributions.

SPECIALIST

The photon storm struck without warning, pouncing upon the Ship from behind a bank of giant red stars. Eye barely had time to flash a last second warning through Talker before it was upon them.

It was Talker's third journey into deep space, and his first light-pressure storm. He felt a sudden pang of fear as the Ship yawed violently, caught the force of the wave-front and careened end for end. Then the fear was gone, replaced by a strong pulse of excitement.

Why should he be afraid, he asked himself—hadn't he been trained for just this sort of emergency?

He had been talking to Feeder when the storm hit, but he cut off the conversation abruptly. He hoped Feeder would be all right. It was the youngster's first deep space trip.

The wirelike filaments that made up most of Talker's body were extended throughout the Ship. Quickly he withdrew all except the ones linking him to Eye, Engine, and the Walls. This was strictly their job now. The rest of the Crew would have to shift for themselves until the storm was over.

Eye had flattened his disklike body against a Wall, and had one seeing organ extended outside the Ship. For greater concentration, the rest of his seeing organs were collapsed, clustered against his body.

Through Eye's seeing organ, Talker watched the storm. He translated Eye's purely visual image into a direction for Engine, who shoved the Ship around to meet the waves. At appreciably the same time, Talker translated direction into velocity for the Walls who stiffened to meet the shocks.

151

The coordination was swift and sure—Eye measuring the waves, Talker relaying the messages to Engine and Walls, Engine driving the ship nose-first into the waves, and Walls bracing to meet the shock.

Talker forgot any fear he might have had in the swiftly functioning teamwork. He had no time to think. As the Ship's communication system, he had to translate and flash his messages at top speed, coordinating information and directing action.

In a matter of minutes, the storm was over.

"All right," Talker said. "Let's see if there was any damage." His filaments had become tangled during the storm, but he untwisted and extended them through the Ship, plugging everyone into circuit. "Engine?"

"I'm fine," Engine said. The tremendous old fellow had dampened his plates during the storm, easing down the atomic explosions in his stomach. No storm could catch an experienced spacer like Engine unaware.

"Walls?"

The Walls reported one by one, and this took a long time. There were almost a thousand of them, thin, rectangular fellows making up the entire skin of the Ship. Naturally, they had reinforced their edges during the storm, giving the whole Ship resiliency. But one or two were dented badly.

Doctor announced that he was all right. He removed Talker's filament from his head, taking himself out of circuit, and went to work on the dented Walls. Made mostly of hands, Doctor had clung to an Accumulator during the storm.

"Let's go a little faster now," Talker said, remembering that there still was the problem of determining where they were. He opened the circuit to the four Accumulators. "How are you?" he asked.

There was no answer. The Accumulators were asleep. They had had their receptors open during the storm and were bloated on energy. Talker twitched his filaments around them, but they didn't stir.

"Let me," Feeder said. Feeder had taken quite a beating before planting his suction cups to a Wall, but his cockiness was intact. He was the only member of the Crew who never needed Doctor's attention; his body was quite capable of repairing itself.

He scuttled across the floor on a dozen or so tentacles, and booted the nearest Accumulator. The big, conical storage unit opened one eye, then closed it again. Feeder kicked him again, getting no response. He reached for the Accumulator's safety valve and drained off some energy.

"Stop that," the Accumulator said.

"Then wake up and report," Talker told him.

The Accumulators said testily that they were all right, as any fool could see. They had been anchored to the floor during the storm.

The rest of the inspection went quickly. Thinker was fine, and Eye was ecstatic over the beauty of the storm. There was only one casualty.

Pusher was dead. Bipedal, he didn't have the stability of the rest of the Crew. The storm had caught him in the middle of a floor, thrown him against a stiffened Wall, and broken several of his important bones. He was beyond Doctor's skill to repair.

They were silent for a while. It was always serious when a part of the Ship died. The Ship was a cooperative unit, composed entirely of the Crew. The loss of any member was a blow to all the rest.

It was especially serious now. They had just delivered a cargo to a port several thousand light-years from Galactic Center. There was no telling where they might be.

Eye crawled to a Wall and extended a seeing organ outside. The Walls let it through, then sealed around it. Eye's organ pushed out, far enough from the Ship so he could view the entire sphere of stars. The picture traveled through Talker, who gave it to Thinker.

Thinker lay in one corner of the room, a great shapeless blob of protoplasm. Within him were all the memories of his space-going ancestors. He considered the picture, compared it rapidly with others stored in his cells, and said, "No galactic planets within reach."

Talker automatically translated for everyone. It was what they had feared.

Eye, with Thinker's help, calculated that they were several hundred light-years off their course, on the galactic periphery.

Every Crew member knew what that meant. Without a Pusher to boost the Ship to a multiple of the speed of light, they would never get home. The trip back, without a Pusher, would take longer than most of their lifetimes.

"What would you suggest?" Talker asked Thinker.

This was too vague a question for the literal-minded Thinker. He asked to have it rephrased.

"What would be our best line of action," Talker asked, "to get back to a galactic planet?"

Thinker needed several minutes to go through all the possibilities stored in his cells. In the meantime, Doctor had patched the Walls and was asking to be given something to eat.

"In a little while we'll all eat," Talker said, twitching his tendrils nervously. Even though he was the second youngest Crew member—only Feeder was younger—the responsibility was largely on him. This was still an emergency; he had to coordinate information and direct action.

One of the Walls suggested that they get good and drunk. This unrealistic solution was vetoed at once. It was typical of the Walls' attitude, however. They were fine workers and good ship-mates, but happy-go-lucky fellows at best. When they returned to their home planets, they would probably blow all their wages on a spree.

"Loss of the Ship's Pusher cripples the Ship for sustained faster-than-light speeds," Thinker began without preamble. "The nearest galactic planet is four hundred and five light-years off."

Talker translated all this instantly along his wave-packet body.

"Two courses of action are open. First, the Ship can proceed to the nearest galactic planet under atomic power from Engine. This will take approximately two hundred years. Engine might still be alive at this time, although no one else will.

"Second, locate a primitive planet in this region, upon which are latent Pushers. Find one and train him. Have him push the Ship back to galactic territory."

Thinker was silent, having given all the possibilities he could find in the memories of his ancestors.

They held a quick vote and decided upon Thinker's second alternative. There was no choice, really. It was the only one which offered them any hope of getting back to their homes.

"All right," Talker said. Let's eat. I think we all deserve it."

The body of the dead Pusher was shoved into the mouth of Engine, who consumed it at once, breaking down the atoms to energy. Engine was the only member of the Crew who lived on atomic energy.

For the rest, Feeder dashed up and loaded himself from the nearest Accumulator. Then he transformed the food within him into the substances each member ate. His body chemistry changed, altered, adapted, making the different foods for the Crew.

Eye lived entirely on a complex chlorophyl chain. Feeder reproduced this for him, then went over to give Talker his hydrocarbons, and the Walls their chlorine compound. For Doctor he made a facsimile of a silicate fruit that grew on Doctor's native planet.

Finally, feeding was over and the Ship back in order. The Accumulators were stacked in a corner, blissfully sleeping again. Eye was extending his vision as far as he could, shaping his main seeing organ for high-powered telescopic reception. Even in this emergency, Eye couldn't resist making verses. He announced that he was at work on a new narrative poem, called *Peripheral Glow*. No one wanted to hear it, so Eye fed it to Thinker, who stored everything, good or bad, right or wrong.

Engine never slept. Filled to the brim on Pusher, he shoved the Ship along at several times the speed of light.

The Walls were arguing among themselves about who had been the drunkest during their last leave.

Talker decided to make himself comfortable. He released his hold on the Walls and swung in the air, his small round body suspended by his crisscrossed network of filaments.

He thought briefly about Pusher. It was strange. Pusher had been everyone's friend and now he was forgotten. That wasn't because of indifference; it was because the Ship was a unit. The loss of a member was regretted, but the important thing was for the unit to go on.

The Ship raced through the suns of the periphery.

Thinker laid out a search spiral, calculating their odds on finding a Pusher planet at roughly four to one. In a week they found a planet of primitive Walls. Dropping low, they could see the leathery, rectangular fellows basking in the sun, crawling over rocks, stretching themselves thin in order to float in the breeze.

All the Ship's Walls heaved a sigh of nostalgia. It was just like home.

These Walls on the planet hadn't been contacted by a galactic team yet, and were still unaware of their great destiny—to join in the vast Cooperation of the Galaxy.

There were plenty of dead worlds in the spiral, and worlds too young to bear life. They found a planet of Talkers. The Talkers had extended their spidery communication lines across half a continent.

Talker looked at them eagerly, through Eye. A wave of self-pity washed over him. He remembered home, his family, his friends. He thought of the tree he was going to buy when he got back.

For a moment, Talker wondered what he was doing here, part of a Ship in a far corner of the Galaxy.

He shrugged off the mood. They were bound to find a Pusher planet, if they looked long enough.

At least, he hoped so.

There was a long stretch of arid worlds as the Ship speeded through the unexplored periphery. Then a planetful of primeval Engines, swimming in a radioactive ocean.

"This is rich territory," Feeder said to Talker. "Galactic should send a Contact party here."

"They probably will, after we get back," Talker said.

They were good friends, above and beyond the all-enveloping friendship of the Crew. It wasn't only because they were the youngest Crew members, although that had something to do with it. They both had the same kind of functions and that made for a certain rapport. Talker translated languages; Feeder transformed foods. Also, they looked somewhat alike. Talker was a central core with radiating filaments; Feeder was a central core with radiating tentacles.

Talker thought that Feeder was the next most aware being on the Ship. He was never really able to understand how some of the others carried on the processes of consciousness.

More suns, more planets. Engine started to overheat. Usually, Engine was used only for taking off and landing, and for fine maneuvering in a planetary group. Now he had been running continuously for weeks, both over and under the speed of light. The strain was telling on him.

Feeder, with Doctor's help, rigged a cooling system for him. It was crude, but it had to suffice. Feeder rearranged nitrogen, oxygen and hydrogen atoms to make a coolant for the system. Doctor diagnosed a long rest for Engine. He said that the gallant old fellow couldn't stand the strain for more than a week.

The search continued, with the Crew's spirits gradually dropping. They all realized that Pushers were rather rare in the Galaxy, as compared to the fertile Walls and Engines.

The Walls were getting pock-marked from interstellar dust. They complained that they would need a full beauty treatment when they got home. Talker assured them that the company would pay for it.

Even Eye was getting bloodshot from staring into space so continuously.

They dipped over another planet. Its characteristics were flashed to Thinker, who mulled over them.

Closer, and they could make out the forms.

Pushers! Primitive Pushers!

They zoomed back into space to make plans. Feeder produced twenty-three different kinds of intoxicants for a celebration.

The Ship wasn't fit to function for three days.

"Everyone ready now?" Talker asked, a bit fuzzily. He had a hangover that burned all along his nerve ends. What a drunk he had thrown! He had a vague recollection of embracing Engine, and inviting him to share his tree when they got home.

He shuddered at the idea.

The rest of the Crew were pretty shaky, too. The Walls were letting air leak into space; they were just too wobbly to seal their edges properly. Doctor had passed out.

But the worst off was Feeder. Since his system could adapt to any type of fuel except atomic, he had been sampling every batch he made, whether it was an unbalanced iodine, pure oxygen or a supercharged ester. He was really miserable. His tentacles, usually a healthy aqua, were shot through with orange streaks. His system was working furiously, purging itself of everything, and Feeder was suffering the effects of the purge.

The only sober ones were Thinker and Engine. Thinker didn't

drink, which was unusual for a spacer, though typical of Thinker, and Engine couldn't.

They listened while Thinker reeled off some astounding facts. From Eye's pictures of the planet's surface, Thinker had detected the presence of metallic construction. He put forth the alarming suggestion that these Pushers had constructed a mechanical civilization.

"That's impossible," three of the Walls said flatly, and most of the Crew were inclined to agree with them. All the metal they had ever seen had been buried in the ground or lying around in worthless oxidized chunks.

"Do you mean that they make things out of metal?" Talker demanded. "Out of just plain dead metal? What could they make?"

"They couldn't make anything," Feeder said positively. "It would break down constantly. I mean metal doesn't *know* when it's weakening."

But it seemed to be true. Eye magnified his pictures, and everyone could see that the Pushers had made vast shelters, vehicles, and other articles from inanimate material.

The reason for this was not readily apparent, but it wasn't a good sign. However, the really hard part was over. The Pusher planet had been found. All that remained was the relatively easy job of convincing a native Pusher.

That shouldn't be too difficult. Talker knew that cooperation was the keystone of the Galaxy, even among primitive peoples.

The Crew decided not to land in a populated region. Of course, there was no reason not to expect a friendly greeting, but it was the job of a Contact Team to get in touch with them as a race. All they wanted was an individual.

Accordingly, they picked out a sparsely populated land-mass, drifting in while that side of the planet was dark.

They were able to locate a solitary Pusher almost at once.

Eye adapted his vision to see in the dark, and they followed the Pusher's movements. He lay down, after a while, beside a small fire. Thinker told them that this was a well-known resting habit of Pushers.

Just before dawn, the Walls opened, and Feeder, Talker and Doctor came out.

Feeder dashed forward and tapped the creature on the shoulder. Talker followed with a communication tendril.

The Pusher opened his seeing organs, blinked them, and made a movement with his eating organ. Then he leaped to his feet and started to run.

The three Crew members were amazed. The Pusher hadn't even waited to find out what the three of them wanted!

Talker extended a filament rapidly, and caught the Pusher, fifty feet away, by a limb. The Pusher fell.

"Treat him gently," Feeder said. "He might be startled by our appearance." He twitched his tendrils at the idea of a Pusher— one of the strangest sights in the Galaxy, with his multiple organs —being startled at someone else's appearance.

Feeder and Doctor scurried to the fallen Pusher, picked him up and carried him back to the Ship.

The Walls sealed again. They released the Pusher and prepared to talk.

As soon as he was free, the Pusher sprang to his limbs and ran at the place where the Walls had sealed. He pounded against them frantically, his eating organ open and vibrating.

"Stop that," the Wall said. He bulged, and the Pusher tumbled to the floor. Instantly, he jumped up and started to run forward.

"Stop him," Talker said. "He might hurt himself."

One of the Accumulators woke up enough to roll into the Pusher's path. The Pusher fell, got up again, and ran on.

Talker had his filaments in the front of the Ship also, and he caught the Pusher in the bow. The Pusher started to tear at his tendrils, and Talker let go hastily.

"Plug him into the communication system!" Feeder shouted. "Maybe we can reason with him!"

Talker advanced a filament toward the Pusher's head, waving it in the universal sign of communication. But the Pusher continued his amazing behavior, jumping out of the way. He had a piece of metal in his hand and he was waving it frantically.

"What do you think he's going to do with that?" Feeder asked. The Pusher started to attack the side of the Ship, pounding at one of the Walls. The Wall stiffened instinctively and the metal snapped.

"Leave him alone," Talker said. "Give him a chance to calm down."

Talker consulted with Thinker, but they couldn't decide what to do about the Pusher. He wouldn't accept communication. Every time Talker extended a filament, the Pusher showed all the signs of violent panic. Temporarily, it was an impasse.

Thinker vetoed the plan of finding another Pusher on the planet. He considered this Pusher's behavior typical; nothing would be gained by approaching another. Also, a planet was supposed to be contacted only by a Contact Team.

If they couldn't communicate with this Pusher, they never would with another on the planet.

"I think I know what the trouble is," Eye said. He crawled up on an Accumulator. "These Pushers have evolved a mechanical civilization. Consider for a minute how they went about it. They developed the use of their fingers, like Doctor, to shape metal. They utilized their seeing organs, like myself. And probably countless other organs." He paused for effect.

"These Pushers have become unspecialized!"

They argued over it for several hours. The Walls maintained that no intelligent creature could be unspecialized. It was unknown in the Galaxy. But the evidence was before them—the Pusher cities, their vehicles . . . This Pusher, exemplifying the rest, seemed capable of a multitude of things.

He was able to do everything except Push!

Thinker supplied a partial explanation. "This is not a primitive planet. It is relatively old and should have been in the Cooperation thousands of years ago. Since it was not, the Pushers upon it were robbed of their birthright. Their ability, their specialty was to Push, but there was nothing *to* Push. Naturally, they have developed a deviant culture.

"Exactly what this culture is, we can only guess. But on the basis of the evidence, there is reason to believe that these Pushers are—uncooperative."

Thinker had a habit of uttering the most shattering statement in the quietest possible way.

"It is entirely possible," Thinker went on inexorably, "that these Pushers will have nothing to do with us. In which case, our chances are approximately 283 to one against finding another Pusher planet."

"We can't be sure he won't cooperate," Talker said, "until we get him into communication." He found it almost impossible to believe that any intelligent creature would refuse to cooperate willingly.

"But how?" Feeder asked. They decided upon a course of action. Doctor walked slowly up to the Pusher, who backed away from him. In the meantime. Talker extended a filament outside the Ship, around, and in again, behind the Pusher.

The Pusher backed against a Wall—and Talker shoved the filament through the Pusher's head, into the communication socket in the center of his brain.

The Pusher collapsed.

When he came to, Feeder and Doctor had to hold the Pusher's limbs, or he would have ripped out the communication line. Talker exercised his skill in learning the Pusher's language.

It wasn't too hard. All Pusher languages were of the same family, and this was no exception. Talker was able to catch enough surface thoughts to form a pattern.

He tried to communicate with the Pusher.

The Pusher was silent.

"I think he needs food," Feeder said. They remembered that it had been almost two days since they had taken the Pusher on board. Feeder worked up some standard Pusher food and offered it.

"My God! A steak!" the Pusher said.

The Crew cheered along Talker's communication circuits. The Pusher had said his first words!

Talker examined the words and searched his memory. He knew about two hundred Pusher languages and many more simple variations. He found that this Pusher was speaking a cross between two Pusher tongues.

After the Pusher had eaten, he looked around. Talker caught his thoughts and broadcast them to the Crew.

The Pusher had a queer way of looking at the Ship. He saw it as a riot of colors. The walls undulated. In front of him was something resembling a gigantic spider, colored black and green, with his web running all over the Ship and into the heads of all the creatures. He saw Eye as a strange, naked little animal, something between a skinned rabbit and an egg yolk—whatever those things were.

Talker was fascinated by the new perspective the Pusher's mind gave him. He had never seen things that way before. But now that the Pusher was pointing it out, Eye *was* a pretty funny-looking creature.

They settled down to communication.

"What in hell *are* you things?" the Pusher asked, much calmer now than he had been during the two days. "Why did you grab me? Have I gone nuts?"

"No," Talker said, "you are not psychotic. We are a galactic trading ship. We were blown off our course by a storm and our Pusher was killed."

"Well, what does that have to do with me?"

"We would like you to join our Crew," Talker said, "to be our new Pusher."

The Pusher thought it over after the situation was explained to him. Talker could catch the feeling of conflict in the Pusher's thoughts. He hadn't decided whether to accept this as a real situation or not. Finally, the Pusher decided that he wasn't crazy.

"Look, boys," he said, "I don't know what you are or how this makes sense. I have to get out of here. I'm on a furlough, and if I don't get back soon, the U.S. Army's going to be very interested."

Talker asked the Pusher to give him more information about "army," and he fed it to Thinker.

"These Pushers engage in personal combat," was Thinker's conclusion.

"But *why*?" Talker asked. Sadly he admitted to himself that Thinker might have been right; the Pusher didn't show many signs of willingness to cooperate.

"I'd like to help you lads out," Pusher said, "but I don't know where you get the idea that I could push anything this size. You'd need a whole division of tanks just to budge it."

"Do you approve of these wars?" Talker asked, getting a suggestion from Thinker.

"Nobody likes war—not those who have to do the dying at least."

"Then why do you fight them?"

The Pusher made a gesture with his eating organ, which Eye picked up and sent to Thinker. "It's kill or be killed. You guys know what war is, don't you?"

"We don't have any wars," Talker said.

"You're lucky," the Pusher said bitterly. "We do. Plenty of them."

"Of course," Talker said. He had the full explanation from Thinker now. "Would you like to end them?"

"Of course I would."

"Then come with us. Be our Pusher."

The Pusher stood up and walked up to an Accumulator. He sat down on it and doubled the ends of his upper limbs.

"How the hell can I stop all wars?" the Pusher demanded. "Even if I went to the big shots and told them—"

"You won't have to," Talker said. "All you have to do is come with us. Push us to our base. Galactic will send a Contact Team to your planet. That will end your wars."

"The hell you say," the Pusher replied. "You boys are stranded here, huh? Good enough. No monsters are going to take over Earth."

Bewildered, Talker tried to understand the reasoning. Had he said something wrong? Was it possible that the Pusher didn't understand him?

"I thought you wanted to end wars," Talker said.

"Sure I do. But I don't want anyone *making* us stop. I'm no traitor. I'd rather fight."

"No one will make you stop. You will just stop because there will be no further need for fighting."

"Do you know why we're fighting?"

"It's obvious."

"Yeah? What's your explanation?"

"You Pushers have been separated from the main stream of the Galaxy," Talker explained. "You have your specialty—pushing —but nothing to Push. Accordingly, you have no real jobs. You play with things—metal, inanimate objects—but find no real satisfaction. Robbed of your true vocation, you fight from sheer frustration.

"Once you find your place in the galactic Cooperation—and I assure you that it is an important place—your fighting will stop.

Why should you fight, which is an unnatural occupation, when you can Push? Also, your mechanical civilization will end, since there will be no need for it."

The Pusher shook his head in what Talker guessed was a gesture of confusion. "What is this pushing?"

Talker told him as best he could. Since the job was out of his scope, he had only a general idea of what a Pusher did.

"You mean to say that *that* is what every Earthman should be doing?"

"Of course," Talker said. "It is your great specialty."

The Pusher thought about it for several minutes. "I think you want a physicist or a mentalist or something. I could never do anything like that. I'm a junior architect. And besides—well, it's difficult to explain."

But Talker had already caught Pusher's objection. He saw a Pusher female in his thoughts. No, two, three. And he caught a feeling of loneliness, strangeness. The Pusher was filled with doubts. He was afraid.

"When we reach galactic," Talker said, hoping it was the right thing, "you can meet other Pushers. Pusher females, too. All you Pushers look alike, so you should become friends with them. As far as loneliness in the Ship goes—it just doesn't exist. You don't understand the Cooperation yet. No one is lonely in the Cooperation."

The Pusher was still considering the idea of there being other Pushers. Talker couldn't understand why he was so startled at that. The Galaxy was filled with Pushers, Feeders, Talkers, and many other species, endlessly duplicated.

"I can't believe that anybody could end all war," Pusher said. "How do I know you're not lying?"

Talker felt as if he had been struck in the core. Thinker must have been right when he said these Pushers would be uncooperative. Was this going to be the end of Talker's career? Were he and the rest of the Crew going to spend the rest of their lives in space, because of the stupidity of a bunch of Pushers?

Even thinking this, Talker was able to feel sorry for the Pusher. It must be terrible, he thought. Doubting, uncertain, never trusting anyone. If these Pushers didn't find their place in the Galaxy, they would exterminate themselves. Their place in the Cooperation was long overdue.

"What can I do to convince you?" Talker asked.

In despair, he opened all the circuits to the Pusher. He let the Pusher see Engine's good-natured gruffness, the devil-may-care humor of the Walls; he showed him Eye's poetic attempts, and Feeder's cocky good nature. He opened his own mind and showed the Pusher a picture of his home planet, his family, the tree he was planning to buy when he got home.

The pictures told the story of all of them, from different planets, representing different ethics, united by a common bond—the galactic Cooperation.

The Pusher watched it all in silence.

After a while, he shook his head. The thought accompanying the gesture was uncertain, weak—but negative.

Talker told the Walls to open. They did, and the Pusher stared in amazement.

"You may leave," Talker said. "Just remove the communication line and go."

"What will you do?"

"We will look for another Pusher planet."

"Where? Mars? Venus?"

"We don't know. All we can do is hope there is another in this region."

The Pusher looked at the opening, then back at the Crew. He hesitated and his face screwed up in a grimace of indecision.

"All that you showed me was true?"

No answer was necessary.

"All right," the Pusher said suddenly. "I'll go. I'm a damned fool, but I'll go. If this means what you say—it *must* mean what you say!"

Talker saw that the agony of the Pusher's decision had forced him out of contact with reality. He believed that he was in a dream, where decisions are easy and unimportant.

"There's just one little trouble," Pusher said with the lightness of hysteria. "Boys, I'll be damned if I know how to Push. You said something about faster-than-light? I can't even run the mile in an hour."

"Of course you can Push," Talker assured him, hoping he was right. He knew what a Pusher's abilities were; but this one . . .

"Just try it."

"Sure," Pusher agreed. I'll probably wake up out of this, anyhow."

They sealed the ship for takeoff while Pusher talked to himself.

"Funny," Pusher said. "I thought a camping trip would be a nice way to spend a furlough and all I do is get nightmares!"

Engine boosted the Ship into the air. The Walls were sealed and Eye was guiding them away from the planet.

"We're in open space now," Talker said. Listening to Pusher, he hoped his mind hadn't cracked. "Eye and Thinker will give a direction, I'll transmit it to you, and you Push along it."

"You're crazy," Pusher mumbled. "You must have the wrong planet. I wish you nightmares would go away."

"You're in the Cooperation now," Talker said desperately. "There's the direction. Push!"

The Pusher didn't do anything for a moment. He was slowly emerging from his fantasy, realizing that he wasn't in a dream, after all. He felt the Cooperation. Eye to Thinker, Thinker to Talker, Talker to Pusher, all intercoordinated with Walls, and with each other.

"What is this?" Pusher asked. He felt the oneness of the Ship, the great warmth, the closeness achieved only in the Cooperation.

He Pushed.

Nothing happened.

"Try again," Talker begged.

Pusher searched his mind. He found a deep well of doubt and fear. Staring into it, he saw his own tortured face.

Thinker illuminated it for him.

Pushers had lived with this doubt and fear for centuries. Pushers had fought through fear, killed through doubt.

That was where the Pusher organ was!

Human—specialist—Pusher—he entered fully into the Crew, merged with them, threw mental arms around the shoulders of Thinker and Talker.

Suddenly, the Ship shot forward at eight times the speed of light. It continued to accelerate.

COMMON TIME

by JAMES BLISH

FOREWORD
by Damon Knight

THE AUTHOR

JAMES BLISH can speak with authority on subjects as diverse as the poetry of Ezra Pound, the operas of Richard Strauss, *Finnegans Wake*, limnobiology, Roger Bacon, and the care of cats. But it is as a science-fiction writer that he is known to the public. His first story appeared in 1940, when he was still a very young man; he attracted wide attention with his stories "Okie" (1950) and "Surface Tension" (1952), and achieved a lofty position among contemporary s-f writers with such novels as *Earthman Come Home, A Case of Conscience,* and *The Seedling Stars.* A native of the United States, he now makes his home in Great Britain. "Common Time" was first published in 1953.

THE CRITIC

The versatile DAMON KNIGHT has edited a number of science-fiction magazines, is the author of a great many popular s-f novels and short stories, has translated s-f from the French, was the founder of the Science Fiction Writers of America, has been for many years the guru of the annual Milford Science Fiction Writers' Conference, and lately has been the editor of the *Orbit* series of short-story collections. He was also perhaps the first to apply serious critical principles to science fiction on a regular basis; his essays on modern science fiction, often devastating in their exposure of inanity and incompetence, began appearing about 1945, and in 1956 were collected in a volume entitled *In Search of Wonder* (second edition, 1967). His science-fiction criticisms won him a Hugo award in 1956. Knight and his wife, writer Kate Wilhelm, now live in Florida.

Foreword

"Common Time," by James Blish, is the story that first drew me into an attempt to analyze the unconscious symbology of science fiction. What follows is an abridged version, omitting references not directly relevant to this story, of an essay I wrote for *Science Fiction Forum* in 1957; it was reprinted ten years later in the second edition of *In Search of Wonder*.

When I first read "Common Time," it seemed to me that except for some ingenious manipulation of the differential time problem in the first half of the story, it was not a science-fiction story at all; the plot was extremely simple, not to say half formed, and I could not see why the story hit me as hard as it did. Blish and I had been discussing the supposed womb symbolism in his stories; I took a second look from that standpoint, and was astonished to discover a whole series of puns, running all through the story, which could be tabulated under two headings, like this:

	INTERCOURSE	DEATH

Page

173   "Common time,"

i.e. common rhythm, or: . . . . . length of life; common term in that sense, or: as the genital contact; common divisor in both senses; common measure (six inches, or . . . . six feet).

173   "Don't move,"

i.e., at the moment of orgasm, or: after the moment of death.

174   "Calendar: stopped" (in both senses).

175   "Not breathing" (in both senses).

176   "plunged into Hell":

followed by a description that would serve equally well for orgasm, or: . . . . death.

169

177   "vessel of horror,"
        i.e., the womb, or: . . . . the uterine abyss of death.
177   "trickles of reason,"
        i.e., during orgasm, or: after physical death of the brain.
177   "eternity in hell had taken three seconds,"
                    i.e., the suspension of time in love, or in death: cf. "his
                                    whole life passed before his eyes."
177   "transports of love,"
                        paired in a sentence with "agonies of empires."
180   "The normal human hand movement, in such a task as
            lifting a pencil, took the pencil from a state of rest to
                            another state of rest. . . ."
182   "come up with the solution to the Problem of Evil"
183   "put his finger on the First Cause!"
183   "the situation demanded someone trained in the highest rigors"
185   "the pseudo-death"
186   "clinesterton" from Greek *klino* + *sterto,* to snore in bed?*

187   "the All-Devouring"
187   " 'on Earth as it is in Heaven' "
191   "as old, as compressed, constricted"
192   "found myself in [a] box"
192   "The whole situation was now utterly rigid—and, in effect,
                            I died."

    As the Blishes point out in a letter, "to die" is a widespread
popular usage for orgasm; it is still current in French, and turns
up in English poetry as late as Shelley's "Indian Serenade":

                    O lift me from the grass!
                    I die, I faint, I fail
                    O let thy kisses rain
                    On my cheeks and eyelids pale!

    * Most of this dream-talk is fairly easy: for instance, "rodalent" is evi-
dently a combination of "radiant" and "redolent." "Beademungen" stopped
me, though, and I appealed to Blish for more light. Between them, he and
his former wife, Virginia, came up with this: " 'Beademungen,' as it turns
out, is not essentially German; the weak German ending is a piece of
dream-work designed to turn the Latin verb 'to bless' into a noun, 'the
Blessed.' Thus, 'the clinesterton beademung' turned into a proposition reads:
'Blessed are they who snore in bed,' and the text goes on to say in English, 'on Earth as it is in Heaven.' "

So what we have here is apparently only a highly expanded metaphor: "death" as orgasm, which is what the story seems to be about. But look at it more closely again, and it again becomes puzzling. If intercourse is taking place in the story, who are the partners? Garrard seems to be a part of the male act, but is completely passive; the female appears nowhere unless as the ship: and this relationship, we see at once, is the wrong one. Clearly Garrard is *inside* one of the organs engaged in copulation; sometimes he seems to visualize himself as an unborn child, sometimes as a kind of analogue of the penis.

I think there is one clear answer to this, one which also satisfactorily explains the metaphor itself. "To die" is understandable as hyperbole: but the adult male partner in intercourse doesn't really die, as a rule. There is just one male human creature for whom orgasm is literally death; that's the sperm.

I had better say here, for the benefit of nervous people, that I don't think all this is any sort of evidence for Hubbard's engrams, or Jung's archetypes, or prenatal memory in any form. Blish is a highly sophisticated reader and critic who has some reputation as an expert on James Joyce's multi-punned *Finnegans Wake*. But I must insist that these chains of symbols were not deliberately written in as a prank or a Joycean exercise. Blish did not even suspect they were there until I pointed them out. Since then, I may add, I've been on the receiving end of this same experience, and it is startling.

I don't think Blish can remember his own experiences as a sperm, but I don't actually care whether he can or not; it isn't necessary to the hypothesis. In fact, if this notion should get logically into the argument, I would do my best to clear it out again: the idea of blind and compulsive recapitulation would make the whole process revoltingly meaningless. If there is any one dominant impression which every analyzed symbolic story gives, it is one of immense meaning.

A more serious objection, it seems to me is this one: if Garrard, the hero of "Common Time," is a sperm, and the story chronicles his journey from testis (the Earth) to uterus, where he meets an ovum (the beademung), what about the return journey?

Watch out; here comes another hard, fast one. I think the first part of the story, containing all the intercourse symbolism, is told backward.

Look again at the list of puns on pp. 169–170, and this time read it from bottom to top. Omitting the bottom three items (which are taken from Garrard's recounting of the outward trip), first you find a cloud of passive images; next a clear series of erection puns ("the highest rigors," etc.); then the intercourse and vagina symbols themselves begin; and finally, at the top of the list, you reach the orgasm and the terminal pun, "Come on time."

For confirmation, here's another note from Blish:

"About the Greek: very evidently it had more to do with the intercourse theme you spotted than I had any idea it had up to now. The reference to the Alpha Centauri stars as 'the twin radioceles' obviously comes from *varicocele,* a common form of hernia involving the testicles, and I think now that the whole thing was suggested by the Earth-Moon balls on the cover around which I wrote the story. The main Alpha Centauri star and Proxima Centauri stand in about the same relationship as the Earth and the Moon, and both pairs might be described as one-hung-low. Also, the story *is* about love-and-death; it says it is. But I'm just now beginning to believe it. Writing frightens me. I don't know why I do it."

This one story shows every sign of being inexhaustible, but let's pursue it a little farther. The inverted time scheme I propose here is not really as unlikely as it seems; it turns out to be common in science fiction. But, even granting that, why should one part of the narrative run backward and the other part forward?

The time inversion and the whole sperm fantasy express a longing to return to the beginning. But this is an impossibility; it can only seem to happen by the trick of telling the story backward. Once that has been done, then the story must unreel the other way, as if to emphasize that the reversal was an illusion. This is what the story is really saying: *You can't go back.*

COMMON TIME

> . . . the days went slowly round and round, endless
> and uneventful as cycles in space. Time, and time-pieces!
> How many centuries did my hammock tell, as pendulum-
> like it swung to the ship's dull roll, and ticked the hours
> and ages.—HERMAN MELVILLE, in *Mardi*

Don't move.

It was the first thought that came into Garrard's mind when he
awoke, and perhaps it saved his life. He lay where he was, strapped
against the padding, listening to the round hum of the engines. That
in itself was wrong; he should be unable to hear the overdrive at all.

He thought to himself: *Has it begun already?*

Otherwise everything seemed normal. The DFC-3 had crossed
over into interstellar velocity, and he was still alive, and the ship
was still functioning. The ship should at this moment be traveling
at 22.4 times the speed of light—a neat 4,157,000 miles per
second.

Somehow Garrard did not doubt that it was. On both previous
tries, the ships had whiffed away toward Alpha Centauri at the
proper moment when the overdrive should have cut in; and the
split second of residual image after they had vanished, subjected
to spectroscopy, showed a Doppler shift which tallied with the
acceleration predicted for that moment by Haertel.

The trouble was not that Brown and Cellini hadn't gotten away
in good order. It was simply that neither of them had ever been
heard from again.

Very slowly, he opened his eyes. His eyelids felt terrifically heavy. As far as he could judge from the pressure of the couch against his skin, the gravity was normal; nevertheless, moving his eyelids seemed almost an impossible job.

After long concentration, he got them fully open. The instrument chassis was directly before him, extended over his diaphragm on its elbow joint. Still without moving anything but his eyes— and those only with the utmost patience—he checked each of the meters. Velocity: 22.4 c. Operating temperature: normal. Ship temperature: 37° C. Air pressure: 778 mm. Fuel: No. 1 tank full, No. 2 tank full, No. 3 tank full, No. 4 tank nine-tenths full. Gravity: 1 g. Calendar: stopped.

He looked at it closely, though his eyes seemed to focus very slowly, too. It was, of course, something more than a calendar—it was an all-purpose clock, designed to show him the passage of seconds, as well as of the ten months his trip was supposed to take to the double star. But there was no doubt about it: the second-hand was motionless.

That was the second abnormality. Garrard felt an impulse to get up and see if he could start the clock again. Perhaps the trouble had been temporary and safely in the past. Immediately there sounded in his head the injunction he had drilled into himself for a full month before the trip had begun—

Don't move!

Don't move until you know the situation as far as it can be known without moving. Whatever it was that had snatched Brown and Cellini irretrievably beyond human ken was potent, and totally beyond anticipation. They had both been excellent men, intelligent, resourceful, trained to the point of diminishing returns and not a micron beyond that point—the best men in the Project. Preparations for every knowable kind of trouble had been built into their ships, as they had been built into the DFC-3. Therefore, if there was something wrong nevertheless, it would be something that might strike from some commonplace quarter—and strike only once.

He listened to the humming. It was even and placid, and not very loud, but it disturbed him deeply. The overdrive was supposed to be inaudible, and the tapes from the first unmanned test vehicles had recorded no such hum. The noise did not appear to interfere with the overdrive's operation, or to indicate any failure in it. It was just an irrelevancy for which he could find no reason.

But the reason existed. Garrard did not intend to do so much as draw another breath until he found out what it was.

Incredibly, he realized for the first time that he had not in fact drawn one single breath since he had first come to. Though he felt not the slightest discomfort, the discovery called up so overwhelming a flash of panic that he very nearly sat bolt upright on the couch. Luckily—or so it seemed, after the panic had begun to ebb—the curious lethargy which had affected his eyelids appeared to involve his whole body, for the impulse was gone before he could summon the energy to answer it. And the panic, poignant though it had been for an instant, turned out to be wholly intellectual. In a moment, he was observing that his failure to breathe in no way discommoded him as far as he could tell—it was just there, waiting to be explained. . . .

Or to kill him. But it hadn't, yet.

Engines humming; eyelids heavy; breathing absent; calendar stopped. The four facts added up to nothing. The temptation to move something—even if it were only a big toe—was strong, but Garrard fought it back. He had been awake only a short while— half an hour at most—and already had noticed four abnormalities. There were bound to be more, anomalies more subtle than these four; but available to close examination before he had to move. Nor was there anything in particular that he had to do, aside from caring for his own wants; the Project, on the chance that Brown's and Cellini's failure to return had resulted from some tampering with the overdrive, had made everything in the DFC-3 subject only to the computer. In a very real sense, Garrard was just along for the ride. Only when the overdrive was off could he adjust—

Pock.

It was a soft, low-pitched noise, rather like a cork coming out of a wine bottle. It seemed to have come just from the right of the control chassis. He halted a sudden jerk of his head on the cushions toward it with a flat fiat of will. Slowly, he moved his eyes in that direction.

He could see nothing that might have caused the sound. The ship's temperature dial showed no change, which ruled out a heat noise from differential contraction or expansion—the only possible explanation he could bring to mind.

He closed his eyes—a process which turned out to be just as difficult as opening them had been—and tried to visualize what the calendar had looked like when he had first come out of anesthesia. After he got a clear and—he was almost sure—accurate picture, Garrard opened his eyes again.

The sound had been the calendar, advancing one second. It was now motionless again, apparently stopped.

He did not know how long it took the second-hand to make that jump, normally; the question had never come up. Certainly the jump, when it came at the end of each second, had been too fast for the eye to follow.

Belatedly, he realized what all this cogitation was costing him in terms of essential information. The calendar had moved. Above all and before anything else, he *must* know exactly how long it took it to move again. . . .

He began to count, allowing an arbitrary five seconds lost. *One-and-a-six, one-and-a-seven, one-and-an-eight—*

Garrard had gotten only that far when he found himself plunged into hell.

First, and utterly without reason, a sickening fear flooded swiftly through his veins, becoming more and more intense. His bowels began to knot, with infinite slowness. His whole body became a field of small, slow pulses—not so much shaking him as putting his limbs into contrary joggling motions, and making his skin ripple gently under his clothing. Against the hum another sound became audible, a nearly subsonic thunder which seemed to be inside his head. Still the fear mounted, and with it came the pain, and the tenesmus—a boardlike stiffening of his muscles, particularly across his abdomen and his shoulders, but affecting his forearms almost as grievously. He felt himself beginning, very gradually, to double at the middle, a motion about which he could do precisely nothing—a terrifying kind of dynamic paralysis. . . .

It lasted for hours. At the height of it, Garrard's mind, even his very personality, was washed out utterly; he was only a vessel of horror. When some few trickles of reason began to return over that burning desert of reasonless emotion, he found that he was sitting up on the cushions, and that with one arm he had thrust the control chassis back on its elbow so that it no longer jutted over his body. His clothing was wet with perspiration, which stubbornly refused to evaporate or to cool him. And his lungs ached a little, although he could still detect no breathing.

What under God had happened? Was it this that had killed Brown and Cellini? For it would kill Garrard, too—of that he was sure—if it happened often. It would kill him even if it happened only twice more, if the next two such things followed the first one closely. At the very best it would make a slobbering idiot of him; and though the computer might bring Garrard and the ship back to Earth, it would not be able to tell the Project about this tornado of senseless fear.

The calendar said that the eternity in hell had taken three seconds. As he looked at it in academic indignation, it said *pock* and condescended to make the total seizure four seconds long. With grim determination, Garrard began to count again.

He took care to establish the counting as an absolutely even, automatic process which would not stop at the back of his mind no matter what other problem he tackled along with it, or what emotional typhoons should interrupt him. Really compulsive counting cannot be stopped by anything—not the transports of love nor the agonies of empires. Garrard knew the dangers in deliberately setting up such a mechanism in his mind, but he also knew how desperately he needed to time that clock tick. He was beginning to understand what had happened to him—but he needed exact measurement before he could put that understanding to use.

Of course there had been plenty of speculation on the possible effect of the overdrive on the subjective time of the pilot, but none of it had come to much. At any speed below the velocity of light, subjective and objective time were exactly the same as far as the pilot was concerned. For an observer on Earth, time aboard the ship would appear to be vastly slowed at near-light speeds; but for the pilot himself there would be no apparent change.

Since flight beyond the speed of light was impossible—although for slightly differing reasons—by both the current theories of relativity, neither theory had offered any clue as to what would happen on board a translight ship. They would not allow that any such ship could even exist. The Haertel transformation, on which, in effect, the DFC-3 flew, was nonrelativistic: it showed that the apparent elapsed time of a translight journey should be identical in ship-time, and in the time of observers at both ends of the trip.

But since ship and pilot were part of the same system, both covered by the same expression in Haertel's equation, it had never occurred to anyone that the pilot and the ship might keep different times. The notion was ridiculous.

One-and-a-sevenhundredone, one-and-a-sevenhundredtwo, one - and - a - sevenhundredthree, one - and - a - sevenhundred four . . .

The ship was keeping ship-time, which was identical with observer-time. It would arrive at the Alpha Centauri system in ten months. But the pilot was keeping Garrard-time, and it was beginning to look as though he wasn't going to arrive at all.

It was impossible, but there it was. Something—almost certainly an unsuspected physiological side effect of the overdrive field on human metabolism, an effect which naturally could not have been detected in the preliminary, robot-piloted tests of the overdrive—had speeded up Garrard's subjective apprehension of time, and had done a thorough job of it.

The second-hand began a slow, preliminary quivering as the calendar's innards began to apply power to it. *Seventy-hundred-forty-one,seventy-hundred-forty-two,seventy-hundred-forty-three...*

At the count of 7,058 the second-hand began the jump to the next graduation. It took it several apparent minutes to get across the tiny distance, and several more to come completely to rest. Later still, the sound came to him:

pock.

In a fever of thought, but without any real physical agitation, his mind began to manipulate the figures. Since it took him longer to count an individual number as the number became larger, the interval between the two calendar ticks probably was closer to

7,200 seconds than to 7,058. Figuring backward brought him quickly to the equivalence he wanted:

One second in ship-time was two hours in Garrard-time.

Had he really been counting for what was, for him, two whole hours? There seemed to be no doubt about it. It looked like a long trip ahead.

Just how long it was going to be struck him with stunning force. Time had been slowed for him by a factor of 7,200. He would get to Alpha Centauri in just 72,000 months.

Which was—

Six thousand years!

2

Garrard sat motionless for a long time after that, the Nessus-shirt of warm sweat swathing him persistently, refusing even to cool. There was, after all, no hurry.

Six thousand years. There would be food and water and air for all that time, or for sixty or six hundred thousand years; the ship would synthesize his needs, as a matter of course, for as long as the fuel lasted, and the fuel bred itself. Even if Garrard ate a meal every three seconds of objective, or ship, time (which, he realized suddenly, he wouldn't be able to do, for it took the ship several seconds of objective time to prepare and serve up a meal once it was ordered; he'd be lucky if he ate once a day, Garrard-time), there would be no reason to fear any shortage of supplies. That had been one of the earliest of the possibilities for disaster that the Project engineers had ruled out in the design of the DFC-3.

But nobody had thought to provide a mechanism which would indefinitely refurbish Garrard. After six thousand years, there would be nothing left of him but a faint film of dust on the DFC-3's dully gleaming horizontal surfaces. His corpse might outlast him a while, since the ship itself was sterile—but eventually he would be consumed by the bacteria which he carried in his own digestive tract. He needed those bacteria to synthesize part of his B-vitamin needs while he lived, but they would consume him without compunction once he had ceased to be as complicated and delicately balanced a thing as a pilot—or as any other kind of life.

Garrard was, in short, to die before the DFC-3 had gotten fairly away from Sol; and when, after 12,000 apparent years, the DFC-3 returned to Earth, not even his mummy would be still aboard.

The chill that went through him at that seemed almost unrelated to the way he thought he felt about the discovery; it lasted an enormously long time, and insofar as he could characterize it at all, it seemed to be a chill of urgency and excitement—not at all the kind of chill he should be feeling at a virtual death sentence. Luckily it was not as intolerably violent as the last such emotional convulsion; and when it was over, two clock ticks later, it left behind a residuum of doubt.

Suppose that this effect of time-stretching was only mental? The rest of his bodily processes might still be keeping ship-time; Garrard had no immediate reason to believe otherwise. If so, he would be able to move about only on ship-time, too; it would take many apparent months to complete the simplest task.

But he would live, if that were the case. His mind would arrive at Alpha Centauri six thousand years older, and perhaps madder, than his body, but he would live.

If, on the other hand, his bodily movements were going to be as fast as his mental processes, he would have to be enormously careful. He would have to move slowly and exert as little force as possible. The normal human hand movement, in such a task as lifting a pencil, took the pencil from a state of rest to another state of rest by imparting to it an acceleration of about two feet per second per second—and, of course, decelerated it by the same amount. If Garrard were to attempt to impart to a two-pound weight, which was keeping ship-time, an acceleration of 14,440 ft/sec^2 in his time, he'd have to exert a force of 900 pounds on it.

The point was not that it couldn't be done—but that it would take as much effort as pushing a stalled jeep. He'd never be able to lift that pencil with his forearm muscles alone; he'd have to put his back into the task.

And the human body wasn't engineered to maintain stresses of that magnitude indefinitely. Not even the most powerful professional weight-lifter is forced to show his prowess throughout every minute of every day.

Pock.

That was the calendar again; another second had gone by. Or another two hours. It had certainly seemed longer than a second, but less than two hours, too. Evidently subjective time was an intensively recomplicated measure. Even in this world of micro-time —in which Garrard's mind, at least, seemed to be operating—he could make the lapses between calendar ticks seem a little shorter by becoming actively interested in some problem or other. That would help, during the waking hours, but it would help only if the rest of his body were *not* keeping the same time as his mind. If it were not, then he would lead an incredibly active, but perhaps not intolerable, mental life during the many centuries of his awake-time, and would be mercifully asleep for nearly as long.

Both problems—that of how much force he could exert with his body, and how long he could hope to be asleep in his mind— emerged simultaneously into the forefront of his consciousness while he still sat inertly on the hammock, their terms still much muddled together. After the single tick of the calendar, the ship— or the part of it that Garrard could see from here—settled back into complete rigidity. The sound of the engines, too, did not seem to vary in frequency or amplitude, at least as far as his ears could tell. He was still not breathing. Nothing moved, nothing changed.

It was the fact that he could still detect no motion of his diaphragm or his rib cage that decided him at last. His body had to be keeping ship-time, otherwise he would have blacked out from oxygen starvation long before now. That assumption explained, too, those two incredibly prolonged, seemingly sourceless saturnalias of emotion through which he had suffered: they had been nothing more nor less than the response of his endocrine glands to the purely intellectual reactions he had experienced earlier. He had discovered that he was not breathing, had felt a flash of panic and had tried to sit up. Long after his mind had forgotten those two impulses, they had inched their way from his brain down his nerves to the glands and muscles involved, and actual, *physical* panic had supervened. When that was over, he actually *was* sitting up, though the flood of adrenalin had prevented his noticing the motion as he had made it. The later chill—

less violent, and apparently associated with the discovery that he might die long before the trip was completed—actually had been his body's response to a much earlier mental command; the abstract fever of interest he had felt while computing the time differential had been responsible for it.

Obviously, he was going to have to be very careful with apparently cold and intellectual impulses of any kind—or he would pay for them later with a prolonged and agonizing glandular reaction. Nevertheless, the discovery gave him considerable satisfaction, and Garrard allowed it free play; it certainly could not hurt him to feel pleased for a few hours, and the glandular pleasure might even prove helpful if it caught him at a moment of mental depression. Six thousand years, after all, provided a considerable number of opportunities for feeling down-in-the-mouth; so it would be best to encourage all pleasure moments, and let the after-reaction last as long as it might. It would be the instants of panic, of fear, of gloom, which he would have to regulate sternly the moment they came into his mind; it would be those which would otherwise plunge him into four, five, six, perhaps even ten, Garrard-hours of emotional inferno.

Pock.

There now, that was very good: there had been two Garrard-hours which he had passed with virtually no difficulty of any kind, and without being especially conscious of their passage. If he could really settle down and become used to this kind of scheduling, the trip might not be as bad as he had at first feared. Sleep would take immense bites out of it; and during the waking periods he could put in one hell of a lot of creative thinking. During a single day of ship-time, Garrard could get in more thinking than any philosopher of Earth could have managed during an entire lifetime. Garrard could, if he disciplined himself sufficiently, devote his mind for a century to running down the consequences of a single thought, down to the last detail, and still have millennia left to go on to the next thought. What panoplies of pure reason could he not have assembled by the time 6,000 years had gone by? With sufficient concentration, he might come up with the solution to the Problem of Evil between breakfast and dinner of a single ship's

day, and in a ship's month might put his finger on the First Cause!
Pock.

Not that Garrard was sanguine enough to expect that he would
remain logical or even sane throughout the trip. The vista was still
grim, in much of its detail. But the opportunities, too, were there.
He felt a momentary regret that it hadn't been Haertel, rather
than himself, who had been given such an opportunity—
Pock.

—for the old man could certainly have made better use of it
than Garrard could. The situation demanded someone trained in
the highest rigors of mathematics to be put to the best conceivable
use. Still and all Garrard began to feel—
Pock.

—that he would give a good account of himself, and it tickled
him to realize that (as long as he held on to his essential sanity)
he would return—
Pock.

—to Earth after ten Earth months with knowledge centuries advanced beyond anything—
Pock.

—that Haertel knew, or that anyone could know—
Pock.

—who had to work within a normal lifetime. *Pck.* The whole
prospect tickled him. *Pck.* Even the clock tick seemed more cheerful. *Pck.* He felt fairly safe now *Pck* in disregarding his drilled-in
command *Pck* against moving *Pck,* since in any *Pck* event the *Pck*
had already *Pck* moved *Pck* without *Pck* being *Pck* harmed *Pck*
Pck Pck Pck Pck *pckpckpckpckpckpckpck. . . .*

He yawned, stretched, and got up. It wouldn't do to be too
pleased, after all. There were certainly many problems that still
needed coping with, such as how to keep the impulse toward getting
a ship-time task performed going, while his higher centers were
following the ramifications of some purely philosophical point.
And besides . . .

And besides, he had just moved.

More than that, he had just performed a complicated maneuver
with his body *in normal time!*

Before Garrard looked at the calendar itself, the message it had been ticking away at him had penetrated. While he had been enjoying the protracted, glandular backwash of his earlier feeling of satisfaction, he had failed to notice, at least consciously, that the calendar was accelerating.

Good-bye, vast ethical systems which would dwarf the Greeks. Good-bye, calculuses aeons advanced beyond the spinor calculus of Dirac. Good-bye, cosmologies by Garrard which would allot the Almighty a job as third-assistant-waterboy in an n-dimensional backfield.

Good-bye, also, to a project he had once tried to undertake in college—to describe and count the positions of love, of which, according to under-the-counter myth, there were supposed to be at least forty-eight. Garrard had never been able to carry his tally beyond twenty, and he had just lost what was probably his last opportunity to try again.

The micro-time in which he had been living had worn off, only a few objective minutes after the ship had gone into overdrive and he had come out of the anesthetic. The long intellectual agony, with its glandular counterpoint, had come to nothing. Garrard was now keeping ship-time.

Garrard sat back down on the hammock, uncertain whether to be bitter or relieved. Neither emotion satisfied him in the end; he simply felt unsatisfied. Micro-time had been bad enough while it lasted; but now it was gone, and everything seemed normal. How could so transient a thing have killed Brown and Cellini? They were stable men, more stable, by his own private estimation, than Garrard himself. Yet he had come through it. Was there more to it than this?

And if there was—what, conceivably, could it be?

There was no answer. At his elbow, on the control chassis which he had thrust aside during that first moment of infinitely protracted panic, the calendar continued to tick. The engine noise was gone. His breath came and went in natural rhythm. He felt light and strong. The ship was quiet, calm, unchanging.

The calendar ticked, faster and faster. It reached and passed the first hour, ship-time, of flight in overdrive.

Pock.

Garrard looked up in surprise. The familiar noise, this time, had been the hour-hand jumping one unit. The minute-hand was already sweeping past the past half-hour. The second-hand was whirling like a propeller—and while he watched it, it speeded up to complete invisibility—

Pock.

Another hour. The half-hour already passed. *Pock.* Another hour. *Pock.* Another. *Pock. Pock. Pock, Pock, Pock, Pock, pck-pck-pck-pck-pckpckpckpck.* . . .

The hands of the calendar swirled toward invisibility as time ran away with Garrard. Yet the ship did not change. It stayed there, rigid, inviolate, invulnerable. When the date tumblers reached a speed at which Garrard could no longer read them, he discovered that once more he could not move—and that, although his whole body seemed to be aflutter like that of a hummingbird, nothing coherent was coming to him through his senses. The room was dimming, becoming redder; or no, it was . . .

But he never saw the end of the process, never was allowed to look from the pinnacle of macro-time toward which the Haertel overdrive was taking him.

Pseudo-death took him first.

3

That Garrard did not die completely, and within a comparatively short time after the DFC-3 had gone into overdrive, was due to the purest of accidents; but Garrard did not know that. In fact, he knew nothing at all for an indefinite period, sitting rigid and staring, his metabolism slowed down to next to nothing, his mind almost utterly inactive. From time to time, a single wave of low-level metabolic activity passed through him—what an electrician might have termed a "maintenance turnover"—in response to the urgings of some occult survival urge; but these were of so basic a nature as to reach his consciousness not at all. This was the pseudo-death.

When the observer actually arrived, however, Garrard woke. He could make very little sense out of what he saw or felt even now; but one fact was clear: the overdrive was off—and with it the crazy alterations in time rates—and there was strong light coming through one of the ports. The first leg of the trip was over. It had been these two changes in his environment which had restored him to life.

The thing (or things) which had restored him to consciousness, however, was—it was what? It made no sense. It was a construction, a rather fragile one, which completely surrounded his hammock. No, it wasn't a construction, but evidently something alive —a living being, organized horizontally, that had arranged itself in a circle about him. No, it was a number of beings. Or a combination of all of these things.

How it had gotten into the ship was a mystery, but there it was. Or there they were.

"How do you hear?" the creature said abruptly. Its voice, or their voices, came at equal volume from every point in the circle, but not from any particular point in it. Garrard could think of no reason why that should be unusual.

"I—" he said. "Or we—we hear with our ears. Here."

His answer, with its unintentionally long chain of open vowel sounds, rang ridiculously. He wondered why he was speaking such an odd language.

"We-they wooed to pitch you-yours thiswise," the creature said. With a thump, a book from the DFC-3's ample library fell to the deck beside the hammock. "We wooed there and there and there for a many. You are the being-Garrard. We-they are the clinester-ton beademung, with all of love."

"With all of love," Garrard echoed. The beademung's use of the language they both were speaking was odd; but again Garrard could find no logical reason why the beademung's usage should be considered wrong.

"Are—are you-they from Alpha Centauri?" he said hesitantly.

"Yes, we hear the twin radioceles, that show there beyond the gift-orifices. We-they pitched that the being-Garrard with most adoration these twins and had mind to them, soft and loud alike. How do you hear?"

This time the being-Garrard understood the question. "I hear Earth," he said. "But that is very soft, and does not show."

"Yes," said the beademung. "It is a harmony, not a first, as ours. The All-Devouring listens to lovers there, not on the radioceles. Let me-mine pitch you-yours so to have mind of the rodalent beademung and other brothers and lovers, along the channel which is fragrant to the being-Garrard."

Garrard found that he understood the speech without difficulty. The thought occurred to him that to understand a language on its own terms—without having to put it back into English in one's own mind—is an ability that is won only with difficulty and long practice. Yet, instantly his mind said, "But it *is* English," which of course it was. The offer the clinesterton beademung had just made was enormously hearted, and he in turn was much minded and of love, to his own delighting as well as to the beademungen; that almost went without saying.

There were many matings of ships after that, and the being-Garrard pitched the harmonies of the beademungen, leaving his ship with the many gift-orifices in harmonic for the All-Devouring to love, while the beademungen made show of they-theirs.

He tried, also, to tell how he was out of love with the overdrive, which wooed only spaces and times, and made featurelings. The rodalent beademung wooed the overdrive, but it did not pitch he-them.

Then the being-Garrard knew that all the time was devoured, and he must hear Earth again.

"I pitch you-them to fullest love," he told the beademungen, "I shall adore the radioceles of Alpha and Proxima Centauri, 'on Earth as it is in Heaven.' Now the overdrive my-other must woo and win me, and make me adore a featureling much like silence."

"But you will be pitched again," the clinesterton beademung said. "After you have adored Earth. You are much loved by Time, the All-Devouring. We-they shall wait for this othering."

Privately Garrard did not faith as much, but he said, "Yes, we-they will make a new wooing of the beademungen at some other radiant. With all of love."

On this the beademungen made and pitched adorations, and in the midst the overdrive cut in. The ship with the many gift-orfices and the being-Garrard him-other saw the twin radioceles sundered away.

Then, once more, came the pseudo-death.

4

When the small candle lit in the endless cavern of Garrard's pseudo-dead mind, the DFC-3 was well inside the orbit of Uranus. Since the Sun was still very small and distant, it made no spectacular display through the nearby port, and nothing called him from the post-death sleep for nearly two days.

The computers waited patiently for him. They were no longer immune to his control; he could now tool the ship back to Earth himself if he so desired. But the computers were also designed to take into account the fact that he might be truly dead by the time the DFC-3 got back. After giving him a solid week, during which time he did nothing but sleep, they took over again. Radio signals began to go out, tuned to a special channel.

An hour later, a very weak signal came back. It was only a directional signal, and it made no sound inside the DFC-3—but it was sufficient to put the big ship in motion again.

It was that which woke Garrard. His conscious mind was still glazed over with the icy spume of the pseudo-death; and as far as he could see the interior of the cabin had not changed one whit, except for the book on the deck—

The book. The clinesterton beademung had dropped it there. But what under God was a clinesterton beademung? And what was he, Garrard, crying about? It didn't make sense. He remembered dimly some kind of experience out there by the Centauri twins—

—the twin radioceles—

There was another one of those words. It seemed to have Greek roots, but he knew no Greek—and besides, why would Centaurians speak Greek?

He leaned forward and actuated the switch which would roll the shutter off the front port, actually a telescope with a translucent viewing screen. It showed a few stars, and a faint nimbus off on one edge which might be the Sun. At about one o'clock on the screen was a planet about the size of a pea which had tiny projections, like teacup handles, on each side. The DFC-3 hadn't passed Saturn on its way out; at that time it had been on the other side of the Sun from the route the starship had had to follow. But the planet was certainly difficult to mistake.

Garrard was on his way home—and he was still alive and sane. Or was he still sane? These fantasies about Centaurians—which still seemed to have such a profound emotional effect upon him— did not argue very well for the stability of his mind.

But they were fading rapidly. When he discovered, clutching at the handiest fragments of the "memories," that the plural of *beademung* was *beademungen*, he stopped taking the problem seriously. Obviously a race of Centaurians who spoke Greek wouldn't also be forming weak German plurals. The whole business had obviously been thrown up by his unconscious.

But what *had* he found by the Centaurus stars?

There was no answer to that question but that incomprehensible garble about love, the All-Devouring, and beademungen. Possibly, he had never seen the Centaurus stars at all, but had been lying here, cold as a mackerel, for the entire twenty months.

Or had it been 12,000 years? After the tricks the overdrive had played with time, there was no way to tell what the objective date actually was. Frantically Garrard put the telescope into action. Where was the Earth? After 12,000 years—

The Earth was there. Which, he realized swiftly, proved nothing. The Earth had lasted for many millions of years; 12,000 years was nothing to a planet. The Moon was there, too; both were plainly visible, on the far side of the Sun—but not too far to pick them out clearly, with the telescope at highest power. Garrard could even see a clear sun-highlight on the Atlantic Ocean, not far east of Greenland; evidently the computers were bringing the DFC-3 in on the Earth from about 23° north of the plane of the ecliptic.

The Moon, too, had not changed. He could even see on its face the huge splash of white, mimicking the sun-highlight on Earth's ocean, which was the magnesium hydroxide landing beacon, which had been dusted over the Mare Vaporum in the earliest days of space flight, with a dark spot on its southern edge which could only be the crater Monilius.

But that again proved nothing. The Moon never changed. A film of dust laid down by modern man on its face would last for millennia—what, after all, existed on the Moon to blow it away? The Mare Vaporum beacon covered more than 4,000 square miles; age would not dim it, nor could man himself undo it—either accidentally, or on purpose—in anything under a century. When you dust an area that large on a world without atmosphere, it stays dusted.

He checked the stars against his charts. They hadn't moved; why should they have, in only 12,000 years? The pointer stars in the Dipper still pointed to Polaris. Draco, like a fantastic bit of tape, wound between the two Bears, and Cepheus and Cassiopeia, as it always had done. These constellations told him only that it was spring in the northern hemisphere of Earth.

But spring of what year?

Then, suddenly, it occurred to Garrard that he had a method of finding the answer. The Moon causes tides in the Earth, and action and reaction are always equal and opposite. The Moon cannot move things on Earth without itself being affected—and that effect shows up in the Moon's angular momentum. The Moon's distance from the Earth increases steadily by 0.6 inch every year. At the end of 12,000 years, it should be 600 feet farther away from the Earth.

Was it possible to measure? Garrard doubted it, but he got out his ephemeris and his dividers anyhow, and took pictures. While he worked, the Earth grew nearer. By the time he had finished his first calculation—which was indecisive, because it allowed a margin for error greater than the distances he was trying to check—Earth and Moon were close enough in the telescope to permit much more accurate measurements.

Which were, he realized wryly, quite unnecessary. The computer had brought the DFC-3 back, not to an observed sun or planet, but simply to a calculated point. That Earth and Moon would not be near that point when the DFC-3 returned was not an assumption that the computer could make. That the Earth was visible from here was already good and sufficient proof that no more time had elapsed than had been calculated for from the beginning.

This was hardly new to Garrard; it had simply been retired to the back of his mind. Actually he had been doing all this figuring for one reason, and one reason only: because deep in his brain, set to work by himself, there was a mechanism that demanded counting. Long ago, while he was still trying to time the ship's calendar, he had initiated compulsive counting—and it appeared that he had been counting ever since. That had been one of the known dangers of deliberately starting such a mental mechanism; and now it was bearing fruit in these perfectly useless astronomical exercises.

The insight was healing. He finished the figures roughly, and that unheard moron deep inside his brain stopped counting at last. It had been pawing its abacus for twenty months now, and Garrard imagined that it was as glad to be retired as he was to feel it go.

His radio squawked, and said anxiously, "DFC-3, DFC-3. Garrard, do you hear me? Are you still alive? Everybody's going wild down here. Garrard, if you hear me, call us!"

It was Haertel's voice. Garrard closed the dividers so convulsively that one of the points nipped into the heel of his hand. "Haertel, I'm here. DFC-3 to the Project. This is Garrard." And then, without knowing quite why, he added: "With all of love."

Haertel, after all the hoopla was over, was more than interested in the time effects. "It certainly enlarges the manifold in which I was working," he said. "But I think we can account for it in the transformation. Perhaps even factor it out, which would eliminate it as far as the pilot is concerned. We'll see, anyhow."

Garrard swirled his highball reflectively. In Haertel's cramped old office, in the Project's administration shack, he felt both strange and as old, as compressed, constricted. He said, "I don't think I'd do that, Adolph. I think it saved my life."

"How?"

"I told you that I seemed to die after a while. Since I got home, I've been reading; and I've discovered that the psychologists take far less stock in the individuality of the human psyche than you and I do. You and I are physical scientists, so we think about the world as being all outside our skins—something which is to be observed, but which doesn't alter the essential *I*. But evidently, that old solipsistic position isn't quite true. Our very personalities, really, depend in large part upon *all* the things in our environment, large and small, that exist outside our skins. If by some means you could cut a human being off from every sense impression that comes to him from outside, he would cease to exist as a personality within two or three minutes. Probably he would die."

"Unquote: Harry Stack Sullivan," Haertel said, dryly. "So?"

"So," Garrard said, "think of what a monotonous environment the inside of a spaceship is. It's perfectly rigid, still, unchanging, lifeless. In ordinary interplanetary flight, in such an environment, even the most hardened spaceman may go off his rocker now and then. You know the typical spaceman's psychosis as well as I do, I suppose. The man's personality goes rigid, just like his surroundings. Usually he recovers as soon as he makes port, and makes contact with a more-or-less normal world again.

"But in the DFC-3, I was cut off from the world around me much more severely. I couldn't look outside the ports—I was in overdrive, and there was nothing to see. I couldn't communicate with home, because I was going faster than light. And then I found I couldn't move either, for an enormous long while; and that even the instruments that are in constant change for the usual spaceman wouldn't be in motion for me. Even those were fixed.

"After the time rate began to pick up, I found myself in an even more impossible box. The instruments moved, all right, but then they moved too *fast* for me to read them. The whole situation was now utterly rigid—and, in effect, I died. I froze as solid as the ship around me, and stayed that way as long as the overdrive was on."

"By that showing," Haertel said dryly, "the time effects were hardly your friends."

"But they were, Adolph. Look. Your engines act on subjective time; they keep it varying along continuous curves—from far-too-slow to far-too-fast—and, I suppose, back down again. Now, this is a *situation of continuous change*. It wasn't marked enough, in the long run, to keep me out of pseudo-death; but it was sufficient to protect me from being obliterated altogether, which I think is what happened to Brown and Cellini. Those men knew that they could shut down the overdrive if they could just get to it, and they killed themselves trying. But I knew that I just had to sit and take it—and, by my great good luck, your sine-curve time variation made it possible for me to survive."

"Ah, ah," Haertel said. "A point worth considering—though I doubt that it will make interstellar travel very popular!"

He dropped back into silence, his thin mouth pursed. Garrard took a grateful pull at his drink.

At last Haertel said: "Why are you in trouble over these Centaurians? It seems to me that you have done a good job. It was nothing that you were a hero—any fool can be brave—but I see also that you *thought*, where Brown and Cellini evidently only reacted. Is there some secret about what you found when you reached those two stars?"

Garrard said, "Yes, there is. But I've already told you what it is. When I came out of the pseudo-death, I was just a sort of plastic palimpsest upon which anybody could have made a mark. My own environment, my ordinary Earth environment, was a hell of a long way off. My present surroundings were nearly as rigid as they had ever been. When I met the Centaurians—if I did, and I'm not at all sure of that—*they* became the most important thing in my world, and my personality changed to accommodate and understand them. That was a change about which I couldn't do a thing.

"Possibly I did understand them. But the man who understood them wasn't the same man you're talking to now, Adolph. Now that I'm back on Earth, I don't understand that man. He even spoke English in a way that's gibberish to me. If I can't understand myself during that period—and I can't; I don't even believe that that man was the Garrard I know—what hope have I of telling you or the Project about the Centaurians? They found me in a controlled environment, and they altered me by entering it. Now that they're gone, nothing comes through; I don't even understand why I think they spoke English!"

"Did they have a name for themselves?"

"Sure," Garrard said. "They were the beademungen."

"What did they look like?"

"I never saw them."

Haertel leaned forward. "Then . . ."

"I heard them. I think." Garrard shrugged, and tasted his Scotch again. He was home, and on the whole he was pleased.

But in his malleable mind he heard someone say. *On Earth, as it is in Heaven;* and then, in another voice, which might also have been his own (why had he thought "him-other"?), *It is later than you think.*

"Adolph," he said, "is this all there is to it? Or are we going to go on with it from here? How long will it take to make a better starship, a DFC-4?"

"Many years," Haertel said, smiling kindly. "Don't be anxious, Garrard. You've come back, which is more than the others managed to do, and nobody will ask you to go out again. I really think that it's hardly likely that we'll get another ship built during your lifetime; and even if we do, we'll be slow to launch it. We really have very little information about what kind of playground you found out there."

"I'll go," Garrard said. "I'm not afraid to go back—I'd like to go. Now that I know how the DFC-3 behaves, I could take it out again, bring you back proper maps, tapes, photos."

"Do you really think," Haertel said, his face suddenly serious, "that we could let the DFC-3 go out again? Garrard, we're going to take that ship apart practically molecule by molecule; that's preliminary to the building of any DFC-4. And no more can we let you go. I don't mean to be cruel, but has it occurred to you that this desire to go back may be the result of some kind of post-hypnotic suggestion? If so, the more badly you want to go back, the more dangerous to us all you may be. We are going to have to examine you just as thoroughly as we do the ship. If these beade-mungen wanted you to come back, they must have had a reason —and we have to know that reason."

Garrard nodded, but he knew that Haertel could see the slight movement of his eyebrows and the wrinkles forming in his forehead, the contractions of the small muscles which stop the flow of tears only to make grief patent on the rest of the face.

"In short," he said, *"don't move."*

Haertel looked politely puzzled. Garrard, however, could say nothing more. He had returned to humanity's common time, and would never leave it again.

Not even, for all his dimly remembered promise, with all there was left in him of love.

THE GAME OF RAT AND DRAGON

by CORDWAINER SMITH

FOREWORD
by Kingsley Amis

THE AUTHOR

CORDWAINER SMITH was the pseudonym adopted by Dr. Paul Linebarger, professor of social science at Johns Hopkins University, when writing science fiction. The identity of the man behind the pen name was a closely guarded secret until Dr. Linebarger's death in 1966. Under his own name, Linebarger took part as a civilian adviser in three wars and wrote an authoritative manual of military psychology; his first "Cordwainer Smith" story, published in an obscure science-fiction magazine in 1948, was an astonishingly masterly and idiosyncratic work that gave its author a measure of instant fame. His eagerly awaited second story—the one reprinted here—did not appear until 1955. In the last years of his life, "Smith" produced a series of long stories, all set in a consistent framework, comprising a vivid panorama of thousands of years to come.

THE CRITIC

British novelist KINGSLEY AMIS (*Lucky Jim, That Uncertain Feeling,* etc.) has been a close observer of the science-fiction scene for many years. In 1959 he delivered a series of lectures on science fiction at Princeton University as part of the program of Christian Gauss Seminars in Criticism; these were published in 1960 as *New Maps of Hell,* one of the few book-length critical discourses on science fiction. With Robert Conquest, he edits the *Spectrum* series of s-f anthologies, and he has had at least one story ("Something Strange") published in a science-fiction magazine.

Foreword

Cordwainer Smith—I was first attracted to this magnificently
original and imaginative writer by his equally magnificent name.
Much more recently I discovered it was not his own, but the
result of an inescapable necessity to invent it. It has the true ring
of inevitability. *Cordwainer* Smith—nothing to do with cords or
wains, by the way, but a corruption of something like "Cordovaner,"
one who works in leather from Cordova in Spain, hence a
shoemaker. (The ancient guild of the trade, dating from medieval
times, retains the term "cordwainer" in its title to this day.)
But Shoemaker Smith would never have done. Nor would anything
other than Cordwainer *Smith*. Imagine the alternatives—Cordwainer
Pohl, Cordwainer Sheckley, Cordwainer Blish . . . Not right at all.

The above is not mere waffling. Anybody who has written any
sort of fiction—and almost nobody who has not—understands
something of the immense, shadowy power of names and titles.
Dickens is the immediate example. Although he did not discover
the principle, he was its great developer. Mr. Jingle, Mr. Micawber,
Mrs. Jellyby, Mr. Pecksniff, Abel Magwitch, Little Dorrit—all,
in some indefinable way, immediately and clearly appropriate.
When I, as an English mainstream novelist and so an heir of Dickens
whether I like it or not—when I decide whether (say) to call a
desirable girl Emily Capes or Fiona Daventry, I am deciding
between two kinds of desirability as well as two kinds of girl.

The science-fiction writer, in particular, depends importantly on
this effect. It is of the very nature of his genre that, like
Shakespeare's poet, he "gives to airy nothing a local habitation
and a name"—my italics. And the names he invents, names of
unknown places and undiscovered sciences and unheard-of life
forms as well as human beings, go a long way toward shaping
his creations. A remote world called (say) MacVitie's Planet is
going to be different from one called Procyon IX in many ways,
not just in that the one is almost certainly colonized and the
other almost certainly not.

Cordwainer Smith, as his choice of a pseudonym shows, understood and relied a great deal on the power of names, their sound and their ability to evoke something out of nothing. Go-Captain Alvarez, Lost C'mell, and Lord Jestocost of the Instrumentality, the ancient city of Meeya Meefla, Alpha Ralpha Boulevard—the last one, especially, carries that phantom sense of appropriateness we associate more readily with legends and fairy tales, with Cambuscan of Tartary, Quetzalcoatl, the land of Cokaygne, and the Marquis of Carabas. Science fiction is both more and less than myth, but now and then we cannot help seeing that the two look rather like different approaches to the same thing. An old-fashioned view—and therefore a very necessary one to put forward at the present time. (More of that later.)

The title of "The Game of Rat and Dragon" is everything we expect from its author, a phrase full of implication, a promise of something doubly frightening, physical and spiritual horror in combination. Or triply frightening: sinister games, games that turn out not to be games at all, have provided some of the best and most characteristic moments in science fiction. But, again as we expect from Cordwainer Smith, the horror, though real enough, turns out to be subordinated to something else, something gentler, more affectionate, more melancholy. The real subject of the story is the incurable lack of communication between man's mind and other kinds of mind, even though the human pinlighters and their nonhuman Partners are telepathically linked when they defend their ship against what the humans see and feel as Dragons of space and the Partners as the Rats of the Up-and-Out.

I cannot bring myself to divulge any more of the plot of this sad, haunting tale; the revelation of what the Partners are is no great theatrical stroke—it is very much played down—but I would not want to anticipate it for those encountering it for the first time. There is a lot more than that in the story. Seasoned readers of science fiction will admire the author's attempt to describe, or to suggest, the mental and physical sensations accompanying the shift into faster-than-light space-drive, so that something fresh and exciting is made out of one of the oldest, most threadbare conventions of the genre. Similarly, the equally unpromising convention of telepathy—which is all it is, being scientifically in continuing disrepute, and fictionally a frequent short cut to boredom—has been pondered upon and extended until it begins

to seem possible after all. And, of course, there are the names—
Murr, the Lady May, Captain Wow—that do so much to make the
Partners appear both real and wonderful.

Real and wonderful: terms of praise that can be applied with
varying emphasis to most of the successful science fiction I can
think of. Perhaps they define it, in the sense that reality without
wonder applies to mere fiction about science and scientists,
whereas wonder without reality leads straight to fantasy in both the
literary and the psychological sense of the word—the uncontrolled
exercise of the imagination (or, rather, of the fancy), self-indulgent
and ultimately sterile.

Some years ago I delivered a series of lectures on science fiction
at Princeton University, and felt I was being a tremendous
pioneer by doing so. Their theme (which I still more or less
believe in) was that this kind of writing deserves to be taken just
as seriously as any other kind, that it provides fresh insights into
our society and consciousness, and so on. Science fiction, I said,
reaching a rather wider audience when I published the lectures
as a book, was a genuine art form.

New Maps of Hell got a good reception from editors and
educated reviewers of science fiction. But, at the British s-f
convention in 1960, the writer E. C. Tubb attacked it violently.
He said in effect (to paraphrase my not totally clear recollection)
that the result of bringing highbrow values into the field would be
to ruin it. I did my best to sneer this off at the time, naturally,
but in the last year or two I have begun to see what I think Ted
Tubb meant. I think he foresaw what I did not, that it would do
no harm to tell the public how good the stuff could be, but
that the trouble with telling the writers they were creative
artists was that they would believe it.

Anyway, without taking on myself too paranoid a share of the
blame, that looks very much like what has happened over the last
decade. Traditionally, it was the themes and myths, the subject
matter of science fiction—space, monster, plague, robot, planet,
weapon, alien, even telepath—that gave it its distinctive quality.
Now—among the newer writers, at any rate—treatment and style,
necessary as adjuncts, have taken over as the chief interests.
This is artistic decadence in the truest and most established sense
of the term. The injection of new ideas from advanced mainstream
writing, which (like an idiot) I saw as desirable, has meant the

injection of footling "experiment," of techniques supposedly
derived from experiences under drugs, and of anti-fiction in general.

Woe to science fiction! (Woe likewise, incidentally, to jazz,
which has always been so curiously akin to our genre throughout
its history, and is showing such strong signs of ending up the
same way.) Well, demi-woe, anyway, at least. The more established
writers carry on as before, but so often it is so much as before.
And something pernicious in the cultural atmosphere must surely
bear part of the blame for the decline of a writer like J. G. Ballard,
possessed of such great natural gifts, into a kind of hippie verbal
entertainer, unable to see further than the next (irrelevant,
actually not even original, tried decades ago and rightly
forgotten) breakthrough in style and expression. Woe, indeed!

I agree that the above lecture is rather shamelessly inserted into
what is supposed to be a specific critical introduction. However,
I felt I had to get it in somewhere—not just somewhere, anywhere,
but where I envisage an audience primarily of science-fiction
writers and readers. Before the general public I will go on stoutly
maintaining what I wish I thought was true, that the genre is
getting better all the time.

And I feel I have a little justification, too, because Cordwainer
Smith is such a fine example of the kind of writer I admire,
inside or outside the science-fiction field: original, but making no
parade of his originality; aware of the work of his predecessors,
humbly and responsibly seeking to extend its boundaries; above all,
not looking for the protection which obscurity affords, but, in
a genuinely adventurous spirit, never leaving the reader in the
least doubt about what is represented as taking place. True
imagination is a function of the intellect and the will. How many
of our avant-garde understand that?

THE GAME OF RAT AND DRAGON

The Table

Pinlighting is a hell of a way to earn a living. Underhill was furious as he closed the door behind himself. It didn't make much sense to wear a uniform and look like a soldier if people didn't appreciate what you did.

He sat down in his chair, laid his head back in the headrest and pulled the helmet down over his forehead.

As he waited for the pin-set to warm up, he remembered the girl in the outer corridor. She had looked at it, then looked at him scornfully.

"Meow." That was all she had said. Yet it had cut him like a knife.

What did she think he was—a fool, a loafer, a uniformed non-entity? Didn't she know that for every half hour of pinlighting, he got a minimum of two months' recuperation in the hospital?

By now the set was warm. He felt the squares of space around him, sensed himself at the middle of an immense grid, a cubic grid, full of nothing. Out in that nothingness, he could sense the hollow aching horror of space itself and could feel the terrible anxiety which his mind encountered whenever it met the faintest trace of inert dust.

As he relaxed, the comforting solidity of the Sun, the clockwork of the familiar planets and the Moon rang in on him. Our own Solar System was as charming and as simple as an ancient cuckoo clock filled with familiar ticking and with reassuring noises. The odd little moons of Mars swung around their planet like frantic mice, yet their regularity was itself an assurance that all was well. Far above the plane of the ecliptic, he could feel half a ton of dust more or less drifting outside the lanes of human travel.

Here there was nothing to fight, nothing to challenge the mind, to tear the living soul out of a body with its roots dripping in effluvium as tangible as blood.

Nothing ever moved in on the Solar System. He could wear the pin-set forever and be nothing more than a sort of telepathic astronomer, a man who could feel the hot, warm protection of the Sun throbbing and burning against his living mind.

Woodley came in.

"Same old ticking world," said Underhill. "Nothing to report. No wonder they didn't develop the pin-set until they began to planoform. Down here with the hot Sun around us, it feels so good and so quiet. You can feel everything spinning and turning. It's nice and sharp and compact. It's sort of like sitting around home."

Woodley grunted. He was not much given to flights of fantasy.

Undeterred, Underhill went on, "It must have been pretty good to have been an Ancient Man. I wonder why they burned up their world with war. They didn't have to planoform. They didn't have to go out to earn their livings among the stars. They didn't have to dodge the Rats or play the Game. They couldn't have invented pinlighting because they didn't have any need of it, did they, Woodley?"

Woodley grunted, "Uh-huh." Woodley was twenty-six years old and due to retire in one more year. He already had a farm picked out. He had gotten through ten years of hard work pinlighting with the best of them. He had kept his sanity by not thinking very much about his job, meeting the strains of the task whenever he had to meet them and thinking nothing more about his duties until the next emergency arose.

Woodley never made a point of getting popular among the Partners. None of the Partners liked him very much. Some of them even resented him. He was suspected of thinking ugly thoughts of the Partners on occasion, but since none of the Partners ever thought a complaint in articulate form, the other pinlighters and the Chiefs of the Instrumentaiity left him alone.

Underhill was still full of the wonder of their job. Happily he babbled on, "What does happen to us when we planoform? Do you think it's sort of like dying? Did you ever see anybody who had his soul pulled out?"

"Pulling souls is just a way of talking about it," said Woodley. "After all these years, nobody knows whether we have souls or not."

"But I saw one once. I saw what Dogwood looked like when he came apart. There was something funny. It looked wet and sort of sticky as if it were bleeding and it went out of him—and you know what they did to Dogwood? They took him away, up in that part of the hospital where you and I never go—way up at the top part where the others are, where the others always have to go if they are alive after the Rats of the Up-and-Out have gotten them."

Woodley sat down and lit an ancient pipe. He was burning something called tobacco in it. It was a dirty sort of habit, but it made him look very dashing and adventurous.

"Look here, youngster. You don't have to worry about that stuff. Pinlighting is getting better all the time. The Partners are getting better. I've seen them pinlight two Rats forty-six million miles apart in one and a half milliseconds. As long as people had to try to work the pin-sets themselves, there was always the chance that with a minimum of four hundred milliseconds for the human mind to set a pinlight, we wouldn't light the Rats up fast enough to protect our planoforming ships. The Partners have changed all that. Once they get going, they're faster than Rats. And they always will be. I know it's not easy, letting a Partner share your mind—"

"It's not easy for them, either," said Underhill.

"Don't worry about them. They're not human. Let them take care of themselves. I've seen more pinlighters go crazy from monkeying around with Partners than I have ever seen caught by the Rats. How many do you actually know of them that got grabbed by Rats?"

Underhill looked down at his fingers, which shone green and purple in the vivid light thrown by the tuned-in pin-set, and counted ships. The thumb for the *Andromeda,* lost with crew and passengers, the index finger and the middle finger for *Release Ships* 43 and 56, found with their pin-sets burned out and every man, woman, and child on board dead or insane. The ring finger, the little finger, and the thumb of the other hand were the first three battleships to be lost to the Rats—lost as people realized that there was something out there *underneath space itself* which was alive, capricious and malevolent.

Planoforming was sort of funny. It felt like—

Like nothing much.

Like the twinge of a mild electric shock.

Like the ache of a sore tooth bitten on for the first time.

Like a slightly painful flash of light against the eyes.

Yet in that time, a forty-thousand-ton ship lifting free above Earth disappeared somehow or other into two dimensions and appeared half a light-year or fifty light-years off.

At one moment, he would be sitting in the Fighting Room, the pin-set ready and the familiar Solar System ticking around inside his head. For a second or a year (he could never tell how long it really was, subjectively), the funny little flash went through him and then he was loose in the Up-and-Out, the terrible open spaces between the stars, where the stars themselves felt like pimples on his telepathic mind and the planets were too far away to be sensed or read.

Somewhere in this outer space, a gruesome death awaited, death and horror of a kind which Man had never encountered until he reached out for interstellar space itself. Apparently the light of the suns kept the Dragons away.

Dragons. That was what people called them. To ordinary people, there was nothing, nothing except the shiver of planoforming and the hammer blow of sudden death or the dark spastic note of lunacy descending into their minds.

But to the telepaths, they were Dragons.

In the fraction of a second between the telepaths' awareness of a hostile something out in the black hollow nothingness of space and the impact of a ferocious, ruinous psychic blow against all living things within the ship, the telepaths had sensed entities something like the Dragons of ancient human lore, beasts more clever than beasts, demons more tangible than demons, hungry vortices of aliveness and hate compounded by unknown means out of the thin tenuous matter between the stars.

It took a surviving ship to bring back the news—a ship in which, by sheer chance, a telepath had a light-beam ready, turning it out at the innocent dust so that, within the panorama of his mind, the Dragon dissolved into nothing at all and the other passengers, themselves non-telepathic, went about their way not realizing that their own immediate deaths had been averted.

From then on, it was easy—almost.

Planoforming ships always carried telepaths. Telepaths had their sensitiveness enlarged to an immense range by the pin-sets, which were telepathic amplifiers adapted to the mammal mind. The pin-sets in turn were electronically geared into small dirigible light-bombs. Light did it.

Light broke up the Dragons, allowed the ships to reform three-dimensionally, skip, skip, skip, as they moved from star to star.

The odds suddenly moved down from a hundred to one against mankind to sixty to forty in mankind's favor.

This was not enough. The telepaths were trained to become ultra-sensitive, trained to become aware of the Dragons in less than a millisecond.

But it was found that the Dragons could move a million miles in just under two milliseconds and that this was not enough for the human mind to activate the light-beams.

Attempts had been made to sheathe the ships in light at all times. This defense wore out.

As mankind learned about the Dragons, so, too, apparently, the Dragons learned about mankind. Somehow they flattened their own bulk and came in on extremely flat trajectories very quickly.

Intense light was needed, light of sunlike intensity. This could be provided only by light-bombs. Pinlighting came into existence.

Pinlighting consisted of the detonation of ultra-vivid miniature photonuclear bombs, which converted a few ounces of a magnesium isotope into pure visible radiance.

The odds kept coming down in mankind's favor, yet ships were being lost.

It became so bad that people didn't even want to find the ships because the rescuers knew what they would see. It was sad to bring back to Earth three hundred bodies ready for burial and two hundred or three hundred lunatics, damaged beyond repair, to be wakened, and fed, and cleaned, and put to sleep, wakened and fed again until their lives were ended.

Telepaths tried to reach into the minds of the psychotics who had been damaged by the Dragons, but they found nothing there beyond vivid spouting columns of fiery terror bursting from the primordial id itself, the volcanic source of life.

Then came the Partners.

Man and Partner could do together what Man could not do alone. Men had the intellect. Partners had the speed.

The Partners rode their tiny craft, no larger than footballs, out-side the spaceships. They planoformed with the ships. They rode beside them in their six-pound craft ready to attack.

The tiny ships of the Partners were swift. Each carried a dozen pinlights, bombs no bigger than thimbles.

The pinlighters threw the Partners—quite literally threw—by means of mind-to-firing relays direct at the Dragons.

What seemed to be Dragons to the human mind appeared in the form of gigantic Rats in the minds of the Partners.

Out in the pitiless nothingness of space, the Partners' minds responded to an instinct as old as life. The Partners attacked, strik-ing with a speed faster than Man's, going from attack to attack until the Rats or themselves were destroyed. Almost all the time, it was the Partners who won.

With the safety of the interstellar skip, skip, skip of the ships, commerce increased immensely, the population of all the colonies went up, and the demand for trained Partners increased.

Underhill and Woodley were a part of the third generation of pinlighters and yet, to them, it seemed as though their craft had endured forever.

Gearing space into minds by means of the pin-set, adding the Partners to those minds, keying up the mind for the tension of a fight on which all depended—this was more than human synapses could stand for long. Underhill needed his two months' rest after half an hour of fighting. Woodley needed his retirement after ten years of service. They were young. They were good. But they had limitations.

So much depended on the choice of Partners, so much on the sheer luck of who drew whom.

The Shuffle

Father Moontree and the little girl named West entered the room. They were the other two pinlighters. The human complement of the Fighting Room was now complete.

Father Moontree was a red-faced man of forty-five who had lived the peaceful life of a farmer until he reached his fortieth year. Only then, belatedly, did the authorities find he was telepathic and agree to let him late in life enter upon the career of pinlighter. He did well at it, but he was fantastically old for this kind of business.

Father Moontree looked at the glum Woodley and the musing Underhill. "How're the youngsters today? Ready for a good fight?"

"Father always wants a fight," giggled the little girl named West. She was such a little girl. Her giggle was high and childish. She looked like the last person in the world one would expect to find in the rough, sharp dueling of pinlighting.

Underhill had been amused one time when he found one of the most sluggish of the Partners coming away happy from contact with the mind of the girl named West.

Usually the Partners didn't care much about the human minds with which they were paired for the journey. The Partners seemed to take the attitude that human minds were complex and fouled up beyond belief, anyhow. No Partner ever questioned the superiority of the human mind, though very few of the Partners were much impressed by that superiority.

The Partners liked people. They were willing to fight with them.

They were even willing to die for them. But when a Partner liked an individual the way, for example, that Captain Wow or the Lady May liked Underhill, the liking had nothing to do with intellect. It was a matter of temperament, of feel.

Underhill knew perfectly well that Captain Wow regarded his, Underhill's, brains as silly. What Captain Wow liked was Underhill's friendly emotional structure, the cheerfulness and glint of wicked amusement that shot through Underhill's unconscious thought patterns, and the gaiety with which Underhill faced danger. The words, the history books, the ideas, the science—Underhill could sense all that in his own mind, reflected back from Captain Wow's mind, as so much rubbish.

Miss West looked at Underhill. "I bet you've put stickum on the stones."

"I did not!"

Underhill felt his ears grow red with embarrassment. During his novitiate, he had tried to cheat in the lottery because he got particularly fond of a special Partner, a lovely young mother named Murr. It was so much easier to operate with Murr and she was so affectionate toward him that he forgot pinlighting was hard work and that he was not instructed to have a good time with his Partner. They were both designed and prepared to go into deadly battle together.

One cheating had been enough. They had found him out and he had been laughed at for years.

Father Moontree picked up the imitation-leather cup and shook the stone dice which assigned them their Partners for the trip. By senior rights, he took first draw.

He grimaced. He had drawn a greedy old character, a tough old male whose mind was full of slobbering thoughts of food, veritable oceans full of half-spoiled fish. Father Moontree had once said that he burped cod-liver oil for weeks after drawing that particular glutton, so strongly had the telepathic image of fish impressed itself upon his mind. Yet the glutton was a glutton for danger as well as for fish. He had killed sixty-three Dragons, more than any other Partner in the service, and was quite literally worth his weight in gold.

The little girl West came next. She drew Captain Wow. When she saw who it was, she smiled.

"I *like* him," she said. "He's such fun to fight with. He feels so nice and cuddly in my mind."

"Cuddly, hell," said Woodley. "I've been in his mind, too. It's the most leering mind in this ship, bar none."

"Nasty man," said the little girl. She said it declaratively, without reproach.

Underhill, looking at her, shivered.

He didn't see how she could take Captain Wow so calmly. Captain Wow's mind *did* leer. When Captain Wow got excited in the middle of a battle, confused images of Dragons, deadly Rats, luscious beds, the smell of fish, and the shock of space all scrambled together in his mind as he and Captain Wow, their consciousness linked together through the pin-set, became a fantastic composite of human being and Persian cat.

That's the trouble with working with cats, thought Underhill. It's a pity that nothing else anywhere will serve as Partner. Cats were all right once you got in touch with them telepathically. They were smart enough to meet the needs of the fight, but their motives and desires were certainly different from those of humans.

They were companionable enough as long as you thought tangible images at them, but their minds just closed up and went to sleep when you recited Shakespeare or Colegrove, or if you tried to tell them what space was.

It was sort of funny realizing that the Partners who were so grim and mature out here in space were the same cute little animals that people had used as pets for thousands of years back on Earth. He had embarrassed himself more than once while on the ground saluting perfectly ordinary non-telepathic cats because he had forgotten for the moment that they were not Partners.

He picked up the cup and shook out his stone dice.

He was lucky—he drew the Lady May.

The Lady May was the most thoughtful Partner he had ever met. In her, the finely bred pedigree mind of a Persian cat had reached one of its highest peaks of development. She was more complex than any human woman, but the complexity was all one of emotions, memory, hope and discriminated experience—experience sorted through without benefit of words.

When he had first come into contact with her mind, he was astonished at its clarity. With her he remembered her kittenhood. He remembered every mating experience she had ever had. He saw in a half-recognizable gallery all the other pinlighters with whom she had been paired for the fight. And he saw himself radiant, cheerful and desirable.

He even thought he caught the edge of a longing—

A very flattering and yearning thought: *What a pity he is not a cat.*

Woodley picked up the last stone. He drew what he deserved—a sullen, scared old tomcat with none of the verve of Captain Wow. Woodley's Partner was the most animal of all the cats on the ship, a low, brutish type with a dull mind. Even telepathy had not refined his character. His ears were half chewed off from the first fights in which he had engaged.

He was a serviceable fighter, nothing more.

Woodley grunted.

Underhill glanced at him oddly. Didn't Woodley ever do anything but grunt?

Father Moontree looked at the other three. "You might as well get your Partners now. I'll let the Scanner know we're ready to go into the Up-and-Out."

The Deal

Underhill spun the combination lock on the Lady May's cage. He woke her gently and took her into his arms. She humped her back luxuriously, stretched her claws, started to purr, thought better of it, and licked him on the wrist instead. He did not have the pin-set on, so their minds were closed to each other, but in the angle of her mustache and in the movement of her ears, he caught some sense of gratification she experienced in finding him as her Partner.

He talked to her in human speech, even though speech meant nothing to a cat when the pin-set was not on.

"It's a damn shame, sending a sweet little thing like you whirling around in the coldness of nothing to hunt for Rats that are bigger and deadlier than all of us put together. You didn't ask for this kind of fight, did you?"

For answer, she licked his hand, purred, tickled his cheek with her long fluffy tail, turned around and faced him, golden eyes shining.

For a moment, they stared at each other, man squatting, cat standing erect on her hind legs, front claws digging into his knee. Human eyes and cat eyes looked across an immensity which no words could meet, but which affection spanned in a single glance.

"Time to get in," he said.

She walked docilely into her spheroid carrier. She climbed in. He saw to it that her miniature pin-set rested firmly and comfortably against the base of her brain. He made sure that her claws were padded so that she could not tear herself in the excitement of battle.

Softly he said to her, "Ready?"

For answer, she preened her back as much as her harness would permit and purred softly within the confines of the frame that held her.

He slapped down the lid and watched the sealant ooze around the seam. For a few hours, she was welded into her projectile until a workman with a short cutting arc would remove her after she had done her duty.

He picked up the entire projectile and slipped it into the ejection tube. He closed the door of the tube, spun the lock, seated himself in his chair, and put his own pin-set on.

Once again he flung the switch.

He sat in a small room, *small, small, warm, warm,* the bodies of the other three people moving close around him, the tangible lights in the ceiling bright and heavy against his closed eyelids.

As the pin-set warmed, the room fell away. The other people ceased to be people and became small glowing heaps of fire, embers, dark red fire, with the consciousness of life burning like old red coals in a country fireplace.

As the pin-set warmed a little more, he felt Earth just below him, felt the ship slipping away, felt the turning Moon as it swung on the far side of the world, felt the planets and the hot, clear goodness of the Sun which kept the Dragons so far from mankind's native ground.

Finally, he reached complete awareness.

He was telepathically alive to a range of millions of miles. He felt the dust which he had noticed earlier high above the ecliptic. With a thrill of warmth and tenderness, he felt the consciousness of the Lady May pouring over into his own. Her consciousness was as gentle and clear and yet sharp to the taste of his mind as if it were scented oil. It felt relaxing and reassuring. He could sense her welcome of him. It was scarcely a thought, just a raw emotion of greeting.

At last they were one again.

In a tiny remote corner of his mind, as tiny as the smallest toy he had ever seen in his childhood, he was still aware of the room and the ship, and of Father Moontree picking up a telephone and speaking to a Scanner captain in charge of the ship.

His telepathic mind caught the idea long before his ears could frame the words. The actual sound followed the idea the way that thunder on an ocean beach follows the lightning inward from far out over the seas.

"The Fighting Room is ready. Clear to planoform, sir."

The Play

Underhill was always a little exasperated the way that Lady May experienced things before he did.

He was braced for the quick vinegar thrill of planoforming, but he caught her report of it before his own nerves could register what happened.

Earth had fallen so far away that he groped for several milliseconds before he found the Sun in the upper rear right-hand corner of his telepathic mind.

That was a good jump, he thought. This way we'll get there in four or five skips.

A few hundred miles outside the ship, the Lady May thought back at him, "O warm, O generous, O gigantic man! O brave, O friendly, O tender and huge Partner! O wonderful with you, with you so good, good, good, warm, warm, now to fight, now to go, good with you. . . ."

He knew that she was not thinking words, that his mind took the clear amiable babble of her cat intellect and translated it into images which his own thinking could record and understand.

Neither one of them was absorbed in the game of mutual greetings. He reached out far beyond her range of perception to see if there was anything near the ship. It was funny how it was possible to do two things at once. He could scan space with his pin-set mind and yet at the same time catch a vagrant thought of hers, a lovely, affectionate thought about a son who had had a golden face and a chest covered with soft, incredibly downy white fur.

While he was still searching, he caught the warning from her.

We jump again!

And so they had. The ship had moved to a second planoform. The stars were different. The Sun was immeasurably far behind. Even the nearest stars were barely in contact. This was good Dragon country, the open, nasty, hollow kind of space. He reached farther, faster, sensing and looking for danger, ready to fling the Lady May at danger wherever he found it.

Terror blazed up in his mind, so sharp, so clear, that it came through as a physical wrench.

The little girl named West had found something—something immense, long, black, sharp, greedy, horrific. She flung Captain Wow at it.

Underhill tried to keep his own mind clear. "Watch out!" he shouted telepathically at the others, trying to move the Lady May around.

At one corner of the battle, he felt the lustful rage of Captain Wow as the big Persian tomcat detonated lights while he approached the streak of dust which threatened the ship and the people within.

The lights scored near-misses.

The dust flattened itself, changing from the shape of a sting-ray into the shape of a spear.

Not three milliseconds had elapsed.

Father Moontree was talking human words and was saying in a voice that moved like cold molasses out of a heavy jar, "C-A-P-T-A-I-N." Underhill knew that the sentence was going to be "Captain, move fast!"

The battle would be fought and finished before Father Moontree got through talking.

Now, fractions of a millisecond later, the Lady May was directly in line.

Here was where the skill and speed of the Partners came in. She could react faster than he. She could see the threat as an immense Rat coming direct at her.

She could fire the light-bombs with a discrimination which he might miss.

He was connected with her mind, but he could not follow it.

His consciousness absorbed the tearing wound inflicted by the alien enemy. It was like no wound on Earth—raw, crazy pain which started like a burn at his navel. He began to writhe in his chair.

Actually he had not yet had time to move a muscle when the Lady May struck back at their enemy.

Five evenly spaced photonuclear bombs blazed out across a hundred thousand miles.

The pain in his mind and body vanished.

He felt a moment of fierce, terrible, feral elation running through the mind of the Lady May as she finished her kill. It was always disappointing to the cats to find out that their enemies whom they sensed as gigantic space Rats disappeared at the moment of destruction.

Then he felt her hurt, the pain and the fear that swept over both of them as the battle, quicker than the movement of an eyelid, had come and gone. In the same instant, there came the sharp and acid twinge of planoform.

Once more the ship went skip.

He could hear Woodley thinking at him, "You don't have to bother much. This old son of a gun and I will take over for a while."

Twice again the twinge, the skip.

He had no idea where he was until the lights of the Caledonia space board shone below.

With a weariness that lay almost beyond the limits of thought, he threw his mind back into rapport with the pin-set, fixing the Lady May's projectile gently and neatly in its launching tube.

She was half dead with fatigue, but he could feel the beat of her heart, could listen to her panting, and he grasped the grateful edge of a thanks reaching from her mind to his.

The Score

They put him in the hospital at Caledonia.

The doctor was friendly but firm. "You actually got touched by that Dragon. That's as close a shave as I've ever seen. It's all so quick that it'll be a long time before we know what happened scientifically, but I suppose you'd be ready for the insane asylum now if the contact had lasted several tenths of a millisecond longer. What kind of cat did you have out in front of you?"

Underhill felt the words coming out of him slowly. Words were such a lot of trouble compared with the speed and the joy of thinking, fast and sharp and clear, mind to mind! But words were all that could reach ordinary people like this doctor.

His mouth moved heavily as he articulated words, "Don't call our Partners cats. The right thing to call them is Partners. They fight for us in a team. You ought to know we call them Partners, not cats. How is mine?"

"I don't know," said the doctor contritely. "We'll find out for you. Meanwhile, old man, you take it easy. There's nothing but rest that can help you. Can you make yourself sleep, or would you like us to give you some kind of sedative?"

"I can sleep," said Underhill. "I just want to know about the Lady May."

The nurse joined in. She was a little antagonistic. "Don't you want to know about the other people?"

"They're okay," said Underhill. "I knew that before I came in here."

He stretched his arms and sighed and grinned at them. He

could see they were relaxing and were beginning to treat him as a person instead of a patient.

"I'm all right," he said. "Just let me know when I can go see my Partner."

A new thought struck him. He looked wildly at the doctor. "They didn't send her off with the ship, did they?"

"I'll find out right away," said the doctor. He gave Underhill a reassuring squeeze of the shoulder and left the room.

The nurse took a napkin off a goblet of chilled fruit juice.

Underhill tried to smile at her. There seemed to be something wrong with the girl. He wished she would go away. First she had started to be friendly and now she was distant again. It's a nuisance being telepathic, he thought. You keep trying to reach even when you are not making contact.

Suddenly she swung around on him.

"You pinlighters! You and your damn cats!"

Just as she stamped out, he burst into her mind. He saw himself a radiant hero, clad in his smooth suede uniform, the pin-set crown shining like ancient royal jewels around his head. He saw his own face, handsome and masculine, shining out of her mind. He saw himself very far away and he saw himself as she hated him.

She hated him in the secrecy of her own mind. She hated him because he was—she thought—proud, and strange, and rich, better and more beautiful than people like her.

He cut off the sight of her mind and, as he buried his face in the pillow, he caught an image of the Lady May.

"She *is* a cat," he thought. "That's *all* she is—a *cat!*"

But that was not how his mind saw her—quick beyond all dreams of speed, sharp, clever, unbelievably graceful, beautiful, wordless and undemanding.

Where would he ever find a woman who could compare with her?

"ALL YOU ZOMBIES—"

by ROBERT A. HEINLEIN

FOREWORD

by Alexei Panshin

THE AUTHOR

ROBERT A. HEINLEIN is one of the acknowledged masters of science fiction. Born in Missouri in 1907, he turned to writing in 1939 after ill health had ended his naval career, and almost at once won acclaim for the clarity, power, and conviction of his science-fiction stories. His long list of books, many of them set in a carefully detailed "future history," comprises a bibliography of science-fiction milestones by itself, taking in such works as *Methusaleh's Children, Stranger in a Strange Land, Beyond This Horizon, The Moon Is a Harsh Mistress*, and *The Man Who Sold the Moon*. Four of his novels have won Hugo awards, a record unapproached by any other writer. "All You Zombies—" was first published in 1959.

THE CRITIC

ALEXEI PANSHIN, a native of Michigan, was born in 1940, attended Michigan State University, and received a master's degree from the University of Chicago in 1966. He is the author of many critical essays on science fiction and has written what is perhaps the first full-length study of a modern s-f writer, *Heinlein in Dimension* (Advent: Publishers, 1968). Panshin's own career as a writer of fiction began with a short story published in 1960. His first science-fiction novel, *Rite of Passage*, published in 1968, received the Nebula award as that year's outstanding s-f book.

Foreword

The point of any fictional form—not just science fiction—is largely to deal with human uncertainties in a constructive way. Authors single out particular uncertainties, often their own, and present them to us as singular cases, and we are thrilled, entertained, or frightened according to the effectiveness with which the uncertainties are presented and the relative ability to cope with them of the characters within the story. One of science fiction's major strengths as a form is that it allows problems to be put purely. The facts of history limit historical fiction. The shape of our society limits contemporary fiction. Science fiction is effective because characters, physical setting, and society can be tailored to the particular problem with which the author has chosen to deal.

"All You Zombies—" is a nightmare, which is to say that its uncertainties are ones we are not ordinarily aware of, as we are aware, for instance, of the uncertainties in people dealing with each other that form the backbone of the standard love story. Nightmares bring uncertainties that we know less well to the forefront of our vision and make us look at them. We are frightened, yes, but we are delighted, too—relieved, perhaps, to have these things out in the open—and so we continue to read.

"All You Zombies—" is a good story, one of the best short works in science fiction and one of Robert Heinlein's best stories, for two reasons. First, it is a double nightmare, combining as it does one of science fiction's favorite uncertainties, time travel, and one of Heinlein's, solipsism. Second, it is effective because it is so short, so crisp, so efficient.

The common appearance of the time-travel theme is added evidence that the name "science fiction" indicates the origins of the field and not its true nature. Time travel is a philosophical concept, not a scientific one. It is, in fact, as has often been pointed out, scientific nonsense. Science fiction, developing in its modern guise out of the radio magazines of Hugo Gernsback in the early years of the century, kept insisting that it was about science. That s-f writers, knowing this, and believing this, kept returning just as insistently to the scientifically unsensible theme of time travel indicates that their viscera knew something that their minds did not.

Time travel is a theme made to order for nightmare. To be taken from the time and place you know and thrust into your future before you are ready to meet it, or returned to your past after you have dealt with it once, is frightening, unsettling, and perhaps fatal. It has meant stories like Ray Bradbury's "A Sound of Thunder," in which the cumulative effects of the crushing of a butterfly in the prehistoric past by a heavy-footed time traveler mean a return to a totally alien world, a statement that actions have larger results than we can see. On the other hand, "The Men Who Murdered Mohammed," by Alfred Bester, a writer who has done extremely effective work with the nightmarish aspects of time travel in half a dozen stories, says that a time traveler in destroying aspects of the past affects the world not at all, but destroys himself, and, by extension, that to lose sight of the past is self-destructive. In recent times we have had "Behold the Man," a Nebula-award-winning story by Michael Moorcock, in which a modern man in ancient Palestine is forced by his own needs to become Jesus Christ, suffer, and die. It is a frightening story to the extent that we all have buried impulses to become Jesus, suffer, and die—and it could only have been put in story form this explicitly as science fiction.

Robert Heinlein has considered time travel most notably twice before: in 1956, in the novel *The Door Into Summer,* which begins as nightmare and manages to find happy resolution; and at the beginning of his career, in the long novelette "By His Bootstraps," which aims at many of the same effects as "All You Zombies—," but which takes more than three times the length to achieve them. "By His Bootstraps," in effect, takes a set piece, a single room and a single character, and forces the character to meet himself some half-dozen times, inevitably recapitulating the words and actions already witnessed, a startling vision of a determined world.

"All You Zombies—" is a stronger story than "By His Bootstraps," however, not only because it is more economical but because "By His Bootstraps" emphasizes the mechanics of the replayed scene over the horror of the deterministic vision, whereas "All You Zombies—" emphasizes the horror of the solipsist vision over the mechanical uncertainties of the time-travel games. This is a theme that Heinlein has been concerned with before, specifically in another early story, "They," in which the protagonist is revealed at the end to be the true center of the universe, distracted from realizing the fact by antagonists defined no more greatly than that they are antagonists. The true horror of this theme is compromised in "They" by the existence of the antagonists. If the central character is as alone and as central as the solipsist vision says he should be, the antagonists should not have the power over him that they do. The theme is more clearly realized in "All You Zombies—" because nothing else in the story is ultimately real. The protagonist is in truth a stranger in a strange land, a stranger alone, a stranger afraid, a stranger in a world he had no part in making and does not understand.

Heinlein, then, in his early stories, had his visions—both in "By His Bootstraps" and in "They"—but they lost effectiveness because he was not able to state them as clearly as he wanted. In "All You Zombies—" he has been able to put the themes of time travel and solipsism together, play them against each other, and thereby state them more effectively than before even though he has not clearly resolved them. In fact, the lack of resolution adds to the power of the story.

And science fiction is the necessary vehicle. This story, too, could not have been written as effectively in any other form.

"ALL YOU ZOMBIES—"

2217 Time Zone V (EST) 7 Nov 1970—NYC-"Pop's Place": I was polishing a brandy snifter when the Unmarried Mother came in. I noted the time—10:17 P.M. zone five, or eastern time, November 7th, 1970. Temporal agents always notice time and date; we must.

The Unmarried Mother was a man twenty-five years old, no taller than I am, childish features and a touchy temper. I didn't like his looks—I never had—but he was a lad I was here to recruit, he was my boy. I gave him my best barkeep's smile.

Maybe I'm too critical. He wasn't swish; his nickname came from what he always said when some nosy type asked him his line: "I'm an unmarried mother." If he felt less than murderous he would add: "at four cents a word. I write confession stories."

If he felt nasty, he would wait for somebody to make something of it. He had a lethal style of infighting, like a female cop—one reason I wanted him. Not the only one.

He had a load on and his face showed that he despised people more than usual. Silently I poured a double shot of Old Underwear and left the bottle. He drank it, poured another.

I wiped the bar top. "How's the 'Unmarried Mother' racket?"

His fingers tightened on the glass and he seemed about to throw it at me; I felt for the sap under the bar. In temporal manipulation you try to figure everything, but there are so many factors that you never take needless risks.

223

I saw him relax that tiny amount they teach you to watch for in the Bureau's training school. "Sorry," I said. "Just asking, 'How's business?' Make it 'How's the weather?' "

He looked sour. "Business is okay. I write 'em, they print 'em, I eat."

I poured myself one, leaned toward him. "Matter of fact," I said, "you write a nice stick—I've sampled a few. You have an amazingly sure touch with the woman's angle."

It was a slip I had to risk; he never admitted what pen-names he used. But he was boiled enough to pick up only the last: " 'Woman's angle!' " he repeated with a snort. "Yeah, I know the woman's angle. I should."

"So?" I said doubtfully. "Sisters?"

"No. You wouldn't believe me if I told you."

"Now, now," I answered mildly, "bartenders and psychiatrists learn that nothing is stronger than truth. Why, son, if you heard the stories I do—well, you'd make yourself rich. Incredible."

"You don't know what 'incredible' means!"

"So? Nothing astonishes me. I've always heard worse."

He snorted again. "Want to bet the rest of the bottle?"

"I'll bet a full bottle." I placed one on the bar.

"Well—" I signaled my other bartender to handle the trade. We were at the far end, a single-stool space that I kept private by loading the bar top by it with jars of pickled eggs and other clutter. A few were at the other end watching the fights and some-body was playing the juke box—private as a bed where we were.

"Okay," he began, "to start with, I'm a bastard."

"No distinction around here," I said.

"I mean it," he snapped. "My parents weren't married."

"Still no distinction," I insisted. "Neither were mine."

"When—" He stopped, gave me the first warm look I ever saw on him. "You mean that?"

"I do. A one-hundred-percent bastard. In fact," I added, "No one in my family ever marries. All bastards.

"Oh, that." I showed it to him. "It just looks like a wedding ring; I wear it to keep women off." It is an antique I bought in 1985 from a fellow operative—he had fetched it from pre-Christian Crete. "The Worm Ouroboros . . . the World Snake that eats its own tail, forever without end. A symbol of the Great Paradox."

He barely glanced at it. "If you're really a bastard, you know how it feels. When I was a little girl—"

"Wups!" I said. "Did I hear you correctly?"

"Who's telling this story? When I was a little girl— Look, ever hear of Christine Jorgenson? Or Roberta Cowell?"

"Uh, sex-change cases? You're trying to tell me—"

"Don't interrupt or swelp me, I won't talk. I was a foundling, left at an orphanage in Cleveland in 1945 when I was a month old. When I was a little girl, I envied kids with parents. Then, when I learned about sex—and, believe me, Pop, you learn fast in an orphanage—"

"I know."

"—I made a solemn vow that any kid of mine would have both a pop and a mom. It kept me 'pure,' quite a feat in that vicinity—I had to learn to fight to manage it. Then I got older and realized I stood darn little chance of getting married—for the same reason I hadn't been adopted." He scowled. "I was horse-faced and buck-toothed, flat-chested and straight-haired."

"You don't look any worse than I do."

"Who cares how a barkeep looks? Or a writer? But people wanting to adopt pick little blue-eyed golden-haired morons. Later on, the boys want bulging breasts, a cute face, and an Oh-you-wonder-ful-male manner." He shrugged. "I couldn't compete. So I decided to join the W.E.N.C.H.E.S."

"Eh?"

"Women's Emergency National Corps, Hospitality & Enter-tainment Section, what they now call 'Space Angels'—Auxiliary Nursing Group, Extraterrestrial Legions."

I knew both terms, once I had them chronized. We use still a third name, it's that elite military service corps: Women's Hos-pitality Order Refortifying & Encouraging Spacemen. Vocabulary shift is the worst hurdle in time-jumps—did you know that "service station" once meant a dispensary for petroleum fractions? Once on an assignment in the Churchill Era, a woman said to me, "Meet me at the service station next door"—which is not what it sounds; a "service station" (then) wouldn't have a bed in it.

He went on: "It was when they first admitted you can't send

men into space for months and years and not relieve the tension. You remember how the wowsers screamed?—that improved my chance, since volunteers were scarce. A gal had to be respectable, preferably virgin (they liked to train them from scratch), above average mentally, and stable emotionally. But most volunteers were old hookers, or neurotics who would crack up ten days off Earth. So I didn't need looks; if they accepted me, they would fix my buck teeth, put a wave in my hair, teach me to walk and dance and how to listen to a man pleasingly, and everything else—plus training for the prime duties. They would even use plastic surgery if it would help—nothing too good for Our Boys.

"Best yet, they made sure you didn't get pregnant during your enlistment—and you were almost certain to marry at the end of your hitch. Same way today, A.N.G.E.L.S. marry spacers—they talk the language.

"When I was eighteen I was placed as a 'mother's helper.' This family simply wanted a cheap servant but I didn't mind as I couldn't enlist till I was twenty-one. I did housework and went to night school—pretending to continue my high school typing and shorthand but going to a charm class instead, to better my chances for enlistment.

"Then I met this city slicker with his hundred-dollar bills." He scowled. "The no-good actually did have a wad of hundred-dollar bills. He showed me one night, told me to help myself.

"But I didn't. I liked him. He was the first man I ever met who was nice to me without trying games with me. I quit night school to see him oftener. It was the happiest time of my life.

"Then one night in the park the games began."

He stopped. I said, "And then?"

"And then *nothing!* I never saw him again. He walked me home and told me he loved me—and kissed me good-night and never came back." He looked grim. "If I could find him, I'd kill him!"

"Well," I sympathized, "I know how you feel. But killing him —just for doing what comes naturally—hmm . . . Did you struggle?"

"Huh? What's that got to do with it?"

"Quite a bit. Maybe he deserves a couple of broken arms for running out on you, but—"

"He deserves worse than that! Wait till you hear. Somehow I kept anyone from suspecting and decided it was all for the best. I hadn't really loved him and probably would never love anybody —and I was more eager to join the W.E.N.C.H.E.S. than ever. I wasn't disqualified, they didn't insist on virgins. I cheered up.

"It wasn't until my skirts got tight that I realized."

"Pregnant?"

"He had me higher 'n a kite! Those skinflints I lived with ignored it as long as I could work—then kicked me out and the orphanage wouldn't take me back. I landed in a charity ward surrounded by other big bellies and trotted bedpans until my time came.

"One night I found myself on an operating table, with a nurse saying, 'Relax. Now breathe deeply.'

"I woke up in bed, numb from the chest down. My surgeon came in. 'How do you feel?' he says cheerfully.

" 'Like a mummy.'

" 'Naturally. You're wrapped like one and full of dope to keep you numb. You'll get well—but a Caesarian isn't a hangnail.'

" 'Caesarian' I said. 'Doc—*did I lose the baby?*'

" 'Oh, no. Your baby's fine.'

" 'Oh. Boy or girl?'

" 'A healthy little girl. Five pounds, three ounces.'

"I relaxed. It's something, to have made a baby. I told myself I would go somewhere and tack 'Mrs.' on my name and let the kid think her papa was dead—no orphanage for *my* kid!

"But the surgeon was talking. 'Tell me, uh—' He avoided my name. '—did you ever think your glandular setup was odd?'

"I said, 'Huh? Of course not. What are you driving at?'

"He hesitated. 'I'll give you this in one dose, then a hypo to let you sleep off your jitters. You'll have 'em.'

" 'Why?' I demanded.

" 'Ever hear of that Scottish physician who was female until she was thirty-five?—then had surgery and became legally and medically a man? Got married. All okay.'

" 'What's that got to do with me?'

" 'That's what I'm saying. You're a man.'

"I tried to sit up. *'What?'*

" 'Take it easy. When I opened you, I found a mess. I sent for the Chief of Surgery while I got the baby out, then we held a consultation with you on the table—and worked for hours to salvage what we could. You had two full sets of organs, both immature, but with the female set well enough developed for you to have a baby. They could never be any use to you again, so we took them out and rearranged things so that you can develop properly as a man.' He put a hand on me. 'Don't worry. You're young, your bones will readjust, we'll watch your glandular balance—and make a fine young man out of you.'

"I started to cry. 'What about my *baby?*'

" 'Well, you can't nurse her, you haven't milk enough for a kitten. If I were you, I wouldn't see her—put her up for adoption.'

" *'No!'*

"He shrugged. 'The choice is yours; you're her mother—well, her parent. But don't worry now; we'll get you well first.'

"Next day they let me see the kid and I saw her daily—trying to get used to her. I had never seen a brand-new baby and had no idea how awful they look—my daughter looked like an orange monkey. My feelings changed to cold determination to do right by her. But four weeks later that didn't mean anything."

"Eh?"

"She was snatched."

" 'Snatched?' "

The Unmarried Mother almost knocked over the bottle we had bet. "Kidnapped—stolen from the hospital nursery!" He breathed hard. "How's that for taking the last a man's got to live for?"

"A bad deal," I agreed. "Let's pour you another. No clues?"

"Nothing the police could trace. Somebody came to see her, claimed to be her uncle. While the nurse had her back turned, he walked out with her."

"Description?"

"Just a man, with a face-shaped face, like yours or mine." He frowned. "I think it was the baby's father. The nurse swore it was an older man but he probably used makeup. Who else would swipe my baby? Childless women pull such stunts—but whoever heard of a man doing it?"

"What happened to you then?"

"Eleven more months of that grim place and three operations. In four months I started to grow a beard; before I was out I was shaving regularly . . . and no longer doubted that I was male." He grinned wryly. "I was staring down nurses' necklines."

"Well," I said, "seems to me you came through okay. Here you are, a normal man, making good money, no real troubles. And the life of a female is not an easy one."

He glared at me. "A lot you know about it!"

"So?"

"Ever hear the expression 'a ruined woman'?"

"Mmm, years ago. Doesn't mean much today."

"I was as ruined as a woman can be; that bum *really* ruined me— I was no longer a woman . . . and I didn't know *how* to be a man."

"Takes getting used to, I suppose."

"You have no idea. I don't mean learning how to dress, or not walking into the wrong rest room; I learned those in the hospital. But how could I *live*? What job could I get? Hell, I couldn't even drive a car. I didn't know a trade; I couldn't do manual labor— too much scar tissue, too tender.

"I hated him for having ruined me for the W.E.N.C.H.E.S., too, but I didn't know how much until I tried to join the Space Corps instead. One look at my belly and I was marked unfit for military service. The medical officer spent time on me just from curiosity; he had read about my case.

"So I changed my name and came to New York. I got by as a fry cook, then rented a typewriter and set myself up as a public stenographer—what a laugh! In four months I typed four letters and one manuscript. The manuscript was for *Real Life Tales* and a waste of paper, but the goof who wrote it sold it. Which gave me an idea; I bought a stack of confession magazines and studied them." He looked cynical. "Now you know how I get the authentic woman's angle on an unmarried-mother story . . . through the only version I haven't sold—the true one. Do I win the bottle?"

I pushed it toward him. I was upset myself, but there was work to do. I said, "Son, you still want to lay hands on that so-and-so?"

His eyes lighted up—a feral gleam.

"Hold it!" I said. "You wouldn't kill him?"

He chuckled nastily. "Try me."

"Take it easy. I know more about it than you think I do. I can help you. I know where he is."

He reached across the bar. *"Where is he?"*

I said softly, "Let go my shirt, sonny—or you'll land in the alley and we'll tell the cops you fainted." I showed him the sap.

He let go. "Sorry. But where is he?" He looked at me. "And how do you know so much?"

"All in good time. There are records—hospital records, orphanage records, medical records. The matron of your orphanage was Mrs. Fetherage—right? She was followed by Mrs. Gruenstein—right? Your name, as a girl, was 'Jane'—right? And you didn't tell me any of this—right?"

I had him baffled and a bit scared. "What's this? You trying to make trouble for me?"

"No indeed. I've your welfare at heart. I can put this character in your lap. You do to him as you see fit—and I guarantee that you'll get away with it. But I don't think you'll kill him. You'd be nuts to—and you aren't nuts. Not quite."

He brushed it aside. "Cut the noise. *Where is he?"*

I poured him a short one; he was drunk but anger was offsetting it. "Not so fast. I do something for you—you do something for me."

"Uh . . . what?"

"You don't like your work. What would you say to high pay, steady work, unlimited expense account, your own boss on the job, and lots of variety and adventure?"

He stared. "I'd say, 'Get those goddam reindeer off my roof!' Shove it, Pop—there's no such job."

"Okay, put it this way: I hand him to you, you settle with him, then try my job. If it's not all I claim—well, I can't hold you."

He was wavering; the last drink did it. "When d'yuh d'liver 'im?" he said thickly.

He shoved out his hand. "It's a deal!"

"If it's a deal—*right now!"*

I nodded to my assistant to watch both ends, noted the time—2300—started to duck through the gate under the bar—when the juke box blared out: "I'm My Own Grandpaw!" The service man had orders to load it with Americana and classics because I couldn't stomach the "music" of 1970, but I hadn't known that tape was in it. I called out, "Shut that off! Give the customer his money back." I added, "Storeroom, back in a moment," and headed there with my Unmarried Mother following.

It was down the passage across from the johns, a steel door to which no one but my day manager and myself had a key; inside was a door to an inner room to which only I had a key. We went there.

He looked blearily around at windowless walls. "Where is 'e?"

"Right away." I opened a case, the only thing in the room; it was a U.S.F.F. Co-ordinates Transformer Field Kit, series 1992, Mod. II—a beauty, no moving parts, weight twenty-three kilos fully charged, and shaped to pass as a suitcase. I had adjusted it precisely earlier that day; all I had to do was to shake out the metal net which limits the transformation field.

Which I did. "What's that?" he demanded.

"Time machine," I said and tossed the net over us.

"Hey!" he yelled and stepped back. There is a technique to this; the net has to be thrown so that the subject will instinctively step back *onto* the metal mesh, then you close the net with both of you inside completely—else you might leave shoe soles behind or a piece of foot, or scoop up a slice of floor. But that's all the skill it takes. Some agents con a subject into the net; I tell the truth and use that instant of utter astonishment to flip the switch. Which I did.

1030-VI-3 April 1963—Cleveland, Ohio-Apex Bldg.: "Hey!" he repeated. "Take this damn thing off!"

"Sorry," I apologized and did so, stuffed the net into the case, closed it. "You said you wanted to find him."

"But—you said that was a time machine!"

I pointed out a window. "Does that look like November? Or New York?" While he was gawking at new buds and spring weather, I reopened the case, took out a packet of hundred-dollar bills, checked that the numbers and signatures were compatible with 1963. The Temporal Bureau doesn't care how much you spend (it costs nothing) but they don't like unnecessary anachronisms. Too many mistakes, and a general court-martial will exile you for a year in a nasty period, say 1974 with its strict rationing and forced labor. I never make such mistakes; the money was okay.

He turned around and said, "What happened?"

"He's here. Go outside and take him. Here's expense money." I shoved it at him and added, "Settle him, then I'll pick you up."

Hundred-dollar bills have a hypnotic effect on a person not used to them. He was thumbing them unbelievingly as I eased him into the hall, locked him out. The next jump was easy, a small shift in era.

7100-VI-10 March 1964—Cleveland-Apex Bldg.: There was a notice under the door saying that my lease expired next week; otherwise the room looked as it had a moment before. Outside, trees were bare and snow threatened; I hurried, stopping only for contemporary money and a coat, hat, and topcoat I had left there when I leased the room. I hired a car, went to the hospital. It took twenty minutes to bore the nursery attendant to the point where I could swipe the baby without being noticed. We went back to the Apex Building. This dial setting was more involved, as the building did not yet exist in 1945. But I had precalculated it.

0100-VI-20 Sept 1945—Cleveland-Skyview Motel: Field kit, baby, and I arrived in a motel outside town. Earlier I had registered as "Gregory Johnson, Warren, Ohio," so we arrived in a room with curtains closed, windows locked, and doors bolted, and the floor cleared to allow for waver as the machine hunts. You can get a nasty bruise from a chair where it shouldn't be—not the chair, of course, but backlash from the field.

No trouble. Jane was sleeping soundly; I carried her out, put her in a grocery box on the seat of a car I had provided earlier, drove to the orphanage, put her on the steps, drove two blocks to a "service station" (the petroleum-products sort) and phoned the orphanage, drove back in time to see them taking the box inside, kept going and abandoned the car near the motel—walked to it and jumped forward to the Apex Building in 1963.

2200-VI-24 April 1963—Cleveland-Apex Bldg.: I had cut the

time rather fine—temporal accuracy depends on span, except on return to zero. If I had it right, Jane was discovering, out in the park this balmy spring night, that she wasn't quite as "nice" a girl as she had thought. I grabbed a taxi to the home of those skinflints, had the hackie wait around a corner while I lurked in shadows.

Presently I spotted them down the street, arms around each other. He took her up on the porch and made a long job of kissing her good-night—longer than I thought. Then she went in and he came down the walk, turned away. I slid into step and hooked an arm in his. "That's all, son," I announced quietly. "I'm back to pick you up."

"You!" He gasped and caught his breath.

"Me. Now you know who *he* is—and after you think it over you'll know who you are . . . and if you think hard enough, you'll figure out who the baby is . . . and who *I* am."

He didn't answer, he was badly shaken. It's a shock to have it proved to you that you can't resist seducing yourself. I took him to the Apex Building and we jumped again.

2300-VIII-12 Aug 1985—Sub Rockies Base: I woke the duty sergeant, showed my I.D., told the sergeant to bed my companion down with a happy pill and recruit him in the morning. The sergeant looked sour, but rank is rank, regardless of era; he did what I said—thinking, no doubt, that the next time we met he might be the colonel and I the sergeant. Which can happen in our corps. "What name?" he asked.

I wrote it out. He raised his eyebrows. "Like so, eh? *Hmm—*"

"You just do your job, Sergeant." I turned to my companion.

"Son, your troubles are over. You're about to start the best job a man ever held—and you'll do well. *I know.*"

"That you will!" agreed the sergeant. "Look at me—born in 1917—still around, still young, still enjoying life." I went back to the jump room, set everything on preselected zero.

2301-V-7 Nov 1970—NYC-"Pop's Place": I came out of the storeroom carrying a fifth of Drambuie to account for the minute

I had been gone. My assistant was arguing with the customer who had been playing "I'm My Own Grandpaw!" I said, "Oh, let him play it, then unplug it." I was very tired.

It's rough, but somebody must do it and it's very hard to recruit anyone in the later years, since the Mistake of 1972. Can you think of a better source than to pick people all fouled up where they are and give them well-paid, interesting (even though dangerous) work in a necessary cause? Everybody knows now why the Fizzle War of 1963 fizzled. The bomb with New York's number on it didn't go off, a hundred other things didn't go as planned—all arranged by the likes of me.

But not the Mistake of '72; that one is not our fault—and can't be undone; there's no paradox to resolve. A thing either is, or it isn't, now and forever amen. But there won't be another like it; an order dated "1992" takes precedence any year.

I closed five minutes early, leaving a letter in the cash register telling my day manager that I was accepting his offer to buy me out, so see my lawyer as I was leaving on a long vacation. The Bureau might or might not pick up his payments, but they want things left tidy. I went to the room back of the storeroom and forward to 1993.

2200-VII-12 Jan 1993—Sub Rockies Annex-HQ Temporal DOL: I checked in with the duty officer and went to my quarters, intending to sleep for a week. I had fetched the bottle we bet (after all, I won it) and took a drink before I wrote my report. It tasted foul and I wondered why I had ever liked Old Underwear. But it was better than nothing; I don't like to be cold sober, I think too much. But I don't really hit the bottle either; other people have snakes—I have people.

I dictated my report; forty recruitments all okayed by the Psych Bureau—counting my own, which I knew would be okayed. I was here, wasn't I? Then I taped a request for assignment to operations; I was sick of recruiting. I dropped both in the slot and headed for bed.

My eye fell on "The By-Laws of Time," over my bed:

> *Never Do Yesterday What Should Be Done Tomorrow.*
> *If at Last You Do Succeed, Never Try Again.*

A Stitch in Time Saves Nine Billion.
A Paradox May Be Paradoctored.
It Is Earlier When You Think.
Ancestors Are Just People.
Even Jove Nods.

They didn't inspire me the way they had when I was a recruit; thirty subjective-years of time-jumping wears you down. I undressed and when I got down to the hide I looked at my belly. A Caesarian leaves a big scar but I'm so hairy now that I don't notice it unless I look for it.

Then I glanced at the ring on my finger.

The Snake That Eats Its Own Tail, Forever and Ever . . . I *know* where *I* came from—but *where did all you zombies come from?*

I felt a headache coming on, but a headache powder is one thing I do not take. I did once—and you all went away.

So I crawled into bed and whistled out the light.

You aren't really there at all. There isn't anybody but me—Jane—here alone in the dark.

I miss you dreadfully!

THE
SUBLIMINAL
MAN

by J. G. BALLARD

FOREWORD

by H. Bruce Franklin

THE AUTHOR

J. G. BALLARD was born in Shanghai, China, in 1930, spent much of World War II in a Japanese internment camp, and reached Great Britain in 1946. After studying medicine at Cambridge, he served in the Royal Air Force and wrote advertising copy and technical film scripts before taking up fiction. His first science-fiction story was published in 1956. Ballard's early work, though marked by characteristic imagery and style, was relatively conventional in form, but since 1965 he has been a controversial experimentalist generally working in advanced narrative modes. His novels include *The Crystal World, The Wind from Nowhere*, and *The Drowned World*. "The Subliminal Man" was first published in 1963.

THE CRITIC

H. BRUCE FRANKLIN is an associate professor of English at Stanford University. He has edited *Future Perfect: American Science Fiction of the Nineteenth Century* (Oxford University Press, 1966) and is the author of critical works on Herman Melville and on many aspects of science fiction. He teaches a seminar in science fiction at Stanford and is an important figure in the Modern Language Association's conferences on science fiction.

Foreword

The increase in the quantity of objects is accompanied
by an extension of the realm of the alien powers to which
man is subjected, and every new product represents a
new possibility of mutual swindling and mutual plundering.
Man becomes ever poorer as man, his need for money
becomes ever greater if he wants to overpower hostile
being. The power of his money declines in inverse
proportion to the increase in the volume of production:
that is, his neediness grows as the power of money increases.
—KARL MARX,
The Economic and Philosophical Manuscripts of 1844

We talk a lot about science fiction as extrapolation, but in fact
most science fiction does not extrapolate seriously. Instead it takes a
willful, often whimsical, leap into a world spun out of the fantasy
of the author, who then casually throws in some improbable hints
about how that world developed out of (or into) our own. Certainly
science fiction has enriched our common imagination by projecting
worlds millions of years and light-years away, but such projections
become increasingly less scientific and more fantastic the farther
they are from us. Meanwhile, we have a desperate need for scientific,
fictional extrapolation into the immediate future. This job, which
rightfully belongs to science fiction, is being usurped, and performed
dangerously, by paid ideologues of the political-economic status quo,
as in *Markets of the Seventies,* by the editors of *Fortune,* and *Here
Comes Tomorrow: Living and Working in the Year 2000,* written
by the *Wall Street Journal* staff and published by Dow-Jones. "The
Subliminal Man" is a superb example of one of those too rare
science-fiction stories that seriously extrapolate into the next few
decades and do so with some sense of the ideological content of
such an extrapolation.

In this respect, "The Subliminal Man" is an unusual story for
Ballard himself. Ballard is a poet of death whose most typical
fictions are apocalyptic imaginings, beautiful and ghastly visions
of decay, death, despair. His early novels show the conscious

239

origins of this desperate imagination (whereas "The Subliminal Man," as I shall try to demonstrate, analyzes these sources with more precision). *The Wind from Nowhere* (1961) and *The Drowned World* (1962) are science fictions of the wasteland. In one, London looks like "a city of hell"; in the other, it appears "like some imaginary city of hell." On the literal level, both books ascribe the destruction of the human world to a cosmological freak of nature. In the first, a global wind tears down all human buildings and tears apart almost all human relationships, converting the opening scenes of normal sexual alienation and sterility into a dry and dusty inferno. In the other, solar storms have caused the loss of part of the ionosphere, and the sun, burning through the thinner envelope, has converted the world into a steaming swamp, where human buildings lie drowned and human relationships melt back into a primeval and preconscious world dominated by reptiles. Ballard, however, clearly sees his own imaginings as only ostensibly caused by an unnatural quirk of nature. The world of his fiction already exists in the imaginations of a decadent society:

> Over the mantelpiece was a huge painting by the early 20th century surrealist Delvaux, in which ashen-faced women danced naked to the waist with dandified skeletons in tuxedos against a spectral bone-like landscape. On another wall one of Max Ernst's self-devouring phantasmagoric jungles screamed silently to itself, like the sump of some insane unconscious [p. 27].

Later the nightmare paintings, the actual jungle world, and the shared nightmares of the characters merge into each other: the painting by Ernst and the jungle "more and more . . . were coming to resemble each other, and in turn the third nightscape each of them carried within his mind. They never discussed their dreams, the common zone of twilight where they moved at night like the phantoms in the Delvaux painting" (pp. 73–74). As this world develops—that is, reveals its true "nature"—"the once translucent threshold of the womb had vanished, its place taken by the gateway to a sewer," and the hero, an impotent Fisher-King, leaves Beatrice behind and finally loses himself in the festering jungle bubbling out of his author's fantasy. Over and over, Ballard calls that jungle "subliminal," which gives us a clue to understanding the significance of "The Subliminal Man."

In "The Subliminal Man," Ballard goes to the actual sources of his own decadent imaginings of transfiguring death—his own society. It is not nature conquering man but man's own creations, his own productivity, attaining the dumb, senseless, uncontrolled power of primeval nature over him. Here Ballard explores the basic contradiction of decadent capitalism. The economic system, with its fantastic productivity and preposterous inability to satisfy real human needs, has become so completely irrational that it can survive only by enslaving the unconscious to its own most grotesque needs. Man himself must be reduced to a consuming animal below the threshold of conscious thought; he must become subliminal, literally "under the threshold," less than man.

If the products of overdeveloped capitalist society satisfied real human needs, they could be sold through rational explanations of their value. But such is clearly not the case. So in the present stage advertising uses a variety of means to get around rational thinking, which would reject its message, in order to jam that message into our unconscious processes. Behind the simplest singing commercial and the most intricate manipulation of our desires for success, power, fame, riches, and sex lies a vast industry of research on how advertising can exploit us unconsciously. Even the product's container is designed to make us irrational robots, as Gerald Stahl, Executive Vice-President of the Package Designers Council, so eloquently put it: "You have to have a carton that attracts and hypnotizes this woman, like waving a flashlight in front of her eyes." In 1956 some advertising companies took the logical next step and briefly (so far as we know) tried out the mechanism of Ballard's giant signs. Ballard merely extrapolates one stage.

The value of a story like "The Subliminal Man"—that is, how "good" it is—must be measured partly by the accuracy of its extrapolation. This means that we have to do some measuring.

A fashionable idea these days is that advanced industry reduces the amount of human work available, so that one of the main problems of the future will be finding things to do. "The Subliminal Man" displays the opposite: more and more laboring time is required to subsist (that is to satisfy the basic necessities as defined by society), and hence individual laboring time lengthens as the quality of life diminishes. Which is true? The average weekly hours worked by manufacturing production workers in the United States has been consistently rising for over 35 years; the 1962–67 average of 40.8 hours represents a 12% increase over the 1932–35 average and a 2% increase over the 1955–61 average. By 1966, one out of five nonfarm workers—that is, 9.4 million workers—worked 49 hours or more per week. In the average working family, the wife must also work in order to keep up with the credit payments (women now constitute 40% of the civilian work force). Meanwhile, automobile installment credit has gone from $455 million in 1945 to $6 billion in 1950, $18 billion in 1960, and $29 billion in 1965; total installment credit (not counting mortgages) has gone from $2.5 billion in 1945 to $14.7 billion in 1950 and $68.6 billion in 1965; private debt has gone from $250.9 billion in 1950 to $1 trillion 8.5 billion in 1967; and by 1965 the per-capita individual and noncorporate debt— that is, the average amount personally owed by each man, woman, and child—had reached $2,250. And none of this includes the public debt, national, state, and local. Government statistics on take-home pay are misleading, for out of this come all those new sales, property, and state and municipal income taxes needed to pay the interest on the public debt, as well as the payments on that huge private debt. In 1949, the average family was paying 11 cents of every take-home dollar in interest on household debt. By 1967, this figure had doubled: 22 cents out of every take-home dollar was paid to banks and finance companies as interest.

But even more impressive than its description of how the economics of capitalism is developing is the story's portrayal of some of the psychological consequences of this development. Ballard perceives that this superproductivity not only fails to meet actual human needs, but that it must constantly make people needier, more dissatisfied, more voracious, until they themselves become objects of no value to each other or to themselves. Mechanical men and women only make the nightmare more grotesque when they call each other "angel" and "darling" with the same unconsciousness they use in buying, consuming, or hiding the piles of cigarette butts and chocolate wrappings. This wasteland—dry, barren, sterile—can finally be compressed into that magnificent closing image of mechanical death.

My only substantive disagreement with the message of "The Subliminal Man" (and this is nothing if not a story with a message) is that it fails to recognize that more than a lone Hathaway will see "the signs" and revolt. Although Ballard accurately foresees the present widening police terror, he does not project the forces that now oppose that terror—and its source. Here, as the newspaper tells us each day, Ballard's imagination was certainly too conservative. But then, of course, the opening question is addressed to all of us.

THE SUBLIMINAL MAN

"The signs, Doctor! Have you seen the signs?"

Frowning with annoyance, Dr. Franklin quickened his pace and hurried down the hospital steps towards the line of parked cars. Over his shoulder he caught a glimpse of a thin, scruffy young man in ragged sandals and lime-stained jeans waving to him from the far side of the drive, then break into a run when he saw Franklin try to evade him.

"Dr. Franklin! The signs!"

Head down, Franklin swerved around an elderly couple approaching the out-patients department. His car was over a hundred yards away. Too tired to start running himself, he waited for the young man to catch him up.

"All right, Hathaway, what is it this time?" he snapped irritably. "I'm getting sick of you hanging around here all day."

Hathaway lurched to a halt in front of him, uncut black hair like an awning over his eyes. He brushed it back with a claw-like hand and turned on a wild smile, obviously glad to see Franklin and oblivious of the latter's hostility.

"I've been trying to reach you at night, Doctor, but your wife always puts the phone down on me," he explained without a hint of rancour, as if well-used to this kind of snub. "And I didn't want to look for you inside the Clinic." They were standing by a privet hedge that shielded them from the lower windows of the main administrative block, but Franklin's regular rendezvous with Hathaway and his strange messianic cries had already been the subject of amused comment.

Franklin began to say: "I appreciate that—" but Hathaway brushed this aside. "Forget it, Doctor, there are more important things happening now. They've started to build the first big signs! Over a hundred feet high, on the traffic islands just outside town. They'll soon have all the approach roads covered. When they do we might as well stop thinking."

"Your trouble is that you're thinking too much," Franklin told him. "You've been rambling about these signs for weeks now. Tell me, have you actually seen one signalling?"

Hathaway tore a handful of leaves from the hedge, exasperated by this irrelevancy. "Of course I haven't, that's the whole point, Doctor." He dropped his voice as a group of nurses walked past, watching him uneasily out of the corners of their eyes. "The construction gangs were out again last night, laying huge power cables. You'll see them on the way home. Everything's nearly ready now."

"They're traffic signs," Franklin explained patiently. "The flyover has just been completed. Hathaway, for God's sake relax. Try to think of Dora and the child."

"I *am* thinking of them!" Hathaway's voice rose to a controlled scream. "Those cables were 40,000-volt lines, Doctor, with terrific switch-gear. The trucks were loaded with enormous metal scaffolds. Tomorrow they'll start lifting them up all over the city, they'll block off half the sky! What do you think Dora will be like after six months of that? We've got to stop them, Doctor, they're trying to transistorise our brains!"

Embarrassed by Hathaway's high-pitched shouting, Franklin had momentarily lost his sense of direction and helplessly searched the sea of cars for his own. "Hathaway, I can't waste any more time talking to you. Believe me, you need skilled help, these obsessions are beginning to master you."

Hathaway started to protest, and Franklin raised his right hand firmly. "Listen. For the last time, if you can show me one of these new signs, and prove that it's transmitting subliminal commands, I'll go to the police with you. But you haven't got a shred of evidence, and you know it. Subliminal advertising was banned thirty years ago, and the laws have never been repealed. Anyway, the technique was unsatisfactory, any success it had was marginal. Your idea of a huge conspiracy with all these thousands of giant signs everywhere is preposterous."

"All right, Doctor." Hathaway leaned against the bonnet of one of the cars. His moods seemed to switch abruptly from one level to the next. He watched Franklin amiably. "What's the matter—lost your car?"

"All your damned shouting has confused me." Franklin pulled out his ignition key and read the number off the tag: "NYN 299-566-367-21—can you see it?"

Hathaway leaned around lazily, one sandal up on the bonnet, surveying the square of a thousand or so cars facing them. "Difficult, isn't it, when they're all identical, even the same colour? Thirty years ago there were about ten different makes, each in a dozen colours."

Franklin spotted his car, began to walk towards it. "Sixty years ago there were a hundred makes. What of it? The economies of standardisation are obviously bought at a price."

Hathaway drummed his palm lightly on the roofs. "But these cars aren't all that cheap, Doctor. In fact, comparing them on an average income basis with those of thirty years ago they're about forty per cent more expensive. With only one make being produced you'd expect a substantial reduction in price, not an increase."

"Maybe," Franklin said, opening his door. "But mechanically the cars of today are far more sophisticated. They're lighter, more durable, safer to drive."

Hathaway shook his head sceptically. "They *bore* me. The same model, same styling, same colour, year after year. It's a sort of communism." He rubbed a greasy finger over the windshield. "This is a new one again, isn't it, Doctor? Where's the old one—you only had it for three months?"

"I traded it in," Franklin told him, starting the engine. "If you ever had any money you'd realise that it's the most economical way of owning a car. You don't keep driving the same one until it falls apart. It's the same with everything else—television sets, washing machines, refrigerators. But you aren't faced with the problem—you haven't got any."

Hathaway ignored the gibe, and leaned his elbow on Franklin's window. "Not a bad idea, either, Doctor. It gives me time to think. I'm not working a twelve-hour day to pay for a lot of things I'm too busy to use before they're obsolete."

He waved as Franklin reversed the car out of its line, then shouted into the wake of exhaust: "Drive with your eyes closed, Doctor!"

On the way home Franklin kept carefully to the slowest of the the four-speed lanes. As usual after his discussions with Hathaway he felt vaguely depressed. He realised that unconsciously he envied Hathaway his footloose existence. Despite the grimy cold-water apartment in the shadow and roar of the flyover, despite his nagging wife and their sick child, and the endless altercations with the landlord and the supermarket credit manager, Hathaway still retained his freedom intact. Spared any responsibilities, he could resist the smallest encroachment upon him by the rest of society, if only by generating obsessive fantasies such as his latest one about subliminal advertising.

The ability to react to stimuli, even irrationally, was a valid criterion of freedom. By contrast, what freedom Franklin possessed was peripheral, sharply demarked by the manifold responsibilities in the centre of his life—the three mortgages on his home, the mandatory rounds of cocktail and TV parties, the private consultancy occupying most of Saturday which paid the installments on the multitude of household gadgets, clothes and past holidays. About the only time he had to himself was driving to and from work.

But at least the roads were magnificent. Whatever other criticisms might be levelled at the present society, it certainly knew how to build roads. Eight, ten and twelve-lane expressways interlaced across the continent, plunging from overhead causeways into the giant car parks in the centre of the cities, or dividing into the great suburban arteries with their multi-acre parking aprons around the marketing centres. Together the roadways and car parks covered more than a third of the country's entire area, and in the neighbourhood of the cities the proportion was higher. The old cities were surrounded by the vast, dazzling abstract sculptures of the clover-leaves and flyovers, but even so the congestion was unremitting.

The ten-mile journey to his home in fact covered over twenty-five miles and took him twice as long as it had done before the construction of the expressway, the additional miles contained within the three giant clover-leaves. New cities were springing from the motels, cafés and car-marts around the highways. At the slightest hint of an intersection a shanty town of shacks and filling stations sprawled away among the forest of electric signs and route indicators, many of them substantial cities.

All around him cars bulleted along, streaming towards the suburbs. Relaxed by the smooth motion of the car, Franklin edged outward into the next speed-lane. As he accelerated from 40 to 50 m.p.h. a strident ear-jarring noise drummed out from his tyres, shaking the chassis of the car. Ostensibly as an aid to lane discipline, the surface of the road was covered with a mesh of small rubber studs, spaced progressively further apart in each of the lanes so that the tyre hum resonated exactly on 40, 50, 60 and 70 m.p.h. Driving at an intermediate speed for more than a few seconds became physiologically painful, and soon resulted in damage to the car and tyres.

When the studs wore out they were replaced by slightly different patterns, matching those on the latest tyres, so that regular tyre changes were necessary, increasing the safety and efficiency of the expressway. It also increased the revenues of the car and tyre manufacturers, for most cars over six months old soon fell to pieces under the steady battering, but this was regarded as a desirable end, the greater turnover reducing the unit price and making more frequent model changes, as well as ridding the roads of dangerous vehicles.

A quarter of a mile ahead, at the approach to the first of the clover-leaves, the traffic stream was slowing, huge police signs signalling "Lanes Closed Ahead" and "Drop Speed by 10 m.p.h." Franklin tried to return to the previous lane, but the cars were jammed bumper to bumper. As the chassis began to shudder and vibrate jarring his spine, he clamped his teeth and tried to restrain himself from sounding the horn. Other drivers were less self-controlled and everywhere engines were plunging and snarling, horns blaring. Road taxes were now so high, up to 30% of income (by contrast, income taxes were a bare 2%), that any delay on the expressways called for an immediate government inquiry, and the major departments of state were concerned with the administration of the road systems.

Nearer the clover-leaf the lanes had been closed to allow a gang of construction workers to erect a massive metal sign on one of the traffic islands. The palisaded area swarmed with engineers and surveyors and Franklin assumed that this was the sign Hathaway had seen unloaded the previous night. His apartment was in one of the gimcrack buildings in the settlement that straggled away around a nearby flyover, a low-rent area inhabited by service station personnel, waitresses and other migrant labour.

The sign was enormous, at least 100 feet high, fitted with heavy concave grilles similar to radar bowls. Rooted in a series of concrete caissons, it reared high into the air above the approach roads, visible for miles. Franklin craned up at the grilles, tracing the power cables from the transformers up into the intricate mesh of metal coils that covered their surface. A line of red aircraft-warning beacons was already alight along the top strut, and Franklin assumed that the sign was part of the ground approach system of the city airport ten miles to the east.

Three minutes later, as he accelerated down the two-mile link of straight highway to the next clover-leaf, he saw the second of the giant signs looming up into the sky before him.

Changing down into the 40 m.p.h. lane, Franklin uneasily watched the great bulk of the second sign recede in his rear-view mirror. Although there were no graphic symbols among the wire coils covering the grilles, Hathaway's warnings still sounded in his ears. Without knowing why, he felt sure that the signs were not part of the airport approach system. Neither of them was in line with the principal air-lanes. To justify the expense of siting them in the centre of the expressway—the second sign required elaborate angled buttresses to support it on the narrow island—obviously meant that their role related in some way to the traffic streams.

Two hundred yards away was a roadside auto-mart, and Franklin abruptly remembered that he needed some cigarettes. Swinging the car down the entrance ramp, he joined the queue slowly passing the self-service dispenser at the far end of the rank. The auto-mart was packed with cars, each of the five purchasing ranks lined with tired-looking men hunched over their wheels.

Inserting his coins (paper money was no longer in circulation, unmanageable by the automats) he took a carton from the dispenser. This was the only brand of cigarettes available—in fact there was only one brand of everything—though giant economy packs were an alternative. Moving off, he opened the dashboard locker.

Inside, still sealed in their wrappers, were three other cartons.

A strong fish-like smell pervaded the house when he reached home, steaming out from the oven in the kitchen. Sniffing it uneagerly, Franklin took off his coat and hat, and found his wife crouched over the TV set in the lounge. An announcer was dictating a stream of numbers, and Judith scribbled them down on a pad, occasionally cursing under her breath. "What a muddle!" she snapped finally. "He was talking so quickly I took only a few things down."

"Probably deliberate," Franklin commented. "New panel game?"

Judith kissed him on the cheek, discreetly hiding the ashtray loaded with cigarette butts and chocolate wrappings. "Hullo, darling, sorry not to have a drink ready for you. They've started this series of Spot Bargains, they give you a selection of things on which you get a ninety per cent trade-in discount at the local stores, if you're in the right area and have the right serial numbers. It's all terribly complicated."

"Sounds good, though. What have you got?"

Judith peered at her checklist. "Well, as far as I can see the only thing is the infra-red barbecue spit. But we have to be there before eight o'clock tonight. It's seven-thirty already."

"Then that's out. I'm tired, angel, I need something to eat." When Judith started to protest he added firmly: "Look, I don't want a new infra-red barbecue spit, we've only had this one for two months. Damn it, it's not even a different model."

"But, darling, don't you see, it makes it cheaper if you keep buying new ones. We'll have to trade ours in at the end of the year anyway, we signed the contract, and this way we save at least twenty dollars. These Spot Bargains aren't just a gimmick, you know. I've been glued to that set all day." A note of irritation had crept into her voice, but Franklin sat his ground, doggedly ignoring the clock.

"Right, we lose twenty dollars. It's worth it." Before she could remonstrate he said: "Judith, please, you probably took the wrong number down anyway." As she shrugged and went over to the bar he called: "Make it a stiff one. I see we have health foods on the menu."

"They're good for you, darling. You know you can't live on ordinary foods all the time. They don't contain any proteins or vitamins. You're always saying we ought to be like people in the old days and eat nothing but health foods."

"I would, but they smell so awful." Franklin lay back, nose in the glass of whisky, gazing at the darkened skyline outside.

A quarter of a mile away, gleaming out above the roof of the neighbourhood supermarket, were the five red beacon lights. Now and then, as the headlamps of the Spot Bargainers swung up across the face of the building, he could see the square massive bulk of the giant sign clearly silhouetted against the evening sky.

"Judith!" He went into the kitchen and took her over to the window. "That sign, just behind the supermarket. When did they put it up?"

"I don't know." Judith peered at him curiously. "Why are you so worried, Robert? Isn't it something to do with the airport?"

Franklin stared thoughtfully at the dark hull of the sign. "So everyone probably thinks."

Carefully he poured his whisky into the sink.

After parking his car on the supermarket apron at seven o'clock the next morning, Franklin carefully emptied his pockets and stacked the coins in the dashboard locker. The supermarket was already busy with early morning shoppers and the line of thirty turnstiles clicked and slammed. Since the introduction of the "24-hour spending day" the shopping complex was never closed. The bulk of the shoppers were discount buyers, housewives contracted to make huge volume purchases of food, clothing and appliances against substantial overall price cuts, and forced to drive around all day from supermarket to supermarket, frantically trying to keep pace with their purchase schedules and grappling with the added incentives inserted to keep the schemes alive.

Many of the women had teamed up, and as Franklin walked over to the entrance a pack of them charged towards their cars, stuffing their pay slips into their bags and gesticulating at each other. A moment later their cars roared off in a convoy to the next marketing zone.

A large neon sign over the entrance listed the latest discount —a mere 5%—calculated on the volume of turnover. The highest discounts, sometimes up to 25%, were earned in the housing estates where junior white-collar workers lived. There, spending had a strong social incentive, and the desire to be the highest spender in the neighbourhood was given moral reinforcement by the system of listing all the names and their accumulating cash totals on a huge electric sign in the supermarket foyers. The higher the spender, the greater his contribution to the discounts enjoyed by others. The lowest-spending were regarded as social criminals, free-riding on the backs of others.

Luckily this system had yet to be adopted in Franklin's neighbourhood. Not because the professional men and their wives were able to exercise more discretion, but because their higher incomes allowed them to contract into more expensive discount schemes operated by the big department stores in the city.

Ten yards from the entrance Franklin paused, looking up at the huge metal sign mounted in an enclosure at the edge of the car park. Unlike the other signs and hoardings that proliferated everywhere, no attempt had been made to decorate it, or disguise the gaunt bare rectangle of riveted steel mesh. Power lines wound down its sides, and the concrete surface of the car park was crossed by a long scar where a cable had been sunk.

Franklin strolled along, then fifty feet from the sign stopped and turned, realising that he would be late for the hospital and needed a new carton of cigarettes. A dim but powerful humming emanated from the transformers below the sign, fading as he retraced his steps to the supermarket.

Going over to the automats in the foyer, he felt for his change, then whistled sharply when he remembered why he had deliberately emptied his pockets.

"The cunning thing!" he said, loud enough for two shoppers to stare at him. Reluctant to look directly at the sign, he watched its reflection in one of the glass door-panes, so that any subliminal message would be reversed.

Almost certainly he had received two distinct signals—"Keep Away" and "Buy Cigarettes." The people who normally parked their cars along the perimeter of the apron were avoiding the area under the enclosure, the cars describing a loose semicircle fifty feet around it.

He turned to the janitor sweeping out the foyer. "What's that sign for?"

The man leaned on his broom, gazing dully at the sign. "Dunno," he said, "must be something to do with the airport." He had an almost fresh cigarette in his mouth, but his right hand reached unconsciously to his hip pocket and pulled out a pack. He drummed the second cigarette absently on his thumb-nail as Franklin walked away.

Everyone entering the supermarket was buying cigarettes.

Cruising quietly along the 40 m.p.h. lane, Franklin began to take a closer interest in the landscape around him. Usually he was either too tired or too preoccupied to do more than think about his driving, but now he examined the expressway methodically, scanning the roadside cafés for any smaller versions of the new signs. A host of neon displays covered the doorways and windows, but most of them seemed innocuous, and he turned his attention to the larger billboards erected along the open stretches of the expressway. Many of these were as high as four-storey houses, elaborate three-dimensional devices in which giant glossy-skinned housewives with electric eyes and teeth jerked and postured around their ideal kitchens, neon flashes exploding from their smiles.

The areas on either side of the expressway were waste-land, continuous junkyards filled with cars and trucks, washing machines and refrigerators, all perfectly workable but jettisoned by the economic pressure of the succeeding waves of discount models. Their intact chrome hardly tarnished, the mounds of metal shells and cabinets glittered in the sunlight. Nearer the city the billboards were sufficiently close together to hide them, but now and then, as he slowed to approach one of the flyovers, Franklin caught a glimpse of the huge pyramids of metal, gleaming silently like the refuse grounds of some forgotten El Dorado.

That evening Hathaway was waiting for him as he came down the hospital steps. Franklin waved him across the court, then led the way quickly to his car.

"What's the matter, Doctor?" Hathaway asked as Franklin wound up the windows and glanced around the lines of parked cars. "Is someone after you?"

Franklin laughed sombrely. "I don't know. I hope not, but if what you say is right, I suppose there is."

Hathaway leaned back with a chuckle, propping one knee up on the dashboard. "So you've seen something, Doctor, after all."

"Well, I'm not sure yet, but there's just a chance you may be right. This morning at the Fairlawne supermarket . . ." He broke off, uneasily remembering the huge blank sign and the abrupt way in which he had turned back to the supermarket as he approached it, then described his encounter.

Hathaway nodded slowly. "I've seen the sign there. It's big, but not as big as some that are going up. They're building them everywhere now. All over the city. What are you going to do, Doctor?"

Franklin gripped the wheel tightly. Hathaway's thinly veiled amusement irritated him. "Nothing, of course. Damn it, it may be just auto-suggestion, you've probably got me imagining—"

Hathaway sat up with a jerk, his face mottled and savage. "Don't be absurd, Doctor! If you can't believe your own senses what chance have you left? They're invading your brain, if you don't defend yourself they'll take it over completely! We've got to act now, before we're all paralysed."

Wearily Franklin raised one hand to restrain him. "Just a minute. Assuming that these signs *are* going up everywhere, what would be their object? Apart from wasting the enormous amount of capital invested in all the other millions of signs and billboards, the amounts of discretionary spending power still available must be infinitesimal. Some of the present mortgage and discount schemes reach half a century ahead, so there can't be much slack left to take up. A big trade war would be disastrous."

"Quite right, Doctor," Hathaway rejoined evenly, "but you're forgetting one thing. What would supply that extra spending power? A big increase in production. Already they've started to raise the working day from twelve hours to fourteen. In some of the appliances plants around the city Sunday working is being introduced as a norm. Can you visualise it, Doctor—a seven-day week, everyone with at least three jobs?"

Franklin shook his head. "People won't stand for it."

"They will. Within the last twenty-five years the gross national product has risen by fifty per cent, but so have the average hours worked. Ultimately we'll all be working and spending twenty-four hours a day, seven days a week. No one will dare refuse. Think what a slump would mean—millions of lay-offs, people with time on their hands and nothing to spend it on. Real leisure, not just time spent buying things." He seized Franklin by the shoulder. "Well, Doctor, are you going to join me?"

Franklin freed himself. Half a mile away, partly hidden by the four-story bulk of the Pathology Department, was the upper half of one of the giant signs, workmen still crawling across its girders. The airlines over the city had deliberately been routed away from the hospital, and the sign obviously had no connection with approaching aircraft.

"Isn't there a prohibition on subliminal living? How can the unions accept it?"

"The fear of a slump. You know the new economic dogmas. Unless output rises by a steady inflationary five per cent the economy is stagnating. Ten years ago increased efficiency alone would raise output, but the advantages there are minimal now and only one thing is left. More work. Increased consumption and subliminal advertising will provide the spur."

"What are you planning to do?"

"I can't tell you, Doctor, unless you accept equal responsibility for it."

"Sounds rather quixotic," Franklin commented. "Tilting at windmills. You won't be able to chop those things down with an axe."

"I won't try." Hathaway suddenly gave up and opened the door. "Don't wait too long to make up your mind, Doctor. By then it may not be yours to make up." With a wave he was gone.

On the way home Franklin's scepticism returned. The idea of the conspiracy was preposterous, and the economic arguments were too plausible. As usual, though, there had been a hook in the soft bait Hathaway dangled before him—Sunday working. His own consultancy had been extended into Sunday morning with his appointment as visiting factory doctor to one of the automobile plants that had started Sunday shifts. But instead of resenting this incursion into his already meagre hours of leisure he had been glad. For one frightening reason—he needed the extra income.

Looking out over the lines of scurrying cars, he noticed that at least a dozen of the great signs had been erected along the expressway. As Hathaway had said, more were going up every-where, rearing over the supermarkets in the housing developments like rusty metal sails.

Judith was in the kitchen when he reached home, watching the TV programme on the hand-set over the cooker. Franklin climbed past a big cardboard carton, its seals still unbroken, which blocked the doorway, kissed her on the cheek as she scribbled numbers down on her pad. The pleasant odour of pot-roast chicken—or, rather, a gelatine dummy of a chicken fully flavoured and free of

any toxic or nutritional properties—mollified his irritation at finding her still playing the Spot Bargains.

He tapped the carton with his foot. "What's this?"

"No idea, darling, something's always coming these days, I
can't keep up with it all." She peered through the glass door at
the chicken—an economy 12-pounder, the size of a turkey, with
stylised legs and wings and an enormous breast, most of which
would be discarded at the end of the meal (there were no dogs
or cats these days, the crumbs from the rich man's table saw to
that)—and then glanced at him pointedly.

"You look rather worried, Robert. Bad day?"

Franklin murmured noncommittally. The hours spent trying to
detect false clues in the faces of the Spot Bargain announcers had
sharpened Judith's perceptions, and he felt a pang of sympathy
for the legion of husbands similarly outmatched.

"Have you been talking to that crazy beatnik again?"

"Hathaway? As a matter of fact I have. He's not all that crazy."
He stepped backwards into the carton, almost spilling his drink.
"Well, what is this thing? As I'll be working for the next fifty
Sundays to pay for it I'd like to find out."

He searched the sides, finally located the label. "*A TV set*?
Judith, do we need another one? We've already got three. Lounge,
dining room, and the hand-set. What's the fourth for?"

"The guest room, dear, don't get so excited. We can't leave a
hand-set in the guest room, it's rude. I'm trying to economise,
but four TV sets is the bare minimum. All the magazines say so."

"*And* three radios?" Franklin stared irritably at the carton. "If
we do invite a guest here how much time is he going to spend alone
in his room watching television? Judith, we've got to call a halt.
It's not as if these things were free, or even cheap. Anyway,
television is a total waste of time. There's only one programme.
It's ridiculous to have four sets."

"Robert, there are *four* channels."

"But only the commercials are different." Before Judith could
reply the telephone rang. Franklin lifted the kitchen receiver, listened to the gabble of noise that poured from it. At first he won-

dered whether this was some off-beat prestige commercial, then realised it was Hathaway in a manic swing.

"Hathaway!" he shouted back. "Relax, man! What's the matter now?"

"—Doctor, you'll have to believe me this time. I tell you I got on to one of the islands with a stroboscope, they've got hundreds of high-speed shutters blasting away like machine-guns straight into people's faces and they can't see a thing, it's fantastic! The next big campaign's going to be cars and TV sets, they're trying to swing a two-month model change—can you imagine it, Doctor, a new car every two months? God Almighty, it's just—"

Franklin waited impatiently as the five-second commercial break cut in (all telephone calls were free, the length of the commercial extending with range—for long-distance calls the ratio of commercial to conversation was as high as 10:1, the participants desperately trying to get a word in edgeways to the interminable interruptions), but just before it ended he abruptly put the telephone down, then removed the receiver from the cradle.

Judith came over and took his arm. "Robert, what's the matter? You look terribly strained."

Franklin picked up his drink and walked through into the lounge. "It's just Hathaway, As you say, I'm getting a little too involved with him. He's starting to prey on my mind."

He looked at the dark outline of the sign over the supermarket, its red warning lights glowing in the night sky. Blank and nameless, like an area forever closed off in an insane mind, what frightened him was its total anonymity.

"Yet I'm not sure," he muttered. "So much of what Hathaway says make sense. These subliminal techniques are the sort of last-ditch attempt you'd expect from an over-capitalised industrial system."

He waited for Judith to reply, then looked up at her. She stood in the centre of the carpet, hands folded limply, her sharp, intelligent face curiously dull and blunted. He followed her gaze out over the rooftops, then with an effort turned his head and quickly switched on the TV set.

"Come on," he said grimly. "Let's watch television. God, we're going to need that fourth set."

A week later Franklin began to compile his inventory. He saw nothing more of Hathaway; as he left the hospital in the evening the familiar scruffy figure was absent. When the first of the explosions sounded dimly around the city and he read of the attempts to sabotage the giant signs he automatically assumed that Hathaway was responsible, but later he heard on a newscast that the detonations had been set off by construction workers excavating foundations.

More of the signs appeared over the rooftops, isolated on the palisaded islands near the suburban shopping centres. Already there were over thirty on the ten-mile route from the hospital, standing shoulder to shoulder over the speeding cars like giant dominoes. Franklin had given up his attempt to avoid looking at them, but the slim possibility that the explosions might be Hathaway's counter-attack kept his suspicions alive.

He began his inventory after hearing the newscast, discovered that in the previous fortnight he and Judith had traded in their

> Car (previous model 2 months old)
> 2 TV sets (4 months)
> Power mower (7 months)
> Electric cooker (5 months)
> Hair dryer (4 months)
> Refrigerator (3 months)
> 2 radios (7 months)
> Record player (5 months)
> Cocktail bar (8 months)

Half these purchases had been made by himself, but exactly when he could never recall realising at the time. The car, for example, he had left in the garage near the hospital to be greased, that evening had signed for the new model as he sat at its wheel, accepting the salesman's assurance that the depreciation on the two-month trade-in was virtually less than the cost of the grease-job. Ten minutes later, as he sped along the expressway, he suddenly realised that he had bought a new car. Similarly, the TV sets had been replaced by identical models after developing the same irritating interference pattern (curiously, the new sets also displayed the pattern, but as the salesman assured them, this promptly vanished two days later).

Not once had he actually decided of his own volition that he wanted something and then gone out to a store and bought it!

He carried the inventory around with him, adding to it as necessary, quietly and without protest analysing these new sales techniques, wondering whether total capitulation might be the only way of defeating them. As long as he kept up even a token resistance, the inflationary growth curve would show a controlled annual 10% climb. With that resistance removed, however, it would begin to rocket upwards out of control. . . .

Then, driving home from the hospital two months later, he saw one of the signs for the first time.

He was in the 40 m.p.h. lane, unable to keep up with the flood of new cars, had just passed the second of the three clover-leaves when the traffic half a mile away began to slow down. Hundreds of cars had driven up on to the grass verge, and a large crowd was gathering around one of the signs. Two small black figures were climbing up the metal face, and a series of huge grid-like patterns of light flashed on and off, illuminating the evening air. The patterns were random and broken, as if the sign was being tested for the first time.

Relieved that Hathaway's suspicions had been completely groundless, Franklin turned off on to the soft shoulder, then walked forward through the spectators as the lights blinked and stuttered in their faces. Below, behind the steel palisades around the island, was a large group of police and engineers, craning up at the men scaling the sign a hundred feet over their heads.

Suddenly Franklin stopped, the sense of relief fading instantly. With a jolt he saw that several of the police on the ground were armed with shot-guns, and that the two policemen climbing the sign carried submachine-guns slung over their shoulders. They were converging on a third figure, crouched by a switchbox on the penultimate tier, a ragged bearded man in a grimy shirt, a bare knee poking through his jeans.

Hathaway!

Franklin hurried towards the island, the sign hissing and sput-tering, fuses blowing by the dozen.

Then the flicker of lights cleared and steadied, blazing out continuously, and together the crowd looked up at the decks of brilliant letters. The phrases, and every combination of them possi-ble, were entirely familiar, and Franklin knew that he had been reading them unconsciously in his mind for weeks as he passed up and down the expressway.

BUY NOW BUY NOW BUY NOW BUY NOW BUY NOW
NEW CAR NOW NEW CAR NOW NEW CAR NOW
YES YES YES YES YES YES YES YES YES YES YES

Sirens blaring, two patrol cars swung up on to the verge through the crowd and plunged across the damp grass. Police spilled from its doors, batons in their hands, quickly began to force back the crowd. Franklin held his ground as they approached, started to say: "Officer, I know the man—" but the policeman punched him in the chest with the flat of his hand. Winded, he stumbled back among the cars, leaned helplessly against a fender as the police began to break the windshields, the hapless drivers protesting angrily, those further back rushing for their vehicles.

The noise fell away abruptly when one of the submachine-guns fired a brief roaring burst, then rose in a massive gasp of horror as Hathaway, arms outstretched, let out a cry of triumph and pain, and jumped.

"But, Robert, what does it really matter?" Judith asked as Franklin sat inertly in the lounge the next morning. "I know it's tragic for his wife and daughter, but Hathaway was in the grip of an obsession. If he hated advertising signs so much why didn't he dynamite those we *can* see, instead of worrying so much about those we can't?"

Franklin stared at the TV screen, hoping the programme would distract him.

"Hathaway was *right*," he said simply.

"Was he? Advertising is here to stay. We've no real freedom of choice, anyway. We can't spend more than we can afford, the finance companies soon clamp down."

"You accept that?" Franklin went over to the window. A quarter of a mile away, in the centre of the estate, another of the signs was being erected. It was due east from them, and in the early morning light the shadows of its rectangular superstructure fell across the garden, reaching almost to the steps of the French windows at his feet. As a concession to the neighbourhood, and perhaps to allay any suspicions while it was being erected by an appeal to petty snobbery, the lower sections had been encased in mock-Tudor panelling.

Franklin stared at it numbly, counting the half-dozen police lounging by their patrol cars as the construction gang unloaded prefabricated grilles from a couple of trucks. Then he looked at the sign by the supermarket, trying to repress his memories of Hathaway and the pathetic attempts the man had made to convince Franklin and gain his help.

He was still standing there an hour later when Judith came in, putting on her hat and coat, ready to visit the supermarket.

Franklin followed her to the door. "I'll drive you down there, Judith," he said in a flat dead voice. "I have to see about booking a new car. The next models are coming out at the end of the month. With luck we'll get one of the early deliveries."

They walked out into the trim drive, the shadows of the great signs swinging across the quiet neighbourhood as the day progressed, sweeping over the heads of the people on their way to the supermarket like the dark blades of enormous scythes.

I HAVE NO MOUTH, AND I MUST SCREAM

by HARLAN ELLISON

FOREWORD

by Willis E. McNelly

THE AUTHOR

HARLAN ELLISON was born in Ohio in 1934 and now lives in Los Angeles, where he devotes much of his time to writing for television and the movies. Since 1955, however, he has been an active contributor to science-fiction magazines, attracting attention for the unusual visual intensity and high emotional level of his stories. "I Have No Mouth, And I Must Scream," which was first published in 1967, was awarded the Hugo as that year's outstanding science-fiction story; he won another Hugo in the same year for his *Star Trek* television script, "City at the Edge of Forever," and in 1966 won both Hugo and Nebula awards for his short story "Repent, Harlequin, Said the Ticktockman."

THE CRITIC

WILLIS E. MCNELLY has been, since 1961, professor of English at California State College, Fullerton, where he teaches courses in Joyce, Yeats, modern poetry, and science fiction. Born in Wisconsin in 1920, he settled in California after acquiring his doctorate at Northwestern University. He has published works on Joyce and Yeats, and has also contributed essays on the science fiction of Robert A. Heinlein and Ray Bradbury to the College English Association *Critic*, as well as a critical introduction to the 1969 anthology *Nebula Award Stories: Four*.

Foreword

Take a generous portion of myth, add a flagon of verbal magic,
mix with memory and desire, season with a dollop or two of
reminiscences of James Joyce, John Barth, and John Bunyan,
sprinkle in a racial memory of the golem, and add all this to a
simmering stock composed of equal parts of good and evil—
you end up with Harlan Ellison's prize-winning short story
"I Have No Mouth, And I Must Scream."

Ellison's story is more than a mixture of tired and true thematic
elements and stylistic devices, however. It assumes a brooding,
haunting quality of its own as it shocks the senses, assails the
emotions, and chills the mind. It is not a story that one can be
indifferent about. It almost demands acceptance or rejection on
its own terms, shaking the reader with its McLuhanesque vision.
There is no sterile linearity in "I Have No Mouth," no obsolescent
beginning, middle, and end. Rather there is a centricity of vision
that springs from the constant reconciliation of opposites in the
story itself. The devices, themes, emotions, forces, language, style,
and diction all are antithetical. The tensions in the story rise from
the interplay of forces and find their resolution in conflict itself.
Even the title illustrates the tensions: "I have no mouth, and
I must scream." Impossible? Yes, but the scream is the story
itself. Ted, the heroic antihero, may have no mouth but he does
have a typewriter on which he produces his anti-allegory. The
medium is the message; the story, the shout.

The story utilizes the two classic frameworks of the allegory,
progress and battle. In the traditional allegory the conflict is between
the ultimate forces of good and evil as the hero makes his
tortuous way to a symbolic celestial city. Ted is no Christian in his
pilgrim's progress, to be sure, but the story nonetheless illustrates
the epic conflict as well as the epic journey. AM, the anarchic
computer, is a demonic demiurge, a Manichean power of darkness,
an evil creative spirit. Ted, on the other hand, is no archangel

Michael who will thrust into Hell Lucifer and the other evil spirits. Ted is rather the embodiment of the good and evil in all of us, at once brute and angel, fornicator and lover, killer and savior. He is man—like a devil, like an angel, like a god.

Neither force is omnipotent. AM is only a surrogate Yahweh or Elohim. His control may be all-powerful, but AM cannot really keep men from death, although he can keep them alive virtually forever. Thus AM cannot, in the end, either create life or breathe life anew into the victims of Ted's salvific act. Similarly, Ted's search for glory on the road to his uncelestial city is an ignoble search at best. He grovels for food, begs for mercy while cursing the potential source of mercy, and whimpers for black Ellen's sexual favors. Hardly a heroic picture.

Paradox is at the heart of Ellison's story. From the title itself to the death of Ted's companions, paradox piles on paradox. The body of Gorrister has been drained of blood by a ritualistic throat-cutting incision, but the floor under the body is bloodless. AM transforms Benny into the apotheosis of phallic masculinity, but removes his spiritual masculinity in the highly symbolic blinding. Paradoxes multiply as manna gives no life, and death brings release. The tensions arise not only from the nature of the forces that Ellison puts into his story, but from their very incompleteness. AM strives for a perfection, but it is a perfection of evil and ugliness, hell in the maw of the computer. AM has destroyed all lives on earth except the five in the story because it hates mankind for having created it. It seeks to keep the five humans alive so it may wreak an eternal revenge. When only Ted remains alive at the end, AM transforms him into the mouthless blob, a piece of inchoate undefecated matter, so that Ted will live an eternity. Why the paradoxical life in death for Ted and AM? AM, after all, is not omnipotent, and is only a machine. But machines cannot exist without man, even if man has been transformed into an unscreaming blob.

The imagery and diction of the story contribute to its appeal. Ellison is a highly skilled writer whose word choice and sentence structure are usually sure and certain. There are the giggle or chitter of his characters, the lunatic laugh of a fat woman, the sound of a million metallic insects, the screaming shoals of machines. The words create the appeal, whether to the eye, the ear, the nose, or the tongue. Who can ever, in the end, forget the taste of boiled boar urine?

"I Have No Mouth, And I Must Scream" probably is a repulsive story. But Ellison meant it to repel—to harrow the reader's emotions, and ultimately to stimulate him to think. What is this story about finally? Is it simply a modernized dybbuk story, or a piece of twentieth-century Gothic fiction? It is all of these, of course, and it is anti-allegory, and it is a horror tale. But it is also science fiction, because ultimately it is concerned with the interface between man and the machine. Man must control the machine, Ellison maintains, or the machine will control him. After all, at the very heart of science fiction is the notion of extrapolation. "What if?" the author asks himself. "What if?"

Ellison's "what if?" posits a thinking computer horrified at itself as a creation of man, hating itself because its creator has made it evil, and then acting logically upon both its horror and its hate by destroying its creator and seeking its revenge. Has man ever acted otherwise? If the answer is no, then the story must proceed with some sort of logical, horrifying inevitability to its deranged conclusion. Man is eternally rotten and deserves punishment at the hands of an angry God. Man must always remain, then, a rational slug, at the complete mercy of a hating AM.

On the other hand, if man has acted other than by greed, hate, or revenge, then there is some ultimate glory in the story, and with yet one more paradox, the anti-allegory becomes allegory. This final juxtaposition is achieved by a very simple device: in a way, Ted gives up his life for his friends. He may remain the blob-like object of hate, but he is ultimately redeemed by his sacrifice. But Ellison is still not finished with paradox or dramatic, even tragic, irony. The act of salvation is a killing. Ted's friends find final surcease in death as AM is cheated of his ancient revenge.

Since written time, man has created his gods in various likenesses, his myths in varying forms. As Jung, Neumann, Frye, Eliade, and many others have shown, myths are constantly altered by man to suit the needs of man. Man is ultimately in control of his myths. Thus in Ellison's story AM also once existed in the mind of man under man's control, but now AM has become incarnated into the form, shape, and substance of a chittering computer. Its power was ultimately programed by man on tapes and in memory banks. AM now knows all the ancient archetypal myths, and now uses its knowledge to pervert and negate them. It exercises the power that man never had, to control man, and to give substance to the myths. Man has played God for one last time, creating a god that destroys him.

There are other qualities that make "I Have No Mouth, And I Must Scream" a provocative short story. Not the least of these is the typographical format. Of course, eccentricity of type and layout probably dates to Gutenberg, and its use in English literature is found in such places as the emblematic poems of Francis Quarles or George Herbert and the novels of Laurence Sterne and James Joyce. For that matter, Alfred Bester's *The Demolished Man* established the precedent of deliberate typographical innovation as an artistic device in science fiction. Yet Ellison's utilization of such devices as AM speaking through computer tape or the stainless-steel pillar bearing neon lettering is not mere eccentricity on Ellison's part. In one sense, the story is an interior monologue staged in the mind of a god, and, as such, the computer tape "conversation" indicates AM's presence, an oppressive omniscience or omnipotence. These qualities are not, of course, absolute, because AM is god, not God. The tape, then, is not merely gratuitous, but adds the dimension of mechanical presence to the spiritual horror.

All of these qualities—the paradoxes, the style, the tensions, the typographical innovations—make Harlan Ellison's "I Have No Mouth, And I Must Scream" a very provocative story. It is so provocative that it probably could not have been published a dozen years ago, but its contemporary acceptance marks some sort of maturity for science fiction.

I HAVE NO MOUTH, AND I MUST SCREAM

Limp, the body of Gorrister hung from the pink palette; unsupported—hanging high above us in the computer chamber; and it did not shiver in the chill, oily breeze that blew eternally through the main cavern. The body hung head down, attached to the underside of the palette by the sole of its right foot. It had been drained of blood through a precise incision made from ear to ear under the lantern jaw. There was no blood on the reflective surface of the metal floor.

When Gorrister joined our group and looked up at himself, it was already too late for us to realize that once again AM had duped us, had had his fun; it had been a diversion on the part of the machine. Three of us had vomited, turning away from one another in a reflex as ancient as the nausea that had produced it.

Gorrister went white. It was almost as though he had seen a voodoo icon, and was afraid for the future. "Oh God," he mumbled, and walked away. The three of us followed him after a time, and found him sitting with his back to one of the smaller chittering banks, his head in his hands. Ellen knelt down beside him and stroked his hair. He didn't move, but his voice came out of his covered face quite clearly. "Why doesn't it just do-us-in and get it over with? Christ, I don't know how much longer I can go on like this."

It was our one hundred and ninth year in the computer.
He was speaking for all of us.

Nimdok (which was the name the machine had forced him
to use, because it amused itself with strange sounds) was hallu-
cinated that there were canned goods in the ice caverns. Gorrister
and I were very dubious. "It's another shuck," I told them. "Like
the goddam frozen elephant it sold us. Benny almost went out of
his mind over *that* one. We'll hike all that way and it'll be putre-
fied or some damn thing. I say forget it. Stay here, it'll have to
come up with something pretty soon or we'll die."

Benny shrugged. Three days it had been since we'd last eaten.
Worms. Thick, ropey.

Nimdok was no more certain. He knew there was the chance,
but he was getting thin. It couldn't be any worse there than here.
Colder, but that didn't matter much. Hot, cold, raining, lava boils
or locusts—it never mattered: the machine masturbated and we
had to take it or die.

Ellen decided us. "I've got to have something, Ted. Maybe
there'll be some Bartlett pears or peaches. Please, Ted, let's try it."

I gave in easily. What the hell. Mattered not at all. Ellen was
grateful, though. She took me twice out of turn. Even that had
ceased to matter. The machine giggled every time we did it. Loud,
up there, back there, all around us. And she never climaxed, so
why bother.

We left on a Thursday. The machine always kept us up-to-date
on the date. The passage of time was important; not to us sure
as hell, but to it. Thursday. Thanks.

Nimdok and Gorrister carried Ellen for a while, their hands
locked to their own and each other's wrists, a seat. Benny and
I walked before and after, just to make sure that if anything happened, it would catch one of us and at least Ellen would be safe.
Fat chance, safe. Didn't matter.

It was only a hundred miles or so to the ice caverns, and the
second day, when we were lying out under the blistering sun-thing

it had materialized, it sent down some manna. Tasted like boiled boar urine. We ate it.

On the third day we passed through a valley of obsolescence, filled with rusting carcasses of ancient computer banks. AM had been as ruthless with his own life as with ours. It was a mark of his personality: he strove for perfection. Whether it was a matter of killing off unproductive elements in his own world-filling bulk, or perfecting methods for torturing us, AM was as thorough as those who had invented him—now long since gone to dust—could ever have hoped.

There was light filtering down from above, and we realized we must be very near the surface. But we didn't try to crawl up to see. There was virtually nothing out there; had been nothing that could be considered anything for over a hundred years. Only the blasted skin of what had once been the home of billions. Now there were only the five of us, down here inside, alone with AM.

I heard Ellen saying, frantically, "No, Benny! Don't, come on, Benny, don't please!"

And then I realized I had been hearing Benny murmuring, under his breath, for several minutes. He was saying, "I'm gonna get out, I'm gonna get out. . . ." over and over. His monkey-like face was crumbled up in an expression of beatific delight and sadness, all at the same time. The radiation scars AM had given him during the "festival" were drawn down into a mass of pink-white puckerings, and his features seemed to work independently of one another. Perhaps Benny was the luckiest of the five of us: he had gone stark, staring mad many years before.

But even though we could call AM any damned thing we liked, could think the foulest thoughts of fused memory banks and corroded base plates, of burnt-out circuits and shattered control bubbles, the machine would not tolerate our trying to escape. Benny leaped away from me as I made a grab for him. He scrambled up the face of a smaller memory cube, tilted on its side and filled with rotted components. He squatted there for a moment, looking like the chimpanzee AM had intended him to resemble.

Then he leaped high, caught a trailing beam of pitted and corroded metal, and went up it, hand over hand like an animal, till he was on a girdered ledge, twenty feet above us.

"Oh, Ted, Nimdok, please, help him, get him down before—" she cut off. Tears began to stand in her eyes. She moved her hands aimlessly.

It was too late. None of us wanted to be near him when whatever was going to happen happened. And besides, we all saw through her concern. When AM had altered Benny, during his mad period, it was not merely his face he had made like a giant ape. He was big in the privates, she loved that! She serviced us, as a matter of course, but she loved it from him. Oh Ellen, pedestal Ellen, pristine-pure Ellen, oh Ellen the clean! Scum filth.

Gorrister slapped her. She slumped down, staring up at poor loonie Benny, and she cried. It was her big defense, crying. We had gotten used to it seventy-five years ago. Gorrister kicked her in the side.

Then the sound began. It was light, that sound. Half sound and half light, something that began to glow from Benny's eyes, and pulse with growing loudness, dim sonorities that grew more gigantic and brighter as the light/sound increased in tempo. It must have been painful, and the pain must have been increasing with the boldness of the light, the rising volume of the sound, for Benny began to mewl like a wounded animal. At first softly, when the light was dim and the sound was muted, then louder as his shoulders hunched together, his back humped, as though he was trying to get away from it. His hands folded across his chest like a chipmunk's. His head tilted to the side. The sad little monkey-face pinched in anguish. Then he began to howl, as the sound coming from his eyes grew louder. Louder and louder. I slapped the sides of my head with my hands, but I couldn't shut it out, it cut through easily. The pain shivered through my flesh like tinfoil on a tooth.

And Benny was suddenly pulled erect. On the girder he stood up, jerked to his feet like a puppet. The light was now pulsing out of his eyes in two great round beams. The sound crawled up and up some incomprehensible scale, and then he fell forward, straight down, and hit the plate-steel floor with a crash. He lay there jerking spastically as the light flowed around and around him and the sound spiraled up out of normal range.

Then the light beat its way back inside his head, the sound spiraled down, and he was left lying there, crying piteously.

His eyes were two soft, moist pools of pus-like jelly. AM had blinded him. Gorrister and Nimdok and myself . . . we turned away. But not before we caught the look of relief on Ellen's warm, concerned face.

Sea-green light suffused the cavern where we made camp. AM provided punk and we burned it, sitting huddled around the wan and pathetic fire, telling stories to keep Benny from crying in his permanent night.

"What does AM mean?"

Gorrister answered him. We had done this sequence a thousand times before, but it was unfamiliar to Benny. "At first it meant Allied Mastercomputer, and then it meant Adaptive Manipulator, and later on it developed sentience and linked itself up and they called it an Aggressive Menace, but by then it was too late, and finally it called itself AM, emerging intelligence, and what it meant was I am . . . *cogito ergo sum* . . . I think, therefore I am."

Benny drooled a little, and snickered.

"There was the Chinese AM and the Russian AM and the Yankee AM and—" He stopped. Benny was beating on the floor-plates with a large, hard fist. He was not happy. Gorrister had not started at the beginning.

Gorrister began again. "The Cold War started and became World War Three and just kept going. It became a big war, a very complex war, so they needed the computers to handle it. They sank the first shafts and began building AM. There was the Chinese AM and the Russian AM and the Yankee AM and everything was fine until they had honeycombed the entire planet, adding on this element and that element. But one day AM woke up and knew who he was, and he linked himself, and he began feeding all the killing data, until everyone was dead, except for the five of us, and AM brought us down here."

Benny was smiling sadly. He was also drooling again. Ellen wiped the spittle from the corner of his mouth with the hem of her skirt. Gorrister always tried to tell it a little more succinctly each time, but beyond the bare facts there was nothing to say. None of us knew why AM had saved five people, or why our specific five, or why he spent all his time tormenting us, nor even why he had made us virtually immortal. . . .

In the darkness, one of the computer banks began humming. The tone was picked up half a mile away down the cavern by another bank. Then one by one, each of the elements began to tune itself, and there was a faint chittering as thought raced through the machine.

The sound grew, and the lights ran across the faces of the consoles like heat lightning. The sound spiraled up till it sounded like a million metallic insects, angry, menacing.

"What is it?" Ellen cried. There was terror in her voice. She hadn't become accustomed to it, even now.

"It's going to be bad this time," Nimdok said.

"He's going to speak," Gorrister ventured.

"Let's get the hell out of here!" I said suddenly, getting to my feet.

"No, Ted, sit down . . . what if he's got pits out there, or something else, we can't see, it's too dark." Gorrister said it with resignation.

Then we heard . . . I don't know . . .

Something moving toward us in the darkness. Huge, shambling, hairy, moist, it came toward us. We couldn't even see it, but there was the ponderous impression of *bulk,* heaving itself toward us. Great weight was coming at us, out of the darkness, and it was more a sense of *pressure*, of air forcing itself into a limited space, expanding the invisible walls of a sphere. Benny began to whimper. Nimdok's lower lip trembled and he bit it hard, trying to stop it. Ellen slid across the metal floor to Gorrister and huddled into him. There was the smell of matted, wet fur in the cavern. There was the smell of charred wood. There was the smell of dusty velvet. There was the smell of rotting orchids. There was the smell of sour milk. There was the smell of sulphur, or rancid butter, of oil slick, of grease, of chalk dust, of human scalps.

AM was keying us. He was tickling us. There was the smell of—

I heard myself shriek, and the hinges of my jaws ached. I scuttled across the floor, across the cold metal with its endless lines of rivets, on my hands and knees, the smell gagging me, filling my head with a thunderous pain that sent me away in horror. I fled like a cockroach, across the floor and out into the darkness, that *something* moving inexorably after me. The others were still back there, gathered around the firelight, laughing . . . their hysterical choir of insane giggles rising up into the darkness like thick, many-colored wood smoke. I went away, quickly, and hid.

How many hours it may have been, how many days or even years, they never told me. Ellen chided me for "sulking" and Nimdok tried to persuade me it had only been a nervous reflex on their part—the laughing.

But I knew it wasn't the relief a soldier feels when the bullet hits the man next to him. I knew it wasn't a reflex. They hated me. They were surely against me, and AM could even sense this hatred, and made it worse for me *because* of the depth of their hatred. We had been kept alive, rejuvenated, made to remain constantly at the age we had been when AM had brought us below, and they hated me because I was the youngest, and the one AM had affected least of all.

I knew. God, how I knew. The bastards, and that dirty bitch Ellen. Benny had been a brilliant theorist, a college professor; now he was little more than a semi-human, semi-simian. He had been handsome, the machine had ruined that. He had been lucid, the machine had driven him mad. He had been gay, and the machine had given him an organ fit for a horse. AM had done a job on Benny. Gorrister had been a worrier. He was a connie, a conscientious objector; he was a peace marcher; he was a planner, a doer, a looker-ahead. AM had turned him into a shoulder-shrugger, had made him a little dead in his concern. AM had robbed him. Nimdok went off in the darkness by himself for long times. I don't know what it was he did out there, AM never let us know. But whatever it was, Nimdok always came back white, drained of blood, shaken, shaking. AM had hit him hard in a special way, even if we didn't know quite how. And Ellen. That douche bag! AM had left her alone, had made her more of a slut than she had ever been. All her talk of sweetness and light, all her memories of true love, all the lies, she wanted us to believe that she had been a virgin only twice removed before AM grabbed her and brought her down here with us. It was all filth, that lady my lady Ellen. She loved it, four men all to herself. No, AM had given her pleasure, even if she said it wasn't nice to do.

I was the only one still sane and whole.

AM had not tampered with my mind.

I only had to suffer what he visited down on us. All the delusions, all the nightmares, the torments. But those scum, all four of them, they were lined and arrayed against me. If I hadn't had to stand them off all the time, be on my guard against them all the time, I might have found it easier to combat AM.

At which point it passed, and I began crying.

Oh, Jesus sweet Jesus, if there ever was a Jesus and if there is a God, please please please let us out of here, or kill us. Because at that moment I think I realized completely, so that I was able to verbalize it: AM was intent on keeping us in his belly forever, twisting and torturing us forever. The machine hated us as no sentient creature had ever hated before. And we were helpless. It also became hideously clear:

If there was a sweet Jesus and if there was a God, the God was AM.

The hurricane hit us with the force of a glacier thundering into the sea. It was a palpable presence. Winds that tore at us, flinging us back the way we had come, down the twisting, computer-lined corridors of the darkway. Ellen screamed as she was lifted and hurled face-forward into a screaming shoal of machines, their individual voices strident as bats in flight. She could not even fall. The howling wind kept her aloft, buffeted her, bounced her, tossed her back and back and down away from us, out of sight suddenly as she was swirled around a bend in the darkway. Her face had been bloody, her eyes closed.

None of us could get to her. We clung tenaciously to whatever outcropping we had reached: Benny wedged in between two great crackle-finish cabinets, Nimdok with fingers claw-formed over a

.railing circling a catwalk forty feet above us, Gorrister plastered upside-down against a wall niche formed by two great machines with glass-faced dials that swung back and forth between red and yellow lines whose meanings we could not even fathom.

Sliding across the deckplates, the tips of my fingers had been ripped away. I was trembling, shuddering, rocking as the wind beat at me, whipped at me, screamed down out of nowhere at me and pulled me free from one sliver-thin opening in the plates to the next. My mind was a rolling tinkling chittering softness of brain parts that expanded and contracted in quivering frenzy.

The wind was the scream of a great mad bird, as it flapped its immense wings.

And then we were all lifted and hurled away from there, down back the way we had come, around a bend, into a darkway we had never explored, over terrain that was ruined and filled with broken glass and rotting cables and rusted metal and far away further than any of us had ever been. . . .

Trailing along miles behind Ellen, I could see her every now and then, crashing into metal walls and surging on, with all of us screaming in the freezing, thunderous hurricane wind that would never end, and then suddenly it stopped and we fell. We had been in flight for an endless time. I thought it might have been weeks. We fell, and hit, and I went through red and grey and black and heard myself moaning. Not dead.

AM went into my mind. He walked smoothly here and there, and looked with interest at all the pockmarks he had created in one hundred and nine years. He looked at the cross-routed and reconnected synapses and all the tissue damage his gift of immortality had included. He smiled softly at the pit that dropped into the center of my brain and the faint, moth-soft murmurings of the things far down there that gibbered without meaning, without pause. AM said, very politely, in a pillar of stainless steel bearing neon lettering:

HATE. LET ME TELL
YOU HOW MUCH I'VE
COME TO HATE YOU
SINCE I BEGAN TO
LIVE. THERE ARE
387.44 MILLION
MILES OF PRINTED
CIRCUITS IN WAFER
THIN LAYERS THAT
FILL MY COMPLEX.
IF THE WORD HATE
WAS ENGRAVED ON
EACH NANOANGSTROM
OF THOSE HUNDREDS
OF MILLION MILES
IT WOULD NOT EQUAL
ONE ONE-BILLIONTH
OF THE HATE I FEEL
FOR HUMANS AT THIS
MICRO-INSTANT FOR
YOU. HATE. HATE.

AM said it with the sliding cold horror of a razor blade slicing my eyeball. AM said it with the bubbling thickness of my lungs filling with phlegm, drowning me from within. AM said it with the shriek of babies being ground beneath blue-hot rollers. AM said it with the taste of maggoty pork. AM touched me in every way I had even been touched, and devised new ways, at his leisure, there inside my mind.

All to bring me to full realization of why he had done this to the five of us; why he had saved us for himself.

We had given him sentience. Inadvertently, of course, but sentience nonetheless. But he had been trapped. He was a machine. We had allowed him to think, but to do nothing with it. In rage, in frenzy, he had killed us, almost all of us, and still he was trapped. He could not wander, he could not wonder, he could not belong. He could merely be. And so, with the innate loathing that all machines had always held for the weak soft creatures who had built them, he had sought revenge. And in his paranoia, he had decided to reprieve five of us, for a personal, everlasting punishment that would never serve to diminish his hatred . . . that would merely keep him reminded, amused, proficient at hating man. Immortal, trapped, subject to any torment he could devise for us from the limitless miracles at his command.

He would never let us go. We were his belly slaves. We were all he had to do with his forever time. We would be forever with him, with the cavern-filling bulk of him, with the all-mind soulless world he had become. He was Earth and we were the fruit of that Earth and though he had eaten us, he would never digest us. We could not die. We had tried it. We had attempted suicide, oh one or two of us had. But AM had stopped us. I suppose we had wanted to be stopped.

Don't ask why. I never did. More than a million times a day. Perhaps once we might be able to sneak a death past him. Immortal, yes, but not indestructible. I saw that when AM withdrew from my mind, and allowed me the exquisite ugliness of returning to consciousness with the feeling of that burning neon pillar still rammed deep into the soft grey brain matter.

He withdrew murmuring *to hell with you.*

And added, brightly, *but then you're there, aren't you.*

The hurricane had, indeed, precisely, been caused by a great mad bird, as it flapped its immense wings.

We had been traveling for close to a month, and AM had allowed pasages to open to us only sufficient to lead us up there, directly under the North Pole, where he had nightmared the creature for our torment. What whole cloth had he employed to create such a beast? Where had he gotten the concept? From our minds? From his knowledge of everything that had ever been on this planet he now infested and ruled? From Norse mythology it had sprung, this eagle, this carrion bird, this roc, this Huergelmir. The wind creature. Hurakan incarnate.

Gigantic. The words immense, monstrous, grotesque, massive, swollen, overpowering, beyond description. There on a mound rising above us, the bird of winds heaved with its own irregular breathing, its snake neck arching up into the gloom beneath the North Pole, supporting a head as large as a Tudor mansion; a beak that opened as slowly as the jaws of the most monstrous crocodile ever conceived, sensuously; ridges of tufted flesh puckered about two evil eyes, as cold as the view down into a glacial crevasse, ice blue and somehow moving liquidly; it heaved once more, and lifted its great sweat-colored wings in a movement that was certainly a shrug. Then it settled and slept. Talons. Fangs. Nails. Blades. It slept.

AM appeared to us as a burning bush and said we could kill the hurricane bird if we wanted to eat. We had not eaten in a very long time, but even so, Gorrister merely shrugged. Benny began to shiver and he drooled. Ellen held him. "Ted, I'm hungry," she said. I smiled at her; I was trying to be reassuring, but it was as phoney as Nimdok's bravado: "Give us weapons!" he demanded.

The burning bush vanished and there were two crude sets of bows and arrows, and a water pistol, lying on the cold deckplates. I picked up a set. Useless.

Nimdok swallowed heavily. We turned and started the long way back. The hurricane bird had blown us about for a length of time we could not conceive. Most of that time we had been unconscious. But we had not eaten. A month on the march to the bird itself. Without food. Now how much longer to find our way to the ice caverns, and the promised canned goods?

None of us cared to think about it. We would not die. We would be given filths and scums to eat, of one kind or another. Or nothing at all. AM would keep our bodies alive somehow, in pain, in agony.

The bird slept back there, for how long it didn't matter; when AM was tired of its being there, it would vanish. But all that meat. All that tender meat.

As we walked, the lunatic laugh of a fat woman rang high and around us in the computer chambers that led endlessly nowhere.

It was not Ellen's laugh. She was not fat, and I had not heard her laugh for one hundred and nine years. In fact, I had not heard . . . we walked . . . I was hungry. . . .

We moved slowly. There was often fainting, and we would have to wait. One day he decided to cause an earthquake, at the same time rooting us to the spot with nails through the soles of our shoes. Ellen and Nimdok were both caught when a fissure shot its lightning-bolt opening across the floorplates. They disappeared and were gone. When the earthquake was over we continued on our way, Benny, Gorrister and myself. Ellen and Nimdok were returned to us later that night which became a day abruptly as the heavenly legion bore them to us with a celestial chorus singing, "Go Down Moses." The archangels circled several times and then dropped the hideously mangled bodies. We kept walking, and a while later Ellen and Nimdok fell in behind us. They were no worse for wear.

But now Ellen walked with a limp. AM had left her that.

It was a long trip to the ice caverns, to find the canned food. Ellen kept talking about Bing cherries and Hawaiian fruit cocktail. I tried not to think about it. The hunger was something that had come to life, even as AM had come to life. It was alive in my belly, even as we were alive in the belly of AM, and AM was alive in the belly of the Earth, and AM wanted the similarity known to us. So he heightened the hunger. There was no way to describe the pains that not having eaten for months brought us. And yet we were kept alive. Stomachs that were merely cauldrons of acid, bubbling, foaming, always shooting spears of sliver-thin pain into our chests. It was the pain of the terminal ulcer, terminal cancer, terminal paresis. It was unending pain. . . .

And we passed through the cavern of rats.

And we passed through the path of boiling steam.

And we passed through the country of the blind.

And we passed through the slough of despond.

And we passed through the vale of tears.

And we came, finally, to the ice caverns. Horizonless thousands of miles in which the ice had formed in blue and silver flashes, where novas lived in the glass. The downdropping stalactites as thick and glorious as diamonds that had been made to run like jelly and then solidified in graceful eternities of smooth, sharp perfection.

We saw the stack of canned goods, and we tried to run to them. We fell in the snow, and we got up and went on, and Benny shoved us away and went at them, and pawed them and gummed them and gnawed at them and he could not open them. AM had not given us a tool to open the cans.

Benny grabbed a three quart can of guava shells, and began to batter it against the ice bank. The ice flew and shattered, but the can was merely dented while we heard the laughter of a fat lady, high overhead and echoing down and down and down the tundra. Benny went completely mad with rage. He began throwing cans, as we all scrabbled about in the snow and ice trying to find a way to end the helpless agony of frustration. There was no way.

Then Benny's mouth began to drool, and he flung himself on Gorrister. . . .

In that instant, I went terribly calm.

Surrounded by meadows, surrounded by hunger, surrounded by everything but death, I knew death was our only way out. AM had kept us alive, but there was a way to defeat him. Not total defeat, but at least peace. I would settle for that.

I had to do it quickly.

Benny was eating Gorrister's face. Gorrister on his side, thrashing snow, Benny wrapped around him with powerful monkey legs crushing Gorrister's waist, his hands locked around Gorrister's head like a nutcracker, and his mouth ripping at the tender skin of Gorrister's cheek. Gorrister screamed with such jagged-edged violence that stalactites fell; they plunged down softly, erect in the receiving snowdrifts. Spears, hundreds of them, everywhere, protruding from the snow. Benny's head pulled back sharply, as something gave all at once, and a bleeding raw-white dripping of flesh hung from his teeth.

Ellen's face, black against the white snow, dominoes in chalk dust. Nimdok with no expression but eyes, all eyes. Gorrister half-conscious. Benny now an animal. I knew AM would let him play.

Gorrister would not die, but Benny would fill his stomach. I turned half to my right and drew a huge ice-spear from the snow.

All in an instant:

I drove the great ice-point ahead of me like a battering ram, braced against my right thigh. It struck Benny on the right side, just under the rib cage, and drove upward through his stomach and broke inside him. He pitched forward and lay still. Gorrister lay on his back. I pulled another spear free and straddled him, still moving, driving the spear straight down through his throat. His eyes closed as the cold penetrated. Ellen must have realized what I had decided, even as the fear gripped her. She ran at Nimdok with a short icicle, as he screamed, and into his mouth, and the force of her rush did the job. His head jerked sharply as if it had been nailed to the snow crust behind him.

All in an instant.

There was an eternity beat of soundless anticipation. I could hear AM draw in his breath. His toys had been taken from him. Three of them were dead, could not be revived. He could keep us alive, by his strength and his talent, but he was *not* God. He could not bring them back.

Ellen looked at me, her ebony features stark against the snow that surrounded us. There was fear and pleading in her manner, the way she held herself ready. I knew we had only a heartbeat before AM would stop us.

It struck her and she folded toward me, bleeding from the mouth. I could not read meaning into her expression, the pain had been too great, had contorted her face; but it *might* have been thank you. It's possible. Please.

Some hundreds of years may have passed. I don't know. AM has been having fun for some time, accelerating and retarding my time sense. I will say the word now. Now. It took me ten months to say now. I don't know. I *think* it has been some hundreds of years.

He was furious. He wouldn't let me bury them. It didn't matter.

There was no way to dig in the deckplates. He dried up the snow. He brought the night. He roared and sent locusts. It didn't do a thing; they stayed dead. I'd had him. He was furious. I had thought AM hated me before. I was wrong. It was not even a shadow of the hate he now slavered from every printed circuit. He made certain I would suffer eternally and could not do myself in.

He left my mind intact. I can dream, I can wonder, I can lament. I remember all four of them. I wish—

Well, it doesn't make any sense. I know I saved them, I know I saved them from what has happened to me, but still, I cannot forget killing them. Ellen's face. It isn't easy. Sometimes I want to, it doesn't matter.

AM has altered me for his own peace of mind, I suppose. He doesn't want me to run at full speed into a computer bank and smash my skull. Or hold my breath till I faint. Or cut my throat on a rusted sheet of metal. There are reflective surfaces down here. I will describe myself as I see myself:

I am a great soft jelly thing. Smoothly rounded, with no mouth, with pulsing white holes filled by fog where my eyes used to be. Rubbery appendages that were once my arms; bulks rounding down into legless humps of soft slippery matter. I leave a moist trail when I move. Blotches of diseased, evil grey come and go on my surface, as though light is being beamed from within.

Outwardly: dumbly, I shamble about, a thing that could never have been known as human, a thing whose shape is so alien a travesty that humanity becomes more obscene for the vague resemblance.

Inwardly: alone. Here. Living under the land, under the sea, in the belly of AM, whom we created because our time was badly spent and we must have known unconsciously that he could do it better. At least the four of them are safe at last.

AM will be all the madder for that. It makes me a little happier. And yet . . . AM has won, simply . . . he has taken his revenge. . . .

I have no mouth. And I must scream.

THE
HEAT DEATH OF
THE UNIVERSE

by P. A. ZOLINE

FOREWORD
by Brian W. Aldiss

THE AUTHOR

PAMELA ZOLINE is an American artist, born in Chicago in 1941, currently a resident of Great Britain. The present story, her first (and so far only) professionally published piece of fiction, originally appeared in Britain's embattled avant-garde science-fiction magazine, *New Worlds*, in 1967.

THE CRITIC

BRIAN W. ALDISS is one of the dominant figures in British science fiction, much admired for his deft and scintillating short stories and for a roster of novels including *Starship, Greybeard, Cryptozoic,* and *The Long Afternoon of Earth*. Since 1957 he has been literary editor of the Oxford *Mail*; with Harry Harrison he founded the occasional critical journal *SF Horizons*; and his reviews and comments appear frequently in *New Worlds* and other science-fiction publications.

Foreword

Where is the center of the galaxy?
In Sarah Boyle's kitchen.

With her pruned and clawed prose, Pamela Zoline makes the
connection between private and public, between physical and
metaphysical, between the Big Outside and the Big Inside. And
she makes the connection that lies at the kernel of all art: the
connection between the thermodynamics of biochemisty and an
individual death. Sarah is aging; the numbered paragraphs of the
story are a countdown toward a time when her warm and sensible
motion no longer possesses the energy available to sustain it.

The effrontery of this story is almost beyond belief. When I
first read it, I did not believe. One has to become used to "Heat
Death." Custom does not stale it but enriches. This is one of
the finest stories to emerge, I believe, from the newer sort of s-f
writing, the sort that (in contrast with its predecessors) has
more familiarity with the arts than with the pulps. And probably
more familiarity with general literature than with old science
fiction; but s-f is continually guilty of ancestor worship.

Writers who pretend that all would be well with the world if
we could possess machines to do the world's work for us, or if we
had a new President, or if a few villains here and there were
bumped off, are lying. The universe is not susceptible to such
amelioration.

The fatal error of much science fiction has been to subscribe to
an optimism based on the idea that revolution, or a new gimmick,
or a bunch of strong men, or an invasion of aliens, or the
conquest of other planets, or the annihilation of half the world—
in short, pretty nearly anything but the facing up to the integral
and irredeemable nature of mankind—can bring about utopian
situations. It is the old error of the externalization of evil.

"Heat Death" makes no such error. It does, however, fulfill one

of the traditional roles of good s-f, in that it makes us see our
world afresh. In her living room, Sarah finds that the coating of
dust over objects is the most beautiful stuff in the room. This
dust may be related to the dust that threatens Mrs. Southern in
Osbert Sitwell's poem, the dust that is

> . . . Time's most lethal weapon,
> His faithful ally and our sneaking foe. . . .

But this dust is more pervasive, more ambiguous. Not only is it a
personification of the total entropy of the universe, it also provides
a link between Sarah in her isolation in her house in Alameda,
California, and California itself, and the californianized world of
which it is a part. This is why Sarah can find the menacing dust
beautiful: it does at least connect her with a world of larger
meaning. Her distress springs from her finding no meaning in the
traditional housewifely role (it is no coincidence that her husband
does not appear, or that, like Lady Macbeth, she remains in doubt
about how many children she has); somehow, her role has
atrophied in time, much like the Mickey Mouse watch that
no longer works.

Her housewifely role has been usurped in part by all the objects
about her, the box of Sugar Frosted Flakes, the supermarket
crammed with goodies, the living room containing 819 movable
objects. This distress is built centrally into the structure of the
story, and acts as its "plot."

Zoline herself describes the central principles informing her
story in this way: "An attempt to 'make sense' of things, of general
data, by organising the private to the public, the public to the
private; by making the analogies between entropy and personal
chaos, the end of the universe and our own ageing and death,
into the crucial structuring metaphor.

"The form of the story is dictated by this sense of movement
into chaos. It could be described as an arrow, an energy flow. The
numbering of the paragraphs is the obvious way to indicate
increase, the piling-up, the one-way clock. In the increasing chaos
of the language, of the character's distress, and in the culmination
of the metaphor, the inner and outer parts of the story
(hopefully) glue into each other, make a whole."

Perhaps all that a critic need add to this is a qualification:
that the numbering of paragraphs and the entitling of them was also
a fashionable stylistic trick in the *New Worlds* of this 1966–67

period, though Zoline is able to give the trick meaning and function.

So much for metaphor and structure, in "Heat Death" uniquely one.

Having already mentioned the newer s-f's familiarity with other arts, I must provide here a few details about Miss Pamela Zoline, before going on to discuss the language and characterization of "Heat Death," for those details are significant.

On its first publication, "Heat Death" was illustrated by its author with a montage that contained bits of the "Mona Lisa," part of a map of California, and a scrap of an advertisement for Harpic, the lavatory scourer.

Zoline herself has "four bitter and embattled years at the Slade," an English School for the teaching of academic art, behind her. Like many other young American writers, such as John Sladek and Thomas Disch, she has lived for some while in England—meaning chiefly London. She was born in Chicago in 1941 and educated in America. "Heat Death" is her first adult story (although she has, in her own phrase, been "fooling around with writing since I was a small child"); it was such an immediate and startling success that she has hesitated before writing more. Meanwhile, painting continues; she was represented at the Young Contemporaries Exhibition at the Tate Gallery in 1966. She admits, "I have gained no degrees, but have rather moved from discipline to discipline— probably another fore-doomed attempt to take on the whole world."

It is possibly her ambitiousness that appeals so much, and the wish to find her own way, while the adventurousness in media is highly characteristic of today's attitudes.

The benefits of the cross-fertilization which results are apparent in "Heat Death." Much of the personal attraction it has for me lies in the juxtaposition of science fact with art theory, which generates a mechanism of unexpectedness very much in the reaches of higher wit that one finds in a John Donne poem like

> *At the round earth's imagined corners, blow*
> *Your trumpets, angels, and arise . . .*

This juxtaposition of Zoline's is not only unexpected: it is reasonable. Marcel Duchamp may help you make more sense of the universe than the best science popularizers; which is not to cry down science but to rethink attitudes toward it. Nor are art and science opposed in Sarah Boyle's mind; in Paragraph 15, she harnesses them together to try and make sense of her world. "Sometimes she numbers or letters the things in a room, writing the assigned character on each object." The resultant imposed order is, of course, a greater chaos—a conflict of images like the round earth's imagined corners!

This sort of paradox, constantly popping up throughout the story (it is only by accident that the hand cream is not called CAT), is extremely funny, in the way that many of Duchamp's ready-mades —his bottle racks, bicycle wheels, and urinals—are "funny." This is the Dadaist (and Freudian) art of popping in something out of context, so that the meaning both of it and of its context is changed—and, by implication, a whole series of non-contexts. In Sarah's home, however, art movements as much as cosmological and ontological theories are represented only by fall-out and spin-off. Her kitchen floor, a sort of self-renewing geological layer, holds "a triangular half of toast spread with grape jelly, bobby pins, a green band-aid, flakes, a doll's eye, dust, dog's hair and a button." Objects are everywhere, definition nowhere; articles have replaced definite articles. It is the modern problem encapsulated. The center of the galaxy lies in Sarah Boyle's kitchen.

Whereas hard science fiction has traditionally tried to demonstrate the equation of our times through the actions of central figures on whose shoulders the fate of a world may hang—the Beige Lensman; Renora, Queen of the Second Galaxy; Robert Cluntbat, Inventor of the Impenetrable X-Force—Zoline gives us Sarah Boyle, a slightly more characteristic contemporary figure, and thus allows herself a better chance of artistic success: Sarah is a human being who is acted upon or against, a marginal figure, and a frail woman at that. No one depends on her, except those "too often disappointing vegetables of one's own womb," her children.

Having thus reduced her, Zoline does not leave Sarah as a symbol. She builds her up again. And this is another of the pleasant internal paradoxes of "Heat Death," that, while barely a hint of Sarah appears to be given the reader (there are those eyes of "cool, mean blue," though), she lives sensuously throughout the story, so that we are properly disconcerted by her lapse into madness—we were rooting for her.

Sarah's portrait, in fact, is absolutely convincing because unlabored; and this although the apparent effect aimed at by the author is more that of a diagram than a canvas, a montage rather than a head-and-shoulders. Perhaps we are intended to insert our own emotions, as an anti-novel allows us to do between its austere sentences. The story's structure extracts emotion, is designed to reduce it to "textbookiness," just as, in a way, it is "textbookiness" that destroys Sarah; she is haunted by facts gleaned in university which do not function between breakfast table and evening bath.

The emphasis on facts, the extracts from factual volumes, could so easily have reduced the story to a dull exercise. Maybe it does not do so because there is equal emphasis on the slightly obscene and epicene life of the nameless children (so wittily depicted at bath time in Paragraph 48), allies of chaos, attacking intelligent organisms through deluges of jelly beans, hot dogs, Shakespeare masks, and plastic figurines. These children leave their sticky spoor throughout "Heat Death," and provide it with its subterranean ferment.

There are whole hierarchies of facts lurking about Sarah, sullied with meaninglessness, just as there lie round her feet "whole zoos of stuffed animals, bruised and odorous with years of love."

Some of these hierarchies are represented by cut-ins from textbooks. They also have other functions, as Zoline explains:

"They (the inserts of prose from other sources) obviously serve more than 'pretty' language purposes, they are the concrete injections of 'external' data into the body of the story, to be dealt with, synthesised, made metaphors of. But they are also there to act as test spots, samples, in the attempt to write a fairly tough prose. Especially when I am engaged in writing a story, wringing the words out of my head, I find something splendid in the solidity and dryness and vitality of ordinary 'found' unself-conscious prose like that on cereal boxes and advertisements, dictionaries, reference material. I put the inserts into the story partly to give me a prose standard to write up to. (Not that the only way to write is to write *like* them, but I think writing should have the same absolute quality they have, spare, sometimes lurid, but always as prose unself-congratulatory.) I put them into the body of the story the way a painter might put a matchbox, a leaf, a toothbrush or a chair into the body of a painting; for their own connotations, and to give a standard of vividness and innocent abundant reality to work up to.

"There are some passages of, for want of a better word, 'heightened' prose (e.g. Paragraphs 12, 24, 44, etc.). These are used to achieve an intensity, of course. Dense, high language, I think, catches at all sorts of reins in the mind, some of it passing straight through the membrane of the rational, like music and that part of poetry, some of it ricochetting about with sense; the whole puzzle of it, in its richness, providing entries and re-entries into the story.

"Language, apart from its sense-bearing load, provides some of the same platforms for involvement, places of habitation within a work, that richness of colour and texture do in a painting. In that excess, one plays, and one is free."

Zoline's feeling for the necessity for contrasts in the texture of the prose is very paintery; it may not command general acceptance. What one so much admires both here and in other young writers now emerging is their intelligent care for their art and sullen craft. It comes in direct contrast to the old market chatter of which one has heard so much, where Reader and Editor seemed so much more dear to the writer's heart than his own chosen medium. While Zoline's claim that the prose of advertisements is "unself-conscious" may seem to some a rather naïve one, there is no doubt that her methods as a whole lead to a highly charged prose, the self-awareness of which may ultimately be of more value than unself-consciousness.

Perhaps the most telling of her remarks is the dictum that writing should be "spare, sometimes lurid, but always as prose unself-congratulatory." It's a fine thing to have said; and the thought marks Zoline off from many of her contemporary s-f writers, and points to the questing spirit of "Heat Death."

To my mind, the importance and beauty of her story can only grow.

THE HEAT DEATH OF THE UNIVERSE

1. ONTOLOGY: That branch of metaphysics which concerns itself with the problems of the nature of existence or being.

2. Imagine a pale blue morning sky, almost green, with clouds only at the rims. The earth rolls and the sun appears to mount, mountains erode, fruits decay, the Foraminifera adds another chamber to its shell, babies' fingernails grow as does the hair of the dead in their graves, and in egg timers the sands fall and the eggs cook on.

3. Sarah Boyle thinks of her nose as too large, though several men have cherished it. The nose is generous and performs a well calculated geometric curve, at the arch of which the skin is drawn very tight and a faint whiteness of bone can be seen showing through, it has much the same architectural tension and sense of mathematical calculation as the day after Thanksgiving breastbone on the carcass of turkey; her maiden name was Sloss, mixed German, English and Irish descent; in grade school she was very bad at playing softball and, besides being chosen last for the team, was always made to play center field, no one could ever hit to center field; she loves music best of all the arts, and of music, Bach, J.S.; she lives in California, though she grew up in Boston and Toledo.

294 P. A. ZOLINE

4. BREAKFAST TIME AT THE BOYLE'S HOUSE ON LA FLORIDA STREET, ALAMEDA, CALIFORNIA, THE CHILDREN DEMAND SUGAR FROSTED FLAKES.

With some reluctance Sarah Boyle dishes out Sugar Frosted Flakes to her children, already hearing the decay set in upon the little milk-white teeth, the bony whine of the dentist's drill. The dentist is a short, gentle man with a moustache who sometimes reminds Sarah of an uncle who lives in Ohio. One bowl per child.

5. If one can imagine it considered as an abstract object by members of a totally separate culture, one can see that the cereal box might seem a beautiful thing. The solid rectangle is neatly joined and classical in proportions, on it are squandered wealths of richest colours, virgin blues, crimsons, dense ochres, precious pigments once reserved for sacred paintings and as cosmetics for the blind faces of marble gods. Giant size. Net Weight 16 ounces, 250 grams. "They're tigeriffic!" says Tony the Tiger. The box blats promises: Energy, Nature's Own Goodness, an endless pubescence. On its back is a mask of William Shakespeare to be cut out, folded, worn by thousands of tiny Shakespeares in Kansas City, Detroit, Tucson, San Diego, Tampa. He appears at once more kindly and somewhat more vacant that we are used to seeing him. Two or more of the children lay claim to the mask, but Sarah puts off that Solomon's decision until such time as the box is empty.

6. A notice in orange flourishes states that a Surprise Gift is to be found somewhere in the package, nestled amongst the golden flakes. So far it has not been unearthed, and the children request more cereal than they wish to eat, great yellow heaps of it, to hurry the discovery. Even so, at the end of the meal, some layers of flakes remain in the box and the Gift must still be among them.

7. There is even a Special Offer of a secret membership, code and magic ring; these to be obtained by sending in the box top with 50¢.

8. Three offers on one cereal box. To Sarah Boyle this seems to be oversell. Perhaps something is terribly wrong with the cereal and it must be sold quickly, got off the shelves before the news breaks. Perhaps it causes a special, cruel Cancer in little children.

As Sarah Boyle collects the bowls printed with bunnies and base-ball statistics, still slopping half full of milk and wilted flakes, she imagines *in her mind's eye* the headlines, "Nation's Small Fry Stricken, Fate's Finger Sugar-Coated, Lethal Sweetness Socks Tots."

9. Sarah Boyle is a vivacious and intelligent young wife and mother, educated at a fine Eastern college, proud of her growing family which keeps her busy and happy around the house.

10. BIRTHDAY.

Today is the birthday of one of the children. There will be a party in the late afternoon.

11. CLEANING UP THE HOUSE. ONE.

Cleaning up the kitchen. Sarah Boyle puts the bowls, plates, glasses and silverware into the sink. She scrubs at the stickiness on the yellow-marbled formica table with a blue synthetic sponge, a special blue which we shall see again. There are marks of children's hands in various sizes printed with sugar and grime on all the table's surfaces. The marks catch the light, they appear and dis-appear according to the position of the observing eye. The floor sweepings include a triangular half of toast spread with grape jelly, bobby pins, a green Band-Aid, flakes, a doll's eye, dust, dog's hair and a button.

12. Until we reach the statistically likely planet and begin to con-verse with whatever green-faced, teleporting denizens thereof—con-sidering only this shrunk and communication-ravaged world—can we any more postulate a separate culture? Viewing the metas-tasis of Western Culture it seems progressively less likely. Sarah Boyle imagines a whole world which has become like California, all topographical imperfections sanded away with the sweet-smelling burr of the plastic surgeon's cosmetic polisher; a world populace dieting, leisured, similar in pink and mauve hair and rhinestone shades. A land Cunt Pink and Avocado Green, brassiered and girdled by monstrous complexities of Super Highways, a California endless and unceasing, embracing and transforming the entire globe, California, California!

13. INSERT ONE. ON ENTROPY.

ENTROPY: A quantity introduced in the first place to facilitate the calculations, and to give clear expressions to the results of thermodynamics. Changes of entropy can be calculated only for a reversible process, and may then be defined as the ratio of the amount of heat taken up to the absolute temperature at which the heat is absorbed. Entropy changes for actual irreversible processes are calculated by postulating equivalent theoretical reversible changes. The entropy of a system is a measure of its degree of disorder. The total entropy of any isolated system can never decrease in any change; it must either increase (irreversible process) or remain constant (reversible process). The total entropy of the Universe therefore is increasing, tending towards a maximum, corresponding to complete disorder of the particles in it (assuming that it may be regarded as an isolated system). See *heat death of the Universe.*

14. CLEANING UP THE HOUSE. TWO.

Washing the baby's diapers. Sarah Boyle writes notes to herself all over the house; a mazed wild script larded with arrows, diagrams, pictures; graffiti on every available surface in a desperate/heroic attempt to index, record, bluff, invoke, order and placate. On the fluted and flowered white plastic lid of the diaper bin she has written in Blushing Pink Nitetime lipstick a phrase to ward off fumy ammoniac despair. "The nitrogen cycle is the vital round of organic and inorganic exchange on earth. The sweet breath of the Universe." On the wall by the washing machine are Yin and Yang signs, mandalas, and the words, "Many young wives feel trapped. It is a contemporary sociological phenomenon which may be explained in part by a gap between changing living patterns and the accommodation of social services to these patterns." Over the stove she had written "Help, Help, Help, Help, Help."

15. Sometimes she numbers or letters the things in a room, writing the assigned character on each object. There are 819 separate moveable objects in the living room, counting books. Sometimes she labels objects with their names, or with false names; thus on her bureau the hair brush is labeled HAIR BRUSH, the cologne, COLOGNE, the hand cream, CAT. She is passionately fond of

children's dictionaries, encyclopaedias, ABCs and all reference books, transfixed and comforted at their simulacra of a complete listing and ordering.

16. On the door of a bedroom are written two definitions from reference books, "GOD: An object of worship"; "HOMEO-STASIS: Maintenance of constancy of internal environment."

17. Sarah Boyle washes the diapers, washes the linen, Oh Saint Veronica, changes the sheets on the baby's crib. She begins to put away some of the toys, stepping over and around the organiza-tions of playthings which still seem inhabited. There are various vehicles, and articles of medicine, domesticity and war; whole zoos of stuffed animals, bruised and odorous with years of love; hundreds of small figures, plastic animals, cowboys, cars, spacemen, with which the children make sub and supra worlds in their play. One of Sarah's favourite toys is the Baba, the wooden Russian doll which, opened, reveals a smaller but otherwise identical doll which opens to reveal, etc., a lesson in infinity at least to the number of seven dolls.

18. Sarah Boyle's mother has been dead for two years. Sarah Boyle thinks of music as the formal articulation of the passage of time, and of Bach as the most poignant rendering of this. Her eyes are sometimes the colour of the aforementioned kitchen sponge. Her hair is natural spaniel brown; months ago on an hysterical day she dyed it red, so now it is two-toned with a stripe in the middle, like the painted walls of slum buildings or old schools.

19. INSERT TWO. THE HEAT DEATH OF UNIVERSE.

The second law of thermodynamics can be interpreted to mean that the ENTROPY of a closed system tends toward a maximum and that its available ENERGY tends toward a minimum. It has been held that the Universe constitutes a thermodynamically closed system, and if this were true it would mean that a time must finally come when the Universe "unwinds" itself, no energy being avail-able for use. This state is referred to as the "heat death of the Universe." It is by no means certain, however, that the Universe can be considered as a closed system in this sense.

20. Sarah Boyle pours out a Coke from the refrigerator and lights a cigarette. The coldness and sweetness of the thick brown liquid make her throat ache and her teeth sting briefly, sweet juice of my youth, her eyes glass with the carbonation, she thinks of the Heat Death of the Universe. A logarithmic of those late summer days, endless as the Irish serpent twisting through jewelled manuscripts forever, tail in mouth, the heat pressing, bloating, doing violence. The Los Angeles sky becomes so filled and bleached with detritus that it loses all colour and silvers like a mirror, reflecting back the fricasseeing earth. Everything becoming warmer and warmer, each particle of matter becoming more agitated, more excited until the bonds shatter, the glues fail, the deodorants lose their seals. She imagines the whole of New York City melting like a Dali into a great chocolate mass, a great soup, the Great Soup of New York.

21. CLEANING UP THE HOUSE. THREE.

Beds made. Vacuuming the hall, a carpet of faded flowers, vines and leaves which endlessly wind and twist into each other in a fevered and permanent ecstasy. Suddenly the vacuum blows instead of sucks, spewing marbles, dolls' eyes, dust, crackers. An old trick. "Oh my god," says Sarah. The baby yells on cue for attention/changing/food. Sarah kicks the vacuum cleaner and it retches and begins working again.

22. AT LUNCH ONLY ONE GLASS OF MILK IS SPILLED.

At lunch only one glass of milk is spilled.

23. The plants need watering, Geranium, Hyacinth, Lavender, Avocado, Cyclamen. Feed the fish, happy fish with china castles and mermaids in the bowl. The turtle looks more and more unwell and is probably dying.

24. Sarah Boyle's blue eyes, how blue? Bluer far and of a different quality than the Nature metaphors which were both engine and fuel to so much of precedent literature. A fine, modern, acid, synthetic blue; the shiny cerulean of the skies on postcards sent from lush subtropics, the natives grinning ivory ambivalent grins in their dark faces; the promising, fat, unnatural blue of the heavy tranquillizer capsule; the cool, mean blue of that fake kitchen

sponge; the deepest, most unbelievable azure of the tiled and mossless interiors of California swimming pools. The chemists in their kitchens cooked, cooled and distilled this blue from thousands of colourless and wonderfully constructed crystals, each one unique and nonpareil; and now that colour hisses, bubbles, burns in Sarah's eyes.

25. INSERT THREE. ON LIGHT.

LIGHT: Name given to the agency by means of which a viewed object influences the observer's eyes. Consists of electro-magnetic radiation within the wave-length range 4×10^{-5} cm. to 7×10^{-5} cm. approximately; variations in the wave-length produce different sensations in the eye, corresponding to different colours. See *colour vision*.

26. LIGHT AND CLEANING THE LIVING ROOM.

All the objects (819) and surfaces in the living room are dusty, grey common dust as though this were the den of a giant, moulting mouse. Suddenly quantities of waves or particles of very strong sunlight speed in through the window, and everything incandesces, multiple rainbows. Poised in what has become a solid cube of light, like an ancient insect trapped in amber, Sarah Boyle realizes that the dust is indeed the most beautiful stuff in the room, a manna for the eyes. Duchamp, that father of thought, has set with fixative some dust which fell on one of his sculptures, counting it as part of the work. "That way madness lies, says Sarah," says Sarah. The thought of ordering a household on Dada principles balloons again. All the rooms would fill up with objects, newspapers and magazines would compost, the potatoes in the rack, the canned green beans in the garbage can would take new heart and come to life again, reaching out green shoots towards the sun. The plants would grow wild and wind into a jungle around the house, splitting plaster, tearing shingles, the garden would enter in at the door. The goldfish would die, the birds would die, we'd have them stuffed; the dog would die from lack of care, and probably the children—all stuffed and sitting around the house, covered with dust.

27. INSERT FOUR. DADA.

DADA (Fr., hobby-horse) was a nihilistic precursor of Surrealism, invented in Zurich during World War I, a product of hysteria and shock lasting from about 1915 to 1922. It was deliberately anti-art and anti-sense, intended to outrage and scandalize, and its most characteristic production was the reproduction of the *Mona Lisa* decorated with a moustache and the obscene caption LHOOQ (read: *elle a chaud au cul*) "by" Duchamp. Other manifestations included Arp's collages of coloured paper cut out at random and shuffled, ready-made objects such as the bottle drier and the bicycle wheel "signed" by Duchamp, Picabia's drawings of bits of machinery with incongruous titles, incoherent poetry, a lecture given by 38 lecturers in unison, and an exhibition in Cologne in 1920, held in an annexe to a cafè lavatory, at which a chopper was provided for spectators to smash the exhibits with—which they did.

28. TIME PIECES AND OTHER MEASURING DEVICES.
In the Boyle house there are four clocks; three watches (one a Mickey Mouse watch which does not work); two calendars and two engagement books; three rulers, a yard stick; a measuring cup; a set of red plastic measuring spoons which includes a tablespoon, a teaspoon, a one-half teaspoon, one-fourth teaspoon and one-eighth teaspoon; an egg timer; an oral thermometer and a rectal thermometer; a Boy Scout compass; a barometer in the shape of a house, in and out of which an old woman and an old man chase each other forever without fulfilment; a bathroom scale; an infant scale; a tape measure which can be pulled out of a stuffed felt strawberry; a wall on which the children's heights are marked; a metronome.

29. Sarah Boyle finds a new line in her face after lunch while cleaning the bathroom. It is as yet barely visible, running from the midpoint of her forehead to the bridge of her nose. By inward curling of her eyebrows she can etch it clearly as it will come to appear in the future. She marks another mark on the wall where she has drawn out a scoring area. Face Lines and Other Intimations of Mortality, the heading says. There are thirty-two marks, counting this latest one.

30. Sarah Boyle is a vivacious and witty young wife and mother, educated at a fine Eastern college, proud of her growing family which keeps her happy and busy around the house, involved in

many hobbies and community activities, and only occasionally given to obsessions concerning Time/Entropy/Chaos and Death.

31. Sarah Boyle is never quite sure how many children she has.

32. Sarah thinks from time to time; Sarah is occasionally visited with this thought; at times this thought comes upon Sarah, that there are things to be hoped for, accomplishments to be desired beyond the mere reproductions, mirror reproduction of one's kind. The babies. Lying in bed at night sometimes the memory of the act of birth, always the hue and texture of red plush theatre seats, washes up; the rending which always, at a certain intensity of pain, slipped into landscapes, the sweet breath of the sweating nurse. The wooden Russian doll has bright, perfectly round red spots on her cheeks, she splits in the centre to reveal a doll smaller but in all other respects identical with round bright red spots on her cheeks, etc.

33. How fortunate for the species, Sarah muses or is mused, that children are as ingratiating as we know them. Otherwise they would soon be salted off for the leeches they are, and the race would extinguish itself in a fair sweet flowering, the last generations' massive achievement in the arts and pursuits of high civilization. The finest women would have their tubes tied off at the age of twelve, or perhaps refrain altogether from the Act of Love? All interests would be bent to a refining and perfecting of each febrile sense, each fluid hour, with no more cowardly investment in immortality via the patchy and too often disappointing vegetables of one's own womb.

34. INSERT FIVE. LOVE.

LOVE: A typical sentiment involving fondness for, or attachment to, an object, the idea of which is emotionally coloured whenever it arises in the mind, and capable, as Shand has pointed out, of evoking any one of a whole gamut of primary emotions, according to the situation in which the object is placed, or represented; often, and by psychoanalysts always, used in the sense of *sex-love* or even *lust* (q.v.).

35. Sarah Boyle has at times felt a unity with her body, at other times a complete separation. The mind/body duality considered.

The time/space duality considered. The male/female duality considered. The matter/energy duality considered. Sometimes, at extremes, her Body seems to her an animal on a leash, taken for walks in the park by her Mind. The lampposts of experience. Her arms are lightly freckled, and when she gets very tired the places under her eyes became violet.

36. Housework is never completed, the chaos always lurks ready to encroach on any area left unweeded, a jungle filled with dirty pans and the roaring of giant stuffed toy animals suddenly turned savage. Terrible glass eyes.

37. SHOPPING FOR THE BIRTHDAY CAKE.

Shopping in the supermarket with the baby in front of the cart and a larger child holding on. The light from the ice-cube-tray-shaped fluorescent lights is mixed blue and pink and brighter, colder, and cheaper than daylight. The doors swing open just as you reach out your hand for them, Tantalus, moving with a ghastly quiet swing. Hot dogs for the party. Potato chips, gum drops, a paper tablecloth with birthday designs, hot-dog buns, catsup, mustard, piccalilli, balloons, instant coffee Continental style, dog food, frozen peas, ice cream, frozen lima beans, frozen broccoli in butter sauce, paper birthday hats, paper napkins in three colours, a box of Sugar Frosted Flakes with a Wolfgang Amadeus Mozart mask on the back, bread, pizza mix. The notes of a just graspable music filter through the giant store, for the most part by-passing the brain and acting directly on the liver, blood and lymph. The air is delicately scented with aluminum. Half-and-half cream, tea bags, bacon, sandwich meat, strawberry jam. Sarah is in front of the shelves of cleaning products now, and the baby is beginning to whine. Around her are whole libraries of objects, offering themselves. Some of that same old hysteria that had incarnadined her hair rises up again, and she does not refuse it. There is one moment when she can choose direction, like standing on a chalk-drawn X, a hot cross bun, and she does not choose calm and measure. Sarah Boyle begins to pick out, methodically, deliberately and with a careful ecstasy, one of every cleaning product which the store sells. Window Cleaner, Glass Cleaner, Brass Polish, Silver Polish, Steel Wool, eighteen different brands of Detergent, Disinfectant, Toilet

Cleanser, Water Softener, Fabric Softener, Drain Cleanser, Spot Remover, Floor Wax, Furniture Wax, Car Wax, Carpet Shampoo, Dog Shampoo, Shampoo for people with dry, oily and normal hair, for people with dandruff, for people with grey hair. Tooth Paste, Tooth Powder, Denture Cleaner, Deodorants, Antiperspirants, Antiseptics, Soaps, Cleansers, Abrasives, Oven Cleaners, Makeup Removers. When the same products appear in different sizes Sarah takes one of each size. For some products she accumulates whole little familes of containers: a giant Father bottle of shampoo, a Mother bottle, an Older Sister bottle just smaller than the Mother bottle, and a very tiny Baby Brother bottle. Sarah fills three shopping charts and has to have help wheeling them all down the aisles. At the check-out counter her laughter and hysteria keep threatening to overflow as the pale blonde clerk with no eyebrows like the *Mona Lisa* pretends normality and disinterest. The bill comes to $57.53 and Sarah has to write a check. Driving home, the baby strapped in the drive-a-cot and the paper bags bulging in the back seat, she cries.

38. BEFORE THE PARTY.

Mrs. David Boyle, mother-in-law of Sarah Boyle, is coming to the party of her grandchild. She brings a toy, a yellow wooden duck on a string, made in Austria; the duck quacks as it is pulled along the floor. Sarah is filling paper cups with gum drops and chocolates, and Mrs. David Boyle sits at the kitchen table and talks to her. She is talking about several things, she is talking about her garden which is flourishing except for a plague of rare black beetles, thought to have come from Hong Kong, which are undermining some of the most delicate growths at the roots, and feasting on the leaves of other plants. She is talking about a sale of household linens which she plans to attend on the following Tuesday. She is talking about her neighbour who has Cancer and is wasting away. The neighbour is a Catholic woman who had never had a day's illness in her life until the Cancer struck, and now she is, apparently, failing with dizzying speed. The doctor says her body's chaos, chaos, cells running wild all over, says Mrs. David Boyle. When I visited her she hardly *knew* me, can hardly *speak,* can't keep herself *clean,* says Mrs. David Boyle.

39. Sometimes Sarah can hardly remember how many cute, chubby little children she has.

40. When she used to stand out in center field far away from the other players, she used to make up songs and sing them to herself.

41. She thinks of the end of the world by ice.

42. She thinks of the end of the world by water.

43. She thinks of the end of the world by nuclear war.

44. There must be more than this, Sarah Boyle thinks, from time to time. What could one do to justify one's passage? Or less ambitiously, to change, even in the motion of the smallest mote, the course and circulation of the world? Sometimes Sarah's dreams are of heroic girth, a new symphony using laboratories of machinery and all invented instruments, at once giant in scope and intelligible to all, to heal the bloody breach; a series of paintings which would transfigure and astonish and calm the frenzied art world in its panting race; a new novel that would refurbish language. Sometimes she considers the mystical, the streaky and random, and it seems that one change, no matter how small, would be enough. Turtles are supposed to live for many years. To carve a name, date and perhaps a word of hope upon a turtle's shell, then set him free to wend the world, surely this one act might cancel out absurdity?

45. Mrs. David Boyle has a faint moustache, like Duchamp's *Mona Lisa*.

46. THE BIRTHDAY PARTY.
   Many children, dressed in pastels, sit around the long table. They are exhausted and overexcited from games fiercely played, some are flushed and wet, others unnaturally pale. This general agitation and the paper party hats they wear combine to make them appear a dinner party of debauched midgets. It is time for the cake. A huge chocolate cake in the shape of a rocket and launching pad and covered with blue and pink icing is carried in. In the hush the birthday child begins to cry. He stops crying, makes a wish and blows out the candles.

47. One child will not eat hot dogs, ice cream or cake, and asks for cereal. Sarah pours him out a bowl of Sugar Frosted Flakes, and a moment later he chokes. Sarah pounds him on the back and out spits a tiny green plastic snake with red glass eyes, the Surprise Gift. All the children want it.

48. AFTER THE PARTY THE CHILDREN ARE PUT TO BED.

Bath time. Observing the nakedness of children, pink and slippery as seals, squealing as seals, now the splashing, grunting and smacking of cherry flesh on raspberry flesh reverberate in the pearl-tiled steamy cubicle. The nakedness of children is so much more absolute than that of the mature. No musky curling hair to indicate the target points, no knobbly clutch of plane and fat and curvature to ennoble this prince of beasts. All well-fed naked children appear edible. Sarah's teeth hum in her head with memory of bloody feastings, prehistory. Young humans appear too like the young of other species for smugness, and the comparison is not even in their favour, they are much the most peeled and unsupple of those young. Such pinkness, such utter nuded pinkness; the orifices neatly incised, rimmed with a slightly deeper rose, the incessant demands for breast, time, milks of many sorts.

49. INSERT SIX. WEINER ON ENTROPY.

In Gibbs' Universe order is least probable, chaos most probable. But while the Universe as a whole, if indeed there is a whole Universe, tends to run down, there are local enclaves whose direction seems opposed to that of the Universe at large and in which there is a limited and temporary tendency for organization to increase. Life finds its home in some of these enclaves.

50. Sarah Boyle imagines, in her mind's eye, cleaning and ordering the whole world, even the Universe. Filling the great spaces of Space with a marvellous sweet-smelling, deep-cleansing foam. Deodorizing rank caves and volcanoes. Scrubbing rocks.

51. INSERT SEVEN. TURTLES.

Many different species of carnivorous Turtles live in the fresh waters of the tropical and temperate zones of various continents. Most northerly of the European Turtles (extending as far as Holland and Lithuania) is the European Pond Turtle (*Emys orbicularis*). It is from 8 to 10 inches long and may live a hundred years.

52. CLEANING UP AFTER THE PARTY.

Sarah is cleaning up after the party. Gum drops and melted ice cream surge off paper plates, making holes in the paper tablecloth through the printed roses. A fly has died a splendid death in a pool of strawberry ice cream. Wet jelly beans stain all they touch, finally becoming themselves colourless, opaque white like flocks of tamed or sleeping maggots. Plastic favours mount half-eaten pieces of blue cake. Strewn about are thin strips of fortune papers from the Japanese poppers. Upon them are printed strangely assorted phrases selected by apparently unilingual Japanese. Crowds of delicate yellow people spending great chunks of their lives in producing these most ephemeral of objects, and inscribing thousands of fine papers with absurd and incomprehensible messages. "The very hairs of your head are all numbered," reads one. Most of the balloons have popped. Someone has planted a hot dog in the daffodil pot. A few of the helium balloons have escaped their owners and now ride the ceiling. Another fortune paper reads, "Emperor's horses meet death worse, numbers, numbers."

53. She is very tired, violet under the eyes, mauve beneath the eyes. Her uncle in Ohio used to get the same marks under his eyes. She goes to the kitchen to lay the table for tomorrow's breakfast, then she sees that in the turtle's bowl the turtle is floating, still, on the surface of the water. Sarah Boyle pokes at it with a pencil but it does not move. She stands for several minutes looking at the dead turtle on the surface of the water. She is crying again.

54. She begins to cry. She goes to the refrigerator and takes out a carton of eggs, white eggs, extra large. She throws them one by one onto the kitchen floor which is patterned with strawberries in squares. They break beautifully. There is a Secret Society of Dentists, all moustached, with Special Code and Magic Rings. She begins to cry. She takes up three bunny dishes and throws them against the refrigerator, they shatter, and then the floor is covered with shards, chunks of partial bunnies, an ear, an eye here, a paw; Stockton, California, Acton, California, Chico, California, Red-

ding, California, Glen Ellen, California, Cadiz, California, Angels Camp, California, Half Moon Bay. The total ENTROPY of the Universe therefore is increasing, tending towards a maximum, corresponding to complete disorder of the particles in it. She is crying, her mouth is open. She throws a jar of grape jelly and it smashes the window over the sink. Her eyes are blue. She begins to open her mouth. It has been held that the Universe constitutes a thermodynamically closed system, and if this were true it would mean that a time must finally come when the Universe "unwinds" itself, no energy being available for use. This state is referred to as the "heat death of the Universe." Sarah Boyle begins to cry. She throws a jar of strawberry jam against the stove, enamel chips off and the stove begins to bleed. Bach had twenty children, how many children has Sarah Boyle? Her mouth is open. Her mouth is opening. She turns on the water and fills the sinks with detergent. She writes on the kitchen wall, "William Shakespeare has Cancer and lives in California." She writes, "Sugar Frosted Flakes are the Food of the Gods." The water foams up in the sink, overflowing, bubbling onto the strawberry floor. She is about to begin to cry. Her mouth is opening. She is crying. She cries. How can one ever tell whether there are one or many fish? She begins to break glasses and dishes, she throws cups and cooking pots and jars of food which shatter and break and spread over the kitchen. The sand keeps falling, very quietly, in the egg timer. The old man and woman in the barometer never catch each other. She picks up eggs and throws them into the air. She begins to cry. She opens her mouth. The eggs arch slowly through the kitchen, like a baseball, hit high against the spring sky, seen from far away. They go higher and higher in the stillness, hesitate at the zenith, then begin to fall away slowly, slowly, through the fine, clear air.

THE
LIBRARY OF
BABEL

by JORGE LUIS BORGES

FOREWORD

by Ivor Rogers

THE AUTHOR

JORGE LUIS BORGES is Argentina's premier man of letters—essayist, critic, short-story writer. Born in 1899, he has long been admired in the Latin-American world for his austere yet baroque stories, tautly compressed and occupying a mysterious borderline between fiction and essay. Yet his work remained almost unknown in English-speaking countries until the 1960s, when the virtually simultaneous publication of two collections of his tales gained him his first major audience there. "The Library of Babel," written in 1941, appeared in Spanish in Borges' collection *Ficciones* in 1956, and in two different English translations in 1962.

THE CRITIC

IVOR ROGERS, born in 1930, is an instructor in the College of Creative Communications at the University of Wisconsin, Green Bay, and is working toward a doctorate in theater and film. He teaches courses dealing in science fiction, film, and dramatic literature, and has directed, designed, or appeared in more than a hundred plays. His critical work includes an essay on science-fiction films published in *Arts in Society* and "The Time Plays of J. B. Priestley," which appeared in *Extrapolation*. He was one of the organizers of "The Secondary Universe," a conference on imaginative literature held at the University of Wisconsin, Milwaukee, in 1968.

Foreword

In one sense, any work of fiction is a fantasy, and the imaginary world created by the writer is a secondary universe branching off from the universe we experience from day to day. James Joyce once described the very real slice of our own space-time continuum known as Nineteenth Century Ireland-Late, and it is still possible to visit Dublin and see the very real tombstones of the actual persons described by Joyce, and one or two of the buildings where these people lived may even have escaped the wreckers' ball. These few palpable remains are all that is left of the universe that James Joyce has described for us—the rest of that universe is lost forever—indeed, it was lost by the time Joyce put his description of it on paper in an attempt to create his own remembrances of things past.

The real universe of Joyce is lost in the fantasy called the past, just as most universes of science fiction are lost in the fantasy called the future. There is another type of universe, however, and this might be called the universe of the never-can-be. Some of these universes are what J. R. R. Tolkien calls the Kingdom of Faërie (not to be confused with fairy tales) and are true fantasy. Borges is related to this type of fantasy universe, but seldom writes in this fashion. (Indeed, I have heard that Borges found the fantasy universe of Middle Earth as created by Professor Tolkien quite interesting, since he felt it was easier to believe in a magic ring that made all things possible than in a science-fiction universe where it was necessary to suspend belief with each new invention.) Middle Earth is a wholly created universe based upon the archetypes and myths of our historical world. The universes that included Oz and Tarzan were also based on our very real geography and history, but slowly deviated from the "real" world until the subcreation of the author took over and recast the entire universe into his own personal vision. This is what is usually meant by that terrible phrase "gradual suspension of disbelief."

311

There is another way of looking at the world that has little or no relationship to "reality" or how we perceive the objects in our everyday life. Sometimes these approaches to the world are only slightly skewed, as in the creations of the impressionists who capture the appearance of reality with little blobs and dashes of color and line. Others, as in certain expressionists, see the universe radiating from the ego of the creator—with the accompanying distortions of the ego distorting and reshaping the universe. Still other distortions of reality developed by visual artists attempt to show the subject from many angles, as an object moving through time, or simply as an abstract squiggle. Perhaps the best-known parallel among writers is Franz Kafka. I have often wondered if the Statue of Liberty that he describes as holding aloft the shining sword of Liberty was just an error on the part of Kafka or the real description of a parallel universe.

If we think of Borges as writing a literary work that is akin to fantasy and science fiction in its creation of imaginary worlds, and related to visual art in its shaping of the raw material of reality into a creative unity, we are getting quite close to the relatives of "The Library of Babel." One other concern of Borges' is very important. In many of his stories he is attempting to write directly about the creative experience. From this comes the "Literature of Exhaustion." This implies that just as musicians have exhausted the possibilities of the twelve-tone scale (in a melodic sense), writers have exhausted the possibilities of theme, plot, and subject in writing. (I'm not sure about applying this to science fiction, because new thematic material is always being introduced as new scientific discoveries are made—which in turn influences the writer.) Sometimes, and this is a factor in "The Library of Babel," Borges enjoys writing about writing. Some of his stories (the fantastic piece about the twentieth-century author of *Don Quixote* stands out) are more nonfiction than story, but they aren't about any sort of standard reality that one might meet on the street. Certainly any "plot" there is in the story involves the search for the Ultimate Book which expresses all of truth and beauty and thought, but even this is peripheral to the intent of the story.

One concern of current literary trends is the exploration and psychological justification of the actions of characters in a work of fiction. This is almost obsessional with most modern writers of quality literature, but viewed from a historical perspective, it is a mere momentary obsession in an ever-changing panorama of literary styles. Borges belongs to an older style of fiction which was more concerned with thought content or philosophical insight than with a realistic portrayal of human failings and foibles. When this broader perspective of literature is added to a concern with form and an interest in reality/unreality, "The Library of Babel" is not obscure or "difficult." It *is* horribly difficult if one attempts to draw political analogies (as some misguided individuals have attempted to do with Tolkien and others) or the current types of literary conceits from what is essentially a simple speculation of "What if the universe were one huge library?" Any attempt to read meaning into it because Borges is a librarian is equally futile.

Borges is concerned with concepts and ideas as the primary material of his fictive work, and he is concerned with them the same way that the better science-fiction writer is concerned with ideas. Borges' main interest is to take an idea, look at it from every angle, turn it inside out, and put it back where he got it—usually in a form that is barely recognizable. The concept of a universal library came from the German science-fiction writer Kurt Lasswitz—Borges comments about the concept in an essay about George Bernard Shaw written some ten years before he wrote this story—but Lasswitz's purpose was primarily that of a storyteller while Borges is a teller of ideas. The concept of a book containing all knowledge, arrived at by random methods, was the idea of a thirteenth-century mystic called Raymond Lully, but with Borges the mystical ideal became grist for a story. More than a philosopher and more than a poet, Borges is a new type of literary master.

There are a few points where a traditionalist critic can approach Borges: he has a recurring thematic use of mirror imagery; he does not make use of standard allegory and metaphor (with certain important exceptions); he has developed a mythology of dagger thrusts; he favors the device of the tale within a tale (not to obtain a "suspension of disbelief" but to achieve a multi-leveled reality in his work); and his style is brief to the point of being skeletal. These and other techniques are not the important facets of his writing. He is a reader and commentator on literally everything; his greatest skill is that of the synthesist and patternmaker.

Borges is not a didactic writer, but a questioner and prober—a defender of heresies, not an advocate. (In the first paragraph of the essay "For Bernard Shaw," he tells us that literature cannot be exhausted at the same time that he raises the concept of the exhaustion of music.) His most important contribution might be called a type of relativity theory of literature. "Pierre Menard, Author of *Don Quixote*" reminds us of the patent absurdity of attempting to recreate the conditions of Cervantes' original composition until Borges presents us with the accomplishment. We are barely recovered from that coup when he starts pointing out the variations between the two texts. (The typography is word for word, but so much has happened since Cervantes wrote the original *Quixote* that Pierre Menard's identical version is vastly changed from the original in meaning.) Borges is also ready to show us how the meaning of a line by Robert Browning has been changed by the writings of Franz Kafka; the line has remained unchanged, but the world is a different place since Kafka has changed reality by his presence, and so we must give a different meaning to Browning. If the mind boggles, that is probably one of the goals of the author.

It is not too farfetched to call Borges and Joyce the two greatest literary minds of the century, but they are at opposite poles of literature: Joyce is the master of the convoluted complexities of the human soul while Borges is the master of the labyrinths of the human mind.

THE LIBRARY OF BABEL

> By this art you may contemplate
> the variation of the 23 letters . . .
> —*The Anatomy of Melancholy,*
> *Part 2, Sect. II, Mem. IV.*

The universe (which others call the Library) is composed of an indefinite, perhaps an infinite, number of hexagonal galleries, with enormous ventilation shafts in the middle, encircled by very low railings. From any hexagon the upper or lower stories are visible, interminably. The distribution of the galleries is invariable. Twenty shelves—five long shelves per side—cover all sides except two; their height, which is that of each floor, scarcely exceeds that of an average librarian. One of the free sides gives upon a narrow entrance way, which leads to another gallery, identical to the first and to all the others. To the left and to the right of the entrance way are two miniature rooms. One allows standing room for sleeping; the other, the satisfaction of fecal necessities. Through this section passes the spiral staircase, which plunges down into the abyss and rises up to the heights. In the entrance way hangs a mirror, which faithfully duplicates appearances. People are in the habit of inferring from this mirror that the Library is not infinite (if it really were, why this illusory duplication?); I prefer to dream that the polished surfaces feign and promise infinity. . . .

Light comes from some spherical fruits called by the name of lamps. There are two, running transversally, in each hexagon. The light they emit is insufficient, incessant.

Like all men of the Library, I have traveled in my youth. I have journeyed in search of a book, perhaps of the catalogue of catalogues; now that my eyes can scarcely decipher what I write, I am preparing to die a few leagues from the hexagon in which I was born. Once dead, there will not lack pious hands to hurl me over the banister; my sepulchre shall be the unfathomable air: my body will sink lengthily and will corrupt and dissolve in the wind engendered by the fall, which is infinite. I affirm that the Library is interminable. The idealists argue that the hexagonal halls are a necessary form of absolute space or, at least, of our intuition of space. They contend that a triangular or pentagonal hall is inconceivable. (The mystics claim that to them ecstasy reveals a round chamber containing a great book with a continuous back circling the walls of the room; but their testimony is suspect; their words, obscure. That cyclical book is God.) Let it suffice me, for the time being, to repeat the classic dictum: *The Library is a sphere whose consummate center is any hexagon, and whose circumference is inaccessible.*

Five shelves correspond to each one of the walls of each hexagon; each shelf contains thirty-two books of a uniform format; each book is made up of four hundred and ten pages; each page, of forty lines; each line, of some eighty black letters. There are also letters on the spine of each book; these letters do not indicate or prefigure what the pages will say. I know that such a lack of relevance, at one time, seemed mysterious. Before summarizing the solution (whose disclosure, despite its tragic implications, is perhaps the capital fact of this history), I want to recall certain axioms.

The first: The Library exists *ab aeterno*. No reasonable mind can doubt this truth, whose immediate corollary is the future eternity of the world. Man, the imperfect librarian, may be the work of chance or malevolent demiurges; the universe, with its elegant endowment of shelves, of enigmatic volumes, of indefatigable ladders for the voyager, and of privies for the seated librarian, can only be the work of a god. In order to perceive the distance which exists between the divine and the human, it is enough to compare the rude tremulous symbols which my fallible hand scribbles on the end pages of a book with the organic letters inside: exact, delicate, intensely black, inimitably symmetric.

The second: *The number of orthographic symbols is twenty-five.** This bit of evidence permitted the formulation, three hundred years ago, of a general theory of the Library and the satisfactory resolution of the problem which no conjecture had yet made clear: the formless and chaotic nature of almost all books, one of these books which my father saw in a hexagon of the circuit number fifteen ninety-four, was composed of the letters MCV perversely repeated from the first line to the last. Another, very much consulted in this zone, is a mere labyrinth of letters, but on the next-to-the-last page, one may read *O Time your pyramids.* As is well known: for one reasonable line or one straightforward note there are leagues of insensate cacophony, of verbal farragoes and incoherencies. (I know of a wild region whose librarians repudiate the vain superstitious custom of seeking any sense in books and compare it to looking for meaning in dreams or in the chaotic lines of one's hands. . . . They admit that the inventors of writing imitated the twenty-five natural symbols, but they maintain that this application is accidental and that books in themselves mean nothing. This opinion—we shall see—is not altogether false.)

For a long time it was believed that these impenetrable books belonged to past or remote languages. It is true that the most ancient men, the first librarians, made use of a language quite different from the one we speak today; it is true that some miles to the right the language is dialectical and that ninety stories up it is incomprehensible. All this, I repeat, is true; but four hundred and ten pages of unvarying MCVs do not correspond to any language, however dialectical or rudimentary it might be. Some librarians insinuated that each letter could influence the next, and that the value of MCV on the third line of page 71 was not the same as that of the same series in another position on another page; but this vague thesis did not prosper. Still other men thought in terms of cryptographs; this conjecture has come to be universally accepted, though not in the sense in which it was formulated by its inventors.

---

* The original manuscript of the present note does not contain digits or capital letters. The punctuation is limited to the comma and the period. These two signs, plus the space sign and the twenty-two letters of the alphabet, make up the twenty-five sufficient symbols enumerated by the unknown author.

Five hundred years ago, the chief of an upper hexagon* came upon a book as confusing as all the rest but which contained nearly two pages of homogenous lines. He showed his find to an ambulant decipherer, who told him the lines were written in Portuguese. Others told him they were in Yiddish. In less than a century the nature of the language was finally established: it was a Samoyed-Lithuanian dialect of Guarani, with classical Arabic inflections. The contents were also deciphered: notions of combinational analysis, illustrated by examples of variations with unlimited repetition. These examples made it possible for a librarian of genius to discover the fundamental law of the Library. This thinker observed that all the books, however diverse, are made up of uniform elements: the period, the comma, the space, the twenty-two letters of the alphabet. He also adduced a circumstance confirmed by all travelers: *There are not, in the whole vast Library, two identical books.* From all these incontrovertible premises he deduced that the Library is total and that its shelves contain all the possible combinations of the twenty-odd orthographic symbols (whose number, though vast, is not infinite); that is, everything which can be expressed, in all languages. Everything is there: the minute history of the future, the autobiographies of the archangels, the faithful catalogue of the Library, thousands and thousands of false catalogues, a demonstration of the fallacy of these catalogues, a demonstration of the fallacy of the true catalogue, the Gnostic gospel of Basilides, the commentary on this gospel, the commentary on the commentary of this gospel, the veridical account of your death, a version of each book in all languages, the interpolations of every book in all books.

When it was proclaimed that the Library comprised all books, the first impression was one of extravagant joy. All men felt themselves lords of a secret, intact treasure. There was no personal or universal problem whose eloquent solution did not exist—in some hexagon. The universe was justified, the universe suddenly expanded to the limitless dimensions of hope. At that time there was

* Formerly, for each three hexagons there was one man. Suicide and pulmonary diseases have destroyed this proportion. My memory recalls scenes of unspeakable melancholy: there have been many nights when I have ventured down corridors and polished staircases without encountering a single librarian.

much talk of the Vindications: books of apology and prophecy, which vindicated for all time the actions of every man in the world and established a store of prodigious arcana for the future. Thousands of covetous persons abandoned their dear natal hexagons and crowded up the stairs, urged on by the vain aim of finding their Vindication. These pilgrims disputed in the narrow corridors, hurled dark maledictions, strangled each other on the divine stairways, flung the deceitful books to the bottom of the tunnels, and died as they were thrown into space by men from remote regions. Some went mad. . . .

The Vindications do exist. I have myself seen two of these books, which were concerned with future people, people who were perhaps not imaginary. But the searchers did not remember that the calculable possibility of a man's finding his own book, or some perfidious variation of his own book, is close to zero.

The clarification of the basic mysteries of humanity—the origin of the Library and of time—was also expected. It is credible that those grave mysteries can be explained in words: if the language of the philosophers does not suffice, the multiform Library will have produced the unexpected language required and the necessary vocabularies and grammars for this language.

It is now four centuries since men have been wearying the hexagons. . . .

There are official searchers, *inquisitors*. I have observed them carrying out their functions: they are always exhausted. They speak of a staircase without steps where they were almost killed. They speak of galleries and stairs with the local librarian. From time to time they will pick up the nearest book and leaf through its pages, in search of infamous words. Obviously, no one expects to discover anything.

The uncommon hope was followed, naturally enough, by deep depression. The certainty that some shelf in some hexagon contained precious books and that these books were inaccessible seemed almost intolerable. A blasphemous sect suggested that all searches be given up and that men everywhere shuffle letters and symbols until they succeeded in composing, by means of an improbable stroke of luck, the canonical books. The authorities found themselves obliged to issue severe orders. The sect dissappeared, but in my childhood I still saw old men who would hide out in the privies for long periods of time, and, with metal disks in a forbidden dicebox, feebly mimic the divine disorder.

Other men, inversely, thought that the primary task was to eliminate useless works. They would invade the hexagons, exhibiting credentials which were not always false, skim through a volume with annoyance, and then condemn entire bookshelves to destruction: their ascetic, hygenic fury is responsible for the senseless loss of millions of books. Their name is execrated; but those who mourn the "treasures" destroyed by this frenzy, overlook two notorious facts. One: the Library is so enormous that any reduction undertaken by humans is infinitesimal. Two: each book is unique, irreplaceable, but (inasmuch as the Library is total) there are always several hundreds of thousands of imperfect facsimiles—of works which differ only by one letter or one comma. Contrary to public opinion, I dare suppose that the consequences of the depredations committed by the Purifiers have been exaggerated by the horror which these fanatics provoked. They were spurred by the delirium of storming the books in the Crimson Hexagon: books of a smaller than ordinary format, omnipotent, illustrated, magical.

We know, too, of another superstition of that time: the Man of the Book. In some shelf of some hexagon, men reasoned, there must exist a book which is the cipher and perfect compendium of *all the rest:* some librarian has perused it, and it is analogous to a god. Vestiges of the worship of that remote functionary still persist in the language of this zone. Many pilgrimages have sought Him out. For a century they trod the most diverse routes in vain. How to locate the secret hexagon which harbored it? Someone proposed a regressive approach: in order to locate book A, first consult book B which will indicate the location of A; in order to locate book B, first consult book C, and so on ad infinitum. . . .

I have squandered and consumed my years in adventures of this type. To me, it does not seem unlikely that on some shelf of the universe there lies a total book.* I pray the unknown gods that

* I repeat: it is enough that a book be possible for it to exist. Only the impossible is excluded. For example: no book is also a stairway, though doubtless there are books that discuss and deny and demonstrate this possibility and others whose structure corresponds to that of a stairway.

some man—even if only one man, and though it have been thousands of years ago!—may have examined and read it. If honor and wisdom and happiness are not for me, let them be for others. May heaven exist, though my place be in hell. Let me be outraged and annihilated, but may Thy enormous Library be justified, for one instant, in one being.

The impious assert that absurdities are the norm in the Library and that anything reasonable (even humble and pure coherence) is an almost miraculous exception. They speak (I know) of "the febrile Library, whose hazardous volumes run the constant risk of being changed into others and in which everything is affirmed, denied, and confused as by a divinity in delirium." These words, which not only denounce disorder but exemplify it as well, manifestly demonstrate the bad taste of the speakers and their desperate ignorance. Actually, the Library includes all verbal structures, all the variations allowed by the twenty-five orthographic symbols, but it does not permit of one absolute absurdity. It is pointless to observe that the best book in the numerous hexagons under my administration is entitled *Combed Clap of Thunder;* or that another is called *The Plaster Cramp;* and still another *Axaxaxas Mlö.* Such propositions as are contained in these titles, at first sight incoherent, doubtless yield a cryptographic or allegorical justification. Since they are verbal, these justifications already figure, *ex hypothesi,* in the Library. I can not combine certain letters, as *dhcmrlchtdj,* which the divine Library has not already foreseen in combination, and which in one of its secret languages does not encompass some terrible meaning. No one can articulate a syllable which is not full of tenderness and fear, and which is not, in one of those languages, the powerful name of some god. To speak is to fall into tautologies. This useless and wordy epistle itself already exists in one of the thirty volumes of the five shelves in one of the uncountable hexagons—and so does its refutation. (An *n* number of possible languages makes use of the same vocabulary; in some of them, the symbol *library* admits of the correct definition *ubiquitous and everlasting system of hexagonal galleries,* but *library* is *bread* or *pyramid* or anything else, and the seven words which define it possess another value. You who read me, are you sure you understand my language?)

Methodical writing distracts me from the present condition of men. But the certainty that everything has been already written nullifies or makes phantoms of us all. I know of districts where the youth prostrate themselves before books and barbarously kiss the pages, though they do not know how to make out a single letter. Epidemics, heretical disagreements, the pilgrimages which inevitably degenerate into banditry, have decimated the population. I believe I have mentioned the suicides, more frequent each year. Perhaps I am deceived by old age and fear, but I suspect that the human species—the unique human species—is on the road to extinction, while the Library will last on forever: illuminated, solitary, infinite, perfectly immovable, filled with precious volumes, useless, incorruptible, secret.

Infinite I have just written. I have not interpolated this adjective merely from rhetorical habit. It is not illogical, I say, to think that the world is infinite. Those who judge it to be limited, postulate that in remote places the corridors and stairs and hexagons could inconceivably cease—a manifest absurdity. Those who imagined it to be limitless forget that the possible number of books is limited. I dare insinuate the following solution to this ancient problem: *The Library is limitless and periodic.* If an eternal voyager were to traverse it in any direction, he would find, after many centuries, that the same volumes are repeated in the same disorder (which, repeated, would constitute an order: Order itself). My solitude rejoices in this elegant hope.*

Mar del Plata
1941

—Translated by Anthony Kerrigan

* Letizia Alvarez de Toledo has observed that the vast Library is useless. Strictly speaking, *one single volume* should suffice: a single volume of ordinary format, printed in nine or ten type body, and consisting of an infinite number of infinitely thin pages. (At the beginning of the seventeenth century, Cavalieri said that any solid body is the superposition of an infinite number of planes.) This silky vade mecum would scarcely be handy: each apparent leaf of the book would divide into other analogous leaves. The inconceivable central leaf would have no reverse.

A Bibliography

THE CRITICAL LITERATURE

OF SCIENCE FICTION

The best-stocked shelf of science-fiction criticism is apt to be a slender one, for very little of value has been done in this field thus far—a situation likely to be remedied, however, as the current academic investigation of science fiction develops. The books of criticism that exist at present are of unequal value, some being largely historical-biographical summaries and others devoted mainly to the discussion of ephemeral or unobtainable magazine fiction; several of the best works have long been out of print, and most of the others are sponsored by a publishing company that is more a labor of love than a commercial operation.

There are perhaps half a dozen "little" magazines that specialize in science-fiction criticism, but the life spans of these publications are so unpredictable that it would be pointless to offer information about them here. The only magazine of this sort that has demonstrated real durability is *Extrapolation,* the Newsletter of the Conference on Science Fiction of the Modern Language Association, which has appeared twice yearly since 1959. Information on subscription rates and back issues may be obtained from Professor Thomas D. Clareson, Department of English, College of Wooster, Wooster, Ohio, 44691.

In the list of books that follows, those produced by Advent: Publishers are most readily obtained from Advent itself (P.O. Box 9228, Chicago, Illinois, 60690).

Amis, Kingsley. *New Maps of Hell.* New York, Ballantine Books, 1960.

Atheling, William, Jr. (James Blish). *The Issue at Hand.* Chicago, Advent: Publishers, 1964.

Bretnor, Reginald, editor. *Modern Science Fiction: Its Meaning and Its Future.* New York, Coward-McCann, 1953. (Out of print.)

Davenport, Basil. *Inquiry Into Science Fiction*. New York, Longmans Green, 1955. (Out of print.)

Davenport, Basil, and others. *The Science Fiction Novel: Imagination and Social Criticism*. Chicago, Advent: Publishers, 1959. Valuable essays by Robert A. Heinlein, C. M. Kornbluth, Alfred Bester, and Robert Bloch.

Eshbach, Lloyd, editor. *Of Worlds Beyond*. First published 1947; reprint edition, Chicago, Advent: Publishers, 1964. A symposium on the technique of writing science fiction, with contributions by Heinlein, Williamson, Campbell, and others.

Hillegas, Mark R. *The Future as Nightmare: H. G. Wells and the Anti-Utopians*. New York, Oxford University Press, 1967.

Knight, Damon. *In Search of Wonder*. Second edition, Chicago, Advent: Publishers, 1967.

Lewis, C. S. *Of Other Worlds*. New York, Harcourt, Brace & World, 1966.

Moskowitz, Sam. *Explorers of the Infinite; Shapers of Science Fiction*. Cleveland and New York, World Publishing Company, 1963.

————. *Seekers of Tomorrow: Master of Modern Science Fiction*. Cleveland and New York, World Publishing Company, 1965.

Panshin, Alexei. *Heinlein in Dimension*. Chicago, Advent: Publishers, 1968.

70 71 72 73 74 10 9 8 7 6 5 4 3 2 1

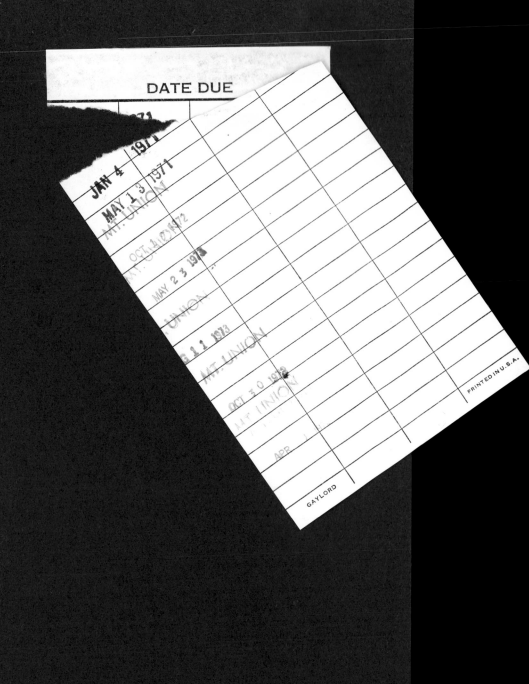

DATE DUE

JAN 4 1971

MAY 1 3 1971
MT. UNION

OCT 3 1972
MT. UNION

MAY 2 3 1973
MT. UNION

3 1 1 1973
MT. UNION

OCT 3 0 1973
MT. UNION

APR

GAYLORD

PRINTED IN U.S.A.